Sweet Wine of Youth

A First World War romance

Ian Cotton

Copyright
Ian Cotton 2023

Holmwood

To Almudena, who helped in so many ways

Part One: Innocence

Chapter One

Oxford, April 1914

Years later she would try to remember. Yet try as she would, she could never quite place it. It was something in his eyes, a kind of recognition, a re-visiting, almost, of something she already knew. But what, precisely? Then once again her memory would fade, all would become vague, and she would flounder.

The event was plain enough. Indeed, it was amusingly familiar. It was four o'clock on a late April afternoon in 1914, and Ingrid was sitting downstairs on a horse bus, as it made its lurching way across St. Giles in Oxford. A man had caught her eye and was staring at her.

This often happened. For Ingrid was eighteen, vividly pretty, with wide blue eyes and the kind of blonde-gold hair that was nearer red than yellow. She shone forth with an inner glow.

Yet she had, too, an air of mild eccentricity: she carried five bags, three of which looked like shopping bags, and every so often, in a whirlwind of elbows and arms, she would drop one of them.

But most striking of all was her manner - for Ingrid was in constant, evident intercourse with the world. Whatever happened right in front of her had her absolute attention, and she gave of herself, unendingly, in an infinite sequence of emotional adventures, each one a little work of art.

At this moment she was laughing at a little girl opposite who was playing peek-a-boo from behind her mother's shopping bag, shouting 'coo-ee!' every time she poked her head out, followed by wildly disproportionate giggles.

She evidently felt she was the first girl in the world to have discovered such a game. And rather than just smiling shiftily, like the other passengers, avoiding the girl's eyes, Ingrid started making her own faces back, which delighted the child still more.

Then she made a little paper ball and threw it to the child, who threw it back. Next she herself ducked down behind her seat and called 'coo-ee' to the child - and lo! a social alchemy! The infection spread. In a flash the whole bus was laughing.

No wonder Ingrid was a woman men found approachable.

With a wide, knowing grin – momentarily this very adult-looking eighteen- year-old looked charmingly child-like, an effect enhanced by a broad gap in her front teeth - Ingrid sat back in her seat and once again surveyed the bus, intent on searching out again the man who had been staring.

She took care, of course, to look around in a general, take-things-in-at-large way, making a series of broad, panoramic sweeps to left and right that included her admirer as a kind of afterthought, so there could be no embarrassment. Yet just two or three of these sweeps, intensely focussed for the millisecond he came into view, were quite sufficient.

Tall, she could tell, even though he was sitting down, at least six foot two. Broad shoulders, long arms, exceptionally long thighs; overall, a sense of weight, of ponderousness even.

A student presumably, from the way he was dressed? And yet his clothes looked as if they were not quite his own, as if they were someone else's idea of what he should be wearing: a tweed suit of the very best quality and yet, too *big*, mysteriously, despite his own, huge size.

It was as if the suit had its own independent existence, a life of its own, thought Ingrid, and smiled again. Then, just as she was smiling, she locked eyes with the man, and something extraordinary happened.

This huge, heavy, authoritative-looking man flashed her a glance of pure alarm. And then, a split second later, he sneaked another, covert glance at her, met her eyes, and looked away. Then a minute later (Ingrid saw this out of the corner of *her* eyes) he risked another glance, peeping and hiding, fluttering his eyelids - almost as if he had been the most bashful of virgin brides. Quite extraordinary.

This is the second game of peek-a-boo I've played in five minutes, thought Ingrid, once again wearing her broad, slightly cracked smile, but thinking it more proper, for the moment, to move her gaze from the bus interior to the view outside, as she consolidated this latest information.

Of course, she thought to herself, the man is English and the English are a race apart; most notable, as all knew, for their world-renowned reserve. How different from the German boys at home! For Ingrid was from the little village of Entlingen, just south of Munich, a village with no less than five amateur choirs, where the exteriors of the houses were painted with brilliantly-coloured angels. Restraint was not a problem *there*- nor eye-fluttering either. **Gott im himmel**, could those young German boys **stare**!

Not that she disliked the curious English shyness - in its own way she found it deeply attractive. Working, as she had, for five months now, as governess to the children of one of the New College dons, she often ran into his students because her employer taught them in his own home. The college was short of rooms and he lived, most conveniently, right under the college walls.

It was surprising how often she bumped into a clutch of these young men arriving for their tutorials and ended up chatting to them; almost as surprising as how often she ran into them as they left.

Raised voices distracted her.

"LOOK, I'm sorry, sir, but it's the rule. No standing."

"But I can't sit down! There's nowhere to sit."

It was the man! He'd moved out of his seat. Now he was standing, holding on to a strap.

"Well, in that case you'll have to get off, I'm afraid; there's no standing on my bus."

"But my dear fellow!" The man looked round with an incredulous smile. "I *was* sitting; I only got up to give my seat to this lady." And it was true; there was an old lady now sitting in his place.

The conductor looked rattled. He'd been upstairs, he hadn't seen.

"Look, I'm not inclined to argue, sir. It's quite simple: no standing on my bus."

"I agree, it *is* quite simple; I'm staying here."

Now Ingrid felt again the massiveness of the man, louring ominously over the little conductor.

But the conductor wouldn't give up.

"Talk about simple? I'll tell you what's simple." He pulled a cord, with a flourish, that caused a loud 'Ping!' in the driver's cabin.

"Bert!"

The driver, resigned, looked round; the bus shuddered to halt.

"Till you get off, mate, this bus ain't moving, not one inch."

And indeed, the bus stayed rooted to the spot, right in the middle of St. Giles, while the traffic threaded its way to left and right of it.

Cries of "Some of us 'as pubs to go to!" and "Come *on*, son!" rent the air and the young man's face, which had looked rather strong and magisterial at first, slowly crumbled.

But Ingrid would not have been Ingrid had she not intervened.

"If it comes to that, he can take MY seat!" she called, and advanced down the aisle, in the sure assumption that the conductor would never take the same stance with a woman.

But the conductor's chivalry was never tested. Just as she approached where he and the young man were standing, a new passenger jumped on board, pushed past all three of them, spotted Ingrid's empty seat at the front of the bus, and sat in it.

Now there were two passengers without seats.

Ingrid and the man, quite friendless now, gazed at each other for a full five seconds till finally they shrugged – and got off the bus.

Chapter Two

The man turned to Ingrid.

"How did that happen?" he asked." I really am most frightfully sorry."

Little gleaming eyes; thoughtful, considerate, intent.

Ingrid laughed.

"Don't worry! It's the funniest thing that's happened to me for weeks. Did you see the look on those peoples' faces? You'd have thought we'd got a bomb!" And she laughed again.

The man, still looking concerned, stood and watched her as she laughed; and there unfolded, to anyone watching them, a remarkable duet.

For if she was striking for her jollity, he was more noticeable still - for the way his mood so swiftly changed. Like sun stealing through a cloud, his face first relaxed, then looked curious, then, abruptly, *he* started laughing too: with a sudden zing of release, like a jack-in-the-box.

"Absolutely!" he cried. "I thought the best bit was the look on the face of the driver, did you see! It was his **resignation** that struck me. He knows his conductor - this has happened before!" He laughed again - till struck by the obvious thought.

"But I've forced you off the bus! Where were you going?"

"Oh, home," she said. "But you've done me a favour. You see, I live just down there" (she pointed to Broad Street, just fifty yards away) "and now I don't have to walk back. I'm actually closer than if I'd got off at the next stop."

Once again, the melting of the cloud. "Divine intervention" said the man.

"Perhaps," said Ingrid.

"So now you walk home."

"Perhaps."

And now Ingrid smiled; adroit at such rhythms, she sensed the looming of what psychologists call ' the moment.' Why, the man was blushing!

"Well then," he said - a pause – " I walk you home," a little hoarsely, putting the wrong stress on ' home' and saying it with an incongruous little squeak. Then adding, as if by way of apology, "I owe you that."

And Ingrid smiled once more. So now, united by choice, not just by accident, they walked off together towards Broad Street.

The man peered down at her. Again the glinting little eyes.

"You know," he said, with an air almost reflective "I wish we could talk."

"We just did," Ingrid grinned.

"We talked, yes, but I would like a conversation. Talk is cheap – conversation is the rarest thing in the world."

"You're a philosopher."

"No, a realist. Conversation is a co-operative enterprise, something that happens between friends "

"ARE we friends?! That's rather sudden, isn't it?

"This whole thing's rather sudden, isn't it?!"

And both laughed.

"Look!" he said, with the mock business-like air of one who sells a brush. " My proposal is this: a conversation. Which means a brief walk over to the Cadena café; where next, we choose a table; then next, two cups of coffee; then next, quite possibly, though by no means certainly, two buns."

Another pause.

"Look, I understand -   we have not been introduced. Me - Alexey Smolensky, poor student, of New College Oxford. And you?"

But before she could answer he took Ingrid's hand and raised it to his lips, leaning toward her with a curiously fawning, almost oriental smile.

And at that moment Ingrid understood what had gradually been dawning on her for some time - this man wasn't English! He was…….. Polish! Yes, Polish, she was sure of it! None but the Poles had that strange fawning way of greeting people – she had seen it time and again, on a Warsaw trip with her family.

"And you?" repeated Alexey.

"Rose La Touche," Ingrid found herself saying, to her own considerable surprise, partly because it sounded more poetic than Ingrid, partly as a way of distancing herself from the impropriety of being picked up, and partly because at eighteen young women, (and men), do things, every now and then, for motives that are utterly obscure

"Rose La Touche " mused Alexey, ten minutes later, as they sat at their table in the Cadena. "A beautiful name………….." Or was that irony?

"……Yes, quite beautiful. Full of literary associations, too - tell me, was that not that the name, or something very like it, of the young woman the art critic John Ruskin fell in love with in his old age?"

Now it was Ingrid's eyes that flashed - in alarm. Of course! Alexey was right. Her mind had floated into the area labelled 'poetic references' and out had dropped the name, like chocolate from a vending machine. And Alexey knew it!

But Ingrid rarely lacked poise. "Really!" she said, in doe-eyed surprise. "What an ***extraordinary*** -"

" – ***coincidence***…. - "

" - Especially" said Ingrid, recovering swiftly, " when you consider that my parents never told me this, and yet they spent half their lives talking to me about Ruskin. They were convinced he was the greatest art critic in Europe."

"Really!" said Alexey. Little glinting eyes. "And where was that, then? Where did you grow up?"

By now Ingrid was back in control.

"Giverny," she said, with joyous devilment. "You know, where Monet lived? And where he built his garden? My father helped design it."

"Really!"

"Really!"

A pause. A quizzical look:

"Tell me - perhaps this is indelicate - but did your father go to Monet's funeral?"

"Why yes, now you mention it, I think he did - yes, I'm quite sure – because I distinctly remember him saying that the flowers all came from Giverny, and how poignant that seemed."

"Well now," said Alexey, sitting back and gazing at her. "That really *is* remarkable."

"Why?"

"Because," said Alexey, "Monet isn't dead. Or not the last I heard, just a fortnight ago." Little glinting eyes, full of intelligence and humour, now. "As you very well know!"

And he sat back in his chair and rocked with laughter; while moments later Ingrid exploded into laughter too, as the other customers stared at them in surprise.

"Tell me, Rose, or Chrysanthemum, or Love-In-The-Mist, or whatever you call yourself, just tell me this – and the truth this time, if you DONT mind – whatever put it into your head to tell me such a farrago of nonsense?"

"I've no idea!" said Ingrid, which was true. "Don't you ever do things without knowing why?"

"All the time!" said Alexey. "Take that bus incident just now. Why on earth did I take it into my mind to give my seat to that old lady?! I knew it might mean trouble, if not quite the trouble that turned out!"

"Well, why did you?"

"Well, as you have confessed all, now I will too. I did it because I had been gazing at you for five minutes and I truly thought I had never seen such a……. vision of loveliness in all my life. Don't laugh! It's true! And I got carried away to such a romantic, chivalrous state of mind that I felt I had to DO something …..chivalrous.

"So I did! I gave up my seat! And perhaps I should confess, too, that I secretly hoped you might notice me; and maybe think "why, what a chivalrous young man" and that we might even meet, one day in the future, and you might remember, and think: 'why, I know that face! It is that nice, chivalrous young man who gave up his seat on the bus for the old lady! He *must* be nice.'

"But I never dreamed, and this I'm sure you do believe, that it would turn out like this."

Alexey leaned back. "Now tell me about yourself."

How on earth to reply!

"There's not much to tell - I work as a governess and look after children. I study literature - and – and - I study the English!"

"Ah, the English! Now there's a subject! I study them too."

Ingrid felt encouraged. "Yes, it's curious, they're not at all what I expected. I'd heard this nation of shopkeepers were rough and blustering, but they're not like that at all. Well, they are in one way - they hate anything abstract and they are remarkably disinclined to lace their talk with art or literature. Yet what does interest them are the everyday details of human behaviour. They analyse each others' behaviour constantly, and are often very acute.

"But the thing that really surprises me, the thing I truly didn't expect, is their strange delicacy, their extraordinarily exaggerated politeness. They have such a sense of the vulnerability of anyone they talk to! This nation of John Bulls are remarkably indirect."

Alexey's eyes lit up. "Ah, indirect! Yes! Exactly! This is what strikes me, too."

Now Ingrid was in full flight. "I'll never forget one particular evening. My employer was holding a New Year's Eve party, and he had invited around twenty people, most of whom hardly knew each other. And we all stood around drinking sherry, and the question arose, what to talk about. And what do you think we DID talk about?"

"I don't! The weather? The Woman Question? Cricket?!"

"No, for forty minutes, without pause, they **discussed how they had reached that place** - their means of transport, and with the two couples who had a car, their route!"

"Wonderful!" Alexey was in paroxysms of giggles, coughing with laughter.

"But this was only half of it. What I gradually realised was that they weren't actually talking about the route at all; it was mere code. Shy, delicate English people that they were, people who had hardly met before, infinitely nervous of hurting others and being hurt, they were flagging up messages about their characters, at one remove, by describing their **philosophy** of travelling!

"There were the pipe-smoking muscular-Christianity ones - of course they walked. There were the ones who came by train - it was the reliability, the common-sense of railway timetables that appealed to them.

"But best of all were the ones who came by car. One couple who had driven in from five miles outside the city described this tortuous, wonderful route through the foggy lanes and then the winding backroads of the city - these were the Romantics! But then these others had come straight up the main road and parked in the High – these were the John Bulls!

"Now, my Bavarians would have simply said what they thought and felt, from the heart; Parisians would have duelled with their intellects, classical and cold; but these English!"

For the second time in half an hour Ingrid surprised herself - shyness was rarely her problem but, even so, it was rare for her to take off quite like this.

But there was good reason. There was something qualitatively different about talking with Alexey. Most of the men she met *addressed* her – with varying degrees of wit and intelligence. Alexey listened. More, he listened creatively. His listening was participatory, his whole manner was one of excitement and surprise, which encouraged her to say more, still more, and more again.

So when the conversation lurched towards national character as expressed in education, and Alexey began to tell her about a very un-British-sounding project he knew - a way of helping children with behavioural problems, its educational philosophy about as far away from the controlling, chauvinist, competitive public school system as you could get - she swiftly discovered educational interests in herself she wasn't even aware of.

And when it turned out Alexey was going to visit this place, just outside Oxford, that very next weekend, and that he wondered, just **wondered**, whether she might be interested in coming along to take a look, it took all her self-control to remain equivocal, and mutter vaguely about employers, and children, and the difficulty she had getting time off.

Still more amusement in Alexey's eyes.

"Look on it as your opportunity to see the English as you have never seen them. They're friends of mine, these revolutionary pedagogues, and they have a whole host of hopelessly un-British virtues - they're gentle, empathic, idealist, messianic. They're quite convinced they're bringing in a brave new world, and they're doing it in the most beautiful English forest imaginable."

Alexey thought for a moment "It's true, they do rather avoid the more theoretical approach of we Russians."

"Russians? I had you definitely down for Polish."

"Polish!" spat Alexey. For the first time since they had been talking he seemed riled. "No, not Polish. Not Polish at all. RRRRussian, *please*" and he reverberated it, like an opera singer, from fathoms deep in his chest.

So struck was Ingrid by this new, unprecedented note in Alexey's manner, this sudden anger, even haughtiness, that it was not till later that she recalled the other odd thing about that moment, something that only surfaced after they had agreed to meet the next day, and she was walking home.

For at that same instant she had also seen that strange fluttering of the eyes, that otherwise out-of-character bashfulness, near-panic even, that she had first registered when their eyes had met, those few short hours earlier, across the bus; and which she had not seen again in all the time they'd talked, till then.

Chapter Three

Nevertheless Saturday morning saw Ingrid sitting in a train at Oxford railway station, waiting for the departure of the ten-twenty-five to Westbury, home of Alexey's 'educational project.' All complications had been forgotten, all mysteries ignored, for here was adventure, Ingrid's favourite thing.

And there was a bonus: the English climate - which Ingrid had decided, in the five short months she had been in the country, was best suited to ducks, fish, or possibly frogs - was for once behaving itself. The familiar great scuds of clouds rushed across the sky, but they were shot through, today, with jagged gashes of blue, some dark, some weirdly pale - all flooded, now and then, by golden sun.

There had been, as she'd expected, no problem getting permission to go out. True, this was the second time this week, but before that she'd not had an evening off for a month. Her employers had promised to make it up to her, and they'd done just that - indeed, they'd said she could stay out the whole day.

For they were honest and upright and liberal, were Mr. and Mrs Crosby: much more liberal than most. Why, they even let her go out on her own, like the other day when she met Alexey, and at her age too! But then this very liberalism was the reason she was staying at their house. The liberal Mr. Crosby was an old university friend of her father, the liberal Herr Uberspeer - twenty years ago they had studied history of art together in Jena - and one of many advanced views they shared was a belief in female emancipation.

Although, as Mr. Crosby liked to say, fairly often if truth be known, *you have to draw the line somewhere*. A local trip like the one when she met Alexey (she had been returning from the Bodleian library) was alright, she could do that on her own; but whole-day, out-of-town jaunts like today were different: for these she had to have a chaperone.

And Ingrid had one, who had become a regular. She was Paula Chase, the statuesque daughter of one of Mr. Crosby's friends, the dean of All Hallows, and she was, remarkably for someone who was only twenty-seven years of age, a widow.

Her husband, an architect aged only thirty, had died, most tragically, in a building accident in Holland. (Only an unkind few said he'd run off with another woman.)

So now, once again living at home, Paula supported herself as a schoolteacher. She was a graduate of one of Oxford's new womens' colleges, St. Hilda's. So that what with her job, her widowed status, and her admirably fulfilled daughterly responsibilities, who could possibly be more trustworthy than she?

Almost anyone, it turned out. For Ingrid and Paula had long made a pact whereby most times they met, they would split up, minutes later, to go and meet friends on their own.

In Paula's case it was because there was a man she wished to see of whom her parents disapproved. And her 'outings' with Ingrid provided a perfect alibi.

While for Ingrid, her motive was simpler still, no more nor less than a young girl's yearning for freedom, or what Ingrid called ' adventure.'

Although Ingrid, unlike Paula, had never previously used this freedom to meet a man.

As for any awkward questions about their 'outings' from either employers or parents...... both had, in abundance, the gift of the gab, so all that was needed was to agree a broad scenario. No problem at all.

And today such shenanigans seemed only more reason to be gay. Was not Paula at Oxford station at that very same moment, due to head out by train, after their usual initial meeting, in the very opposite direction – to see her own, albeit secret, man?

Which brought forth yet another of Ingrid's boyish, gap-toothed grins, drawing the routine fascination from the three other passengers, two young men and their fat, preoccupied mother, sitting opposite. Not, of course, that Ingrid was only thinking about Paula. For as the train lurched away she was, inevitably, also thinking about Alexey.

Like all eighteen- year-olds she had convinced herself this man was different... different in intelligence, in understanding, in empathy, in sensitivity....alright, in looks.....

There'd been a moment when they were talking that time in the Cadena when they'd argued, briefly, about education. For he had explained to her that the 'disablement' of the boys at the camp where she was heading was above all emotional, and that they suffered, almost all of them, from being excessively withdrawn; they were obsessive, pedantic, remote.

But they could also be quite dangerous: ' like islands – volcanic islands' he had said. Yet their helpers were nearly all boys, too, of the same age; and these helpers were, apparently, the polar opposite of their charges. Ordinary East End cockneys, warm, fun-loving and spontaneous.

A marriage of true opposites – this much Ingrid could see. But children looking after children? Wasn't that dangerous?

Alexey disagreed. "They're actually far *better* at such work than adults; they've no prejudices, which makes them better observers, which means that when they act it's with better information."

But what Ingrid remembered, later, was not what he'd said but the way he'd said it; how he gestured between them as he spoke; broad, slow, manly gestures, curving solemnly from his chest over to hers. It was as if he wanted reduce the whole debate to something personal, something between *them*.

Then she'd been struck, too, by the way he had taken one position, she'd taken another and then - magically – they'd arrived at a third: a hybrid of them both.

Indeed, Ingrid thought to herself, her face stretching yet again into one of her grins, we've only known each other four days and we've had our first baby!

What would they talk about today?

Soon, far more swiftly than Ingrid expected - so remote had her daydreaming made her - the train braked suddenly at what Ingrid saw, with a flash of alarm, was Westbury station.

Grabbing her bags, she got up, ready to get out. But she never did: because the train didn't stop.

With a lurch of alarm she realised the train wasn't *meant* to stop there. Of course, Alexey had warned her! Get the wrong train, he'd explained, and it would pass through Westbury, without stopping. This was such a train. She'd have to get out at the next station and come back.

One in three Worcester line trains were fast. Two stoppers for every through train, that should have been pretty good odds. But, absent-minded as ever, Ingrid had chosen the one that went straight through. And she had no idea when the next stop might be. However could she manage to be so *stupid* - why must she always manage to *mess everything up*?

And yet the crisis was not so bad. There was, confirmed the family opposite - only too pleased to find a reason, at last, to engage this intriguing-looking young woman in conversation - a train coming back within half an hour.

And in forty - five minutes Ingrid was duly back at Westbury, almost falling out of the window this time, as she leaned out to make sure she didn't again go flying past, and scooped herself, rather than alighted, onto the platform. The train disappeared into the distance.

Chapter Four

She stepped into silence. No sign of Alexey. He'd said he would come down to meet her; he must have given her up. The platform, vibrating in the unseasonable heat, stretched lifeless in both directions - which way to go?

After a short, panic-stricken search, she pulled out Alexey's directions. She tried hard to make the writing out, squinting in the noonday light.

"Can I help you?"

It was a porter, seemingly dropped from heaven. Ingrid knew enough about English idioms to know that genuine 'help' was rarely offered in this guise.

"I hope so! Could you tell me the way to Westbury Camp? I'm told it is quite near this station."

"*Westbury Camp*?"

He stared at her for a full five seconds. Then he shrugged.

"Across the bridge again; out of the gate; left turn and walk down to the road; two miles along and you'll see it, on the hills way up on your right: a boundary fence and some huts."

"Two miles!" Now Ingrid was aghast.

"About that. Didn't they tell you?"

"No they did not."

"Well then they should have done."

After ten yards walking, Ingrid stopped.

"You should have done that extra week!" she yelled.
"What extra week?"

"At charm school !"

And she walked on.

Alexey had indeed warned about the trains, that mistake was assuredly hers, but what about this two mile trek? The white, chalky track - half path, half road - stretched away until a bend, and for all that length there was no-one to be seen.

Nevertheless - 'nothing to do but to do it' as her mother would say, and with hausfrau doggedness Ingrid set off with a will, soon working herself up to her natural cruising speed of three miles an hour. So in forty minutes she'd reached the bend and could see beyond it. And there, as promised, was what looked like the camp perimeter.

Thank God she'd arrived...... and the place did look rather magical.... but then Ingrid could move as fast from wrath to cheerfulness as the reverse.

True, the huts were undistinguished. Clad with long, grey planks, some with the kind of porches you could sit out on, they looked for all the world like something out of the Wild West. But the trees that stood amongst them, arching high above their roofs, were different again.

Tall and slender, some as high as sixty feet, they swayed like poplars in the gusts of early spring. But poplars they were not - what were they?

Then Ingrid saw their leaves. Why, they were oaks! Oaks slender as poplars, nothing like the squat, Henry-the-Eighth oaks of which the English were so proud. Then she remembered, dimly, something she had long ago heard from her father. Any tree, even an oak, grew slenderly if it was in a group like these - they reached for the light - all the more so if they were constantly trimmed. And these were trimmed alright, of course they were, in a young boys' camp, for safety. They were a new species!

And Ingrid was gazing, motionless, at the tallest of all, whose summit glittered like a fountain, when there was a cry:

"Ingrid!"

It was Alexey! Running up toward her now, waving furiously, slowing down ten yards away into that slow, rather muscle-bound walk that she remembered, his arms stretched wide in welcome, his face stretched into a broad, magisterial grin.

Ingrid's resentment....vapourised.

"Alexey!"

They rushed toward each other - almost kissed; not quite.

"I thought we'd lost you!"

"Well, you nearly did!"

"What happened?"

And Ingrid duly spelled out story; while Alexey stood there smiling, nodding at her with amused, sympathetic eyes.

"Let me take your bags! My, what a *lot* of bags! Sit down! Let me get you a drink! You must be thirsty, as well as exhausted, you poor thing!"

Alexey showed Ingrid to a sunny seat at the head of a trestle table, and vanished indoors to get her drink. Ingrid settled herself and once more gazed around.

Two wings of wood stretched down like arms beside the path she had come up; beyond lay a flat, gleaming plain of many miles. It was like looking seaward from a port. Add to this the rancid smell of last year's bracken; the sweet smell of wood chippings, just like fruitcake, Ingrid thought; and everywhere, the trees - trees right in the middle of the camp, regardless of the possibility that their roots might undermine the huts. So that the camp felt part of, rather than apart from, the woods.

Someone must have planned all this, thought Ingrid.

She glanced over her shoulder. Something was cooking. Herrgott, it was an animal, skewered on a spit! Whatever it was, it smelled delicious. Then came a crack, like a pistol shot. Had it come from the fire? No. On the edge of the clearing, half a dozen fawn-like figures had appeared, and were standing motionless in the gloaming. What were they? They were little boys!

And now, over on her left, she saw four more… and two on the right….all standing there, motionless, staring. It was as if they had been brought into being, elf-like, by the wood. They were barefoot, scruffy, and one at least was so totally covered in mud that he looked like he'd fallen into a swamp. Still they stood there, staring, seemingly sizing her up.

For a moment, despite their youth, Ingrid felt a superstitious chill. But the spell soon broke. Suddenly, arrow-like, two boys from her left came running frantically toward her, at which, a split second later, two others came hurtling from the right, all cannoning into each other about five yards from her seat, all rolling and punching and scrabbling around on the ground, like dogs.

"She's ours!"

"No she ain't!"

"You done the last one!"

" No we never!"

"You *did*!"

"We did *not*!"

At which the fighting began again, and all the other boys joined in, and the screaming rose to fever pitch. One boy already had a bleeding nose, another a black eye, when Alexey, laughing, reappeared from the hut, plus two other men who came rushing round from behind it. The three grown-ups waded in among the boys, scattering blows with an abandon that made Ingrid gasp, and had peace established in a moment.

Holding what looked like the two ringleaders by the scruff of their necks, Alexey said:

"You know what you're going to do? You're going to toss for it. And you know what you're going to do after that? You're going to abide by my decision." A coin was produced: someone called; the scruffier of the two, the one covered in mud, won.

"Alright," said Alexey,"now say it."

The boy - barrel chested, round as a ball, with a crewcut hairstyle that made him look, Ingrid reckoned, just like a baby chick - walked up to Ingrid and said:

" Jer fancya cu' a' tea?"

At which he wiped his nose (he too had a slight nose-bleed) and gave Ingrid a rhapsodic smile.

Ingrid said she'd be delighted, at which the boy, plus his accomplice, darted off. Everyone laughed. A huge, tawny Alsatian, who'd been stirred from his place in the sun, lay down again, with the air of one who'd seen it all before.

Alexey grabbed a chair and sat down opposite Ingrid.

"Believe it or not," he said, " All that was about welcome."

He explained that it was a time-honoured tradition at the camp - a tradition that had been brought down from the East End of London - that the very first thing that happened to any visitor, before all else, was that they should get a cup of tea. "And as you can see, the boys take it so seriously they'll fight for the privilege." So that now Alexey had, as he put it, been 'sacked' from his job of drink provider, he could come and talk to her.

"By the way" he said, indicating a shock- headed young man standing beside him, "This is George. He is also at New College and has very kindly come out here to help. George is very good at fighting, as you can see, but he is also rather good at carpentry, and is helping me add an extension to the boys' sick room. "
George surged forward, grinning and holding out his hand; he reminded Ingrid of a friendly, plunging sheepdog. "And this is Henry, " indicating a tall, fresh- faced young man with a long, curved nose. So freshfaced, thought Ingrid, he could almost be a vicar, though his profile was more Roman than Home Counties.

" Now Henry is good at fighting too - though not quite so good at building - and Henry has an even greater commitment to this place than the rest of us, because ……he lives here! With his wife! Because he's married!"(Now there's a surprise, thought Ingrid: not the cock-virgin he looks.) "Even though he too is a New College student, and studies music, and writes poetry, and all that."

Henry levered his mighty head in Ingrid's direction, caught her eye, gazed intently, flickered a smile, then turned away. Like a mystic, socially dysfunctional dinosaur, Ingrid thought.

Alexey explained a little of the camp's background. It had started, he said, ten years ago, as the summer camp of a youth group from Hackney in London. The founder had been an educator of genius, Anthony Parsons. He'd soon decided that for all Westbury's beauty, the best therapy of all, for his boys, (many of whom had dire problems) was to befriend others even worse off than themselves.

They'd begun with the disabled child of a local family who'd wandered into their camp while out for a walk. And now they looked after at least a hundred every year. While for two years now, Oxford students – including Alexey and his friends - had been helping Parsons out.

Yet the really intriguing question, said Alexey, so far as the kids were concerned, was who benefited most - the disabled children, or the boys who did the caring. "Personally, I'd put my money on the carers, " said Alexey. Because the crucial point Parsons had grasped, Alexey continued, was how much children *need* to help others. "And the more they do, the happier they are themselves."

"This Anthony Parsons sounds quite a fellow," said Ingrid. "Is he here?"

"Oh, he's here alright," said Alexey, "But he's in the back reading. He lets the place run itself. You may very well not see him all day" (She never did.) "Or as he puts it: 'Adults should be seen and not heard.' "

Ingrid sat there and let all this wash over her. It didn't sound much like education as she'd known it, but it seemed to make sense.

Suddenly Alexey looked concerned. "Oh dear!" he said, gazing over Ingrid's shoulder, " The fire's going out. There goes our lunch. To the rescue, everyone, quick!" And in another switch from quietude to wild freneticism a dozen boys rushed toward the fire .

Led by Alexey and his friends, the boys crowded around the dying embers and started on a caricature of frantic blowing, some lying flat, others stooping or leaning over. One pasty-faced boy grabbed a bit of broken flowerpot and started fanning the fire with that.

In seconds the fire revived; now more wood was brought over from the store and Alexey, with two boys, started banking it up, placing a piece in place, blowing on it, placing another, blowing again, all done with remarkably deft movements, Ingrid noticed, for a man of Alexey's size. The boys improvised a chain, throwing logs along it from one to the other with a rather beautiful, balletic rhythmn.

Although the other thing that struck Ingrid was that it all seemed somehow overblown. Clearly the boys *enjoyed* all this excitement.

And now, more drama still.

"Don't do it!"yelled one of them, arms stretched out, wild-eyed, and next moment, WHOOOMPH! a rush of heat came from behind her. A boy had thrown something on the fire. Ten kids jumped on him, while the smell made clear what had happened. He'd thrown petrol! Which he'd got, it turned out later, from the store where they kept the camp's automobile.

The boys hustled him away, while yet another turned to Ingrid with a grotesque grin."There you are you see, " he said, his arms spread wide."Don't say we don 't look after yer. Our very own Westbury recipe. Beef flambe!"

Chapter Five

Ten minutes later, the same boy – his name was John – pronounced the meat cooked.

It was hauled off the fire and hustled into the kitchen, where the kids and the adults, including a sun-bronzed woman Ingrid hadn't noticed before, were putting the finishing touches to lunch.

Once again, Ingrid was struck by Alexey's deftness.. This huge, heavy man was cutting up raw carrot: chop chop chop he went, slicing the carrots into slivers unbelievably fast, while little boys darted around getting plates out, and ladling potatoes.

Then Ingrid noticed another small boy carving the meat, cutting long, thin slices of beef with strokes as swift as Alexey's. In five minutes he had cut enough for everyone. With a start, Ingrid realised it was the same boy who had thrown the petrol. Alexey noticed her surprise. "He's an excellent carver," he said.

The whole crowd of them, around twenty adults and children, moved outside to eat.

Alexey sat down beside her and started talking about the petrol-thrower. He was, it emerged, one of the boys the others looked after. He'd noticed the fire was going out, and thought petrol would revive it.

"What you might call a hyper-logical mind" grinned Alexey. "But as you could see with the carving, he's excellent with his hands - in certain practical ways, like many boys of his sort, he's ***cleverer***, rather than *less* clever, than average."

"***You*** certainly didn't seem too bothered by the blow-up, "said Ingrid. "And as for the boys, they looked delighted! The way they laughed!"

"Well, they would, wouldn't they," said Alexey. "Kids love drama above all else. It's only boring old grown ups who love peace."
Now the woman Ingrid had seen inside the kitchen came out and joined them. Alexey introduced her. She was Henry's wife, Mary. Firm-featured and stolid, her face was transformed by her smile.

Alexey put down his plate and fussed round the two women, checking their drinks, thrusting cushions down behind their backs, asking if they wanted more vegetables, or butter, or maybe a little French dressing? More radiant smiles from Mary. She obviously appreciated Alexey's care.

Across the trestle table, somehow separate, sat Henry. He gazed quietly and thoughtfully, while wolfing, Ingrid noticed, quite remarkable amounts food. What he didn't do, she also noted, was take pains to look after them, like Alexey.

Indeed, so striking was Henry's self-absorption that this may have been why Mary started on a quick check-list of Henry's virtues. While hopeless, she said, with his hands - which was why Alexey and George were here to help with the building - Henry was strangely adept, physically, in other ways. He was a fine games player and loved to coach the boys at cricket. He'd had a trial for the University eleven.

But above all he had a remarkable flair for animals, especially horses. They kept horses at Westbury, she explained, for the boys to ride. And when Henry rode, she said, it was less as if he *rode*, more as if he and the horse quite simply fused together. While if ever the horses became anxious - strange noises, say, or the onset of a thunderstorm - his mere presence among them, and above all his touch, would calm them instantly.

" Yet the strangest thing is horses have the same effect on Henry. Any irritations, any anxieties troubling *him* and off he goes to his beloved horses , and they calm him down.

"To be absolutely honest, I think they think he's one of them! And you know what? At times I think they' re right!"

Alexey sat and listened to all this, looking amused. He said there'd be a chance to test such notions shortly, as they'd be riding after lunch.

And, indeed, as lunch finished, out of the shifting, sun-and-shadow motley of the woods, there appeared no less than twelve horses. Slowly, ponderously, heads nodding as in kindly resignation, they made their way up into the camp, each led by one of the boys, each with a disabled child on its back. The Londoners had clearly managed to saddle them up themselves.

Well, every horse but one, that is. True, there was a rider on it - but, to the visible delight of the boys, he was lying on the horse face down, pointing backwards. His boy went up to Alexey and explained. The rider had got on like this and refused to move. Could Alexey help?

Alexey approached him.

"Why are you lying like that, Jimmy?"

"Because I'm scared."

"What are you scared of?"

"That he might bite me."

"Well he can't bite you if you lie away from his head like that."

"That's why I'm doin' it."

At which the boys once more rocked with laughter. But Alexey waved them gently aside. He went up to the rider's shoulder and stood still, whispering in his ear. After two minutes the boy sat up, turned round, and assumed a normal seat.

'We'll go now' said Alexey, with a wink and a grin. And off they went. George, like Alexey, led one of the disabled boys, as did Henry, while the boys from London looked after the others. Mary suggested Ingrid join them, and they walked together at the back.

The warmth of the morning had turned into an even sunnier afternoon. A louring heaviness lay over everything. The boys subsided into silence.

There was nothing to be heard but the rustle of the wind, the snorts of the horses and the pad pad pad of the horses' hooves, drumming on the leaves of last year. Once more the day was turning into a dream.

Up front Ingrid could see Henry, leading the first horse in the queue; as he walked, leaning slightly forward, his great head moved up and down in perfect synchronisation with those of the horses. "My God, you're right" Ingrid said to Mary. " He really IS a horse."

"Didn't I tell you ? " said Mary.

Half-way up the line was Alexey, still leading his boy who was sitting upright, looking much more confident now. As with Henry there was a wonderful rightness about this duo too.There was something indefinable in Alexey's posture, in the way he bent toward the child, in the way he chatted gently to him, in the manner in which one hand held the boy's back, the other his reins. What was it ? Then Ingrid realised; it was the ***femininity*** of his tenderness.

Just behind him walked sheepdog George, far noisier, and with far more chat - but his boy looked happy too.And now, because the head of the column was threading along a path that wound like a river, and came back, for twenty yards, straight toward her, she got a full view, this time from the front, of Henry.

The child he was leading - one of the disabled - was one of the most beautiful children she'd ever seen. Big enough to be, what? twelve years old, yet with a face as luminous and unlined as a toddler's. More, his mood was writ large. For while the other children looked happy, Henry's child looked rhapsodic.

For nearly a minute he rode through a pool of sunlight, beyond the shadow of the trees. His face and body were outlined, by the sun, as with an aura. Once more Ingrid felt a flash of superstition. And all the time, neither Henry nor the child said a word, but moved in silence, in unison with the horse.

Mary whispered:

"Don't you think that young boy looks remarkable?"

"I certainly do."

"Any idea why?"

"Well - I've rarely seen a boy look quite so content."

"Anything else?"

"Well- I really don't know…"

"He's asleep."

"*Asleep*? His eyes are wide open."

"He's asleep. You know how soldiers can fall asleep on the march and still keep going? The boy's asleep. It happens often during these rides."

And for some reason, she added, it happened most frequently to children led by Henry.

For two idyllic hours the walk went on; eventually, their course took them round in a great circle back to the camp. The boys were dismounted and the horses taken back to the stables; then everyone had tea, sitting round the camp fire.

Now Alexey suggested he showed Ingrid more of the site. There was this grove, he said, where the boys liked to play a chasing game, invented by themselves, in a wood at the top of the hill - the most beautiful place in the whole forest. Would Ingrid care to see it?

Of course she would - for one thing this would be the first time, that day, that she and Alexey would be alone. So off they went, slogging up a long, straggly path through half-grown trees to the full-grown woodland on the hill's top; the darkest, greenest woodland on the site. The oaks were left behind now, for here the trees were beech: their sheen, silky trunks soaring branchless to their summits, their leaves bursting out in shimmering clouds.

Ingrid stared upward with a look of wonder - which nearly brought disaster. For, caught out by her endemic clumsiness, she fowled her foot on a root and down she went.- or would have done, had not Alexey moved like lightning.

The moment she slipped he streaked the three yards between them - then caught her, cradled her, and sat her down on a tree stump. His speed amazed her. Pure reflex, she felt , beyond thought. What was the phrase at the back of her mind? 'Like a mother' - that was the phrase. Or just like that same feminine tenderness she'd seen earlier between Alexey and the boy.

They sat together in silence, then Ingrid said:

"Tell me - could it really be true that one of the boys fell asleep on horseback?"

At once, the light of interest in Alexey's eyes.

"Oh, you saw that, did you?"

"Well, I did when Mary pointed it out. She says it often happens."

"Well it does, actually, she's quite right, and it *is* extraordinary - but it especially tends to happen around Henry."

"Ah yes, she said that. But then she said he virtually *is* a horse!"

"That's putting it mildly."

And Alexey explained that not only did Henry, in particular, have the knack of getting these highly nervous riders so relaxed they'd fall asleep, but that still stranger things had happened on other rides. Deaf children had regained their hearing. Mute children had talked. And then, most remarkable of all, however delicate the children, their helpers never had to choose considerate horses, because **all** the horses acted considerately.They adapted their behaviour to the kids. However ill behaved the horses might be with anyone else, the moment a disabled child got on their back, they'd be the soul of gentleness.

"My God!" said Ingrid, "That's remarkable! Back in Bavaria, the stables I use, like yours, sometimes helps the disabled – and one of the helpers told me the precise same thing!"

"Really!"

"Yes, really! And there's more too. He said an especially good sign is when a horse starts playing up. It means the child is getting better - they'll never misbehave when the child is ill."

Alexey crowed with delight."That's wonderful!" He thought for a moment."So the horse no longer feels the need…… to make allowances."

"Exactly!"

"Wonderful!"

It was as if an electric charge had flown between them; as if, like old-established couples taking turns to tell the same story, they'd become one mind. They grinned at each other, they laughed and shouted, they were breathless with excitement.

Mein Gott, thought Ingrid, we've had our *second* baby.

And on Alexey's face there was a look she was already coming to recognise; a kind of triumphant, tearaway excitement, like a runner breasting the tape .

Yet gradually that look changed, as he continued to gaze back. It became, instead, a glance of the most pure and penetrating attention, that seemed to see through her into something far beyond, something quite wonderful that she didn't even know about herself. Whatever it was, it seemed to delight him !

He stared some more, smiled again ………… and ……didn't kiss her.

"How beautiful it is here," he said.

"And the company is beautiful too" said Ingrid.

"Yes it is," Alexey agreed, "the company *is*, *very* beautiful, too."

They sat some more in silence, strangely unselfconscious despite the hovering sexual tension between them. Once again, like a couple who had been married thirty years - full of trust. In the distance the shouts of the boys; in the foreground the sun, making firm, bright panels in the glade; around them the wind, caressing them like a friend.

Intimacy, at this moment, was more vital for both than even desire.

"So how is your ankle now?" Alexey asked.

"Much better " said Ingrid." But I'd better take it carefully."

"You'd better take my arm."

" I better had."

Alexey gave her his arm; and Ingrid took it; and moments later, Ingrid leaning on Alexey's shoulder, they walked back to the camp.

Chapter Six

All of which gave Ingrid plenty to think about, on the train back to Oxford. A strange bird, this Alexey! She'd never met anyone like him.

She'd understood, back in Bavaria, the young admirers she called 'Siegfrieds'- would-be Wagnerian heroes - not that there was overmuch to understand. She had met - usually children of her father's friends – Entlingen's so-called 'intellectuals'; but they seemed quite different from Alexey, another species.

Indeed, when she compared them to Alexey, she realised she found these ' intellectuals' even less attractive than the Siegfrieds. It wasn't just that they were often such poor specimens physically - too thin, too fat, too clumsy – it was something their very spirits, weirdly, seemed to write upon their bodies.

"They have no bearing", was how a soldier friend had put it. A strange grey tiredness in their faces: a flat, even tone in their voices: no cadence, no bounce, no enthusiasm, full of spluttery, loquacious fountains of words that were, for all their importunity…. lifeless. Whereas Alexey was above all else, alive…

Most memorable had been the time she met a law student, one evening, whose ambition was to be a judge. 'Judge not that ye be not judged' grinned Ingrid and asked him what he thought of *that;* he spluttered, he laughed, he went a rather fetching shade of green, and then, he said - very politely - "Well, yes; yes, yes indeed; that's very interesting, isn't it? D'you know, I've never actually *thought* of that." And the conversation……. stopped.

Which was where Alexey was such a contrast. Ask Alexey something serious and, yes, the conversation stopped with him, too, but in a different way.

Because Alexey would stop…..and think. Indeed Ingrid had realised since meeting him how extraordinarily rare thought was, and how little of it she'd ever come across.

Offhand, in fact, she couldn't think of anyone else she'd met who actually thought, really *thought,* at all. Not even her father, let alone the academic Mr. Crosby, however delightful he was in other ways. Instead, they reached from the lumber room of their minds for something they already 'knew'; something prefabricated, something someone else, in fact, had thought of first.

Yes, Alexey would stop, and think….. and act.

One instance of which had got him working at Westbury. Alexey had, he explained, met Westbury's founder, Anthony Parsons, two years ago at a party. They'd talked, and Parsons had told two particular stories. One described the day when Anthony found one of his youth group stealing.

" 'As I've done before,' said Anthony,' I gave him exactly the same amount of money, as a gift, that he had taken. He never stole again. It never fails!' "

Then there was a different, twelve-year-old recruit, already a criminal veteran, due to travel down to Westbury for the first time. Anthony had been busy, apparently, and couldn't escort him. So he'd given the boy his fare and his blessing, and sent him on his way. "But was that *all* you did? " asked the other party-goers. " Didn't you ginger him up a bit, tell him he must go straight on down there, not spend a penny of the money on anything else?"

Absolutely not, said Anthony; because it would have shown the boy he didn't trust him, and he would never have seen him again. "What counts," said Alexey, "What the child, in fact, will always act on, is not what we *want* him to do, but what we *expect*."

In the event, the boy bought his ticket, took his train, and went down to Westbury like a lamb.

"Everything Anthony said that evening was true" said Alexey. "I thought about it for a day or two, then I took steps. First I fixed to spend the whole of the summer holidays working at the camp. Then, come the new term, I resigned from the rowing club and spent the time that gave me working at Westbury."

Just like that! thought Ingrid. This man does take ideas seriously.

Chapter Seven

"Good morning, Ingrid!"

Breakfast next day.

"Good morning, Mr. Crosby. Good morning, children!"

"Good morning, Ingrid, *darling*!" - this last sung with rhapsodic giggles by the two Crosby children, six year-old Harold and four year-old Jane. They loved their Ingrid.

Mr. Crosby, her employer, sat at the table's head; his wife sat twelve feet from him down the other end. Somehow, especially in the early moments of a meal, he seemed less a father than the chairman of a board. Yet he was a first-rate listener, especially with Ingrid, who had always been his favourite. The Crosbys and the Uberspeers often stayed with each other for summer holidays.

"So tell us, Ingrid," he said, "Was yesterday productive? How go your studies of the English? Are you bullish about John Bull?"

"It was a very good day," said Ingrid, feeling her usual amusement, tinged with guilt, as she embarked on the familiar process of dissembling. "I love the Ashmolean, and the primroses by the river were superb."

"But that's almost exactly what you did last week!" Mrs. Crosby eyed Ingrid archly. "Don't you get the tiniest bit bored?"

A flash of alarm. But no, Mrs. Crosby was continuing:

"Now tell me, Ingrid, the truth: did you really go to the Ashmolean? Or did you, as I suspect, eschew the paintings for the real thing – the sun and the flowers?

Ah, that was alright then. It was merely Mrs. Crosby making one of her routine digs at Ingrid's supposed intellectual shortcomings. Mrs. Crosby was a thin, dark woman, evidently beautiful in her youth, whose eyes were surrounded by two broad fans of kindly lines, like childrens' drawings of a sunrise; yet also, around her lips, deep furrows of disappointment.

This disappointment clearly manifested itself, in her relations with Ingrid, in rivalry. And the way it revealed itself, perversely, was in an ongoing need to 'help' the under-achieving Ingrid toward her better self – a self defined, given the Crosbys' value system, as academic. Mrs. Crosby was determined Ingrid should go to university, and hence must nurture her brain.

Mr. Crosby rescued her.

"Come Lucy," he said, "Be reasonable! She didn't do too badly the other day, did she, the time she met that feller on the bus?" Ingrid had given the Crosbys an edited version of her first meeting with Alexey. "That was adventurous, surely, and intellectually adventurous at that. Some young ladies might have settled for merely being bought tea. But, no, not Ingrid! Before he knew it she'd got her young man talking about sociology, national identity - even Impressionism!"

He turned to Ingrid. "Alexey Smolensky, wasn't it? As I said then, I know him. Comes to my political economy class. Now, if you are going to be assailed in the street by anyone, he's the man to choose."

He turned back to his wife. "He's charming, this Smolensky, and quite bright, too. He has this rarest of qualities among young men: he *thinks*. What's more, he listens" (Ingrid nodded, enthusiastically) "which is rarer still - quite different from some of the young men in his circle, I can tell you."

"Take that Ernst Hoffman, for instance." Mr. Crosby's face, untypically, darkened. "Much narrower in his view. One of the German Rhodes Scholars, of course, and even more susceptible than the rest of them to naïf nationalism. Why, he even thinks Nietzsche was a nationalist, and no, he won't be told! Not a mistake, incidentally, Ingrid, your father would ever make - but then he represents an older, very different kind of Germany."

"He certainly does," said Mrs. Crosby. "Intellectual Germany, liberal Germany, the Germany we had briefly in 1848 and will again."

"We will indeed," said Mr. Crosby who rarely had a pessimistic thought for ten seconds. And now Ingrid felt him revving himself up for one of his periods: and here it came, his thoughts - lucid, ordered, disciplined – wheeling out like soldiers on parade.

"Indeed, we're already beginning to see it. German socialism, which is something of which I only partly approve, nevertheless represents an utterly different spirit from that of the Hohenzollerns. Not to mention its first cousin, Bismarck's old-age pensions. And this new mood has its cultural language too – Higher Criticism, with its rationalisation of religion; German expressionism; the new psychology. Even Nietzsche himself, properly understood- ...

"Two Germanys," said his wife, " The battle between Weimar and Berlin, as one might put it, which is, incidentally, as much a battle of male and female sensibility as one of 'Kultur'. Little wonder the Junkers hate feminism – it could transform German national consciousness. That's why I'm always nagging you, Ingrid, to make use of your very considerable intellectual gifts. Your country needs you! No ulterior motive, I promise you, as you very well know."

No motive you are conscious of, thought Ingrid.

But at this high-falutin' moment the conversation was subverted by.............. a marmalade pot. First Ingrid, having buttered her toast, reached out for it; then six-year-old Harold, also at the toast stage, reached out for it too; then, instead of reprimanding her son, Mrs. Crosby, lunged, remarkably, for the pot ***herself***, so that for a split second the hands of all three were on it, like a game of One Potato. At which moment, with a sly movement of her other hand, Mrs. Crosby snatched the pot from underneath.

A little gesture, and yet in its own way quite extraordinary. It was as if, for one moment, Mrs. Crosby had ceased to be a mother and had become a child. Briefly the whole table sat there open-mouthed - but now, once again, Mr. Crosby came to the rescue, this time as peacemaker to the family at large.

"I think this is the moment," he said, "to unveil my gifts."

Reaching behind him to the tea trolley, he produced four miniature pots of marmalade, all different. He had, he said, bought them in town the day before.

"Your favourite" he said, passing a lime marmalade to his wife.

"And one for you, Harold, and one for you, little Jane……And now, Ingrid," he said, producing yet another pot, "we come to you. Good old English rough-cut marmalade, just like you said you like so much, and like you will never, ever, find back home in Entlingen.

"Very important of course, for all good feminists to develop their tastes in every way! Quite as much in marmalade as in Monet or Van Gogh. Was it not Oscar Wilde who said – very truly in my view – that all the serious things in life are trivial, and all the trivial, serious?"

Not that Mr. Crosby meant it for a moment. Nevertheless, like many such men, he admired wit, as it were, from afar - it was one of the things which had attracted him to Ingrid's father. And a reference to Oscar Wilde, or anyone else with social or artistic clout, always helped when trying to push something past his wife. He used intellectual flattery like some men use pearls.

For Mrs. Crosby's childlike eruptions happened regularly. And when they did, they could make Ingrid feel quite as much a rival ***sibling*** as ever she did a young and pretty woman.

Meanwhile, these undertones meant Ingrid's relationship with her employers was nothing if not complex. At different times Mrs. Crosby could make Ingrid feel 1) a rival mother figure - the childrens' adoration was plain; 2) a rival sexually - at forty-eight, Mrs. Crosby was, inevitably, losing her looks; 3) most bizarrely of all - as now - a rival child.

Remarkably, in the light of this, Ingrid and Mrs. Crosby got on - most of the time, anyway - rather well.

But then Ingrid could be childlike too; perhaps she and Lucy had more in common than they knew.

As usual, with breakfast done, she took the children upstairs for their lessons. Today they'd do some history.

Ingrid loved the room, at the very top of the house, where she taught them. With windows on each side, and bright, white walls, it was sunny all day. And those white walls made a perfect backdrop for the educational pictures that Ingrid – with the busy help of Mrs. Crosby – had brought in. Five brilliantly coloured dinosaurs, in gaudy reds and greens; a copy of the Bayeux Tapestry, straggling right around the room; a view of the Coliseum, with serene Italian sky – plus a whole wall of paintings done by the children.

Then add in her charges' physical beauty: Harold, bold and upright, like a little hussar, Jane, a tangle of pale yellow curls with huge, blue, dreamy eyes.

Little wonder, perhaps, that Ingrid found the nursery idyllic. Indeed, given its position at the top of the house, virtually merging into the sky, she often confused it, half-consciously, with heaven.

In the middle of the nursery was a large desk for Ingrid and two miniature ones for the children. Beside Ingrid's desk was a blackboard, with coloured chalks.

As ever, with a slowness amazing to Ingrid, the children got their books out and began to settle down. And yet…… did it take even longer, with even more hiccups, today?

Nevertheless, Ingrid got out the yellow chalk, the childrens' favourite colour, and turned to the blackboard. She wrote:

'1066.'

"What's that?" she asked.

The children stared hard, screwed up their eyes, appraised the blackboard thoughtfully.

"A number," said Jane.

"Very good," smiled Ingrid. "But any number in particular? Anything special about it?"

"It's a *big* number," said Harold. "Very big. One ….thous…and… and…. sixty-six." "One thous….and….and….and… sixty six" repeated Jane.

"Not thousand….and…*and*…. silly," said Harold, "just thousand and. That's all."

"Not sixty-six?"

"Yes, that too, silly – you need that as well, of course – but not till after the 'and' – "

"Don't call me silly"

"You *are* silly- it's so easy-peasy -"

"Not as silly as you!"

"YOU *ARE* SILLY!"

"SILLY YOURSELF!"

"SILLY!"

"SILLY!"

"Ingriiiiiid!"

This last in unison – the customary climax to their rows.

Swiftly as ever, with kisses and smiles, Ingrid pacified them; but she remained mystified by their mood. They'd been flighty, over-excited, from the start. She tried again.

"1066" she declared. "It's not a number, actually, it's a date. Well, it *is* a number, of course, but it's a date as well, which is a special kind of number which records a year, a year when something happened, that is, not that things don't happen every year, of course, but a date records a year when something BIG happened, like what happened in 1066 - "

"Ingrid?"

Much frantic, conspiratorial giggling among the kids.

"Can I ask a question?" Harold held up his hand.

"Certainly!"

More giggling- a thump in Harold' ribs from Jane.

"Are you – I mean will you - " and then, in a rush, "***going-to-marry-Alexey?***"

So that was it! Of course. The children had been sitting there silent, during breakfast, but they'd picked up - ignoring everything else - Ingrid's fondness for her new friend.

"Marry him! I think it might be just a little early for that, don't you? I've met him, yes, I like him, very much, but I think actually ***marrying*** him might be just a little bit previous at this stage…"

"I think she's going to marry him," said Jane.

"I think she is too" said Harold philosophically. "But I don't want her to! If you marry Alexey, Ingrid, won't you have to go and live with him, without us, in another house?" An inspiration. "I tell you what - ***I'll*** marry you, and then you won't have to go away at all. I love you far more than that soppy Alexey and if he comes here to marry you, I'll kill him!"

"I love Ingrid much more than you *ever* could," cried Jane. "I love Ingrid" she pointed upward, "as high as the sky, and *I* want her to marry ***me***!"

"Girls can't marry girls, silly!"

"Yes they can if they want to, silly!"

"Don't call me silly, silly!"

"I'll call you silly if I want to, silly!"

Once more, in unison, "Ingriiiiiid!"

"Harold, Jane," cried Ingrid, "You'll end up killing each other, forget about Alexey. I tell you what: how about this?" Instant attention. "We can all get married ***together***. All of us! You come to my wedding as a bridesmaid, Jane, and you come, Harold, as a page and the wedding will be for ***us all***. It's quite the usual thing, everybody does it, and it means we can all have a lovely wedding together, and nobody need be left out!"

"That's brilliant," cried Harold, "and Alexey can come and live with us, in our house!"

"He could sleep up here," said Jane. "Where the billiard table used to be. Or in the garden, out in the shed."

"That's a lovely idea," said Ingrid, "and the sweetest thought. I tell you what. When the time comes - which may not be ***just*** yet, I have to say - I'll suggest it to your mummy and daddy."

"They'll love it," said Jane.

And for the rest of the morning the children were fine.

Chapter Eight

Three days later Ingrid was striding energetically from New College toward the town centre, a spark in her eye, a bounce in her step, with the air of brisk, wide-eyed attention that turned the heads of passers-by.

For just after the childrens' lessons finished, a hand-delivered note had dropped through the Crosbys' letterbox, containing an invitation, from Alexey, to a meeting of the 'St. Ebbe's Socialist Society' - a group Alexey had told Ingrid about – on Thursday, just two days away.

He'd said Ingrid would hopefully agree - they'd talked about this on Saturday – that if the fine, free, twentieth century they all looked forward to was ever going to happen it was as important to act nationally, in the field of broad politics, as ever to act locally, as at the camp.

Added to which, said Alexey, for 'students of English culture' like themselves the natives she'd meet at St. Ebbe's would be even more un-English than those she'd met on Saturday. Idealist, ideological, passionate (a description, thought Ingrid, that mainly described Alexey himself) - whatever else, he said, it would surely be an education.

Though all this was nonsense, the letter suddenly declared - because all he really wanted to do, of course, was see her, whether at the meeting, in a park, or up a tree; and what he really wanted to say, was how very, very much he had enjoyed their time together the previous Saturday…..

And so forth. Which was good enough for Ingrid. Of course she'd go! Little difficulty fixing it, either - because it was, pretty much, an intellectual evening, which should play well with Mrs. Crosby.

So the sole question was the availability of the chaperoning Paula, which was swiftly established by the usual exchange of notes. So swiftly, indeed, that Ingrid sensed Paula, as so often, fancied the jaunt for reasons of her own.

For once again they'd fixed a rendezvous at the Radcliffe Camera at seven o'clock - as Ingrid had duly told the Crosbys - and once again both turned up on the dot. Then went their separate ways.

So off Ingrid strode along the Broad toward the Randolph Hotel, where she'd arranged to meet Alexey. Past the Sheldonian on the left, with its comical classical busts, past Trinity College on the right, so much larger than it seemed, then on to the gaunt, train-terminus neo-Gothic of Balliol (' c'est magnifique, mais ca n'est pas la gare' was the local wise-crack.)

Balliol, famous for its pioneering welcoming of sub-continent Indians - "Balliol, bring out your black men!" students from less advanced colleges would chant outside. The same students, Ingrid suspected, who'd been in a music hall she'd gone to one evening with the Crosbys, when every time the comic hit a punch-line, this mob shouted "Har, har, har, damned funny!" in perfect unison. In the end the comic offered to take them outside.

Which only seemed, tonight, more food for jollity. She crossed the little lane next to St. Ebbe's church; crossed again, to the West side of Magdalen Street; then once more, to the West side of St. Giles, where they had agreed to meet at seven fifteen. She turned into Beaumont Street, which contained their rendezvous, the Randolph hotel's main entrance, and found…….nothing.

She glanced at her watch. Twenty past - she was slightly late. They'd said seven-fifteen, hadn't they? He'd be along in a moment.

She adopted a pose she hoped looked elegant. She wanted very much to look beautiful the first moment he saw her. She straightened her back, pulled in her stomach till it hurt and puffed out her breasts; then decided that looked a bit stiff, so she shifted her weight onto her left leg, and stood there rather lop-sided - more jaunty, more easy-going, she thought. He'll probably approach from Magdalen Street. She hoped so, that was her best profile.

8 o'clock. A new thought struck her: she was pretty sure about the time – 7.15 - but could she have mistaken the *place*? ' The corner of Beaumont street, outside the Randolph' - could he have meant the other side? Come to that, could she have got the wrong *day* ? They did say ' Thursday' didn't they? That's to say, this Thursday? Not Thursday next week?

And then she saw him! A hundred yards away along St. Giles, striding quickly down towards her. His head and shoulders, a foot higher than those around him, bobbed up and down like a cork. Wait a minute - it wasn't him at all! Wait, wait, yes it *was*! But as the man got closer she realised that while he was indeed Alexey's height, he moved all wrong and Ingrid knew that how people move is their deepest signature of all. Had she not had it explained to her, at some length, by one of her Siegfrieds?

And how differently, come to think of it, men walked from women! Take this woman, for instance, heading towards her right now: upright, splendid, like a galleon in full sail. No bumps and lurches here - she slid as if on casters.

Yet, as she got closer, Ingrid sensed something familiar about her.

Closer still, and she saw why: it was Paula.

Her friend was grinning. She walked right up to Ingrid; nudged her knowingly in the ribs and said:

'Look, I know this sounds very strange, but I was actually at the meeting you're supposed to be going to, and I've been sent to fetch you, because Alexey's got stuck. A bit of an emergency!"

And before Ingrid could react:

" Yes, I do know Alexey! I've known him for months! Yes, I know it all seems weird, but I'll explain it as we go, because we've really got to scoot if you can bear it, I'm on a deadline."

And off Paula shot, chin lifted proudly, trailing Ingrid in her wake, as Paula began a brisk, breathless explanation of her surprising re-appearance, and why she'd long known Ingrid's new friend.

How she had indeed been at the St. Ebbe's meeting – she joined them regularly. (Ingrid knew Paula was interested in socialism, but she hadn't mentioned anything like this.)

How at this particular meeting, there'd been some problem with the fabric of the building - the gas playing up or something – which was potentially so dangerous that it had to be dealt with urgently, which was why Alexey hadn't been able to come down. For which he apologised.

And how Alexey was a friend of another very good friend – *her* friend - had she mentioned Tom? (She had not.) How long had Ingrid known Alexey?

Ingrid explained their strange meeting on the bus.

Paula laughed. "Strange indeed! Well, quite strange, anyway! Just like Alexey. Such things always happen to him. What a surprise, when he twigs that you and I are acquainted! So he's recruited you! That's wonderful! That's another of his talents - bringing in new members."

"I am not a member yet " said Ingrid, but Paula only sped off again, throwing back over her shoulder: "I do apologise for all this rush. You see, the thing is I'm supposed to be speaking myself – on feminism, can you believe – and I'm due on in just five minutes. Hello, what's this?"

For as they turned the corner into St. Margaret's Street, where the St. Ebbe's Society had their meeting place, they were met by a swarming crowd of students, pensioners, and cloth-capped locals. They looked like they'd come from the hall.

"Oh God," said Paula, "Don't tell me they've called it off."

And indeed, it soon emerged, they had. The gas emergency had escalated. Then, near the hall doors, Ingrid recognised a series of faces she knew: Henry Thornton from the camp, sheep-dog George, and behind them, Alexey.

Surprisingly, there was a jolly, bank holiday air about it all, as there so often is when things go wrong. Even Alexey was smiling, as he waved hello to Ingrid and Paula.

"The millennium is postponed!" he said. "Until next week. Our gas hiccup turned out to be a gas debacle, I'm afraid, and our caretaker warned us we were on the verge of blowing the place up. Which is what our neighbours, of course, have always expected..... ."

He moved over to Ingrid and smiled, briefly, deep into her eyes. "How wonderful to see you. Such nonsense, this! But I'll explain."

And then, to the others, "But what to do now? We're snookered here for the evening, I'm afraid."

"We could go to the pub."

"That was last night."

"We could go to the park."

"It's nearly sunset!"

"I've got it!" cried Alexey." Why don't we go back to New College? To my rooms. We could have a conversation! I feel in just the mood for a conversation. And it's so much easier to talk in one's rooms than in a pub. *Or* a park."

But colleges were men-only. Ingrid felt a rush of disappointment.

"But what about me!" she blurted. "About us, I mean," she laughed, turning towards Paula. "New College counts us out. You may not have noticed, Alexey, but two of us are women."

"I assure you I *had* noticed," said Alexey. "But fear not; the situation may yet be saved. We'll disguise you! We'll smuggle you in. We've done it before," he said, and Ingrid wondered what *that* meant. "We'll create a diversion and distract the porters. We'll make a man of you, Ingrid!" he cried, grinning at her with that same bantering, teasing air that had so struck her when they first met.

"You will do it, won't you, Ingrid?" he asked again, his manner changing to a boyishness that was near-wistful; and to her surprise, Ingrid found herself saying: "Yes."

And Paula? Paula threw her eyes to heaven – but agreed; and Henry did too - with his secret smile. Then George, then some new fellow who seemed to have attached himself to the group - his name was Ernst - could he be German? - agreed as well. So that was everyone, and off they went.

Yet what struck Ingrid as a little strange, nevertheless, was that Alexey hadn't made any personal apology for not meeting her. Nevertheless, for the moment, she forgot about it.

Not least because she was intrigued by all this dressing-up, which sounded hilarious. The plan was to go to George's lodgings where he kept a whole range of outfits which belonged to the college drama society. George's landlady was away, so they could change there.
The group walked on, back down the Broad toward New College. George's lodgings were the Magdalen side of New College, in Longwall.

Ingrid edged up beside Paula.

"So you've really known Alexey all this time? I'm surprised you never mentioned it."

"Well, I think I *did* mention it, actually, but, as I said before, he's a friend of a friend. It was probably the most fleeting of mentions, and it may not have sunk in."

They walked on.

" He seems an interesting kind of man, " said Ingrid.

"Oh yes," said Paula. " Very interesting."

"He's a remarkable listener, isn't he? A *creative* listener. Listening like that seems almost to *magic* conversation out of the air!"

"Yes, he's good at that."

"So unusual in anyone, but especially in a man!" sang Ingrid.

"Yes, it is unusual in anyone," repeated Paula. "But perhaps that's precisely why he does it. To be unusual."

Which took Ingrid back a little, but not that much; this wasn't the first sardonic conversation she'd had with Paula about men. Let alone lovers - Paula wouldn't talk about them at all. Men at large she rarely spoke about without irony, though usually laced with such wit you scarce noticed any subtext of disappointment. But then Ingrid had heard, from the Crosbys, about Paula's marital debacle. She put her sexual weltschmerz down to that.

Yet by the time they got to George's all was forgotten in the excitement of the coming stunt. George found them their men's clothes, they put them on, and soon Paula, in particular, was palpably loving the masquerade. Most striking of all, when a little mild padding had been contrived, was how convincingly she came over as a man.

"You should team up with George!" laughed Ingrid. "With George as the woman. It's a match made in Heaven. Spend an evening together - go to a dinner party – try it!"

"Spend a lifetime together," said Henry. "Get married! We'll all come to the wedding. Now that would be a moment – when the priest calls out 'let any man who knows just hindrance,' and all that - for once there'd be a *real* hindrance, something to get your teeth into – the kind of hindrance the poor, bored priest has been longing for all his life...."

Ingrid, predictably, looked far less masculine than Paula - there was always something hopelessly female about Ingrid - yet she still, aided by Paula's swift, clever adjustments to her hair, looked plausible enough. At which moment Alexey re-appeared, finally back from the meeting.

So all six 'men' set off for New College, trying very hard indeed to look like the most normal young people in the world.

Chapter Nine

An hour later, they were in Alexey's rooms. It had been surprisingly easy to get in. True, Ingrid and Paula had had to go a step further than merely change sex, they had had to pose as cricketing 'bloods', returning, they claimed, from early season net practice - but meanwhile the others swarmed through the other side of the wide doorway.

Moments later they were in the main quad, then vanished through the gothic arch at its end into the stately, eighteenth-century Garden Quad, whose wings stretched out into the college gardens. Here, Alexey had his rooms, on the second floor. The group clattered up the staircase and burst in.

Alexey disappeared to hang up the women's' coats. George, Henry, and three newcomers, who they'd picked up en route - were they Germans, like Ernst? Ingrid thought she recognized the accent - disposed themselves on chairs around the room, the taller of them swinging his feet over the sofa like some latter-day Beau Brummel.

Alexey explained the "hidden agenda, or gender" of Ingrid and Paula; the 'Germans' looked amused, but, Ingrid noted, singularly unsurprised.

Ingrid glanced round Alexey's room. Her first thought was: 'superb taste'. As well as a Bechstein piano, there was a row of eighteenth-century-looking walnut chairs, three large oak bookcases, a writing desk pleasantly placed underneath the window, and - a surprising touch for a young man - a Queen Anne grandfather clock in a corner.

But there were modern things as well, notably something abstract Ingrid couldn't make out. It looked like a geometry exercise gone mad, a tangle of curves, lines and right angles with underneath a title: "Nude Descending."

Now Alexey was again the perfect host. "So what are you drinking?" he asked the two women. "Will you have some wine? And Ingrid, how awful, I never introduced you to Ernst. Guess what, he's a fellow German" (Well, I got that right, thought Ingrid). "As, too, is Albert!" he added, indicating a small, serious-looking man on the sofa, one of the three who had joined them as they crossed the quad. At Alexey's words Albert's face lit up in a strange, amazed grin – like a cat, thought Ingrid, who had, expecting a sardine, been given a salmon. "And as for this one here " Alexey indicated the long-legged one on the sofa, "....he's a Von."

"Yvonne!" laughed Ingrid. "You don't look like a girl!"

"A ' Von', you ass" cried Alexey, pitching a cushion at her. "Von Leckburg to be precise; by Christian name, one Rudi."

"No, call me Yvonne!" cried Rudi. " I prefer it."

"Ignore him. But I have a confession to make: We have quite a Deutsch clique here Ingrid, as you can see. You should feel at home! Rhodes scholars you know, hands across the sea, bringing together the Anglo-Saxon peoples, all that. But, before even confessions, however cathartic, I have to start on apologies: for our aborted meeting, of course, especially to Ernst, who was going to speak, but also to Paula, who was going to cap Ernst with her feminist jibes; and then to Ingrid, who was left naked on a street corner, well, nearly naked, oh dear oh dear, it gets worse ….."

"Oh stop it Alexey," said Paula. "It was pure routine and you know it - the same thing happened last week, and the week before, though I grant you this was the first time you've actually had to shut up shop. Who cares? There's something irredeemably amateurish about the St. Ebbe's Society and there always will be. That's its charm - "

"Well ….."

For the first time since Ingrid had met him, she thought Alexey looked taken aback. But he recovered.

"Paula's right," he said. "What she generously calls charm is actually wild impracticality and we can't afford it. We must reform."

"What we really need, " said Ernst, who'd been silent but now plunged, "is to get in touch with the more working-class elements locally, of whom there are so few among the members of St Ebbe's. It's not as if the likes of us even *matter*; for Heaven's sake; it's the rise of the masses which is the story of our time, and they're always practical, they have no choice. And it's happening in Oxford like it's happening worldwide. Right here indeed, smack bang amidst the spires!"

"It's true, " agreed George. "It's the grand story of the age. It's in the poetry! Think of John Masefield's 'The Everlasting Mercy." On the face of it, it's about one workingman's individual salvation; in reality, it's about the redemption of a whole class."

"It's more than that, " said Alexey. For now the flame of optimism was rushing round them all. Alexey strode across to the bookcase, grabbed a small volume and rushed back to his seat. "Listen to this: it's that poet D. H. Lawrence - do you know him Henry? He's rather fine. It's a review he wrote of the collection 'Georgian Poets, 19II-1912.' Funnily enough, he was in the collection himself, but that didn't stop him reviewing it. Anyway, he said, "This collection is like a big breath taken when we are waking up after a night of oppressive dreams. The nihilists, the intellectual, hopeless people – Ibsen, Flaubert, Thomas Hardy – represent the dream we are waking from, but now we are awake again. Our lungs are full of new air, our eyes of morning….

"We are drunk with the joy of it, having got away from the fear. In almost every poem in the book comes this note of exultation after fear, the exultation in the vast freedom, the illimitable wealth that we have suddenly got…."

But at that moment there was a loud roar from the quadrangle outside, followed by a crash, a thump and a screech.

"Al…..ex…..ey! Bring out your hun - men!"

"Oh God," said Henry. "Hearties!"

"*Eton* hearties!"

"Al…….ex…..ey! Bring out your wim - men!"

"This is intolerable!" cried Alexey. "How do they know you're here, for heaven's sake? Not that you are, of course. "

Alexey strode over to the window and leaned out : a cheer welled up from below.

"Having a bit of a **bonners** down here, Alexey," cried an absurdly fruity voice. "Thought you might like to *float* down and help us out."

"Bring down your hun-men!" cried another voice.

"And your wim-men!" cried yet another.

"Har, har, har, damned funny!" they all cried in unison, and collapsed into drunken laughter, which in turn switched to mock-terrified wails as Alexey, grabbing a nearby fire-bucket full of water, pitched the contents out of the window. Roars of wrath now, swiftly followed by more wails; and Alexey, leaning out, could see why.

Below him were around eight assorted hearties, mostly Etonians, and they had indeed assembled a half-baked bonfire, made out of what looked like bits of chairs and tables, probably raided from someone's room, plus some unfortunate's poetry books. But the wails were caused, not by the water, nor by the advent of the college porters but by the sight of a huge, heavy young man heading across the courtyard, remarkably swiftly for a man of his weight.

This man was plainly intent on taking on the whole pack of them single-handed. In a flash, seven fled; one, bolder than the rest, remained. The newcomer caught up with him, and, sweeping his arm backwards in a wide arc, swung it round on the side of the young man's head. There was a pistol-shot crack: the young man fell like a stone, and lay there motionless.

"Hello, Alexey" waved the assailant, unabashed. "Having trouble?"

"Not any more, thanks to you," called Alexey. "Why don't you come up?"

"Don't mind if I do," shouted back the other, "especially if there's a drink in it."

And he jogged off toward Alexey's staircase; while his victim stirred, got to his feet, and made as if to resume the fight. A moment later, realising he was alone, he staggered off to join his friends, who had retreated to the porter-free safety, fifty yards away, of the college garden.

Soon there was a shove at the door, and in lumbered one of the strangest people Ingrid had ever seen. A broad, stout young man who could have been thirty - but presumably was twenty like the rest. He had the chiselled, classic features of a Greek God, yet the heavy-lidded, muscle-bound manner of a Yorkshire farmer; the far-off, eternity-contemplating gaze of a philosopher, yet the tiny, rose-bud mouth of a little girl.
He was drunk.

"Welcome the conquering hero!" cried Alexey, and thrust a mug of wine into his hand. The man swigged, spilled a dollop on the carpet, shot a wild-eyed grin at Ingrid, mouthed a strange, secret ' hello' to Paula, and collapsed into a chair.

Alexey, aware that Ingrid was the only one who had never previously met him, explained: "Dear Ingrid, please to meet Tom Huntingdon, the philosopher-pugilist of our times."

"My God you're beautiful! " he said, wide-eyed. "Wherejew get her from?" he asked Alexey. "Was that the one you picked up on the bus?"

"We did indeed meet on the bus" said Alexey," but I wouldn't say I picked her up."

"I would, " said Paula.

"So!" said Tom, with the air of one who takes charge. "What's all this then? What are you at? Is it a party? If not, then why the women? If so, then where's the bar?" He threw two great paws up in mock horror." Not women smuggled in again!?Alexey I'm ashamed of you!" (aside to Ingrid) "He wants watching – *really.* Or are you talking philosophy?"

"Well yes, it *is* philosophy, actually - before your striking advent we were just saying…."

"Oh the Hell with it! How dare you, Alexey, say anything, express *anything* in this room that isn't an articulation of pure, simple appreciation of feminine beauty with this *stunner* sitting here! - Stunners, I mean!" (He turned his fish-eyed gaze on Paula) "You, too, stun me. You stun me, too. Errrrerp. Oh Paula, I do apologise, this is terrible." Paula once more rolled her eyes; at this moment Ingrid guessed, correctly, that this was the Tom Paula mentioned earlier. Some 'friend'!

"Nevertheless!" went on Tom, "Here you are, Alexey, graced by the presence of one of life's great truths - female beauty, the vital agency of our species survival - and you insult them with the trivialities of *philosophy*? I hope you are insulted, Ingrid. *And* you, Paula. And if you aren't, I'll be, on both your behalf's."

"Why so?" asked Alexey.

"Well, any young man or woman who meets someone of the opposite sex and gets asked round to talk philosophy when the real reason for their being there is actually procreation, will be offended in their soul, whatever they may feel on the surface Alright! I admit! That maybe it is better, in our strangely convoluted world, to *pretend* to talk such nonsense out of politeness - all I ask is that it should be absolutely clear you don't mean it."

"Tom, you are impossible."

"No I'm not- I'm entirely possible. Don't you think I'm possible, Ingrid? There you are, you see, she agrees - she thinks I'm possible, too. She sees me as a possibility, in fact, and that's all I ask; not a probability, even, let alone a likelihood, but a humble, unassuming possibility, and I'll settle for that. By the way, what WERE you philosophising about?

"Ernst was saying – well, Alexey that is – well, D. H. Lawrence, really - that we stand on the very brink of a New Age, of a reinvention of the human species, of a resurrection of the body, of a rediscovery of the soul, of a clambering out of Nineteenth century lies and obfuscation into reason, honesty, the glaring clarity of twentieth century light........."

"Really? All that? And all at once? A kind of Wind in the Willows of the spirit, if you recall the first chapter of that estimable animal book in which dear little 'Mole', or 'Moley' as his particular friends, I believe, like to call him, rushes out one bright spring day from his dank little hole where he has been spring-cleaning into the lush spring grass and daylight up above? Learned critics have explained the cultural metaphor. But isn't there just one problem here? Isn't this - I'll put it delicately - the most utter, dire, unforgivable bollocks? Isn't this stone Romanticism, pure fantasy out of Rousseau via Morris and Oscar Wilde? Believe me, there are no revolutions in this world, no progress, no change of human nature, we are the same now as we were in the days of the Ancient Greeks. What it all comes down to, in fact, is original sin…"

"Original blessing you mean." This was Ernst. They evidently disliked each other.

"Eh?"

"Original blessing - human kind is born good - not bad."

"No: it's born bad, not good."

"Bad."

"Good."

"No, it's not."

"Yes, it is."

Tom lurched up out of his seat.

"You wanna *fight* about it?"

And he put his fists up like an old-fashioned pugilist, jumped back and forth, swayed, and collapsed back into his seat again, laughing helplessly, coughing and spluttering.

Suddenly George pointed to Henry. "Henry, Come back to us ! Where have you gone, darling! What have you seen!"

For Henry was staring wide-eyed out of the window.

"I was looking at the stars. Do you know there are galaxies we can see whose light set out billions of years ago? Looking at them is like staring into a time machine; we are gazing directly at the past, the billion-year-old, unthinkably remote past. Which means, as well, that one day, when *our* light reaches *them*, they will also see the past…. The billion- year - old past…which will, for them, be us…....it……made me think a bit."

Henry's friends cheered, while Henry submerged once more into silence. He'd clearly heard nothing anyone had said for half an hour.

The crisis, nevertheless, was over. Yet despite the renewed jollity, Ingrid felt vaguely disturbed. For one thing she'd felt left out of this male-dominated conversation. (What she missed, of course, was that the men had been competing for her attention.) But most of all because she'd felt ignored by Alexey. And he'd never really explained why he had left her standing on a street corner for three quarters of an hour.

However, the observant Alexey, once freed from the distractions of argument, spotted this.

The others went on bantering; but Alexey motioned Ingrid, for privacy, into his bedroom. They sat together on the edge of his bed. (Ingrid felt the daringness, but thought it wrong to object.) Placed close beside her, leaning forward a little and staring her full in the face, with an expression that combined frankness with a kind of playful, yet delicate humour, he began to explain.

He said that at the very moment he'd been about to set out, he'd been grabbed by one of the caretakers, who'd told him there was a real possibility of a full-blown explosion; and that - and here he looked just like Ingrid's twelve year old cousin when caught out in naughtiness - in the excitement and chaos he had, to be absolutely honest, momentarily forgotten about their rendezvous. Then to add to the fun, Ernst had suddenly turned up - unannounced - and had even been persuaded to speak - assuming, like the rest of them, that the emergency would be defused.

And it was then, realising a speech by Ernst would be just the kind of un-British manifestation he'd earlier promised Ingrid, that he'd sent Paula, who was the only person then available, down pell-mell to fetch Ingrid. Ernst's slot was in just ten minutes. All of which was in vain.... as Ingrid knew... because the whole show had collapsed when they'd been forced to close the hall.

It still sounded a little strange to Ingrid, but now Alexey's attention, flooding toward her, sweet and enfolding as ever, increasingly mollified her. Once more, Alexey's superlative listening - his gaze like a caress.

Better still, he was adamant they should meet again soon - on the stern understanding that this time they would *definitely* be on their own. "We need time together," he said. "No? Just you and me. After all, it's hard to believe - at least for me - that it's still only the third time - apart from that day we met on the bus - that we have been together at all. It's strange, " he said. "For me it feels much longer."

"For me too," said Ingrid, and now for the first time in the conversation, she shot Alexey a trusting, even voluptuous look. Which was the moment she found herself recognising the piece someone was playing on Alexey's piano– 'Sleepers awake', her most favourite Bach chorale of all. How noble it sounded, how calm, how exquisitely grave! How well it went with these interesting young men who were surely, she found herself once again thinking, so original and so nice!

Of course, said Ingrid, something could be arranged. It was just a question, as ever, of her talking to her employers, the Crosbys.

The evening wound down. By eleven o'clock Ingrid had to go.

Conveniently, it emerged that leaving the college was much easier than getting in - there was a door in one of the college walls which could be opened from the inside.

Paula joined her and Henry said he would see them on their way. Remarkably, he was walking back to Westbury Camp, through the night, a distance of six miles.

Alexey and George saw them down to the door. Yet despite Henry's protestations the girls insisted they could go home alone. Ingrid lived mere yards from the college while Paula felt her male attire would protect her adequately for the half mile to hers. So the men said goodbye to the women at the exit, though not before Alexey had firmed up his arrangement to see Ingrid the following Saturday, - "a deux."

The women's' road home, it turned out, went right by the Crosbys' house, while the first fifty yards took them past New College garden.

Floatings of conversation came over the college wall; the hearties were still there.

"So we lost a ***hundred*** and went to the Grid, then another ***hundred*** and went to the Bull……." the lazy, fruity, strangely nasal accents droned gently on " So you can see ***why***" (pause) " we thought, ***Hell"*** (pause) "let's ***float*** back to college and have a ***bonners***….."

Ingrid laughed out loud.

"I love their, how you call it, slang," she said. "The way they make all these words end in 'er'." When I first came here I found it impenetrable."

"I'm not surprised," said Paula. "After all, they sometimes make a point of using 'er' words and no others at all."

Ingrid chortled with delight.

"It's like a code! Their own secret language! We have the same thing in Germany - our ' corps' students, you know the ones who fight duels, and scar their faces? It's all the same desire to show their distinctness, their specialness - and their manliness, too."

"Yes," said Paula. "They're like boys, these men."

"Innocence, strange innocence. But then their whole lives they've had everything laid out and arranged, schools, morals, marriages, careers…. one can't help wondering how they'd shape up in a ***real*** crisis."

"They won't have to. Their lives will be like their parents', predictable, deadly dull, but above all easy. Products of what someone called "The Hundred Years Peace."

They walked on ruminatively, down the empty, dim-lit street. Of course what Ingrid really wanted to talk about was Alexey, and the strange coincidence of Paula already knowing him. Yet Paula did little more than repeat what she'd said earlier. The whole thing, she agreed, was indeed a surprise, yet not quite so strange when you considered her membership of the St. Ebbe's socialist society. Which was how she'd got to know more or less everyone they'd met that evening, come to that.

Ingrid tried another tack.

"They all seem very different."

"They certainly are. And as for Tom - he's the most different of them all. Tell me, Ingrid, as someone who's just met him, what do you reckon?"

This was not what Ingrid intended but she was flattered Paula asked. She laughed.

" Well, he seemed very jolly, but not much like a student – more like a farmer, say, or even a gamekeeper!"

"Now Ingrid, how dare you be polite! Of course the fellow seemed like a complete and utter slob – would ***Dummkopf*** be the appropriate German word? But actually, you know, he's the brightest of them all - the only true original. Would you believe, he writes more poetry than any of them, even Henry! And he's been published, too, in a London review! But he keeps it well hidden. A bit like George, can you believe, who writes poetry too? Come to that, they ***all*** write poetry, all of them, that is, except Alexey."

Ah! Alexey.

"If Tom is the cleverest," said Ingrid," and George the nicest, and they're all poets, what about the unpoetical Alexey? What's he, the warmest? That's how he struck me."

"Well, I can see that. That's how he struck ME, at first, too. But he's more complicated than that. In fact that's the best…." she thought for a moment " ….the ***fairest*** way to describe him, really….. 'complicated'…. talk about hidden depths." Paula faltered, plainly caught between honesty and discretion. "My first conversation with him was in front of Claude's 'Landscape with Ascanius' in the Ashmolean. He came up and asked me what I thought of it. He was very charming." Once again, she seemed to check herself. "Of course your experience was very different, clearly, because it seemed like an accident."

Ingrid pondered this; a strange thing to say, surely, because ***her*** meeting with Alexey was obviously an accident.

"How to say… " said Paula, "No-one has ever accused Alexey of being shy. Not on the surface, anyway. He talks to who he likes, when he likes, and the last thing he bothers about is introductions. That's why he knows so many people."

Again Paula hesitated.

"I mean, he's the sort of person people do things for. Take me " she grinned. ""There I was, just getting ready to watch Ernst speak, who I always enjoy, when Alexey rushed up and next thing he persuaded me to dash off and get you and, of course, he probably could have gone and got you himself, the lazy sod, even if he did have a thousand things to do. I mean he'd certainly managed to get down to meet you earlier ….."

"Earlier?"

"Yes, he went down to meet you earlier, and waited, but you weren't there, so he rushed back because he was needed back in the hall."

"I see."

Yet more for Ingrid to ponder! So Alexey must have got there bang on seven - why yes, of course, she'd been five minutes late! But he hadn't mentioned it - hardly surprising, if true, because that would have suggested that while Ingrid had thought Alexey was worth waiting nearly an hour for, Alexey had allowed her just five minutes.

Chapter Ten

After saying goodnight to Ingrid and Pauline, Henry Thornton set out to walk home.

He wasn't bothered by the distance. He loved to walk. He hoped very much it would lift his mood; for tonight, as so often in his uncertain, difficult life, he felt depressed. And the night, and the stars, and the countryside, might help him.

Ah, if only he didn't feel so lonely! That evening he had felt the worst loneliness of all – that of one in a crowd. Not for nothing had he stayed so quiet in Alexey's rooms. This time the feeling had begun when Alexey and the others started, as they so often did, on their wild euphoria about the splendours of modern times, their declaration that the world was awakening, Lazarus-like, into a whole new age of plenitude and joy..... and Henry had felt utterly shut off. For Henry didn't feel like that at all.

Rather, he felt the opposite – with a feeling far more intense than Tom Huntingdon's jokey scepticism. He felt a strange, impending doom underlying everything, a doom that was paradoxical, he quite understood, given the economic boom, sexual emancipation and burgeoning social equality that seemed so obvious to everyone else. Yet a doom he felt the deepest truth of all.

It was as if some strange, inexplicable monstrosity was gaining on them all. Yet he was at a loss to say what it could be. A European War? Impossible, everyone agreed - the international credit system wouldn't stand it. Economic crash? More impossible still – look at the capital reserves built up by the industrial revolution. Well, what else? He had no idea – although whatever it was he felt it was 'written backwards', as he put it to himself, in the rabid optimism of the times. Above all in its louche, extreme, over-lush material display. Yet this was hardly an argument.

So what else was he supposed to tell his friends? That he felt something ominous and deadly in Mahler's symphonies? That he knew what Nietzsche meant by the 'coming century of terrible wars'? That modern painting and sculpture, even, seemed to crackle with violence and angst? These were just feelings; and his friends were only impressed by fact. 'Henry's off again', they would laugh– by no means unkindly - whenever he tried to put such notions into words. So he learned to keep quiet.

Walking swiftly, with his characteristic swinging, rolling gait, he quickly reached the Banbury Road in North Oxford. Soon he would be out of town and into the countryside. He would walk home, as he so often had before, by the light of the moon. Perhaps the natural world, his oldest, truest friend, might work its magic.

For when Henry walked in the countryside, above all on his own, far from feeling lonely he would feel more closely accompanied than when he was with another human being. His companion was nature. The result was more than mere 'therapy:' it was the most successful device he knew for lifting the depressions to which he was prone.

He certainly needed help right now. Because for two days, on and off, he had been arguing with his wife Mary, bitter, searing arguments that had rent and torn their relationship, and reduced his wife, not to mention their children, to tears. And the worst was that he knew it was almost all his fault.

He'd not felt right since that recent visit to Westbury Camp by George, Alexey and the young German woman who was, apparently, Alexey's latest 'conquest.' From the start he'd felt bad about having to ask the others for help with the building work – but he was so cack-handed, he could never do anything like that on his own.

Worse, Alexey, especially, had made him feel his incompetence acutely. Not in any obvious way, true, but by asking Henry to help with things, casually, and publicly, that he must have known Henry would find difficult (he asked him, for instance, to shape joints in the timber struts they were using, in plain view of all, on the work table outside; simple enough, but still demanding a certain basic flair.)

Then add on the further embarrassment - after Henry had got angry and begun his withdrawal - when Alexey made a further point of acting out flagrant concern for the women present, not least Mary. A concern, his manner seemed to underscore, not demonstrated by Henry himself.

With the result that by the time Alexey and co. had left, Henry was feeling utterly hopeless, both practically and emotionally. Soon he started snapping at the children, soon afterwards at Mary too, and then started the sequence of arguments that had been rumbling right up to now.

Henry swung on, out of the suburbs now and into a broad, glistening stretch of moon-lit meadow, no trees, so the full panoply of stars stretched out above him.

Sometimes, especially in summer, Henry had known the night-sky to breathe, seemingly, pure luxury, as if garlanded with wreaths of gold - but not to-night. Tonight the stars felt threatening; they spoke to him as they'd spoken earlier, when he'd been gazing through the window of Alexey's room.

And Henry remembered Pascal:

'Le silence eternel de ces espaces infinis m'effraie.'

Eternal silence!......yes .... silence infinite and unimaginable....an eternity of time.

At which moment, as if dictated, there came into his mind the lines:

'We are the old ones sere
Lost in the vastness of the night-sky drear...'

What was that! Where did it come from? What remarkable words! But from where? Had he read them? Like many people with a hyper-active subconscious, words and phrases often floated into his mind which he later realised he'd got out of books.

But he felt a spark of possibility. ***Could*** these be his own words? Surely not - they felt too authoritative. Henry suffered from the gifted man's fault of underestimating his own abilities. Yet - ***could*** they be? It had happened before. And if they were, might they not have the makings of a poem?

Now the spark of possibility flared into excitement: for whether these words were his or no, there ***was,*** surely, a poem in this strange, lighthouse flash of perception.

"We are the old ones sere," he muttered again to himself, "Lost in the vastness of the night-sky drear," and now other words were coming, looming large out of the mental gloom, tipping over the horizon of his mind:

".....And cold, unimaginably cold, and far, inconceivably far,
Billions upon billions of light years far, beyond the balance of the mind..."

Yes, that sounded powerful too – and that, at least, was certainly his own – so now he needed just one more line to round that initial riff off... and here it came...

"...to those who will be seeing us from the future…" Not so poetic this, but vital in another way - vital, quite simply, for the thought. What had Tolstoy said ? Thought and feeling must stand side by side, twin pillars indispensably supporting the whole. Lacking either, the whole artistic edifice comes crashing down. Having said which, that last line needed trimming – maybe ' to those who will *view* us from the future' – yes, that was better, just a touch more crisp. Yes, that was about it. That was a start.

And whipping out the torch he always carried on such jaunts Henry quickly jotted down the lines on the back of an envelope. So there they were, now, all the lines together, a real beginning:

"We are the old ones sere
Lost in the vastness of the night-sky drear
And cold, unimaginably cold, and far, inconceivably far,
Billions upon billions of light years far, beyond the balance of the mind,
To those who will view us from the future...."

And already this small, but real achievement was having its effect. Henry was feeling less depressed. Indeed he was feeling different, even, about his surroundings. He glanced up at the stars: austere, still, but they now felt austerely beautiful, glowing chastely against the night.

He felt almost happy.

Yet underneath his uncertainties rumbled on.

Let's be honest, Henry told himself, he'd made a pig's dinner of his life. He was married, yes, but why? Because he'd got Mary pregnant while she was still living at home, a mere seventeen, and this was in Henry's second year of music studies at New College.

A disaster for all, a huge embarrassment to both their families, and an event which came within a hair's breadth of getting him sent down. Only the intervention of friends - Alexey, for instance, who had wheeled out his rich and influential uncle - had led to a compromise, which included a donation to New College Chapel's Roof Fund and Henry and Mary's semi-exile to Westbury Camp.

For Alexey's uncle knew Westbury's founder, Anthony Parsons, and had long - there had been other donations - supported his work.

Then there were Henry's endemic difficulties with money. His father, a grinning, peace-and -progress chemist from Macclesfield, who disliked him, had decided that as part of the settlement of Henry's 'disaster' he would indeed continue to pay Henry's Oxford fees - but would withdraw his small allowance. Earning money might make his feckless son grow up.

So in addition to his regular music studies Henry had taken on other earning jobs like freelance violin playing - as well as earning anything he could by selling poetry, or articles, to London journals. In this he had had considerable success for one so young.....but little money.

All of which led to the fundamental conundrum of Henry's life: was he a success or a failure?

Many said his poetry was 'wonderful' - but his carpentry was dire. Or that he was brilliant at cricket - yet dreadful with machines. He himself knew he had a flair for horses, but he was hopeless at mathematics and emotionally inconsistent, to say the least, with his children.

Was he a prick or a prodigy? Who could say?

Chapter Eleven

And then he saw it. Rounding a bend of utter darkness, rearing abruptly in front of him, a cliff of rock. At least twenty feet high, with a face of dark grey iron: its top, crested with grass, surreally yellow in the brilliant moonlight. He'd seen the cliff before, on previous walks. It always spooked him.

He froze. Just a small green hill, but it felt like so much more. A viewpoint perhaps, even the plinth for a statue; a place that demanded a presence. And yet the weird thing was it was *his* presence, seemingly, it required. Though Henry had no idea why.

Come, it said, come and join me, this place is yours. Come and drink in its beauty, however fearsome – if you dare.

Henry stood and stared. A shiver ran down his back. This was how he always felt when he saw this place. How strongly he wanted to go up there; how desperately he did not! But he had never climbed it.

Yet now, he took a step forward; and then another; and then a third; he turned back for a moment; then suddenly, in a little rush, he was up the side and onto the top.

He stood and tried to fix his feet, still trembling. Around him the woods glowed ghostly in the dark, the moon cast shadows sharp-edged as the day; yet this was not what absorbed him.

Rather it was what he could see beneath. One false step and he would tumble twenty feet, he'd break his back, even his neck! He could end everything! No more failure, no more self-criticism, no more torturing all those he loved…….

Nevertheless, he moved back from the top - then suddenly slipped, slithered, and with a spasm of terror **knew** he was sliding over the edge. Thankfully he fell down where the slope was gentle, and in a turmoil of arms and legs he rolled to the ground .

For a minute he lay prone.

And started chuckling. Hitting the ground had literally brought him back to earth, and feelings that had overwhelmed him moments ago seemed suddenly small. Who *cared*, for God's sake, if he was an idiot or no? Nevertheless, as he continued his walk, he still felt subdued, until, turning a corner, he saw his second vision of the night.

This was different. As before, the moonlit meadow; once again, the louring trees; but now the meadow was dotted with black lumps. Three lumps, five, twenty – no, forty! What were they? Surely not cattle, they were too small. Nor horses, either. Why, they were deer! Wild roe deer, not the dumpy apologies you so often saw locally, called muntjacs. These, rather, were the kind you saw in parks, big, statuesque, with dappled coats. On two of them, gleaming in the moonlight, there were antlers.

They must have escaped from the local estate, Winchmore House, which had a deer park.

Truly, a vision. And Henry stopped, and stood, and drank it in. What were the deer doing, frozen motionless like this? Could they be asleep, standing up, like horses or cows? Or were they grazing, at this time of night? Yet such crowding questions were swiftly swallowed by one overriding feeling: the utter, magical beauty of these delicate creatures, so close in spirit to the meadows and the stars. Henry's earlier preoccupations vanished. All that was left now was wonder – and joy.

He stood there for five minutes watching them. Eventually the deer stirred, drifting slowly across the meadow, still utterly silent. Henry stepped gingerly forward. Instantly one deer, then two, then all of them, slipped lissomly away toward the wood. In a flash they were gone.

But their magic remained. The healing process Henry had so hoped for, when he set out earlier that evening, had begun. And now, as he gazed again at the grandeur and enormity of the sky, more lines came to him, yet more of his new poem:

".......We are the stars that they will see....
...... Staring down on them like eyes...
    Watching, waiting......

He stumbled for a moment, and then it came.... 'knowing....' yes, **knowing**, that was the word.... ' as the past , now, stares at us...'

And now, clear as a bell, came the rest of it - of this section, anyway:

"...The remote, glittering, billion-year-old past,
In the cold night."

Henry stopped, got out his notebook again, and wrote it down without correction. He had, as he put it to himself, 'got the head out.' The worst of the birthing process was done and he knew, now, that he would finish it.

And why not? He had finished all the others - over the years his poems had run into hundreds. Even though only fifty, in Henry's view, were remotely worth keeping.

One, appropriately enough for such a quiet patriot as Henry, was called 'England.' It described a moment he'd experienced a couple of years back, when he'd had a spare half hour and walked into Salisbury cathedral. He'd been deeply moved, not by any sense of Christianity, but by his feeling that the whole entity – building, monuments, music, even visitors - was like a shrine to Englishness: utterly pagan and beautiful, soaked through with the national spirit.

But it was another poem, 'Memory', which pleased him most of all. And this view was shared, emphatically, by most who read it.

Overtly it was about the Boer war, and the lies with which this, and all other wars, become encrusted the moment they were over – unlike the fleshly corruption of their victims, the young men. Whose bones, divested of their rotting flesh, would rapidly ' shine clean and white in morning's sight,' as Henry put it.

'How deep then must we cut to find war's bones!' he'd said – but this was just the kind of thing some readers didn't like. They felt the only corruption that mattered in the Boer War was the worldview of the Boers themselves. As for any other wars Henry might have in mind, they didn't care.

Which was fortunate, really, because if they'd known the war Henry actually meant they'd have thought him crazier still. For what Henry had in mind had nothing to do with the past or the Boers (though it applied to them too) rather the European Armageddon he so strongly sensed was coming.

The poem was not really about 'Memory' at all: it was prophetic.

But Henry only ever told his wife this, and commanded her discretion. He'd had enough of being laughed at by his friends.

Nevertheless, ' Memory' was why he knew he was a poet. If he had done it once he could do it again. And now there came, as through an unblocked stream, the last lines of his new 'Stars' poem. After a little more stopping and starting, he had the whole thing:

"We are the old ones sere
Lost in the vastness of the night-sky drear
And cold, unimaginably cold, and far, inconceivably far,
Billions upon billions of light years far, beyond the balance of the mind,
To those who will view us from the future;
We are the stars that they will see
Staring down on them like eyes,
Watching, waiting, knowing, as the past, now, stares at us;
The remote, glittering, billion-year-old past,
In the cold night.

All our loves, hates, plans, sly histories, despairs
Our hard-won oases of security,
The bloom on our childrens' cheeks, our warmths, our fears,
All just a gleam, an unutterably miniscule prick
On the broad dark back of eternity

Stretching billions upon billions of light years across space
Billions upon billions of stars, stretching before and after."

He sat and thought about it; jotted it down; lit a pipe. He gazed, again, at the momentous stars. He felt satisfied.

'I've laid an egg' he told himself.

Chapter Twelve

By six o-clock he arrived at the hillside overlooking Westbury Camp. The daybreak was lovely: the first rays of early sun, where it burst through the gaps in the trees, burned brilliant shafts of green across the frost.

So idyllic was the scene that for a moment Henry had, for him, the rarest of feelings: a sense of privilege. Down there was everything he cared for: his home, his wife, and the children he adored. And at that very moment a door opened in the side of the long, low hut his family lived in, and out came his youngest daughter, Josephine, carrying a white bowl, flanked by her mother.

Josephine disappeared round a corner, evidently to feed the chickens; Mary stood with arched back and hand to her forehead, staring upwards toward the ridge where Henry was standing.

She didn't see him, he was too high amid the trees. He waved and shouted but she didn't hear. Back came his daughter, and, with her mother's arm around her, she peered upward too. And Henry's heart went out to both of them. Above all to Josephine, the youngest and his favourite.

For Josephine was the one creature on the planet for whom he felt pure, uncomplicated love - and felt loved back.

At which moment he felt a wallop on his back, which plunged him to the ground. He looked up to see a shotgun pointed at his nose.

"Gotcha!" cried a grinning face. It was Fred Parsons, the son of Anthony Parsons' brother, Joe Parsons - the farmer who owned the Camp Holmbury site. Three other laughing faces surrounded Fred – two farmworkers, Ted Molesley and Ben Tennant, both of whom Henry knew – and old Joe Parsons himself.

"You're nicked!" said Joe. "We told you we was doing a push on poachers – you should have been warned!"

"One move and you're horse-meat" said Fred.

"Unfair on the horse!" said Ben.

And as one they reached down and hauled Henry to his feet, slapping him on his back.

"Good to see you, mate!" cried red-faced, vast-stomached Joe, thrusting his tweed cap to the back of his head with a broad grin, as if their mode of greeting had been the most natural thing in the world. "What have you been up to? Not another of your walks!"

"Of course," said Henry, grinning back, and shaking Joe's hand. "I've just walked all the way from Oxford."

"Go on!"

"And I saw some deer."

"Bang-bang!" cried Fred.

"Not that you'd ever hit them - "

"Oh yeah?" And Fred put his gun to his shoulder and let fly at a passing wood pigeon. He missed by a mile. A cluster of leaves floated forlornly down.

"My point precisely."

"Go on!"

And so the banter continued. Joe Parsons and his men were, indeed, on the lookout for poachers and had been out, as they so often were, since first light that morning.

More surprising perhaps, given their huge difference in manner, was how well they got on with Henry. Yet they were, in fact, just the kind of jolly, unpretentious people Henry liked. Joe especially, who Henry preferred, if truth were told, to his do-gooding brother Anthony - more Alexey's taste than his own.

Standing there, bright-breathed and cheery, the countrymen were like an artist's evocation of old-time rural England.

On an impulse Henry said:

"Come and have some breakfast!"

"What, all of us?" said Joe.

"Yes, all of you, of course! It'll be no trouble!"

"No trouble to you, maybe," said Joe, with another huge grin, "but what about Mary?"

"Oh she'll be fine," said Henry. "There's loads of food."

Which was more than he knew, in fact, though what he hoped.

But then Henry would often make kingly offers of this kind, while it would fall to others, it must be said, to carry them out.

Yet if Henry's wife *was* thrown by this, she kept it well hidden. When Henry, with his add-on of four guests, strode down into the camp, she came running out and, regardless of the company, threw her arms round him, smothering him in kisses. Henry's two daughters bolted after her, each grasping one of Henry's legs or an arm, hugging them and whooping with delight.

So evidently overjoyed was Mary to see Henry that it was clear she would accommodate anything he required. Four extra places for breakfast, it seemed, were nothing. Moments later she and the girls disappeared inside; shortly afterward a wonderful smell of bacon, eggs and sausages wafted out. Plates were laid on one of the worktables outside and the whole company began eating in the morning sun.

"So have you caught any, Joe?" asked Henry, spluttering through his sausages and eggs. "Any poachers, I mean? Real ones?

"We had one two days ago. Winged him. Young bloke, I think, by the way he run."

"How could he run if you'd winged him?"

"Only clipped him up the arse. Probably made him run all the faster."

"That's the spirit Joe!" cried Henry. "He shoots the rabbits; you shoot him; Fred shoots you, probably by mistake...."

"Probably on purpose."

"That's not very nice! Not very nice, eh Henry?"

And Joe sat there waving a sausage around on the end of a fork with his gap-toothed grin, while Henry thought how good his coffee tasted, how happy he felt, and how different life seemed from just a few hours earlier.

Yet there was a further reason why Mary had greeted him so fulsomely.

It was relief. Because, a couple of days earlier, rummaging through one of their bedroom cupboards, she'd found a jewelled, imitation Spanish 'poniard', or miniature dagger, behind his notebooks. He must have bought it in a second-hand shop, thought Mary. How like him to choose something so medieval-looking and florid! But then - some strange, instinctive anxiety came over her. ***Why*** had he bought it?

Henry had talked, recently, of a friend of theirs who'd slit his wrists. No, come now, this was ridiculous! However bad his depressions, suicide had never been his style. Even so, she was used to those black, terrible moods when he would leave the camp and disappear for hours, even days on end......

And she had wondered.

She wondered sufficiently, given their dreadful recent arguments, that after Henry had left the previous evening she'd found herself checking the cupboard to make sure the poniard was still there. And it had gone! A stab of fear.

So that she'd found herself counting the minutes till he came back. From the moment it was light, in fact – she couldn't sleep. Which was why Henry had seen her standing there looking out for him.

But he'd returned! Quite clearly, in the best of spirits! On the face of it, her concerns had been just as she had suspected – absurd.

Nevertheless, she could not resist just one more act, the most ridiculous, she had to admit, of all. Waiting till Henry had gone off to rest, she slipped into their cloakroom. And there she rummaged through the great tweed jacket, with its huge pockets, specially tailored for notebooks and maps, that Henry always used for walks, and had worn that night.

In the right hand pocket she found his pipe – and little else.

But in the left she found tobacco, coins, a map, some handkerchiefs…. ….and …..at the very bottom of the pocket …….Henry's 'poniard' .

That gleaming, threatening little knife.

Chapter Thirteen

Henry slept till the early afternoon. Shocked by what she had discovered, Mary let him be.

Come two o-clock Mary, peeling potatoes in the kitchen, heard thumps from the bedroom. It was Henry, starting to stir. Soon, en route to the bathroom, he poked his head round the door; grinned at her, tickled her ribs and was gone. There followed a fearsome rendering of 'The Lincolnshire Poacher', echoing through the walls. Mary smiled. They both loved English folk songs. When Henry sang, it was a sure sign he was happy.

He reappeared, naked to the waist, rubbing his hair dry. Mary offered him something for lunch, a ham sandwich perhaps? But no, Henry declared that he was still 'stuffed', as he put it, from breakfast and food was the last thing he wanted right now.

"What do you want then?" said Mary.

"You" he said, staring laughingly into her eyes. "I request the privilege of sexual intercourse."

This mock-formal 'request' was their standing joke.

"Sexual intercourse? That's rather sudden isn't it? I'll have to think about that."

Mary rocked her head from side to side.

"Hmmmm. I wonder. Hmmmmm. Well, you've got one thing right, anyway – it *is* a privilege. And one a very great many other men might value too, unless I much mistake them."

"Oh, which men?"

"Oh, quite a lot. Now let me see: One two, three...." Mary started counting off on her fingers....... "eight, nine, ten, dear me, I've run out of fingers. By the way, what *is* sexual intercourse? You know how big words puzzle me."

"Fear not - I'll show you."

"How sweet of you! There's just one problem."

"What's that?

"You'll have to catch me first."

And Mary was off and away, with a quicksilver speediness startling in one so stolid. They tore out into the yard, plunged through the chicken coop, then rushed back into the kitchen where Mary scooped up the potato bowl and, cocking it under one arm, threw potatoes as she ran. Finally, with a great leap, Henry cornered her on the balcony outside. He scooped her up, fists flailing, and slung her over his shoulder.

Transferring her to his arms, like a cliché bridegroom, he marched into the bedroom, shoved open the door, and moments later they were making love, with the naive ardour of newlyweds.

For one thing they never lost, in all their difficulties, was their delight in each other's bodies.

Nor something else, which had been with them from the start: Henry's everlasting ability to infect Mary with his moods, which could swing as violently upward as ever they swung down. Overwhelmed by Henry's jollity, Mary's anxieties, however temporarily, disappeared.

After making love they fell asleep, curled into one another like puppies. Eventually, both stirred. And Henry's face broke into a deep, rich smile, his happiest look of all. How different, Mary thought, from his desperate, haggard look when they had rows! But this, now, was the man she loved and, above all, admired: how much had he taught her over the years, about literature, music, nature, sex, everything really, despite being only a year or two older than she.

"You know" he stumbled, ".... I wish...... I love you. I...... ......love you. And I love the kids. I just wanted to say that. I don't say it often enough."

Mary smiled back, and snuggled up to his shoulder.

"I love you too, dear," she said.

"You know.....all the other stuff....... it's like a kind of pretence. I don't know why I do it. But *this* is real; it's beneath it all. The truth is, I'm like two people. But," Henry repeated, "this is me, now, here. This is real."

He chuckled. "Realer, certainly, than all that poetry. And yet......." he laughed again. " I've a confession to make! I've just written another poem! I've had intercourse with your rival - you know, the White Goddess, my muse? Spiritual rather than physical intercourse, **naturally."**

This too, Mary had been expecting. He'd come back from Oxford with his depression vanished, and she'd long known that only three things could achieve this. One, the most reliable of all, was time spent with nature; another, violin-playing; the third, writing poetry. She knew he'd walked from Oxford in hope of the first; if he'd written a poem en route then he'd achieved the third, too. He'd been doubly blessed, and Mary rejoiced for him.

Her only sadness was that she herself could not have cured him.

Mary swung out of bed to make some tea.

"You've spoiled me, now I shall spoil you," she said.

She reached out to him and they clasped hands, both sliding their fingers over the other's as she moved on. With her customary firm tread, but with a buoyancy, now, that was new, she stepped into the kitchen.

For all the love of art she shared with Henry, she had a woman's delight in homely things. And now, as she filled the kettle, opened the tea tin and spooned some into the teapot, each action gave her a small, but definite, pleasure.

The kettle whistled. She got up to rescue it; and as she approached the hob, she noticed, for the first time, three letters by the front door. The post!

She felt a stab of alarm: letters so often meant trouble, and could threaten this oasis of good mood.

Three letters: one, made out of fine, creamy manilla paper, was postmarked Oxford. Probably one of Henry's New College friends, almost certainly Alexey. Another, judging by the scratchy, spidery handwriting, was from her father. That would be fine.

The third, however, she eyed with alarm. She recognized it for sure: it was from the Criterion – there was the name, printed in rather startling Prussian blue, in the top left-hand corner. This was the monthly magazine to which Henry had been contributing for upwards of a year, and which had developed into a key source of income.

Since two months now, the Criterion had got itself a new editor, someone Henry only knew slightly, and this interloper had brought his own, new gang of contributors. The last two articles Henry had sent them had been rejected. This too could be a rejection! And then what?

She gazed hatefully at the envelope. She squeezed it: oh dear oh dear, there was an enclosure – yet another article sent back! Three in a row, that surely spelt the end! She made a quick calculation: Henry had been selling them roughly two a month, at three pounds apiece: six pounds. Yet even then they had been running a monthly loss of two pounds; now this could shoot up to eight!

And Rosemary had worn her overcoat a winter too long; and Josephine's shoes were not only letting in water, they were catching the ankle where the leather had worn, giving her a sore. The firm set of Mary's eyebrows was now joined by a line of worry, one that was giving her the face she'd surely have in middle age. Oh dear oh dear, just when she'd hoped for some calm!

She gritted her teeth and took Henry's envelopes into the bedroom.

"Post, dear," she said, offhand.

Henry, too, looked studiously indifferent; until, that is, he saw the dreaded word 'Criterion.'

"Oh, God," he said.

He ripped it open. Mary studied his face. Enclosed, indeed, was one of his articles, a piece he'd written about ' lost villages'. Also a letter.

He read it to the very end: his mouth set; for five seconds he sat in silence.

"Good God !" He cried. And his face broke into a grin.

"Mary! Really! You wouldn't believe! Listen to this!"

The letter, it turned out was from Godfrey Wilder, a London friend, some years his senior. A poet, like Henry, who wrote articles too. He'd been made associate editor of the Criterion! And was determined, his letter explained, to reverse their late, anti-Henry tendency there and make sure that in future Henry's stuff was once again used.

Starting indeed, with the enclosed - which Godfrey loved, he said, but about which the editor had made just a few small criticisms - easily accommodated. So easily indeed, and so harmlessly, that Godfrey had taken the liberty of pencilling in the emendations himself, to save Henry the trouble. All he and Henry had to do, he said, was sway, 'poplar-like' to the wind of the editor's recommendations, 'sway back when his attention is diverted', and all would be well.

And having published this, there should be many more.

Oh, and one other thing. The new management were paying new fees. From now on, Henry would be on " £6 a throw". Mary noted the encouraging informality.

"How wonderful!" cried Mary doing the lightning mental arithmetic she did six times a day. Instead of eight pounds a month deficit, four pounds ahead!

"Well doesn't that just show you," she declared, the tension draining from her face. "In life, you never know."

Never indeed. Because a moment later, Henry opened the last remaining letter, the one from Alexey. Once more, the concentration. But this time, no smile. Mary flinched.

"What is it, dear?"

"It's from father."

"Your *father*? I thought it was from....."

"I thought so too. My father stayed a night in Oxford, apparently, and must have posted it there."

"Oh, I see." Mary drooped like a flower; she knew what this could mean.

And indeed Henry said nothing, but sat in silence, glaring. Oh dear, oh dear, how well Mary knew that silence and that look! But she knew better than to say anything: eventually, still silent, but with the gaze with which one stares into a tomb, Henry passed the letter to her.

It started breezily enough - how were they all, how was Mary, how were the children? How was the new piano? Was Josephine still 'boxing'?! All routine. As was the section that followed, when Mr. Thornton got on, as usual, to health. His asthma was worse, his wife's arthritis better, but now something new: a mysterious neuralgia in his wife's neck. She'd been for tests but the doctors, as usual! seemed incapable of diagnosis.

The subtext of which – again, routine - was: " And you think YOU'VE got problems?"

And now, the nub. For the letter turned out to be a demand for money.

A new chemist had opened up fifty yards away from his father's shop, just down the high street. For years, Henry's father had had a virtual monopoly of the chemist business in his part of town. But now he would be forced to compete, and that meant expansion, building work, more staff – which meant money. What he was asking was that Henry should help out. 'We've helped you, rather often if you consider it - perhaps now you could help us."

He would like Henry to contribute an agreed, fixed sum every month. Frankly, Henry should look on it as an investment. Without such help the Thornton business might be in peril and Henry's father might not be able to continue to pay Henry's fees. In short: 'we stand or fall together.'

His father suggested......maybe …. six pounds a month?

The daffodils under the apple trees, he finished up, were blooming quite beautifully, and as for the climbing roses – the ones on the stable – to judge by the buds it should be a cracking year for those as well.

"Glad about the climbers", said Mary, putting the letter down.

"Yes, characteristic, that," said Henry.

"Well, I suppose we might be able to give them something," said Mary, "if not quite what he asks."

Henry exploded. "Don't you *realise*? If we give him six pounds that will neatly, perfectly, account for all the extra we might have got from Godfrey. To the very penny!"

"Only if we give him all of it. I mean, if we should give him, say, half...."

"Oh dear, Mary" and now there was a terrible, dead disappointment in Henry's voice, the tone that Mary dreaded most of all "Will you ever, ever, grasp the REALITY of what it means to be a freelance? It's not a job! The money is not regular! That six pounds is at best an estimate, and a singularly optimistic estimate at that! It could still very easily go wrong….."

"I thought Godfrey said you only had to make minor adjustments, and he's already - ...."

"- Yes, yes, I did say that, but we still don't know if the editor will approve them, not to mention how I feel about Godfrey changing my work! Some of his suggestions are okay, but some aren't trivial at all, they change things quite significantly – the truth is Godfrey's got some nerve, unilaterally rewriting my stuff - "

 "But surely he was only trying to ..."

"Yes, yes, but it still remains my own piece of writing, a piece of *me*. It's just not something a fellow-writer should ever do. Oh dear, why do I even bother? We've been over this so many times! I feel about my writing like you feel about....about........having babies . But then ….." ….reflectively….."it's something you've never experienced, it's not your fault."

"No! No! You're quite right! It isn't my fault!" Now Mary was erupting. It took a lot to provoke her but when she did she was a Vesuvius.

"There *is* a great deal I don't understand! I don't understand why I'm supposed to live on twopence a week when I've got two children to support AND be expected to teach! I don't understand why everything must come back to your self-obsession with 'possibly' creating 'art' when what we know *for sure* is we've got children to feed and no money to do it with! It's beyond me why - "

" - I've always been honest with you – we've never done anything that hasn't been agreed by both of us - "

"Have we? Have we agreed everything? Did we agree last night when you took it into your head to stroll back eight hours after your meeting?"

"Well yes, I told you that I - "

"Did you? Did you r*eally*? Did you really tell me *everything* that happened on that walk?"

Mary stared wide eyed at Henry, while he, equally distraught, stared back. The reality was in both their eyes.

Henry spun on his heel, strode into the bedroom and got dressed. Moments later he reappeared, carrying a map, walked past Mary without a word and opened the front door. "I'm going out," he said. "I don't know how long I'll be. I'm sorry but I don't always know these things. Oh, and I hope we've *agreed* this, incidentally, or putting it another way, that I have your permission."

And he strode off, slamming the door. Mary heard a strangled sob. She turned toward the childrens' room. Rosemary and Josephine were standing in the doorway, wide-eyed.

Chapter Fourteen

For Mary, this was a watershed. For weeks now, there'd been a sea change in her feelings about Henry but this was different. She finally realised how unwell he really was.

The situation was impossible. How could it go on? This mad oscillation between hilarity and despair! One moment she would know, in her gut, that Henry was on the very verge of suicide; the next he would be full of fulsome love; the next, of tempestuous self-hate. The main symptom of which would be his casual, almost whimsical aggression toward whoever happened to be around - usually Mary.

Indeed it had reached the stage, lately, when she was beginning to think she too was going crazy. She'd had dizzy spells for weeks, and two nights ago had woken up, momentarily, unable to breathe ....

Let alone - she shuddered at the thought – what all this might be doing to her daughters. What kind of adults do children become who've been brought up in such an atmosphere? The answer being obvious she tried, very hard, to dismiss it from her mind.

Something must be done.

Having said which she knew very well the root cause of this latest outburst –of nearly all of them, if truth were known.

Henry felt, acutely, his inability to earn.

This conventional view might seem surprising given Henry's seeming bohemianism, yet there it was. But it was connected to one of the qualities that made him unusual: unlike most intellectuals, unlike, certainly, nearly all his Oxford friends, he identified better, in many ways, with the values and mores of ordinary people than ever he did with those of 'art.' And a key ethic of 'ordinary' husbands was earning power.

And these money matters were entwined with something deeper still - Henry's relationship with his father. Throughout Henry's life his father, himself insecure, had been at pains to make Henry feel a fool. This had taken, over the years, many forms but in Henry's adulthood the main one had been Henry's failure, in Mr. Thornton's eyes, to support his family. "It is the first and last responsibility of every man," he would pronounce, "to provide for his wife and children."

True, Henry was only 25, and was living, to say the least, a difficult life. Not one of his friends - some of whom, like Alexey, were very well off indeed - had even to *think* of supporting a family while finishing a degree. But his father was innocent of such understanding.

Neither from this paternal source, then, nor, to be honest, from any other – not even from his beloved Alexey - had Henry ever been consistently supported.

Mary pondered all this, that day, for many hours. What could she do? While Henry's deepest difficulties were lost in the obscurities of his childhood, the one thing which would, right now, make an immediate difference would be to help his over-riding ambition to be a poet.

And this would naturally, in the right circumstances, simultaneously address that other central question, money.

But what on earth could that something be?

Mary thought and thought. But after revolving in a seemingly endless series of parabolas, she always came back to the same place. However improbable it might seem, however wildly impractical, the only person who could truly help Henry was the one person who had been utterly, unreservedly committed to him from the start, through thick and thin... ....herself.

She was the one, above all others – however amateurish her taste – who genuinely revered his work; she was the one, loving him as she did, who longed for his success; she was the one - with her own happiness, even sanity, and that of her children! – at stake, for whom his failure was, quite simply, unthinkable.

Of course she lacked the necessary sophistication. Of course she lacked the contacts. But she did have one quality in superabundance: faith. Perhaps she, Mary Thornton, energetic, unknown she, without reputation, without contacts, without social clout of any kind ......might somehow, somewhere, enable Henry's dream. And she would do it by exercising the one quality she ***did*** have: .... willpower.

And as this last thought came over her, her demeanour changed as swiftly as ever did her husband's. The worry lines faded. Even her colour changed. Instead, her thick firm eyebrows once more seemed to dominate her face, plus a new, jutting certainty around her mouth – everything implied, in fact, by that other seeming incongruity, the heavy tread of her walk.

Not for nothing had George once described her as "a strong character masquerading as a weak."

Chapter Fifteen

So after putting on the children's lunch, and doing her swiftest-ever tidying-up, Mary began.

She strode to the bureau in the corner of the kitchen and pulled out a sheet of paper. She wrote at the top, in capital letters: HENRY'S POETRY. She sucked her pen like a little girl. Then underneath: **Steps to take.**

And stopped dead. What on earth to write next? Well.... the key to it all, clearly, was getting the right person, with the right connections, to read Henry's stuff. But who could that possibly be? She reviewed the options. The process was alarmingly quick. In their limited rural acquaintance there was, frankly, no-one all who could possibly help at all. Except……ah, possibly…….yes!........ Alexey. At least he was discreet.

So the next day, when Henry had left for Oxford for a tutorial, she wrote a short note to Alexey saying there was something she would like to talk about over lunch. And as she expected, back, by the next post, came a charming letter offering to meet. They duly met, he was utterly understanding, and suggested he spoke to his uncle, Sergey Smolensky, who 'knew everyone.'

And his uncle promptly got in touch with Ronny Henderson, a friend, who in turn put him onto Eric Rother, a civil servant who was also a distinguished critic, and who especially liked poetry.

And Rother was immediately interested: not least because it turned out, most fortunately, that Rother was just about to make his debut as a small publisher - publishing poems.

But also because Ronny Henderson had told him, in a casual, throwaway line, that Henry Thornton's wife, this Mary who he would almost certainly meet, without her husband, was charming, bright....... and very, very pretty .

Not that Henderson had ever met her – but he knew what worked with Rother.

So within a week, back came word that Rother would be delighted to read Henry's work, and here was his Albany address to which Mary might send a selection.

So Mary sent Henry's latest - the ' Stars' poem he'd just written, and 'Memory', and ' England'; the other two that Henry thought his best.

Rother's reply was prompt.

He'd been most struck by the poems, he wrote, and would very much like to include them in his forthcoming anthology. Indeed his sole reservation was that he needed more - each poet would be represented by a minimum of six. Were there others he could see?

He gathered that at this stage, for understandable reasons, Mary would prefer that Henry, personally, should not be involved. Well, would she like to come and see him herself? And bring the extra poems? As well as the Albany, he had rooms in New College, Oxford; the very same college where Henry and his friends were students. (Strange that he should have managed this, but Sergey Smolensky, a college donor , had got him in there.)

Nothing so bad as going all the way to London.

Rother would be there from Thursday to Tuesday next week, and then from Friday onward the week after. Would any of these days suit? Please let him know.

Well!.. ….At one level the news was wonderful. This could be just the opportunity Mary had hoped for.

But Rother's letter begged other questions too. There was, Mary presumed, a difference between ' liking' to publish something and making a definite offer. And how would he feel about any new poems she might send?

More, Mary was inexperienced but no fool. Much though she wanted to believe this was all about Henry's poetry….. meeting her on her own, in his 'office' - come now!

Nevertheless she accepted by return, and was already planning her toilette for the trip. She would look affluent but sedate, rather than chic. Indeed, for once in her life, she'd try very hard to look ten years older than her age.

Chapter Sixteen

Next week, at New College, she knocked on Eric Rother's door. It was flung wide by a middle aged man with swept- back, glistening hair, who looked like he enjoyed a drink. He wore a short white linen jacket; he smiled, with just a touch of insolence.

"Mrs. Thornton?"

Mary nodded.

"We're expecting you."

A whoop from somewhere inside. "Oh, excellent!" cried a high tenor voice, with a slight squeak. "Do ask her in."

And Mary understood. The doorman was a college servant.

As she entered, she saw an elaborate-looking lunch table in one corner of the room, and the servant was plainly there to service it. A gleam of silver; a snow-white table-cloth; even candles. Eric Rother evidently had a clear idea of how their interview might develop.

With landscapes on the walls, and a long, ancient settee, slightly musty, plus armchairs, in front of the fire..... the room looked like the drawing room of a country house. Except, that is, for a kind of 'display' (or so Mary thought of it) that lurked in a corner.

This was startling. A long, low Eastern-looking sedan filled up with scatter cushions; still more, much larger, cushions built up around it, with tapestry covers; up above, at a height of ten feet, a canopy such as you might see on a four-poster bed, draped with Egyptian curtains. All climaxed, at the very very top, with peacock feathers spread out in a fan.

Mary had heard Eric Rother had spent years in the Middle East and was an expert on Omar Khayyam, but this wasn't how this weird confection felt. It felt, quite simply, like some naïf, pocket harem: the louche fantasy of an overgrown adolescent.

Nevertheless, Rother greeted her charmingly.

"How delightful to meet you, Mrs. Thornton. ***Do*** sit down. I ***do*** appreciate your coming all this way. So you found it alright? Perhaps a drink? Sherry? Do let me take your coat."

Eric Rother looked sixtyish, all pink and white ebullience, with much waving of arms.

"Perhaps some water," said Mary, arranging herself on the sofa, while the servant vanished with her coat. Moments later he reappeared with a glass, on a silver tray. Then he left.

"Well! I have read your husband's poems!" Suddenly Rother's manner became exaggeratedly business-like. He strode across the room and swept up a file from his desk. "And to be honest, as I said in my letter, I find them quite – quite.......superb." A look of alarm, almost- even a laugh.

"They're original, imaginative, and beautifully worked. Tell me, let me guess - your husband is a Keats lover, is he not?

"Keats is his favourite," smiled Mary.

A squeaking whoop. Eric Rother looked pleased as a boy. "I knew it! These poems are truly Keatsian – they have the same luxuriance of phrase, the sensual extravagance, and – and - a breadth of sensibility which is near-medieval.

" I especially enjoyed the poem ' Memory'. A quite extraordinary image, I thought, that of the bones?......."

"It's his favourite. He thinks it's the best he's ever written."

"Well, *I* think it's one of the best I've read! Anyway! **Did** you bring those other poems we talked about?"

"I certainly did," said Mary, pulling her own folder out of her bag, and handing them to him.

"Thankyou! Thankyou! That really is most kind. I'll put them with the others. I'll look forward very much to reading them just as soon as I can. Tonight I hope! And I'll give you my thoughts, I promise, very promptly indeed."

At that moment the servant - his name was Edward - reappeared with the food, brought up from the kitchens under metal covers.

He opened a bottle of 1898 Nuits St. Georges, and decanted it.

Rother wondered if Mary might like to sit down? With a rustle of her ample skirts Mary moved across and joined him at the lunch table.

Edward removed the metal covers – the lunch was pheasant - and helped Mary and Rother to peas, Vichy carrots and new potatoes. With a flourish Edward added gravy; with another flourish he lit the candles. Once again he left.

The overture is over, thought Mary. Now for the show.

For Eric Rother's self-consciously business-like air had vanished. Now, his manner seemed to imply, the human stuff began.

"We've talked a lot about your husband" he said, " but what about you?" And he leaned back expectantly. For if there was one thing Rother knew about women it was the sine qua non of getting them to talk about ***themselves***. It was, paradoxically, the thing that got them interested in you. But first:

"Oh, by the way" he said, as if forgetting something, "allow me" and made as if to pour some of the decanted wine into Mary's glass. She covered it with her hand. Rother drew back, but poured a little into his own. He took a sip, and smiled encouragingly.

"Well, I'm not sure what to say," stumbled Mary. "I'm a housewife; I look after my children, I do some teaching....."

"Oh yes, I heard about the teaching, " said Rother. " Henderson mentioned it. I'll confess, I'm not surprised. It's obvious you have empathy. And if I'm not mistaken, though it's a subtler point, you've no difficulty with discipline either. Is not that firmness I see there in your eyebrows? However politely you try to hide it?! Empathy ***and*** firmness, yes, I can see it. Ideal for teaching - iron hands in velvet gloves."

"Well, it has been said of me that I'm a 'strong character masquerading as a weak' laughed Mary. "Though why, I've no idea."

"Really? Believe me, *I* can see it. Indeed, I've heard of still more virtues from those who know you. To whit, for instance, that you're ' the ideal wife for a poet.'"

"Who said that?"

"Now that I am not at liberty to tell you. But be assured I am quite sure it is correct."

"How so?"

"Because I have been observing you, very carefully, since you came in. You are, *yourself*, poetical - very different from being, say, academic. You love nature, children and laughter: poetic tastes. But above all you love your husband – and it is the poet in your husband that you admire. Is that not why you are here? To promote his work? You are his ardent champion and God knows a poet, of all people, needs one. All I can say is that I hope he appreciates you."

"Well, sometimes he does," said Mary.

And this time she accepted Eric Rother's offer of wine.

First one glass, and then, under pressure - why not? - one more. No doubt this was why she quickly found herself, with Rother's gentle encouragement, telling him a great deal more than she intended about life with Henry.

"He has these extraordinary mood swings," she said. "Sometimes within half an hour. They really frighten me."

Now she found herself telling Rother about Henry's sudden disappearances, then next about his still more sudden, *re*-appearances (like the morning of the poniard, though she left the poniard out.) Then above all, however much everything she was describing terrified *her*, how still more scared she was of its effect on the children.

Her voice broke as she spoke. Yet Rother, while deeply sympathetic, didn't seem remotely surprised.

"It's insupportable," he agreed. "And quite impossible to live with. Yet what you just might not have quite realised is that the one thing it is *not* is unusual. I have to tell you, I've yet to meet a creative artist - certainly a genuinely *original* one - who was any different. Indeed, perversely, it's a sign – a sine qua non, almost – of Henry's talent."

"Really?" said Mary, wide eyed. "Have you really met a lot of poets like this?"

"Innumerable, I'm afraid," said Rother. "In fact, as I've often told myself, my lifelong ambition is finding one who's *not* like that – an ambition which has so far singularly failed.

"And the extraordinary thing is that in their 'up' moods they are if anything rather *sweeter* and full of loving-kindness– certainly of understanding - than other men."

"That's exactly how it is with Henry," said Mary.

Yet what happened next was stranger still.

Mary, increasingly fascinated by their talk, began to hope that somewhere in all this might lie the golden apercu she'd been seeking for years that would finally unravel Henry. Connecting madness and creativity was one thing - 'great wits are sure to madness near allied' and all that - but how could craziness actually *help* the productive process? One would have thought, she said, the precise opposite?

"Loneliness, in a word," replied Rother, "or aloneness."

The average person, he said – including everyone conventional, however talented - above all wants to be *in the herd*. "Their ideas change, yes, but only like birds in a flock or fish in a shoal, when everyone else changes too."

But the artist of true originality - usually due to some childhood trauma, or some such – grows up emotionally separate. "Horrible - lonely – but making it possible to see life directly, like a child."

"The Emperor's new clothes," said Mary.

"Exactly. Yet this is merely a starting point. Most mad and lonely people have no talent at all. Take me, for instance - I'm quite mad, so everyone tells me, and certainly very lonely....."

"You, lonely – I don't believe it! You see people all the time!"

"Yes, but only superficially. That's why...... that's why......I find a conversation like this so.....interesting. With you, I feel a connection.......I feel sympathy."

"That's because *you* have sympathy! It's catching! But tell me, really, Mr. Rother - forgive my forwardness - whatever could make anyone as *simpatico* as yourself - lonely?"

"What makes anyone anything? Well – as you've been so honest now I'll be honest with you too: my father, is the simple, and honest answer."

"But how?"

"He's dead of course. But to answer your question...... he was a doctor, but he was utterly remote, emotionally and I never got near him. And yet" and now, incredibly, Eric Rother's voice, like Mary's earlier, began to break - " he did this wonderful work, and even though we could never talk, deep down I had the profoundest respect for him."

Visibly struggling, he went on.

"There's one thing I always remember. How every now and then, as a family, we'd come across some medical emergency when we were out, perhaps an accident .There was a railway crash once, I remember, this train de-railed right near where we lived, and there were children hurt and ordinary, confident people running about screaming..... and then my father, this shy, diffident, retiring man..... walked up..... and took charge."

Eric Rother was now almost in tears. He looked hugely embarrassed.

"I'm sorry, this always happens when I talk like this."

The whole thing, in fact, had been one of those conversational accidents that transform an encounter. For the truth was, of course, that both Mary and Rother were, in different ways, out to seduce.

Mary, to promote her husband's interests and, for all her wariness, to exploit her sexual power; Rother, however much he denied it to himself, to do what he had always done with women - bed Mary. Yet both, by a fluke, had stumbled on something more human and more true. By the time Mary left, just after five in the afternoon, they were firm friends.

And the upshot, for Mary, was that she ended up manipulating Rother far more effectively than ever she could have done by plan.

Because, more than a little ashamed of his more louche intentions, Rother finished their lunch utterly determined to help Mary and her remarkable, if complex husband. A determination further enhanced when he read those extra poems.

Within a week he sent a letter to Westbury Camp. Not only would he publish the six poems as part of the anthology; more, he had now shown Henry's work to his old friend Cecil Hampton. Were Mary and Henry familiar with Cecil's company, Landmark Books?

And Cecil, it turned out, was yet more enthusiastic than Rother himself. Indeed, he'd said he wanted to publish Henry's poetry in a new, exclusive edition, devoted to Henry's work alone; which would require yet more poems - maybe sixty or seventy in all. Did Mary think Henry had that many to hand?

"Do I think so?" cried Henry when she told him. "Well, yes, I think so, just about, oh yes, I think so, bloody marvellous - "

And grabbing Mary he swung her high above his head.

"Yes of course I do, because I've got the most marvellous bloody wife in the whole bloody marvellous world!"

Which was fortunate, really, because he'd yet again been behaving badly for the previous few days. He'd sensed that Oxford trip had been about anything except shopping, wondered what it really *was* about, and felt jealous.

But now, with Mary's revelations, all was forgiven. Indeed, from now on their relationship would be transformed: a new era, he announced (not for the first time) had dawned.

Of the three poems Mary initially sent Rother, the first was ' Stars' in the chapter above.

The second was 'Memory', written 8th August 1911.

When young men die, their flesh hangs grey,
Then green, then black, then breaks, and shatters quite;
They stink like pigs, so, by the night
That greets their passing, none can say:
'Here is the smile that warmed me like the day.'

They're chucked in ditches; lime-dosed; kicked; enslimed;
Stifled, they're just a meal for worms and mice;
The putrefaction that is time clamps on its vice
And rot and filth and fungus hold their sway.

Yet time has mercy. Break their tombs apart,
A year, ten years ahead, and all is changed;
The filth and rot are gone, the slime estranged; instead
Their bones shine clean and white in morning's sight.
What lives is pure. The putrid's taken flight.

But when wars die, no likewise cleansing comes.
What started real, if cruel and drenched in spite,
Decays from that hard truth, and tales erupt;
A thousand lies infest each tale of fight
And glory, legend, honour, all corrupt.

How deep we must then cut to find war's bones!
For here, if ever, to be cruel is kind.
For all convention's sighs, and placemens' groans
We'll gouge the dirt out that would make us blind.

And the third was 'England', below.

       Angry, unkempt, exhausted, ill let-down,
       My urgent needs ignored, contemptuously,
       I slouched into the cathedral's west door,
       To kill an hour.

       And found a miracle. I knew it instantly;
       A spirit old, and true, and quietly beautiful,
       A virtue slow-matured across the centuries
       Held the whole building in its spell.
       And everyone around me knew it too;
       They moved in awe, as if within a dream,
       As if within an antique, well-loved masque
       With parts for all, and each one had their part.

      The snot-nosed boys, the clerks, the too-loud officers,
      The pinch-faced, hurrying housewives veiled in black
      The sun in shafts making the dust dance
      The stained-glass windows opening like flowers,
      The tattered banners, and the sounds that broke,
      And rippled out, like stones thrown in a pool,
      And vanished into hushed and vaulted nothingness;
      The organ murmuring nobly at the back.

      The place was holy; but its sanctity was not
      That loved by priests, nor yet Jehovah's wrath,
      Nor yet the sweet forgiving touch of Christ.
      The place was pagan, charged unto the brim
      With all the savage history of our land,
      With fights, adventures, battles, glorious lusts,
      Yet still, the green of meadows and slow streams.
       St. George was there. The Christian God was not.

      England was there.

Chapter Eighteen

Two days after that uproarious evening in his rooms, Alexey woke early.

As always, his mind reviewed the day. He felt, instinctively, a rush of warm anticipation, even before he remembered why.

It expressed itself as a picture. A warm spring day, he and Ingrid on the river, fresh blossom, spring meadows, sunshine……. For at two o'clock that afternoon, Alexey had fixed to meet Ingrid at Magdalen Bridge. They were going punting.

Why punting? Simple enough. He was hugely looking forward to their meeting and wanted to impress her. All Oxford women loved being punted, above all by a man - and surely this would be especially true of Ingrid, with her marked romanticism. He'd seen how her face lit up when he'd suggested it, that night at New College. For it turned out that even though she'd been in Oxford five months, she'd never yet been in a boat.

The problem was the time of year. Still late April, the summer season had yet to start, the punting firms had yet to open, and it was only by calling in favours that an exception was made. And the weather? There were excellent reasons why punting didn't start till May.

He got up and stuck his head out of the window. The dawn was already dimly alive, and at first seemed grey; but, craning his head a bit further out of the window, he could make out, over Magdalen, a yellow glow.

What he'd read as cloud was morning mist, and hopefully should burn off. Wonderful! He'd withdrawn two pounds from the bank, so he'd be able buy any little things they might need. Not that they were likely to need much because he'd already arranged, with his college servant, to be provided with a picnic tea - and, unofficially, wine.

His college servant, who looked after Alexey and the other people on his staircase, was in no way obliged to help out like this, but Alexey had a kind of genius when it came to getting people to do more for him than they should.

Half an hour, still, before breakfast.

He returned to bed and lay there, thinking about Ingrid, and the spring day to come.

Yes indeed, Ingrid…….. what a lovely young woman! That extraordinary smile, with those dimples making it like two smiles in one; that warm, almost throaty voice, despite her youth; that glittering red-gold hair…..nor was it just physical attractiveness: he remembered, too, Ingrid's acuity socially, not least when she'd talked about the English character, and those guests she'd described at her employers' party.

For he too had had endless conversations of this sort with the relatives with whom he had grown up. Because Alexey's uncle, Sergey Smolensky, with whom he lived, was a political refugee from Russia who had come to England during the conservative backlash of the eighteen eighties.

Born into one of the lesser nobilities of European Russia, with estates a hundred miles west of Moscow, he'd managed to get out enough money to live on. Then with considerable acumen, he'd taken this pot of money into the City and, over a generation, turned an initial £10,000 into something approaching a quarter of a million.

So now he had a leased house in London, a freehold villa in the Surrey hills, and had been able to send Alexey to one of the better English public schools – Charterhouse, not so very far from his country home.

And why was Alexey living with his uncle and not his father, his uncle's younger brother? Because his parents, while Alexey was still five, had been involved – in come way Alexey still didn't fully understand – in the same political rumpus as his uncle, but in a way viewed more seriously by the authorities. And the one whose behaviour had been viewed most seriously of all, remarkably, had been Alexey's mother, who had been exiled to Siberia, though she later returned.

An unthinkable tragedy; the tragedy of Alexey's life. And his father? In the United States, apparently - he had left Russia, in a hurry, two years before his elder brother. Indeed the whole episode seemed to have involved, though it had never been made explicit, some form of terrorism.

All of which meant his whole family- his uncle, his aunt, who had been very close to his mother, Alexey himself, indeed - had felt wary, ever since, about any form of political extremism. So different, as his uncle would so often say, from that urbanely English political pragmatism.

And Alexey had inherited this Anglophilia.

But his family history had left scars.

He reached Magdalen steps bang on two. Given what had happened on Tuesday, he'd better be punctual.

Ingrid was there. She looked superb, even better than Alexey remembered. He'd forgotten how tanned she was, (how did she get a tan to last through the winter - did she ski?) while the snowy whiteness of what looked like a brand new blouse set off the glow of her skin.

The blouse was trimmed with just the right amount of lace around the collar, so that her face rose out of it like a climax, much like a choirboy's emerging from a ruff ; while the climax of the climax, even above her face, was the most deliciously outrageous hat, one of the absurd extravagances in vogue that year.

A red velvet rim (red suited Ingrid and she knew it) and a deluge of white goose feathers, with one long feather trailing a good foot behind her, gave her the venturesome air of some latterday cavalier.

And there, as ever, was the grin - as if to say: 'We both know this young-man-punts-a-woman lark is a cliche but it's still fun, isn't it? And we know how masterful and commanding you are expected to be."

Which was a light-heartedness Alexey appreciated because he was, in fact, an utter ingenue at punting and the last time he had tried, the previous September, he had not only finished up in the river himself but had been joined there by three of his passengers. He eyed the hat with alarm - he hoped it didn't cost much.

Why, even getting into the punt was an adventure. Nevertheless, Alexey finally managed it, with his familiar adroit movements. And as Ingrid followed him, he reached out to steady her. The sleeve of her blouse drew back to reveal her forearm; brown as her face, it was covered with a down of light, white hairs that felt, to Alexey, at once delicate and curiously animal. He felt a thrill of privilege in touching her.

He stood up, made a slow, deep thrust into the water, and they were away. At first Ingrid sat bolt upright; but soon she leaned carefully back and began trailing her hand in the water. Then she caught Alexey's eye and laughed again. Yet another punting cliché, their eyes seemed to say, and this one as hilarious as the rest.

And out they floated into the River Cherwell, that Oxford tributary of the River Thames.

And now, a surprise. For Alexey soon he found he'd become mysteriously more competent than that last, disastrous time. The punting movements, which had felt so extraneous back in September, were now part of him. Each push seemed to thrust the punt along at near-double his earlier speed.

Then he remembered a Russian saying - 'you learn to swim in the winter, and to ski in the summer' by which he'd understood that it's when you *stop* consciously trying to learn something that the real learning process takes place….. subconsciously.

He opened his arms, thrust deeper and more certainly, and began to find a rhythm in this still-novel sequence of movements.

As for Ingrid, she was having the time of her life. Guaranteed, at last, Alexey's full attention, she lolled back like the Queen of Sheba, supported by three cushions, amusedly appraising Alexey's capabilities.

Nor was she disappointed. For from the moment he first got into the punt - with that confidence she was coming to know so well - she'd seen the innate athleticism, the natural physicality of the man.

How well he did it, how spare and uncluttered his movements, what instinctive rhythm!

He plainly knew exactly what he was doing.

Yet for all such drole misapprehensions, the truly curious thing about this, their third tete a tete, was that both of them, now, said scarcely anything at all.

They were as communicative as before, maybe more so, but no longer with words.

Rather they used looks, smiles, gestures. Ingrid's languidly feminine, Alex actively male.

It was a ballet.

Helped by the absence of other craft on the river they proceeded upstream towards University Parks. Here were meadows, where Alexey thought they could eat.

Slowly, carefully, manoeuvring the punt to the bank, he stopped, tied the stern to a branch, loped carefully out and stretched his hand across to help Ingrid land.

Once more, the privilege of touch! He smiled at her again, and, this time, the pleasure must have been plain in his eyes; because the warmth of the moment made Ingrid feel this was the time to ask him about the other night.

She plunged.

"I have something to ask you."

Said straightforwardly enough.

"And what might that be?" smiled Alexey.

"It is….."

"Something!…"

"……..to do with Tuesday."

"Oh really! That's no surprise - I can see where you could have something to ask me about *Tuesday*!"

"No, its more to do with….. us… .."

Why was she feeling so nervous!

"Us, is it! That's *good*! Fire away!"

Alexey saw her uncertainty. He tried hard to look encouraging.

"Well, I know it sounds ridiculous, and I'm sure it's very silly, and that there's a very good reason, and all that, but I heard - from some of the people at the meeting-" (some instinct told her to be vague) "that before Paula came down to meet me, you actually came down yourself, and then you went…" a pause, a little rush. "….. you went back…… and left me!"

And now she was almost crying!

What on earth… it was hard to know who was more surprised by the intense, faltering note in her voice - Ingrid or Alexey.

"'Left me?', thought Alexey " *'Left me?'* What language is this?"

His face must have registered his astonishment, because Ingrid instantly drew back:

"Oh, of course," she said, with her familiar self-deprecating grin, "I don't *mean* 'left me,' that's ridiculous - I wasn't even there!"

She tried again.

"I waited three quarters of an hour for you, and would have waited longer, but you waited just five minutes, and then you…. went!"

Again the uncharacteristic, plaintive tone, so surprising to them both.

"I mean, I know, you've already explained why you had to go - you had to get back to the meeting , you explained that, and I know it sounds silly, it's totally irrational, but I felt I had to say it, because I've been thinking about it ever since!"

Another amazed look from Alexey.

" I mean, what you did was quite logical, and utterly understandable" – more flooding words, wide eyes - "it was just something about how it felt. Surely you could have waited a bit longer than that?"

And then, perhaps to make it sound more conventional:

"I mean, was it really…….. polite?"

Polite! Now, more than astonishing, this was beginning to sound, to Alexey, absurd. Yet how often do people, like Ingrid, say things that sound ridiculous, just because they don't dare say what is really on their mind!

But Alexey was taking this at face value, and was rapidly getting riled. If Ingrid had to raise such a matter at all - and frankly it *was* ridiculous, as she herself said - why raise it now? Just when the atmosphere between them had become so warm? Why spoil it?

What he missed, of course, was that it was precisely her sense of the moment - Alexey's demonstrably good mood - that had made Ingrid choose that particular time.

"Now look" said Alexey, controlling himself, " we have talked about this already, but of course I can explain it again. As I said, it was weird, almost comic really. There was a brief moment when it truly looked like the place might explode! It was a genuine , physical emergency! I had no choice but to stay.

"In fact - " (and the point began to strike Alexey more forcibly, the more he talked) " the whole thing was that I *didn't* stay, I came down to meet you, which I shouldn't really have done, but I came anyway precisely because I *had* made a promise, because I *did* value you and how you felt, and it was only the fact that you were late, only a tiny bit late I grant you, but in the context it happened to matter, that I had to rush off again before you arrived!"

"Yes, I know, I know," said Ingrid, caught between near-laughter at the absurdity of it all, and the continuing sense, nevertheless, that there was something important in all this she had to nail.

"Even so" (and as she pursued the point she felt like one who launches herself, oblivious, off a diving board) "Why didn't you send someone along more quickly - say, as soon as you got back? Surely you could have done that, rather than leave me standing on a street corner? To leave somebody standing on a street corner is something I would never do." A flash of anger. "I mean," she said again, "it is *not* polite." And again she laughed, embarrassed by the absurdity of what she'd said, and the very fact it seemed to matter.

It was the laugh that finished Alexey. What was all this weird flippancy, this *fuss*? Above all, was not this *small*? He'd been late because he'd been trying to run a political meeting, not lying about drinking beer!

So this time he let his anger rip. "That too I have explained! And I've apologised! I simply forgot! I'm sorry! Truly I am! I should not have forgotten, of course, and in any normal situation I would not have done!"

And he shot Ingrid such a look of hot, hurt anger that she finally burst into tears, aghast at his crossness, amazed at her own feelings, appalled, after such a delightful start to the day, at how it had turned out.

And now another silence, but how different from that silence earlier. Alexey sat grim-faced, his face frozen into a tense, set glower; Ingrid, too, sat staring, but in the opposite direction - utterly distraught. How had this happened? More weird, precisely *what* had happened?

So they sat in silence, for two minutes, five minutes, ten …… till there occurred what Ingrid, thinking about it later, christened ' the miracle.'

She was still looking away from him, so she never saw the change in his face. She just heard his voice. Suddenly, extraordinarily, all its harshness and tension were gone. It had become again the caress she knew so well.

" Look, Ingrid," he was saying, excessively gently, "I do see what you mean. I do see why you feel as you do. It was thoughtless of me - it *is* ridiculous to leave someone standing on a street corner. It is I who should be apologising. And I do apologise."

And he stared once again into her eyes in that way of his which seemed to penetrate right into her soul, his gaze drifting about her face, as if on the kindest and most considerate of quests, as if searching for the tiniest sign of friendship and reconciliation.

"I can only say again, in mild mitigation, that I had an awful lot on my mind. Silly things, "he said hurriedly, "things that seemed so important at the time, silly though they were. Things that crowded from my mind all the things that really count – and that was even *before* the gas emergency. Things like - well, I mean….. things like *you*….. though you're not a thing!"

In the minutes they'd been silent Ingrid, too, had felt regret; indeed she'd felt the full gamut of emotions, remorse, surprise, anger, and finally- a flash of the old Ingrid - laughter.

So she fell on this like a lifeline.

"*You're* the thing! A *silly* thing! You silly old thing! But not a bad thing, really!"

"How can I put it more simply," said Alexey, and now he had that boyish, pleading air of his. He looked her straight in the eye.

"Will you forgive me?"

And Ingrid gave him a smile he remembered for the rest of his life.

"It is rather you," she stumbled, "who should forgive *me*."

And Alexey, looking solemn, kissed her gently on the forehead; softly, tenderly, and with the utmost consideration.

Which once again bemused her. Now there's a thing a Siegfried would never have done, she thought, who had, in her few years of puberty, been kissed full-heartedly, square on the lips, with far less reason, if rather more clumsiness, than that.

There was still an hour before Ingrid had to go back to her family. So they ate their picnic and, shortly afterward, Alexey suggested they drift back. And off they went, punting slowly and amiably down the stream, peace restored - though there was, now, a mild undertone they'd never felt before.

You could measure it, strangely, by the simple fact that they were once again talking. For now, like that first time they'd talked in the café, their exchange was all banter, jokes, ideas. Even the subject matter was the same - the English character - as if by returning to their first theme they might resurrect old feelings.

Ingrid, especially, chattered happily away, relieved the crisis was past, though mystified as to why.

And as for Alexey - what Ingrid didn't know was the real reason he'd changed. For while sitting apart, he'd come to a conclusion.

'There's no point in my pursuing this,' he'd said to himself , "there *is* something strange about Ingrid's behaviour and I'm going to have to make allowances. She's hyper-sensitive. No doubt, as with us all, it's caused by something I don't know about. Past insecurities, early difficulties, whatever. I'll find out eventually, but meanwhile, I must remember that it's beyond her conscious control. For *her* sake- forget mine - I must be considerate."

But what struck him most vividly of all, and very much moved him, was the sense he got of Ingrid's *vulnerability,* a quality especially appealing to Alexey. Indeed, he had long been struck by the vulnerability of women in general, and how readily men could trigger it. This male bullying, as he saw it, was dreadful. And now he was doing it himself! Of course she had, in one sense, 'over-reacted', but so what? Vulnerable as she was, it was up to him to protect her.

Nevertheless, when they parted, despite their newfound warmth, he still didn't kiss her - not on the lips.

Instead, he clasped her hands, stared deep into her eyes (at least he's looking at me with his old look, thought Ingrid) and…again…. and it took long enough …… the forehead kiss! And this time she felt irritated as well as surprised.

This man thinks I'm a child, she thought. I'm surprised he didn't chuck me under the chin.

Chapter Nineteen

Nor, when they parted that evening, was anything definite arranged.

Indeed, Alexey waited a few days before he even considered what to do next.

He had other concerns anyway. He had a looming essay crisis and he'd still not read Weber, as recommended by his tutor, or Sombart, as also recommended, and now he'd heard about one Ernst Troeltsch, who'd said similar things to both Sombart and Weber, and he'd not read a word of him either. Then add in his endless, ongoing work for socialism……..

And yet, despite this host of impeccably good reasons why he should put his emotional life on hold, perhaps his real motive was less conscious. There had been moments, with Ingrid, in that brief but intense exchange, when Alexey had felt profoundly disturbed. Much like Ingrid, in fact, in his own way,…… sufficient, certainly, to alarm him.

The truth was, he needed a breathing space.

His 'commitments', you could say, became his alibi.

By the third day he began to feel better. Or, as he told himself, more clear about things.

His attraction for Ingrid returned, albeit in more cautious form. Why not meet her, yes, but in a different way- why not compromise, as it were, by meeting her in the company of others?

Why not ask her on the next walk arranged by the landscape-loving Henry? For Henry, curiously evangelical about the therapeutic effects of nature, generally led such a walk every month.

There was one due a week next Thursday. Why not ask Ingrid on that?

Nevertheless, Alexey decided to write to Ingrid rather than ask her face to face.

True, in those days letters were much more widely used than now. It felt perfectly natural, even, for a married couple to write to each other in the same house.

But for Alexey, it was more than that. In a letter you had some degree of control. There was no chance, as in a talk, of the conversation getting out of hand. And he had seen what could be the result of that.

So on the Tuesday after the punting trip, Alexey sat down and wrote the following.

Dear Inger,

How are you? I hope very much you are well. I hope you have recovered from the emotional shocks of Saturday - I refer of course to my punting. Did I tell you that the last time I went punting I put no less than four of us, myself included, deep in the drink? But, as you saw, with diligence I have improved....

I enjoyed our trip immensely, as I hope you did too. I hope, also, you were not too upset by our little exchange.

As I said at the time, perhaps I was, quite simply, insensitive. Indeed there's no perhaps about it - clearly I was. I should have had more consideration. I should never have allowed myself to be distracted from what was, I assure you, the one truly important thing in my mind that day....your delightful self.

What can I do now but say again how much, how very much, I apologise?

Anyway Ingrid, to make a long story short, to cut to the chase, to seize the hour, to indulge, in fact, in every cliché of decisiveness imaginable, would you consent to meet up with this miserable sinner just one more time (or maybe even twice, but once more, say, for a start) and come a walk with me, and Henry, and Henry's wife, and Ernst, and George, and yes - I confess it with a blush - the outrageous Tom - and enjoy what is quickly emerging as the most delightful Spring?

As ever - Henry always ensures these jaunts have meaning as well as beauty - the venue will be fascinating, and historically improving - a lost village, he says, *tres* atmospheric. While the valley it's in - I know, because I've visited it before - is arguably the most exquisite in Oxfordshire. By the way, I read somewhere that such and such a village 'was, inevitably, shot through with the vulgarity of the Thames Valley.' Now what do you make of that? Can a valley be vulgar? Can a hill be posh? Enlighten me. For my part, certainly, I don't find the Thames Valley vulgar - I think it's wonderful - and Henry's village, surely, is a peach; but who knows? Some would say peaches are vulgar. Maybe I am too.

Let me know if you can come. DO COME, DO! And assuming you can, let's meet just outside New College main gate at IO.OO AM, this Saturday, May Third. *I must see you* – I really must.

I look forward to Saturday,

                your devoted (and apologetic)

                        Alexey

Reading it over, he knocked out the bracketed phrase "and apologetic" but left 'devoted', slipped the letter into an envelope, and was faced with a final conundrum: he wanted to post it, but although he knew the Crosbys' street and their house's physical position, he didn't know the number.

So he wrote out Ingrid's name, plus the address without the number, added a stamp, and waited till dark to walk out into Longwall. Then he strode quickly past the Crosbys' house, glimpsed the number out of the corner of his eye, went a hundred yards up the street, took out his pen and added it. Finally he popped it into the letter box in Broad Street and walked off.

Surprising, perhaps, in someone so outwardly confident as Alexey.

Next day, as Ingrid's family sat at breakfast, the letter arrived. Blushing scarlet, she fled to her room.

There she quickly slit the letter open, confirmed, from the first line, that it was from Alexey, then jumped to the end - to see how he signed off. This would tell her how he felt.

' Your devoted Alexey' he said. That sounded alright…thank God. Thank God! Because among a galaxy of feelings since their outing, a major one was terror that she had cut the relationship off at the bud. A fear enhanced by not hearing from Alexey for five days. But now she had….

She went back to the start, she skimmed down… he sounded friendly….. and here again, in the third paragraph, was another apology. Then later, all this DO, DO and MUST, MUST! No lack of positive feelings there…….

Even so, a bit like Alexey, Ingrid was thankful that he was *writing* to her, rather than speaking to her direct, as it meant that she, too, could control her reply. More, by showing a little address - she felt, with reason, she had some talent for this - she would compose a letter which would be, she hoped, a little jewel.

So when the children were having their nap after lunch, she went back to her room to write.

Dear Alexey, (she wrote)

Thank you so much for your letter. Like you, I had a wonderful time on Saturday and was only sorry it was marred by our 'little exchange', as you so tactfully call it! However, we are surely friends again now and, as you wisely say, it is a situation from which we can both learn.

Of course I accept, and will be there at 10.00 on Saturday at New College for I am quite sure we will both mend our ways now and be on time! After all, in fairness to you, I was the first to be late, if only by five minutes! And in fairness to both of us, we were both punctiliously (is that the right English word - wait- I look it up - yes!) punctual, if it's possible to be something with so many Ps and Us, the second time we met. Long may we thus successfully mind our Ps and Us, if not our Qs.

Believe me, I look forward very much to seeing you on Saturday. I am sure it will be delightful.

With my very best wishes, Alexey,

Your

Ingrid

PS: Kindly note correct spelling of name. You Russians are notorious for setting your own rules, but really now.

And Ingrid got it right - her letter charmed Alexey, so much of her bright spirit did she distil into such a small space.

Indeed the whole thing felt, to Alexey, almost physical - especially that pert little P.S., which felt, for reasons Alexey couldn't begin to explain, less a sentence, more a poke in the ribs. (In fact the misspelling of Ingrid's name had only happened once, at the very start of his letter.)

At one stage he used it as a book mark, forgot that he had done so, and lost it for a whole afternoon. He fussed after it like an old woman, and became so distraught - then fascinated at his own distraughtness - that he realised losing the letter felt like losing her, and was struck by how much that seemed to matter.

There were no difficulties, for Ingrid, in fixing things. By chance the Crosbys were joining friends at a hotel that weekend - a hotel with a nursery, that looked after guests' children as required. And partly because they were temporarily a little short of money, they suggested Ingrid stayed behind, taking the weekend off. "Unwonted your holiday may be, but not, I suspect, unwanted" said Mr. Crosby.

Chapter Twenty

So promptly at ten on May the third, with a hair-trigger punctuality only their previous unpunctuality could have brought about, Ingrid and Alexey met at New College gate.

By eleven-fifteen they were in the Cotswolds. They left the station, walked up one lane, turned into another, then onto a track, then found themselves in a gentle but swiftly deepening valley, steep hills on either side.

It was the same crowd who had been in Alexey's rooms - Alexey, George, Henry Thornton - plus a more restrained, slightly sheepish-looking Tom.

Notably absent, however, were the Germans. Ernst had been due but had pulled out at the last minute. Alexey seemed annoyed. But Paula and Henry's wife Mary were there. As at the camp, Mary's smile of greeting transformed her.

Henry Thornton had pre-planned their route, and moved to the little column's head. He lead them into the valley, with many waves and cries of "This way, children, this way!" '

"So where 's our lost village?" cried George. " And how does a village get lost, anyway? That's what *I'd* like to know. Lost children I can understand, lost dogs, lost parrots even, but a village? When did you last see a village, wandering hopelessly around, saying, ' Help me, I'm lost?' Enlighten us."

"What you lack, " said Henry, forging ahead, " is faith. There *was* a village once – it's been abandoned. That's why it's lost. But its surrounds are still to be seen: just enter my time machine - surrender yourself - and all will be revealed."

"I surrender."

"Very good. This valley you see before you is magic; perhaps the oldest and most magical I know. Yet the cause of its magic is quite prosaic. Very simply, everything around it has changed, but the valley hasn't. Thus the further you proceed– and here comes the magic - the further you go back in time. Start walking and you shed fifty years; a little further, and you've shed a century - while just round the bend, over there, (he pointed to an ebony wood, plunging steep into a corner) you're in the seventeenth century."

And, in its own way, it was true. Minutes later the group reached the bend, turning the corner into a previously unseen section of the valley. And it was indeed as if they had fled back in time. The forest covered every hill in sight: each wooded ridge, seemingly, with a wooded ridge behind, in the all-embracing way characteristic, we are told, of early England.

Yet in the foreground the woods had been cleared and the sun shone on hills as bright and empty as downs.

And as the young people saw them, green and gay against the blue, their hearts leapt.

No-one felt this more strongly than Ingrid. She knew and loved her Bavarian springs, when, for two months before the summer heat, every meadow was ablaze with wild flowers; starlike, gleaming, quite literally, in the German word, 'Schön'. But this was different. The landscape seemed more lush, more brim-full, bursting with new life. The hawthorn, especially, was pendulous with blossom, as if someone had taken a giant scoop of cream and drenched it over every branch - but over-generous, too many scoops, so the boughs sagged under the weight.

The whole world had become a garden.

Then Alexey, walking up the front with Henry, lifted a finger.

"Hark hark!" he cried.

"A lark!" This from Tom.

"Not a lark, you silly ass - a cuckoo."

"A cuckoo?"

"Yes, a cuckoo. Listen to its sound: First cuck……then ooooo. First cuck….then oooooo. See? That's a cuckoo. Could be the first of the year. I'm going to write to the Times about it."

"That's not a cuckoo, it's a pigeon!"

"It's a cuckoo!"

"Just because it *goes* cuckoo, doesn't mean it *is* a cuckoo, you ass. Lots of things go cuckoo that aren't. A duck goes cuckoo in a funny way, haven't you heard? A cockerel makes a kind of cuckoo sound too, if you really listen, and as for a pigeon, like this one, a pigeon goes "Cuck…oooooo. Cuck……oooooo." Tom made a wailing sound plus distraught look - a perfect imitation of the sound they'd heard.

His sudden, ringing treble, so seemingly out of character, brought gales of laughter from his friends.

"Having said that," he went on " I really don't want to be discouraging. Why shouldn't you write to the Times about it? Just explain that it's the first pigeon you've heard and not a cuckoo. Or maybe it's a duck? Why not? Someone somewhere must hear the first duck - the first *flying* duck, anyway, the ones who fly in from abroad, so why not say so? Don't laugh, it's interesting! Alright, I know what you're going to say, you're going to say the Times readers couldn't give a flying duck *what* you've heard but what I say is….."

"Hark hark!"

"What's that?"

"A flying cow pat, Tom. Plumb on your bum."

Tom swung a blow at Alexey but now the argument was taken away, with furious, arm-waving energy, by Tom, Alexey, and George. They shot off ahead of the others, leaving them trailing by half a mile.

Suddenly they re-appeared. Every so often they would reach down to the ground and grab something – a dried cow pat? - which they threw at each other. Alexey, in seeming full retreat, was running in Ingrid's direction but at an angle of about forty five degrees from the path. "Stop him! Head him off!" she could dimly hear George shouting, with still more waving of arms.

Far be it from Ingrid to turn down any form of play! Pausing only to scoop up her own cow pat, and a little straw, she headed off to intersect Alexey: seeing her coming he altered course again, veered round, running like a hare, and vanished over the ridge.

As far as she could manage, given the restrictions of her ankle-length skirt, Ingrid followed him, - while George and Tom drew up short, evidently out of breath, and happy, clearly, to leave the denouement to Ingrid.

She stumbled over the ridge; there, fifty yards away, was a grinning Alexey. He made a face at her, scooped up a cow pat, and started running, yelling 'You'll never catch me!"

Hoping to trick him, Ingrid walked, at first, quite slowly toward him, her cow pat behind her back; then having successfully lured (she hoped) Alexey into a sense of false security, she waited till she got within twenty yards, and held her side as if she had a stitch.

Then suddenly, with cries of wrath and monstrous energy, she rushed at him when all at once - disaster! Her feet got mixed up with her skirt, she lost her stride, and one foot went plumb down a rabbit hole. With a shriek she fell head over heels, a parody of flailing arms and legs, and hit the ground with a thump that knocked her breathless.

Alexey was at her side like lightning.

"Are you alright?" he said, helping her to her feet.

"I'm fine. Fine!" she said, until she moved - and felt a pain .

"My knee hurts a bit " she said, "that's all." So now Alexey thrust one arm round her waist, then drew her right arm over his shoulder, and then, with a series of shuffling, bumbling movements, like a soldier with a wounded comrade, brought her to the shade of a tree. This is the second time he's done this in a week, thought Ingrid.

"Put your weight on it, " he said, gently supporting her, and encouraging her to try and move the limb. They quickly established there was no break, but Ingrid still felt shaken.

"I tell you what," said Alexey, portentously. "We've reached a moment in our relationship when you must trust me."

"Of course I do, " said Ingrid, looking at him quizzically. "But what do you mean?"

"What I mean," said Alexey, "is that I have some small knowledge of such injuries - no, really I do! And I know that to head them off you must act preventatively; because unless you do, the body sends the wrong chemicals to the source of stress. And it is these chemicals, believe it or not, which cause the real problem, the 'protective' swelling that is the source of pain. "

Ingrid nodded. It sounded plausible.

"But you can head this process off," Alexey went on. "It takes massage."

Here he caught Ingrid's eye - and both laughed.

"This is what I mean by trusting me, "said Alexey, trying very hard to look serious. For what he'd said was true. He'd been in the First Aid section at school - he'd done a course.

"And what sort of massage would you have in mind?"

"Only your knee, "said Alexey. "What would you have in mind? No, you must trust me" and, without more ado, he led her gently in front of him, then sat down on a handy tree trunk just in front of her, his head conveniently just level with her waist.

Before Ingrid even knew it his hand was on her knee. Moments later, as the material was too thick to penetrate, his hand slipped deftly under her skirt and now was touching her skin; rubbing and kneading the muscles like dough, but tenderly. It reminded Ingrid, above all else, of the muzzling of her dog Katya back at home.

After a moment he looked up.

"How does that feel?"

"Very good."

"Any better?"

"Hard to tell."

"Why so?"

"It's the wrong knee."

And they laughed again.

So now, just as deftly, Alexey slipped his hand across to her other knee, while she loured over him….. and here once more was his touch, still warm and muzzling.

Utter silence. One minute, two minutes of massage. Alexey's eyes, because of the way he was sitting, staring straight ahead at Ingrid's stomach, while Ingrid, in turn, stared straight over Alexey's head.

A bizarre situation and utter silence, except a hint of Alexey's breathing and, all around, the country sounds which are anything but quiet: the wind rustling in the poplar opposite; the wood pigeons in the distance; the odd mysterious thump and crack.

Then suddenly, a gasp from Ingrid: for Alexey's touch had changed.

No longer was he kneading, pushing, almost bruising her knee, with a touch that was plainly clinical; now his fingertips were sliding over her skin in the most delicate, searching glissando.

The touch that had been so invasive, yet somehow abstract, had now become the most intimate and sensitive of receiving mechanisms - Ingrid could sense the electric messages flashing back to *his* brain. And, partly because she could sense this, they rushed to hers, too.

It felt like he was touching her to the quick, as if he was feeling for her very life; she knew it ! Extraordinarily, she could feel his fingertips at the back of her scalp, as if some surge of electricity had travelled right up her body. Yet still he only touched her knee.

She gasped again - and now she caught his eye. He, too, looked almost alarmed - he, too, had been surprised by his own feelings.

Though had he better understood himself he might have felt less so. After all, what was the once-again injured Ingrid, if not - once again - vulnerable? And did not vulnerability move Alexey more than anything in the world?

Now Alexey slid his other hand upward and deftly, incredibly swiftly, unbuttoned her blouse. A gentle movement of her clothing, and he had revealed one breast; moments more and his lips were on it, first extraordinarily delicately, seconds later sucking as warmly, richly, as a babe-in-arms.

Still his other hand moved in those glissando patterns on her knee; still the wind, the leaves, the bursts and plunges of warm air.

If Ingrid's scalp had been alight before, now her whole body was. Mysteriously she felt Alexey's touch everywhere, thrilling, voluptuous and tender all at once. How on earth could this be happening, she thought; he's only touching bits of me!

Yet now, with the same union of desire and tenderness, it was Ingrid who moved her hand down onto Alexey's hair, and began caressing his scalp in just the same loving, searching and yet gentle way. It was how a mother caresses a child; so now it was Alexey, to his amazement, who was feeling her touch in his ribs, his thighs, his toes.

"Dear boy. Dearest boy." At last one of them had spoken.

"My beautiful, my dear, my only Ingrid."

And nothing else. Then after a moment:

"You do realise, don't you," said Ingrid, with one of her most conspiratorial grins, "That you still haven't kissed me, Alexey."

"It depends what you mean by kiss."

What a beautiful blush!

"I mean a kiss on the lips."

"On the lips?"

"Yes, on the lips."

"Oh, like *this* you mean," said Alexey, in sudden mock-realisation.

And now yet another surprise. No more the delicate touch, the searching fingertips which seemed to give as much as take; now Alexey stepped forward, put his arm clear round her waist, drew her straight to him, thrust his left leg between hers, and kissed her forcefully, full on the mouth.

Now his body, thrust against her, *was* invasive, rigid, tense - ' like a knife', she thought later. While that same hand that had touched her knee so delicately now grasped her buttocks, thrusting them deep back into his loins.

"Like that you mean?" he repeated.

"Not quite like that," she said. And again she blushed.

"But I .... do not mind."

Five minutes later, they rejoined the others.

Chapter Twenty-One

It was remarkable how much Henry's new-found recognition changed his mood. Soon his angst had largely been forgotten.

Now the Thorntons began working together on Henry's poems, something Mary had dreamed of for years.

Sitting opposite each other at the kitchen table, both armed with pens and writing paper, they began the selection: a task especially suited to Mary's organizational skills.

It was Mary who invented their filing system; Henry who edited its contents. She it was who made the basic division into 'definites', 'possibles' and 'still-to-be-writtens'; Henry who graded the material, and who groaned, if far more humorously than in the past, at the ever-burgeoning pile of 'still-to-be writtens.'

For they soon found a shortage of what they called 'human' material as opposed to poetry about landscape, animals or even skies. That poem from the walk, 'Stars,' was typical, as was the mood piece ' England.' And the gaps had to be filled.

Sometimes, however, the required work already existed. Mary had a genius for remembering Henry's obscurer poems - she'd read them all – and, just as important, finding them.

And off she would go, hunting them down in the farthest reaches of Henry's study - she found one in a shoe-box, another wedged in a window to block out drafts – and back she would come, triumphant, dangling the poem from a hand raised high above her head, grinning like a cat.

In a week they found, and collated, all the poems needed for the Eric Rother section, and in a fortnight 75 per cent of what was needed for the new, Henry-only volume - including three new poems which Henry had somehow managed to conjure up afresh.

All of which gratified Henry, but Mary's reaction was delight.

Because for Mary it was about a great deal more than helping out. It fulfilled a dream she'd cherished ever since they met: the chance to be part of some truly great enterprise, to live out, at last, the life of brilliant, heady adventure she'd always felt possible with Henry. Together they would take on the world! 'To strive, to seek, to find, and not to yield!' There was a medieval quality to her vision, more squire than merely helper. Squire, that is, to the glittering white knight which was how she saw Henry in their more upbeat moments.

"You knight, me Squire" she would say, cuddling his shoulder and batting her eyelids, while Henry smiled back one of his most secret smiles.

"Okay by me squire," he would say.

So Henry and Mary's project went swimmingly until they'd found all the finished poems for the Henry-only volume - and addressed the challenge of topping up with new ones, as required for 'balance'.

And here they hit the buffers. For while Mary had been a tower of strength at the earlier, organisational stage, now, with creativity required, she became irrelevant. For the problem, as Henry constantly explained, was that he was being asked to do something on demand that either came spontaneously or not at all.

"How can I *instruct* myself to be inspired?" he demanded with a flash of the old, haggard look. "It's like ordering someone to appreciate Mozart, or fall in love. There are things in life where willpower is positively pernicious; the harder you try, the likelier you are to fail."

"Well....... maybe you should forget about it for a bit."

"How can I? We need them by the end of the month. The printers are waiting. Eric said so."

"Well......why don't you take the afternoon off and walk over to Heston wood? One day won't hurt and unwinding may inspire you."

"Inspire me to write a love poem? How can communing with nature do that?"

Mary thought it might - ' With how sad steps, O moon, thou climbst the skies' and all that – till she realised her mistake in being seen by Henry to give advice directly. Far better go round the houses.

So after they'd sat side by side for five minutes in total silence, Henry periodically cracking his fingers, Mary said:

"Changing the subject, have you noticed how Jason is lately?"

Jason was one of the shire horses at the camp who worked the water wheel as well as giving rides to the kids.

"Something seems to be upsetting him; he's been charging round the paddock as if half crazy."

Instantly Henry looked interested. "Jason? He's generally the calmest of them all. Nothing bothers him."

"Well, he's not been right for two days, I assure you. And he seems to be infecting the others, too – I saw a whole crowd of them rushing about just half an hour ago."

She gazed at Henry.

"And they're supposed to be riding with the boys this afternoon."

"Really!" said Henry. "Why didn't you mention it before? That means something must be done *at once* and, let's face it, it's me that should be doing it. I'd really better go and take a look."

"Perhaps you should," said Mary.

"***Someone*** should be doing something anyway," said Henry, getting up with a jerk. And he strode out of the room.

Mary gazed after him thoughtfully. Based on experience, this might even work.

Henry strode briskly toward the horses' meadow.

As so often, the moment he left the house he felt different. How lovely this simple woodland path, this summer morning!

He rounded a corner, and there, stretched before him, was the long, yellow, downward-sloping field where Westbury's horses were kept. And, as so often, its nobility overwhelmed him. Here truly was the centuries-old spirit of his race, pure essence of Old England! And yet the reason he especially felt it here, he realised, was above all the horses. It was ***their*** nobility, their quiet, majestic restfulness, which transformed the view.

On most days, that is. As he further rounded the bend he saw, unlike the three calm horses he had glimpsed at first, a wild disturbance now happening to the rest. Ten horses, twenty, thirty now, were galloping in wild ellipses round and round the field, then turning and rushing, in the same crazed semi-circle, to where they'd started from. On each turn they'd rear and plunge and try to bite each other, then charge off and away again, then rush back - so friskily, so weirdly wild, they might have been playing. Though a moment later Henry found himself wondering if they'd gone mad.

And then he realised one horse had detached itself from the herd and was tearing straight towards him. There was a fence between them but, as the horse thundered up, Henry felt a rush of horror at this onrush of massive, maverick weight. More than weight, even - wild-eyed craziness.

Above all he felt this when he realised which horse it was. For the horse was Jason.

Jason tore right up to the fence, reared, let out a neigh like a shriek, spun violently and rushed off again. Forty yards later he spun round again and came tearing back, and this time, before Henry even thought it possible, jumped clean over the fence, missed Henry by a hairsbreadth, landed a yard behind him and shot off into the wood. Where a moment later he skidded to a halt, spun yet again and this time stood stationary, staring straight into Henry's eyes, snorting, gasping, ears flat against his head, pawing the ground.

Henry stood still and stared back. As did the horse. Then gradually, scarcely moving, Henry half closed his eyes, softened his expression, and turned away. Moments later Jason half-turned also, and began standing at an angle of forty-five degrees, his rump toward him.

Silence again. Still both motionless. And now Henry started focusing with all his soul on what might be the cause of Jason's distress. For Jason's whole posture, his entire being, radiated terror and pain.

And gradually the pain seemed to flow into Henry too, followed, a moment later, by the most intense, grieving sympathy for this suffering fellow-creature.

Jason turned to him and, diffidently at first, and then more surely, took one step and then another toward him; and Henry stood still, head down, submissive, and waited. And the horse came right up and stopped just two foot away, raising its head. He stared straight at Henry now, with great brown tortured eyes. And Henry reached out and began stroking Jason's nose, touching the warm, coarse, bony flesh, with utmost delicacy.

Pouring love into him, Henry hoped, through his finger-tips - the tenderness that had welled up in his soul.

Then suddenly, like an electric shock, a rush of pain shot through the right side of Henry's head. Ear-ache and toothache, seemingly, in demonic combination! And moments later Henry *knew* this was what

Jason had been suffering all along, and in some extraordinary way he was feeling precisely what Jason was feeling himself.

Still, he carried on stroking Jason's nose; while as he did this, his own pain subsided. Soon Jason seemed calmer too.

Jason turned toward the field. Henry followed him. They reached the fence that Jason had jumped. Henry led Jason to the gate, just ten yards from where he had been standing, opened it, and let Jason in.

Now, not just Jason, but all the horses were tranquil again. The crisis - the immediate crisis, anyway – was past. And Henry would have to think about a vet.

At which moment, with the cracking of a twig and a slight cough, he sensed a presence. He turned. It was Anthony Parsons, the founder of Westbury Camp.

He had, as ever, manifested, rather than appeared. But then this most self-effacing of men was always like that. How different from his brother, Joe!

Both men were short, but where Joe was round and ruddy, Anthony was slim and pale. And Anthony had the keen sharp features of an intellectual - most strikingly a long, angular nose - aquiline, acute.

He wore a strange, disconcerting grin.

"I've a confession," he said. "I've been watching you from the wood, these last ten minutes. Quite remarkable, what you just did with that horse!"

"Yes, he does seem better," said Henry. "But of course it's temporary. The real problem remains unaddressed."

"And what might that be?"

"Well - maybe toothache."

"Toothache? Just toothache? With all that hysterical behaviour, really? He's been like that for days – I've seen him."

"So I've heard. Mary told me. But maybe the toothache – if that's what it is – is on the surface. Maybe there's something deeper bothering him underneath."

"Maybe."

A pause.

"I have another confession to make" said Anthony quietly.

"Oh, what's that?"

" I've been thinking. About the future. You know I'm going away for a while?"

Henry confessed he'd heard a rumour.

"My sister's husband just died. Heart attack, very sudden. She lives in France. She needs someone to sort out their affairs, which are a mess. It could take weeks, if not months, but I'm going to have to go and help her. She's eighty- five, and frankly I'm frightened for her."

"I understand. You've got to go."

"Yes indeed. But it's rather awkward, as you can guess. We' re just gearing up here for the summer camp. We'll have thirty boys on site within a month, and you know as well as I do someone's going to have to hold things together."

"That's true enough. But who?"

"It's quite a question. It needs someone with authority, who can be here permanently, someone the boys get on with, but, above all, who grasps the ethos of the place."

"A tall order," said Henry.

"Very tall. In fact the more I think about there's really only one person I can think of ."

"Who's that?"

"You,", said Anthony, with his most disconcerting grin.

"ME?" Henry was genuinely flabbergasted. "Why me?"

"Because I think - well, to be honest I'm quite sure - you can do it. Look at the *feel* you have for the place - not just the horses. Think how you get on with the boys!" This was true - like many aloof adults Henry found children easier to relate to than grown-ups.

"Think of the cricket, last year." Henry had first coached, then formed a team among the boys from London. With a little help from Henry's New College friends, they had played, and very nearly beaten, the local village.

"Think of - "

" - But Anthony! This is most flattering, but really! You know organisation's really not my thing –

"Precisely! An organisation man is exactly what I *don't* want."

" - nor is mechanics, nor anything practical, really...."

"But that's precisely why I'm asking you, and not anyone else!"

"I don't understand. Surely you need a manager?"

"Yes, I do need a manager, but managers are frankly two a penny. We can always get someone to help you with all *that*. What I need is something much more rare, and something that you *are*, believe me, even if you don't know it....."

"And what is that, pray?"

Anthony fixed Henry with his most intense gaze, that look which had had such a hypnotic effect on everyone he'd worked with for twenty years.

"A leader."

Chapter Twenty-Two

A leader! At this, Henry finally laughed out loud. Minutes later, the two men parted, Henry still chuckling at Anthony Parsons' suggestion. After all, whatever Anthony said, whoever fulfilled this daunting role would inevitably, also, be an organiser.... and Henry? Piss-ups and breweries came to mind. But even as he walked back to the camp the idea began to reverberate around his head. *A leader*. Anthony certainly knew how to manipulate.

Because, in fact, with that improbable phrase, Anthony had lobbed a time bomb into Henry's subconscious, where it began to fester.

And this was because part of Henry did see himself like that. Not for nothing, for instance, did Henry the poet especially love the patriotic harangues in Shakespeare's Henry the Fifth, above all the ones that could move the mind so swiftly from depression to exaltation. Notably Henry's answer to the French herald before Agincourt:

"......our gayness and our gilt are all besmirch'd

"With rainy marching in the painful field

"And time has worn us into slovenry... "

........pause, a marvellous upswing of valour, now–

" BUT! -

" BY THE MASS! -

"OUR HEARTS ARE IN THE TRIM!"

How often Henry would mutter those lines to himself, above all when he himself felt down. And how they would inspire him! More surprising, perhaps, was that the emotional journey they involved, so reminiscent of the switchback moods Henry experienced himself, was something Henry found he could pass on to others – notably, for instance, the boys at Westbury camp. In the half dozen cricket matches they'd played last summer there had been more than one collapse, usually of morale – and Henry had always known, instinctively, what to say to turn the boys around. And in each case they had duly recovered their poise... and won. Henry the poet? Henry the Fifth!

And, truth to tell, he knew he had other qualities too, also relevant to his improbable candidacy for 'leadership.' He could, for instance, spot talents in people they never knew about - and develop them. In this respect he was an educator as much as ever he was a captain. ("Educo, Latin," as Anthony loved to say: ' I draw out.')

Most notable had been the time one of the most troubled London boys, John Croome, had begun disappearing, mysteriously, from the site. One day Henry, out walking, had stumbled across John in the woods, a good mile away.

And there, in this remote place, in a clearing that caught just enough sunshine to make the project possible, were lines of beans, on poles, and lettuces and cabbages too. The boy had made his own, secret vegetable garden.!

Soon John began asking Henry for gardening tips. Then their chats ranged wider still. Yet what really surprised Henry was how John's broader behaviour, back in the camp, changed as this project developed. The self-belief John won in this little corner of his life spread out to encompass the whole.

And it had all started with Henry *noticing* something; not imposing some arcane pedagogic doctrine, but *noticing* something; and then, with the talent spotted, fertilising it – drawing it out.

But whatever Henry's aptitude, there was, significantly, the further temptation of money. Anthony had offered to pay him. And pay him handsomely - no less than eight pounds a week! A fortune in Henry and Mary's terms. And for all the promise of Henry's new-found projects, they were desperate as ever, right now, for cash.

Nevertheless, though Anthony's offer came back to haunt Henry over the next few days, he still dismissed such vagaries from his mind. He had some of the necessary qualities, yes, however well hidden, but what about his far more obvious defects? His absent mindedness, for instance? His inability, virtually, to change a fuse?

Let alone those wild oscillations of mood which so scared him and Mary, and which Anthony hardly knew about, as they usually happened when Henry was at home.

And then there was the biggest, simplest objection of them all. How could he possibly do what Anthony suggested and continue preparing his poetry for publication? The task was hard enough already: a commitment like this would make it impossible.

Which Anthony, naturally, denied to the hilt. But then he would, wouldn't he, thought Henry, chuckling to himself, not unsympathetically.

After, all, if getting people to do things, however deviously, had not been one of Anthony's talents, Westbury Camp would not exist. And he thought again of Anthony's incongruous, corrupt-looking grin. And once more, he laughed.

Chapter Twenty-Three

Nevertheless, in the next few days Anthony's time-bomb continued to ferment in Henry's mind. And his uncertainties, disturbing him, reignited the difficulties with his wife.

So once again the rumbling, sniping rows, the gloomy silences, till, finally, their most shrieking spectacular yet – which turned out, unexpectedly, to spark off a resolution.

For, as so often, Henry climaxed the argument by storming out of the house, pausing only to scoop the post up as he went. A gesture that always annoyed Mary, as Henry well knew, with its implication that the only post that mattered was for him. And as so often, he headed for the woods.

While walking, he pulled the letters out of his pocket. There were four. The first was from his parents. Their problems had hit crisis point; his father had missed payments on his loan and it was being called in. It was guaranteed against his property – he could lose his home.

But his father had cried wolf before.

The second was from his sister, saying she had already sent their parents a contribution – well, her husband had.

The third looked different. It had an officious-looking address on the front. He guessed, correctly, it was from the childrens' school. He tore it open: inside was a letter from the head, reminding the Thorntons' that the school had not yet received their contribution for the seaside weekend planned in August. They really did need payments promptly.

And this caught Henry at his most vulnerable point.

Because he knew how much this holiday meant to Rosemary. In the intense politics of her school life – politics in which she had been lately distinctly marginalised - it was one of those things, were she to keep her friends, she had to do. The seaside! Few at the village school had even seen it, let alone stayed there for any length of time. It was vital, socially, that she went on this trip. And, of course, the sole reason why the Thorntons had not yet paid their contribution was, as ever, money: £2.

He got up and began walking down the other side of the hill. Already, as generally happened when he argued with Mary, his mood, like a psychic weather vane, was swinging round to its opposite. He began to feel sad, regretful, even benign.

He walked for two hours, drinking in the beauty of his surrounds. He walked in a perfect circle right back to the beech grove where he'd started, and, by the time he got there he was feeling so contrite, so eager to help his relatives, above all his wife and daughters, that he was beginning to wonder whether he could not do exactly what he had earlier been so sure had been impossible: accommodate **all** the demands being made on him, both artistic and personal.

Or at least try. With faith and hope, yes, he'd find a way.....

Then he remembered he still had one more letter in his pocket, the fourth. It was from his publisher, Eric's friend Cecil Hampton. He opened it.

And the first thing it asked was whether Henry was sitting down. It then declared, most apologetically, that for all the previous rush and urgency, publication of Henry's poems – the 'Henry-only' edition that he was handling – would be delayed. By at least a year.

Put simply, Hampton had reached his overdraft limit and his accountant had declared he had no choice but to push certain projects into the next financial year. And one of these, alas! would have to be Henry's. He really could not apologise enough, but what he could do was assure Henry that his work *would* be published eventually, albeit after this most trying delay.

And as a further indication of good faith, please find enclosed a cheque for thirty percent of the sum they had already agreed in advance – twenty pounds. He hoped Henry would be encouraged by his readiness to advance money on work he had not seen.

Henry put down the paper and sat for a moment, stunned. Why, it was as if it was all planned! The mere possibilities of a moment earlier had, in a flash, become clear practicalities.

For he could stop writing altogether, devote himself one hundred percent to the camp for the full three months that Anthony was away, and use the huge rates of pay Anthony was offering to subsidise the *next* six months, working exclusively on his book.

It was as if fate was choosing for him. Indeed, at this moment, he felt his own faint glimmerings of self-belief. What was that quote of Napoleon's? Ah yes....'First commit yourself …..and then see.' Yes! That's what he should do. Commit himself. And then he'd see.

He would accept Anthony's offer.

Chapter Twenty-Four

After Alexey had kissed Ingrid in Henry's valley, she'd felt a rush of joy, even relief, the rest of the afternoon. God knows, his touch, when it had finally come, had been more than 'erotic' - it had been inspired. "He certainly knows how a woman's body works" she told herself. Some contrast to the fumbling, stumbling, over-eager young Bavarians at home!

Yet soon there emerged a quite new worry. Did Alexey respect her? Was that scene in the field, despite its deep eroticism, all he wanted? Maybe the rest was mere build-up! She'd seen his friends grin knowingly when they'd re-joined them. Was she latest in a string?

They next met a week later - Ingrid had had difficulty, till then, getting time off. They returned, for afternoon tea, to the Cadena cafe, the place they'd gone the very first time they met. And for all Ingrid's concerns, the electric charge that so readily flew between them once again worked overtime.

From the start they were talking, nineteen to the dozen; while here again came the same Bavarian waiter as that first afternoon, grinning delightedly. He was evidently amused that this couple, who he remembered, were now self-evidently lovers. But it was above all the spirit behind their exchanges that struck Ingrid. Each thing they said seemed less like words than a caress: stroke…stroke… stroke… was how it felt, first his stroke to her, then hers to him - the content seemed irrelevant.

Shortly afterward they finished tea and left to go – where? Nothing had been said. They were heading down the street when Ingrid suddenly, mysteriously, lurched right into Alexey. It was an accident surely. And yet – for an instant her body enfolded his, warmly, deliciously - it *felt,* to Alexey, like an embrace. So much so that he was emboldened to ask her back to his rooms - to hear his new phonograph! (he blushed at himself.) And she refused! Which surprised him….he'd thought he'd sensed…..but Ingrid went on refusing, however hard he tried. And shortly afterwards she went home.

Well well, thought Alexey, I must have misread her.

Then Ingrid failed to turn up for their next meeting (her excuse was impeccable), then two days later Alexey did the same (his was better still), till finally, no less than three weeks after the clinch in the field, Alexey did manage to inveigle Ingrid back to his rooms.

By waiting till someone left the college, he got her in the side door, the one without porters.

And now, again, the gentle, sensual kisses of their time in the field, the infinitely delicate touch, that same languid combination of eroticism and romance. And there followed no less than three such encounters within ten days - the sensuality of each episode escalating.

One day Alexey even persuaded Ingrid to parade round his room nude to the waist, Alexey gazing at her with fixed intensity, Ingrid strutting like a mannequin, giggling helplessly. By the fourth visit they were lying together, nude, on his bed, when Ingrid suddenly announced, by way of explaining her reluctance to consummate, that she was 'a fucking virgin!' (language courtesy Paula). To which Alexey, suavely unfazed, merely answered that this was one of the more memorable contradictions-in-terms *he'd* heard.

Three visits more they teetered likewise on the brink, each time Ingrid fending off, with yet more difficulty, an ever- more-ardent Alexey. Yet his reaction, soulful as ever, was to re-affirm that he absolutely understood, and that any kind of compulsion was, for him, unthinkable. Which Ingrid appreciated.

Chapter Twenty-Five

Three days later Ingrid met Paula. She desperately needed to talk to someone. Hopefully Paula, as the older woman, would understand. Ingrid was in awe of Paula's 'sophistication'.

And Paula, it turned out, *was* remarkably unshocked by everything Ingrid said. As Ingrid stumbled out her complex tale, with only the very mildest acts of censorship, her friend seemed to know Ingrid's story almost before she told it.

"You see," said Ingrid, with a young girl's doe-eyed seriousness, bringing a smile to Paula's lips, "I think this truly, finally, is the ***real thing***."

The '***real thing***', and how you recognised it, had been the subject of previous seminars.

"Real thing or surreal thing?" said Paula. "It sounds like you and Alexey dance quite a quadrille."

"I know, I know," said Ingrid. "But I do feel terribly confused. Part of me wants him terribly, another part is just as terrified of getting hurt. And you know what's craziest of all? The other day we were in bed together, just playing," (Paula smiled) " and I suddenly leapt up and walked straight out of the room! I had this sudden, overpowering sense that I'd been forced into this against my will! And of course I hadn't. Then a day later I felt the absolute opposite and wanted Alexey more than ever, and now – well, now – I don't know what to think. What do YOU think, Paula?"

Paula continued to look, above all, sympathetic. Perhaps, thought Ingrid, because she too had experienced such virginal teeterings, however long ago.

"Put it this way" said Paula finally. "One thing I really wouldn't worry about, with someone like Alexey, is that he only wants you physically."

"You think so?"

"I know so."

"Then what should I do?"

"You should bring him to the point," said Paula. "Stop the fart-arsing around."

"Sleep with him?"

"Sleep with him tonight if possible, this afternoon better still, but above all else -"

"Above all else what?"

"*Stop the fart-arsing around.*"

So now Ingrid wrote Alexey a letter. She dropped the flirtatiousness and told the truth. She said she'd been utterly confused, had been acting out of character, and only hoped Alexey might consider the possibility that it was the very intensity of her feelings - and her youth (she allowed herself this much manipulation) - that led her into such unwonted ways.

Nevertheless, she still feared he would spurn her. Though Paula seemed convinced that he would not. "Not his style" she said. "He's nothing if not understanding, is our Alexey."

And Paula proved right. Back winged an impeccably generous response, which only stopped short at one thing – Alexey didn't actually specify a meeting. He's hurt! decided Ingrid, with another flood-tide of remorse.

So now, dropping one more veil of convention, she took the bull by the horns and invited *him.*

They should meet at St. Mary's church in the High, she said, at 2.30 that coming Friday - the tower door. And Alexey agreed, and come the day, at 2.25 sharp, Ingrid was there. Alexey had yet to appear.

The child in Ingrid, so central to her charm, could nevertheless get her into scrapes. Today she thought it would be amusing to go up the tower and watch Alexey arrive. She could see how he looked – she could read his mood - without him seeing her! So she skipped up two flights and there, just as she peered out of a second floor window, was Alexey, strolling up with that familiar, stooping walk. Ingrid smiled to herself. Now she would see how Alexey reacted to just the situation she had been in that time, weeks earlier, when he'd left *her* on a street corner!

But as she peered more closely - a surprise. He seemed perfectly at ease. He glanced casually about him, lit a cigarette. In fact he looked *pleased* with himself. Well, he would be, wouldn't he, she thought, now he knew Ingrid was pursuing him. It could only have one meaning. And she continued watching him, intending to rescue him shortly, but not right away.

Then another surprise. He threw down his cigarette with an air of irritation, stamped on it, and walked off. He'd given up! Yet again, he'd allowed her just five minutes! Aghast, Ingrid thrust open the window and yelled his name – but while several passers-by jerked their heads up in surprise, Alexey didn't hear her, and now, striding swiftly and angrily, he'd crossed the square and was about to swing round behind the Radcliffe Camera.

Ingrid flew down the stairs but by the time she reached the bottom Alexey had disappeared. She sped to the Radcliffe and rushed round it. Not a glimpse, and Alexey could have gone one of four different ways. She tried the Broad, she gazed down Holywell; no sign.

Oh my God, she said to herself (her childlike accidents were always followed by equally childlike outbursts of remorse) why oh why must she always, unfailingly, mess everything up?

That evening she wrote again to Alexey, once more apologising, but this time more effusively than before. And once again, he wrote back. But his tone was peremptory. And in a short letter there was just one brief phrase Ingrid remembered: "I'm sick of this' he said, and the phrase reverberated in her brain.

This time she really ***had*** messed everything up.

Chapter Twenty-Six

All of which may seem strange. Yet such behaviour is less unusual than many realise. For if there is one thing people learn early, for social survival, it is to cover their tracks by a thick veil of seeming convention – and most of us are fooled.

And outwardly Ingrid and Alexey did cover their tracks. Alexey's male friends, for instance, continued to see Alexey's on-off relationship with

Ingrid as the latest in something that had long become, among them, a cliche - Alexey the Lothario. And as for Ingrid, almost all who knew saw only her confidence and charm. That vulnerability, for instance, which Alexey so strongly sensed, eluded them.

Yet her vulnerability was real, and had a history.

She'd had an unhappy love affair. It happened in Bavaria, just before she came to England. The boy concerned had been a young chemist in Entlingen. Heinrich was tall and blonde and a touch overblown - thus far he fulfilled the Bavarian male convention. But otherwise he was utterly different from Ingrid's other followers.

For one thing, all he ever talked about was his work – intermolecular energy! – the kind of thing most young men avoided like a smell. Nor did he listen to anything Ingrid said. Yet Ingrid's interest, to her own amazement, never flagged.

Not that she felt, at first, consciously attracted. What she did feel was an acute sense of Heinrich's ***strangeness***, a sense that grew. Soon this strangeness began to shade into fascination; but then perhaps 'strangeness' is not so far from a sense of the unique.

Soon, too, Heinrich began to show quite different sides of himself. He took her for walks in the meadows. He talked like a poet: never before had Ingrid felt so strongly, vividly, the beauty of the world. And she began visiting him in his room. Soon after they ended up in bed, the first time Ingrid had ever allowed a man such liberties.

And yet, mysteriously, though she and Heinrich tried very hard to make love, it remained unclear whether they had actually succeeded. For one thing, she never bled. But then she understood a woman's hymen could be broken in a number of ways, even riding a horse. Ingrid rode every week.

Nevertheless, she quickly plunged into her first real, adolescent, passion. And soon her parents realised it. Her mother in particular sensed that, if not yet sleeping together, they were on the very verge.

After a month of questions, insinuations, door slammings and flouncings-out by Ingrid, Herr Uberspeer went off, one day, to visit Heinrich's father in Salzburg. So successfully did he convince his old friend that both Heinrich and Ingrid were on the verge of being compromised for life, that he persuaded the father to call the son back home, on the pretext he was needed for the family business.

None of which backstairs dealings were even hinted at to Ingrid. So when she wrote to Heinrich after his departure - he left very suddenly - and he failed to respond, she never knew either that he had been compelled to leave very much against his will or that he had been forced, in addition, to ignore her letters.

Yet it was how she then reacted that was the surprise. For now this warm, gregarious girl went into precipitate decline. She stayed in her room and avoided friends. She walked around with a ghostly, pre-Raphaelite pallor and lost weight. She even took up evangelical religion. This last especially disturbed Herr Uberspeer, as advanced theologically as he was in other ways.

Then one day her mother, looking in Ingrid's bedroom for a brush, found one of her own leather-bound diary-books which Ingrid had appropriated. She opened it to find a long, depressive diatribe by Ingrid, climaxing in a threat of suicide.

That did it. Ingrid's mother went straight down to her husband's study, burst in on him while working – an unprecedented intrusion - and, in floods of tears, demanded that Herr Uberspeer DO SOMETHING to save her daughter from herself. "While," she gasped tremulously, "there is still time."

Six weeks later, after yet more letters – this time to Mr. Crosby, that other old friend, who'd always got on especially well with Ingrid - it was fixed that she should go to stay in Oxford for a year.

And from that moment, everyone noted, Ingrid began to recover. Herr Uberspeer congratulated himself, and thanked God he had such understanding of adolescent psychology. While Frau Uberspeer, less advanced, merely thanked God.

And when Ingrid came to England her improvement continued, especially at first. Oxford was everything she had hoped for. A city that was a real city, yet full of gardens - in almost every college! A fairy-tale.

On the surface, indeed, she had quite regained her normal self. But underneath the old angst lingered on - which was all the more reason why she strived, every day, to act so cheerily.

Chapter Twenty-Seven

It was into this brittle, unstable chirpiness that Alexey had burst. And if Ingrid's susceptibility to Alexey's charm was predictable, so, given her history, was the effect of his rejection.

Once again she entered a decline. Yet this time, with Ingrid resolute to control herself, it showed itself at a remove. The knee she twisted that day with Alexey started playing up - she developed a limp. While a cough she caught became quite violent, and lingered on.

Strangest of all, she found herself getting worried about 'ghosts.' Mrs Crosby had told her about an undergraduate who had been stabbed in a town-and-gown riot, fifty years ago, right under their windows, and how a previous nanny had heard unexplained screaming at night. Mrs. Crosby meant merely to amuse but the result, now, was that if ever the Crosbys took the children out and left Ingrid at home, she rapidly got spooked - although she noticed , too, she felt no such fears if others were around. Even little Jane was sufficient for her to feel safe. Remarkable, really, because the poor mite could hardly protect her.

But she found consolations. One day she wandered into a nursery garden just down the road and, on impulse, bought five hyacinths in a pot. As a child she'd loved seeing hyacinths bloom in spring, and now she revisited this simple joy. She watered them lovingly every day. She talked to them and fed them sugar. Soon, the buds turned into blooms, and filled her bedroom with their rich, pure aroma, which felt strong and sure as ever it felt sweet….. gazing forward, with quiet confidence, to the spring.

First three buds were produced by her new friends, then five, then soon, a remarkable thirteen. Ingrid convinced herself they grew even as she watched.

One day, as she tended them, there was a tap at the door. It was the children. They often dropped by in this way and Ingrid encouraged it. They'd always been friendly but of late seemed even more so. Almost as if they'd understood her history with Alexey, though naturally they could only have known the essence.

They stood there staring at her, smiling shyly, as she fussed over her flowers.

"They're lovely," said little Jane, at length.

"They certainly are," said Ingrid. "Look at this one." She lifted a fledgling bloom, cradling it with her palm just underneath the bud, as by the neck. "It's pink, yes, but look at the other colours, too - mauve, look, green, and even white."

"You should talk to them," said Harold.

"I do."

"Tell them they're beautiful – and tell them how YOU feel, too."

"I do."

"They'll grow better if you do, you know."

"I do know."

"They're very nice, flowers – very kind. Do you *really* tell them how you feel?"

"Yes, I do – but why do you keep asking? What do *you* think I should be telling them? How do *you* think I feel?"

"Sad", said Jane.

At which the tears welled in Ingrid's eyes. Little though the children knew about her and Alexey in one sense, in another they knew everything. Far more, certainly, than the Crosbys, or even Paula.

"You're sad about Alexey, aren't you," said Harold. He turned to Jane. " I *told* you I should have killed him. Now look what he's done to Ingrid!"

"Don't talk about killing," said Jane, "you'll make her sadder still." She turned to Ingrid. "But I suppose it is a bit like someone's died," she said. "I felt the same when I lost my hamster."

Ingrid drew both children into her arms.

Gradually, Harold and Jane became her lifeline. She did everything she'd always done with them, but new things too; she even played cricket with them, a game veiled in mystery to Ingrid heretofore. She was touched by the look of Harold while he waited for her to bowl, squirming and wriggling with delight.

Bath-time was more intimate still, a time for halting, heartfelt tales of friendship and betrayal. But what moved Ingrid most, and what she needed most herself, was something simpler still: the endless, spontaneous hugs the children gave her. Jane, especially, would do this, with a tactile eloquence remarkable in one so young.

Indeed, thought Ingrid, whose fondness for Harold and Jane was swiftly turning into love, it was possible, when holding the children, to feel everything she felt for Alexey - only lacking the sex. How sweetly, delicately, Jane would kiss her on the cheek, with what intuition that the lighter the touch, the more moving for the one she was touching! Where on earth did she learn such things, at such an age?

And yet the thought of Alexey was always there. She'd forget him for three days then back would come his memory, like knocking a bruise. Time and again she'd pick up her pen to write to him, then throw it down after the first few words; on two separate occasions she wrote a whole letter, but never posted it.

She tried writing to her parents - but the inevitable self-censorship made her lonelier still. She tried talking to Paula; it helped a bit, but Paula's prescription was new activities and new people. So off they went to parties and concerts and met young men, but charming as these new friends were, they only started Ingrid thinking about Alexey all the more. And she compared them, inevitably, to their disadvantage.

Then one day she was walking down New College Lane, approaching a right angle bend, and there was Alexey, large as life, coming straight toward her! They almost collided. Then next – surrealism. A polite hello, a half-smile such as you grant an acquaintance……and they were past.

Stranger still was her reaction: a sudden, tingling rush of alarm, like a cold douche, setting her pulse racing as madly as if she'd seen one of the children hit by a car. And simultaneously a great surge of desire. Aghast, she ploughed remorselessly on. She daren't look back for twenty yards – and when she did, Alexey had disappeared.

Three weeks passed. Ingrid's plants died, but her relationship with the children grew stronger. Cricket took an ever growing part - not least, perhaps, because Ingrid's very incompetence, plus enthusiasm, made Harold and Jane feel all the more appreciated. As ever, they felt Ingrid was ***on their side.***

One day, she decided to take them to play in University Parks, just half a mile north of New College. The very place where she and Alexey had so memorably stopped, weeks earlier, for their picnic. They took a tennis ball and four miniature stumps, one stump for the bowler, three to make up the batsman's wicket. Even bails! Harold insisted the game should be 'grown-up' cricket.

The weather was scorching, more like August than May. Brick walls threw out heat like radiators; windows, flung wide, seemed to beckon in the sun. After playing with the children for an hour Ingrid lay down. They carried on playing happily enough, till gradually she heard Harold getting more and more cross with Jane, who was having great difficulty, when bowling, getting the ball within three feet of the wicket. Eventually, after much bickering, there was a row and Harold threw down the bat and stomped off. Ingrid sat up to see him disappearing far away over the grass, Jane in outraged and tearful pursuit.

The two passed other children, who pointed at them and laughed. They cannoned into an old lady who bawled at them. They passed a young man with some kind of sack slung over his shoulder, with something familiar in his stooping, plodding gait. Ingrid screwed up her eyes and stared some more. Good God – once again - it was Alexey!

Yet again the wild alarm, the thumping heart. But now there was no escape. Alexey was coming straight at her. She stared wildly around. What should she do? In the event she froze, still lying prone; and moments later there he was, right in front of her, towering high. And, yes, he was smiling- with surprise, yes, but also with that same humorous, quizzical gaze she knew so well. He seemed far less bothered by the confrontation than she.

"Exhausted?" he said.

"Well - very tired."

He nodded.

"Hello again," he said.

"Hello."

"Long time no see."

"Yes, it has been long."

"That *was* you the other day, wasn't it?"

There was no need to spell out where.

"Indeed it was."

"Well, it *was* me too, of that you can be quite sure. I - "

He smiled again, and looked about him.

"Here on your own?"

"No, I'm with the children. They're over there."

They were standing a few yards back, gazing intently. Of course, thought Ingrid, they'd no idea who Alexey was, they'd only heard of him by name. Better not introduce him, either – heaven knows what Harold might do.

Alexey gestured toward his bag. "It's got a shirt in it" he said. "I'm making my own. I often come here to sew. I like to sit and work on it - in the sun." Ingrid believed him. She remembered his cleverness with his hands, his love of craftsmanship.

"We're playing cricket," she said.

"YOU'RE not playing cricket - you're lying on the ground."

"Well, I was, it's just that I got a bit -"

"Exhausted?"

"Yes."

This time Ingrid allowed herself a glimmering smile; but she didn't feel up to banter. She turned to the children "This is: …..a friend of mine," she announced. "Oh yes. A very …*old*…..friend."

The children smiled shyly and Alexey grinned back, then settled himself cross legged on the ground, adopting that plain man's, no-nonsense air he often affected when being playful.

"Now," he said. "What you don't know, is that I am actually very good at cricket. Amazing, eh? And me a Russian! I learned it at Charterhouse. But, do you know, the very best game of all is **French** cricket, not English." He turned to the children. "Have you ever played French cricket ? You should try. It's the best game in the world! You don't even need stumps! Watch me! "

And now he was up again, picking up the bat, and soon he was showing the children how to play this 'much easier' game, wherein the wicket became the batsman himself - his legs.

The children took to it, and to Alexey, in a flash. But then, thought Ingrid, he's always been wonderful with children.

He stood behind Jane, supporting her arm, and helped her bowl. He bowled, himself, the most amazing, skidding spins along the ground, that described a perfect curve as they rushed between him and the batsman. Then he took the bat and Jane, bowling close to him, released the ball so late it flew straight up and hit him on the forehead: he dropped like a stone. As the children rushed toward him, aghast, he leapt up with a roar and chased them, screaming delightedly, all round the park.

Soon other children, attracted by the excitement, joined in. Within minutes there were a dozen playing, and Jane and Harold's mood had been transformed. And gradually, the infection spread to Ingrid. As she sat there, watching the joy Alexey was giving the children, she found her alarm fading - to be replaced by its first cousin, that intense attraction she had felt for him from the start.

Years later, looking back, Ingrid decided this was the moment when she knew she was in love. And as Alexey sat panting with her and the children on the grass, the game over, all reserve between the two grown-ups seemed, once again, to have disappeared.

So when Ingrid and the children had to leave, Alexey naturally saw them to the Crosbys' front door.

The children leapt like dogs to kiss Alexey goodbye. While Ingrid and Alexey, gazing into each other's eyes in quite the old way, said of course they'd meet again very soon.

From the depths Ingrid hurtled back up to the heights. The Crosbys, noticing, were amazed by the transformation - not merely of her mood, but of her looks. It was as if someone had run a flat-iron over her face. The lines of stress had disappeared, while her skin regained all its former creaminess.

True, there were aftershocks. She did, for instance, have to explain to the children, after an appropriate pause, that their delightful new friend was in fact the fiendish-beyond-belief Alexey. Which they, at first, refused to believe. How *could* he be?

Eventually they took their first step toward adult complexity, and accepted it. Soon, with the almost occult ability of children to absorb the emotions of those around them, Ingrid's happiness became theirs as well.

That night she dreamed about him.

And what a dream! His face and body were as she knew them, but covered, bizarrely, by an inch of fur.

She felt all the familiar tenderness. But now, as she stroked his chest, her hand slid downward to his stomach, then lower still, and in a moment she was doing what her dream told her, without question, was what she wanted: she was stroking, caressing, that place between his legs where he did have real-life 'fur.' Soon she was grasping his erect penis, which in her dream had become immense. And she was drawing it, with luxurious urgency, between her legs, when she woke up.

For a moment she lay stunned. Where was she? Wakefulness felt less real than her dream. And then – but how grotesque! She knew she wanted

Alexey, but like *that*? Was her love *quite* so grossly physical? Well, clearly it was. And as she gradually, over the next hour, digested this directive from her subconscious, she began to feel quite grateful, because at least she knew where she stood. She knew her real feelings.

Like Paula said, no more fart-arsing around. This time she would deal with the situation directly. Seize fate by the throat! By something, anyway.

So two days later, come her evening off, she once more announced that she would go out with Paula, set off for what she presented to the Crosbys as a literary 'talk', described a perfect ellipse away from New College then back again, and finished up at its main entrance.

Living so close by, she had often noticed female domestic staff going in and out, sometimes with hoods against possible rain, sometimes with bags. So she took a tip from that first New College evening and put together a disguise. She had her own rather fetching Tyrolean hood, so she wore that, grabbed a cumbrous-looking bag, filled it with potatoes, and off she went. It was a gamble, of course, because Alexey might well not be in. But the chances were he would be, as she knew he had no less than two separate tutorials the next day. So he would work into the night.

At nine o-clock, at dusk, just as college dinner was finishing, she appeared outside the lodge gates. Hood up, bag weighing her down, assuming the lurching, martyred walk of the female college servants, she was through the gate in a flash. The porters never blinked.

And yes, Alexey *was* in; and yes, he was delighted to see her, albeit amazed; and yes, within half an hour of her arrival they were in bed together and at last they consummated....but did they really? Try as Alexey might, he never entered her.

For regardless of her Freudian vision of Alexey's penis, Alexey failed to achieve any erection at all, whatever they tried. Like stuffing jelly up a pipe, thought Ingrid irreverently, not quite the manly invasion she had hoped for. While the more things went wrong, the more Alexey ***talked***:

talked, in fact, with a meaninglessness as profound as those verbose and spluttery intellectuals back in Entlingen.

For his ramblings implied the difficulties would soon pass. But they did not. Nor did they on the three further occasions Ingrid came back to visit him. Finally, by tacit agreement, they gave up.

Then a week later, a note from Alexey suggesting a meeting. Which Ingrid attended. No Alexey. Then the day after, another letter; so sorry about the non-appearance, etc, a crisis had cropped up – but even this, he went on, was as nothing compared to what had erupted now. For with the spring holidays looming, he suddenly had to go away!

To the Mediterranean, would you believe, with his uncle! It meant he had to get special dispensation from New College to leave early. They'd had an invitation from Countess Sorkozy, an old family friend, and for some reason his uncle was adamant he must come.

Had he mentioned the Countess? He thought he had. It really was quite dreadful being hustled away like this. It was *too* ridiculous, it was like being kidnapped! He'd be away for at least two months, he feared, possibly longer.

He'd write, of course, and be in touch the moment he returned.

Yet there was one other thing Ingrid now remembered. Throughout their attempted lovemaking, amidst all that flooding verbosity, Alexey had periodically flashed her that same glance of panic and alarm that had so struck her – and had seemed, then, so out of character - the very first time they'd met.

Part Two: Experience

Chapter Twenty-Eight

Once Henry decided to accept Anthony Parsons' offer, they moved swiftly to agreement.

So Henry bent himself to his new task. And was faced with the eternal conundrum - like Mary when she'd set out to promote his poetry - where should he *start*?

Though there was this difference. Mary had to *do* things – things she'd never previously attempted. Henry had to get *other people* to do things....to administrate. Where would he find them?

So curiously enough, his first managerial act was to go down the pub.

The Roebuck was in a mean street just off the village green - a pub Mary hated. For Mary found it, as she put it, 'rough'. It brought out the latent bourgeois in this journalist's daughter. With its chipped, ill-painted sign, with its mangey plaster walls, with its vague, pervasive odour of lime, presumably to do with cleaning, it offended something deep within her gentle middle-class soul.

Which was precisely why Henry liked it. For almost any evening you could be sure the Roebuck's customers would include Joe Parsons - Anthony Parsons' farmer brother– and a fair few of his men. The gang the Thorntons had given breakfast to after Henry's all-night walk.

And Henry would sit there quietly, sucking his pipe, and listen with his puckish smile to their talk. And they - sensing his genuine enjoyment of their company - happily accepted him, little though he said.

As for Henry, he loved his times there, full of rich, enfolding working-class warmth. 'Sumptuous' was the way he described it to himself. So different from the world he had grown up in, that of the mean-spirited bourgeoisie.

So down to the Roebuck went Henry, for three full evenings, the week after he shook hands with Anthony. And he sat, and smoked, and listened, as was his wont. And said nothing at all about his coming role at the camp; partly because he felt reluctant to use friends, but also because he sensed, correctly, that should he do so the trick was to take his time, to wait until the Joe Parsons workforce came to ***him.***

He knew they'd hear about the new developments shortly, via the unfailing tom-tom of country rumour. And so they did. By the third evening Ben Tennant, one of Joe Parsons' herdsmen, sat down beside him and carefully worked the conversation around to the rumoured changes at the camp, wondering if Henry could tell him anything about it.

And having established what they'd heard was true, Ben said they'd be only too pleased to do anything they could to help, especially – a grin – anything mechanical. Henry had but to ask. At which Henry, grinning back, said it was very kind of them to offer, and he would bear them gratefully in mind, but right now there was nothing pressing. Though there might be eventually.

So the chic of these things was maintained. And now Henry bought Ben a pint, then Joe bought Henry one, then Henry bought one for Mike ***and*** Fred.... and there were jokes and banter and all parted the best of friends.

Nevertheless, very soon, just the kind of problem Henry feared did crop up – one of mechanics.

For Jason - the horse who'd had toothache, now recovered - was strapped up, three times a day, to a huge iron capstan, just off the grassy area in the middle of the site. And there, helped on by Bluebell, another Westbury horse, he pulled the capstan round and round and thereby hauled up water from the well.

For a week now Jason had been bucking, when hitched up to the capstan, in a way never before seen. And Henry gradually realised the problem lay in the capstan itself. It kept catching. Something was clearly awry. But what? And how to fix it? This was where Henry needed help.

And how readily Ben responded, when Henry raised it at the pub! Once more the flooding, working class warmth, but this time linked to practicalities. True, Ben explained, he couldn't do the work himself, as, like Henry, his thing was animals. But he shouted across the bar to Ted

Molesley, who was there playing darts with Joe's son Fred. And Ted *did* have a mechanical mind, as did Fred, and both agreed, instantly, to take a look the following day. Tom Rowbottam and Harry Pick, friends of theirs Henry hadn't even met, came along too – and short, slouching, Cayleb, the village blacksmith, with his tools.

In an hour the fault was found - a cracked cylinder. Using Cayleb's tools, they removed it; then they took it, on the camp cart, down to Cayleb's forge; within an hour he'd welded it into shape. By late afternoon the cylinder was back. By supper it was fitted. And the day ended with Mary serving Irish stew to everyone, on the deal table on the camp green.

Bit by bit, Henry and Mary got into their new life as administrators.

The horse-riding was organised as every year – this, naturally, was one of Henry's strengths. The swimming, in the nearby river Thames, went beautifully too; but then this, also, was part of the athletic world Henry understood. The marquees, on the other hand, which were put up every year for extra space, mystified him: so he backed off and left the raising thereof to a cheery combination of Ben Tennant, Ted Molesley and half a dozen East Enders. In the event Henry joined in too, but strictly as an underling.

For in Henry's regime, different people became the boss for different tasks. If the problem was psychological - if one of the backward children, say, ran amok - Henry took charge. If one of catering - twenty people, say, needing a meal - then Mary took charge. If the capstan needed a tweak, or the pump played up a bit - Cayleb took charge. A kind of flexible, revolving hierarchy – and it happened without anybody mentioning it.

And if things went wrong, especially humorously, who cared?

Typical was the day when three iron beds were due to be delivered to a neighbour's farm. Ben Tennant announced that he would drive the horse Bluebell, hitched up to the cart, the three miles over there 'without maps, no nonsense like that.' Because Bluebell 'knew the route.'

In the event Bluebell did find his way, impeccably. He did the whole trip by memory. But there was just one drawback: it was the wrong farm. Yet when Ben and Bluebell arrived back, six hours later, still with the beds, they were greeted at Westbury with rapture, cheered up the lane by a good twenty of the boys. Joe Parsons, especially, nearly died laughing.

For Henry's running of Westbury was above all about spirit. To Henry, a quote of Tolstoy's, attacking force-fed education, summed it up:

"Every such attempt does not advance the pupil, but only removes him from the aim toward which he is to tend, like the rude hand of a man, which, wishing to help the flower to open, crushes everything all around and violently opens the flower by its petals.'

Freedom, autonomy, humour – these were Henry's watchwords. Especially freedom.

Chapter Twenty-Nine

Meanwhile Ingrid's life was changing too.

She never did manage to contact Alexey. George had been given an address and she tried writing more than once, but got no reply. At first she felt as devastated as before, complete with tears, mooning, and Gothic pallor; but then, one evening, something new.

She was gazing at her reflection in the mirror. She looked exhausted, spectre-pale, with soulful, woebegone eyes. And yet…she reminded herself of something. What could it be? Mein Gott, but it was Katya, her pet dog back in Bavaria, the night she'd turned up after vanishing for three days! She looked like her pet dog!

At which she laughed out loud.

Then gradually she understood. It was what Freudians called the 'laugh of recognition'. Some evolutionary process had taken place and suddenly she saw her experience in a completely new way. She was a victim! She'd conspired in her own demise! She of all people, Ingrid the golden, Ingrid the toast of every Siegfried in Bavaria ……. was a compulsive, creeping victim!

Or rather, she was *not* - she had come to the end of that particular road. She saw, now, what had been going on with both Alexey and Heinrich (not really with Heinrich but she included him anyway.) Herr Gott, how had she stood any of it for five minutes? Looking back, both relationships had been doomed from the start - Heinrich with his autistic self-absorption, Alexey with his compulsion to fail at the simplest, primary form of contact: the fundamental process of *meeting*, for heaven's sake. What could be more basic than that?

And as for the charm, the 'understanding,' the exquisite listening, the way he would spoil her, if they were in a teashop, with cream and cakes! This was clearly but the flip side of his avoidance – a massive act.

He acted *more* kind, *more* empathic, *more* protective than other men - precisely because he was actually less so. Two sides of the same coin. And now something else struck her, something which had never dawned on her till then - the *theatricality* of her relationship with Alexey.

That first conversation in the Cadena, for instance, why, it could have been a scene out of a play! (Ingrid forgot this also applied to a young lady posing as Rose La Touche). What was the Greek word for one who plays a part? Hupokrites! The key to Alexey's character was that he was above all else a hypocrite, an *actor*.

She glanced at herself once more and now, another surprise- she was transformed. Gone was the pallor, the pre-Raphaelite angst. Instead there was a quite new fire and fury in her face, a near-cynical humorousness that had as little to do with her misery as with the chirpy Ingrid of old. Why, she looked positively devilish!

A week later, there took place a pseudo-modern-art exhibition, put on at the Oxford Union. Paula had corralled Ingrid into it - the scam being that the 'modern art' had either been cobbled together by the students themselves (one picture had been painted by Ernst in a mirror, with his left hand) or, in the case of three colourful and much-praised pieces, had been produced by Harold and Jane. Jane's attempt at a rabbit, titled 'Woman in love' won many learned plaudits.

All Alexey's friends were there, and everyone saw how Ingrid had changed.

Satire had never been her chosen mode, yet here she was as fiercely glad as any of them at the pious appreciation of their audience. This crowd was made up of everyone from the more up-to-date dons, through two bright-eyed chaplains, to a sedate and pince-nezed group of women students, the art club from St. Hugh's. Everything in Oxford, in fact, that might be conveyed by the eternal mantra 'advanced'; everything, now thought Ingrid, she despised.

She'd even helped with the accountancy (the Crosbys had put in a small sum, assuming the exhibition was conventional) but above all she'd demanded, and been given, the prime position at the table where sales were made. This meant she had the further, fierce joy of taking money off these 'mugs.' (Profits to charity.) More, it was she who had suggested, and then contrived, the evening's climax - a stand-up row, followed by exchange of blows, between one of the young 'artists' (played with verve by a be-wigged and bearded Ernst) and a pompous middle aged 'bourgeois' (played with still more verve by Tom.)

Added to which Ingrid was now, potentially, famous. For the moment the fight broke out, and Ingrid had been trying to 'separate' the protagonists, the local newspaper photographer had snapped his camera. She might yet appear on the front page.

All this was viewed with amusement by those who knew her. Yet they also sensed something wrong. For ever since Alexey's departure, his friends had been much touched by - and had much gossiped about - Ingrid's evident melancholy. And all had done their best, in different ways, to help. Ernst, florid and romantic, had been the soul of gallantry, forever offering understanding, trips out for tea, and even flowers; while George – steady, good natured George - had said little, but arguably helped more. For his support consisted above all in his manner, which Ingrid found deeply sympathetic.

Then there was Paula. She, too, had shown a delicacy that was new. So as the two women extricated themselves from the exhibition, at five o'clock, leaving the men to do the dismantling, she made a point of walking Ingrid back home.

She suggested tea, which Ingrid gaily accepted. By some instinct Paula avoided the Cadena and took Ingrid to the Poor Student, a smaller and more intimate place just down the road.

And as they sat down Paula was struck by Ingrid's friskiness. Ingrid glanced round cheerily enough, checking the place out, but her movements were jerky and ill-timed.

"Well," she declared, "all I can say is I hope they've plenty of cream cakes. I need a sugar charge! Fighting is so exhausting, don't you find?"

"I haven't done a huge amount of fighting. Only with my sisters, and they let me win. Oh, and there's fighting the sex battle with men, naturally, but that's different."

"Why's that?"

"That's fighting to lose. Or rather to make them think they've won. It's sweet, really, their need to believe in 'conquest.' "

"*Do* they need to believe that?"

"Oh, I think so. Behind most men, however tender, lies this need to be the grand initiator, the arch seducer, the omnipotent controller of each emotional event. Without it they feel weapon-less; they feel.... well... impotent."

This struck a nerve, because Ingrid had recurrently wondered, since Alexey's disappearance, whether her sexual assertiveness had been part of the problem.

"Are there any who don't feel this?

"Very few, I fear. And the more they say they don't, the more they do."

This too struck a nerve. Now Ingrid's 'gaiety' was replaced by an air of deep thought; indeed her mood swing was so striking Paula was quite taken aback. Was it her imagination, or was Ingrid on the verge of *tears*?

What on earth could have made her feel quite so strongly, and so suddenly, at that moment?

The answer being in one sense obvious – Alexey - Paula regretted her clumsiness. But now she wondered how she could help. Finally, falteringly, she began to talk. Some instinct told her that the way to start was to suggest that she, too, had suffered comparable agonies in the past.

For the first time in their relationship Paula described her marriage - that strange, continental debacle that Ingrid had only heard about, till now, through rumour. Yes, she had been married for five years to a Dutch architect, Jan, who she had met while he was studying at Oxford and who she had accompanied back to Amsterdam. And, yes, he had in many ways been remarkable, interested in all the latest architectural ideas. "His mecca was the Eiffel Tower." said Paula. "Steel-framed buildings, the house as a machine, huge windows, sunlight, no clutter." He made contacts, became successful, and they were happy.

Yet gradually Paula realised her husband didn't like sex. Not least, she suspected, because he didn't want children and for someone as clean-lined and functional as Jan, what was the point of sex without procreation? "For Jan, everything was always a means to an end, not an end in itself."

But Paula did want sex - as an end in itself. And soon came the inevitable: she got involved with a psychology tutor, one Friedrich Paul. They became lovers. There was little romanticism in Friedrich's approach, no especial delicacy, but he was uninhibited, hugely potent, and Paula found him extraordinarily satisfying. They talked, too – he was full of free love ideology – but sex was the main thing. Two amicable, amiable, love-making animals.

If Paula hoped these revelations would transform Ingrid's mood she was right. Both Ingrid's tearfulness and fervid gaiety vanished. Instead, her eyes opened wide in fascination. Never before had Paula spoken to her so directly; never at all about anything like this.

"So what happened?" Ingrid asked.

"Jan found out! He came across letters - in a place I never put them but where, conceivably, they might have been left out by the housemaid." Paula's familiar ironical smile. "Coincidence being the wonderful thing it is, Jan later married her. Then shortly afterward, he fell off a building and that was the end of *him*. Schadenfreude! And the housemaid inherited."

"I *see*. And Friedrich?"

"Oh, we carried on through it all and after Jan's death, too: but I was out on my ear. Nevertheless I had a flat paid for, like a traditional mistress, by Friedrich. Less traditional, though, were the parameters Friedrich now laid down for our relationship.

"Till then he had seemed the exception to the rule, that eternal male need to be in control. But now he let his sexual libertarianism rip and he declared – a kind of dominance in reverse - that we should both enjoy our sexual freedom. And indeed we did; he slept with others and so did I."

"Really?"

"Yes, *really*! I slept with two of his friends. He suggested it."

"Really?"

"Yes, *really* - why not? After all, we had plenty in common – our tastes, our interest in psychology …..Friedrich….. the friends were delightful, they attracted me, so why not? Why not express our friendship physically? As Friedrich said, expression before repression, a thousand times so, or 'nichts verdrangen' in his favoured phrase."

"But wasn't he jealous?"

A glimmering smile.

"Perhaps a little. But, as I said, he suggested it."

A pause, while Ingrid digested this. Then a maverick thought.

"So how *was* it with the other two?"

"Very good." A wide grin, now. "But not as good as Friedrich."

And thus it was, in this and subsequent talks, that the two friends' camaraderie ripened into intimacy. And Ingrid learned ever more about her friend.

She learned, for instance, about the inevitable ending, quite soon, of Paula's relationship with Friedrich. Because for Friedrich it had essentially been an episode.

And she learned how Paula, imbued with her new-found sexual libertarianism, found the split from Friedrich less difficult than she'd expected. Indeed, she'd felt enhanced by the experience. So, on her return to England, though for money reasons she'd moved in with her parents, she looked for a similar set-up in the UK.

And who did she choose? Why yes, as Ingrid had possibly guessed (Ingrid had indeed at least half-guessed) none other than….. Alexey!……. who had originally approached her - as she thought she'd described? - in the Ashmolean….. though she'd had plenty of other offers, she had to say, which she'd turned down.

While what followed, with Alexey, explained why she'd reacted with as much recognition as sympathy to Ingrid's earlier tales of woe. Because Paula, like Ingrid, had at first been captivated, then later hugely let down by Alexey's behaviour. "More erratic than erotic," she said. She ended up angry and frustrated.

Although, like Ingrid, she'd felt great sympathy for Alexey's vulnerability. And hence the need, so faithfully fulfilled till then, to remain discreet.

But her final revelation was most startling of all: after Alexey, she announced, she had taken up with Tom! (Though Ingrid, it must be said, had sensed this too.)

And Tom, unlike Alexey, had not been frustrating at all. His very conservatism, Paula felt, was to do with a certain deep self-satisfaction which translated into huge sexual potency - reminiscent, perversely, of the left wing Friedrich Paul. That he and Paula were at daggers drawn, politically, only added piquancy to their relationship. The chemistry was electric.

Not to mention his poetry - quite good poetry, actually, rather better than his friends …………..perhaps he was more romantic than he seemed.

And it emerged, too, that Paula had used their 'chaperone' meetings for her own purposes! For when Ingrid had gone off to meet Alexey, Paula had met Tom.

But by then, in fact, Paula's need for discretion had been monumental. Not only had all the protagonists in her English love life known each other, but there was the primary necessity, ever present, of keeping all this away from her parents.

Above all from her father - a college dean. A higher form of vicar! It might have killed him.

Chapter Thirty

June came, and with it the full blooming of an Oxford summer. The college gardens sagged with flowers; mowers rattled on the lawns; the grey old courtyards rang with the shrieks of the young.

To Ingrid the city's bells, striking the hour, were most suggestive of all. Bong bam bim boom would go the clock of New College, re-echoing through the shining, hanging stillness, then Queen's would join in, then another college half a mile away, and then another.

It was as if Oxford itself was talking, as if kindly, centuries-old friends were bestirring themselves to greet the young. Enjoy yourself, the bells seemed to say: we were young once too, we've seen it all, there's very little you can do to shock us. Be happy. It is your right.

Although the effect on Ingrid was mainly disturbing. How could you live in such an atmosphere without romance? Or if not 'romance', at least a lover, like Paula? And now Paula, too, had gone away, for a fortnight! A sick aunt in Scotland, apparently. 'Everyone's going away except me' thought Ingrid, then laughed at her own self-pity.

Laughter had certainly been key to her and Paula's attempts to square Paula's theories of male predominance with sexual libertarianism. The trick, they decided, was for men to be led to believe the precise opposite of what was true – that women were actually calling the shots.

In particular was this necessary with the likes of the conservative Tom. For the truth, of course, with Tom, had been that Paula had had many offers, but Tom's had been the offer she chose. And the art lay in Tom never getting a glimpse, not the remotest hunch, of the truth. "Like a clever chancellor working with a stupid king," said Paula. "The king keeps having these brilliant ideas."

Though why, ruminated Ingrid, should a woman have to go through all this rigmarole at all? Why shouldn't her 'right to choose' be as overt as any man's? Bernard Shaw had said (Ingrid thought it was Bernard Shaw) that he looked forward to an era of honest, pragmatic sexual relationships when if a man were walking down the street and saw a woman he desired, he could walk straight up to her, and, politely and reasonably, ask her to make love. And the woman should treat this as an entirely reasonable suggestion.

Yes, but why not the reverse position as well? Why shouldn't the woman ask? Now that **would** be different.

Let's have a world, thought Ingrid, where I could choose any genuinely attractive man straight off the street and we could proceed to bed right away. I could solve my virginity problem in half an hour, rather than half a century, as with Alexey.

And at that moment her fundamental concern became clear. The plain first step toward this glittering new world, at least her part in it, was to cease all this flaffing around and have sex. Real sex. Delicious, abandoned, sensual, Paulaesque sex (Ingrid remained impressed by her older friend) and to have it now.

Not that sex showed any sign of actually happening, at least not yet. The only real male friends she'd made since coming to Oxford were the New College crowd and she sensed they still felt she was 'Lothario' Alexey's property, whatever they thought of his behaviour. Not that she would dream of getting involved with anyone Alexey knew anyway. She'd leave such complexities to Paula.

Then there was that sub-sect of the New College crew, the German Rhodes scholars, and their attentions – lacking the quaint reserve of the English – had been more fulsome. Above all Ernst's. But quite how far he meant it, and quite how far he merely enjoyed admiring his own rather far-fetched chivalry remained unclear.

One memorable moment occurred at the Holywell Music Rooms, when the friends gathered to watch Henry Thornton rehearse. Suddenly, during a pause, Ernst slipped onto the piano and started playing Bach's Bist Du Bei Mir, one of Ingrid's most favourite songs. And what quickly became plain was that he was directing his performance toward Ingrid - complete with full repertoire of dreamy, love-lorn looks.

"Bist du bei mir," he sang, " geh' ich mit Freuden,
Zum Sterben und zu meiner Ruh,
Ach, wie vernugt war' so meine Ende………"

"With you beside me, I'd go with gladness.
To death and to my rest.
Ah, how my end would bring contentment….."

The 'ach', especially, was pronounced memorably - so much so that the Englishmen present, notably Henry and Tom, laughed out loud. Which annoyed Ernst, but also hugely embarrassed Ingrid. Never could she conceive of being the object of Ernst's romantic attentions, however ardently felt.

As a Bavarian, she knew the type.

One day she became pro-active. In weird reprise of that first meeting with Alexey, it was on a bus. The vehicle was swirling up the High in heavy traffic, and - as with Alexey - Ingrid was sitting downstairs. And across the walkway, three rows along, was the most beautiful young man she'd ever seen. Huge shoulders, the dreamiest, most languidly poetic face imaginable, pensive, far-off eyes as if lost in the most tender reverie of poetic delight ……or, in the way Ingrid tended to think these days, in the deepest luxury of post-coital satisfaction.

Now it was Ingrid doing the staring, full of frank and joyous sexual appraisal, a Mona Lisa smile around her lips.

And as the man became aware of her glance, and surely of its meaning, he gave her a look of what was surely his own, unabashed desire.

And then an old lady got on the bus! And the conductor came clattering downstairs! And he ordered the old lady off, as it was the rush hour! Still more déjà vu. And in a sudden inspiration, touching eyes with Adonis as she moved, Ingrid got up and offered the old lady her seat – convinced the young man would offer his seat, too, and that somehow this would lead to conversation.

But instead, a quite different young man got up and offered her his. And he was fat, bald and ugly. So Ingrid turned him down.

And now the conductor, with many apologies, explained that someone would have to get off and it looked like it would have to be…..well…. Ingrid. And still Adonis made no offer…….. nor did anyone else … and the whole thing was embarrassing and absurd…. and anyway, the bus was stuck in a jam and they were within a hundred yards of the Crosbys' home.

So Ingrid got off, and ended up on the pavement, alone.

Sexual assertiveness, in fact, was harder to realise than she'd thought. Nevertheless, the Great Bus Debacle had this effect – it set Ingrid thinking, once again, about Alexey, though in a different spirit from before. What an amazing rodomontade they had achieved together, to be sure! Now if SHE had been Alexey, she would have had herself in bed before you could say Ingrid Uberspeer. So to speak.

So when, one sunny June morning, an envelope flopped onto her place at breakfast - 'It's for you, Ingrid!' followed by the usual gaze of concentrated attention from the Crosbys - her reaction was, above all, one of irritation.

Because the letter was postmarked Paris, and there really was only one person who would be writing to her from Paris. She laid the letter aside for the moment, then read it in privacy, up in her room.

It was on hotel paper, headed 'Auberge Cinq Moulins', under a rather scratchy etching of five windmills. Curious, thought Ingrid, that Alexey and his rich relatives should be staying somewhere so cheap. And then, as usual, she jumped to the letter's end to see how Alexey had signed off.

But weirdly his writing, too, looked wrong, not at all as she remembered it. And the last two lines, when she reached them, read:

"I dearly hope that you will come. Not least because that will enable me to fulfil my duty and I'm sure you sense how dutiful I am; but also because if you don't you'll make me miserable, and I'll cry.

So – in sure expectation - I remain, dear Ingrid,

> Your helpless and yet hopeful admirer,
>
> Tom Huntingdon."

***What*?!** Tom Huntingdon, of all people - and writing to her in those terms?! Ingrid was so amazed she almost forgot to be angry. And what was he doing in France, anyway? Come to think of it, she did remember Paula saying something about Tom and a conference in Paris - that must be it. She flicked urgently to the start of the letter, and read:

Auberge Cinq Moulins,
21 Rue de la défense,
Paris

May 10, 1914

Dear Ingrid,

Tom speaking. Tom Huntingdon. Last seen swapping blows with that dastardly modern painter, Ernst, at the 'art' exhibition, despite your energetic and appreciated intervention.

I am in Paris for a brief 'convention of progressive European poets ' to which I was, amazingly, invited, though for such a brevity that by the time you get this I will probably not be in Paris at all, but back in Oxford, so perhaps you should ignore this aspect altogether.

Now, Ingrid! Do you believe in mixing business with pleasure? I do. Because so successful was that art exhibition you helped with that myself and other friends have decided to follow it up with a sculpture exhibition, also very modern indeed, in London. And I am commissioned to ask you this: would you help with this one too?

We wondered if you might do a little bit more accountancy, and we thought, too, of having conversation pieces that might include say, a strangulated cat, or a pile of bricks (believe me, the way things are going, one day someone really will exhibit a pile of bricks at the Tate in deadly earnest).And then we thought of a section along the lines of 'Is real life superior to art?' and in the Female Beauty section thereof we thought of exhibiting the following remarkable piece: you.

Would you consent to be exhibited, Ingrid, in the flesh? (NB *Not* nude, please, what can you be thinking!) We shall, of course, provide all necessaries, such as dresses, a pedestal etc. plus copious cups of tea; indeed, at such moments we would also produce large cardboard placards saying things like 'Female Beauty Taking Tea,' to avoid any possible confusion, and to play big, also, with the social realists.

We did consider exploring the feminist aspect, given those rioting talents you showed with me and Ernst, not least because of the further, hurling, possibilities for the bricks, but decided to keep it simple. Or as George inimitably put it: "Who needs a punch-up when we've got Panther - good old Panther?"

At which moment you may reasonably ask:

"But who is Panther? Who is she
That all the swains commend her?"

And the answer is that 'Panther' is you; 'Panther' being what you have lately been christened by those who know you, as it seems to convey so succinctly the dashing, jungly quality of your Female Beauty as well as being wonderfully in tune with the spirit of the age.

By which I mean that wild, predatory zeitgeist so notably expressed in the Russian ballet, not to mention the fact that Mr. Winston Churchill's mother, Jenny Jerome, who has allegedly predated 2OO lovers, is nicknamed 'Panther', nor forgetting that the German cruiser with which your Kaiser so nearly precipitated a European war at Agadir was also called 'Panther'. Coincidence? I think not. Jungly, leonine, predatory, that's you, and that's early-twentieth- century we, too; or as future generations will surely see us, anyhow.

Whew. Where was I? I'm sure there was a point in there somewhere. Ah! That, believe it or not, was the business: now for the pleasure.

Before Paula left she specially asked me to 'look after' you while she was away. She's very fond of you, you know. I naturally said I would be delighted to do any looking after necessary.

So what I suggest is the following: that we meet up, very shortly, to discuss the business aspect of all this but combine it with the pleasure of discussing the whole thing over lunch. How about the Cosa Nostra, in the Turl, at 12.3O, say, on Thursday?

There remains only for me to make the following confession; that for me, the pleasure will far outweigh the business; that 'looking after' you, were you to allow me, is probably the least dutiful duty I will ever undertake; and that that is, of course, because you are the most ravishing, charming, vivacious and amusing young woman I can off hand remember meeting.

I dearly hope that you will come. Not least because that will enable me to fulfil my duty and I'm sure you sense how dutiful I am. But also because if you don't you'll make me miserable, and I'll cry.

So – in expectation - I remain, dear Ingrid,

        Sincerely,

                Your helpless and yet hopeful admirer,

                      Tom Huntingdon.'

Well! Now, after reading the whole thing through, Ingrid exploded. The cheek of it! How dare he assume so much – assume, at the least, the right to flirt! 'Look after her' indeed! Oh yes, that was likely, that was - that Paula should fix her man up with her friend while she was away.

Indeed, the whole thing was so ridiculous Ingrid once again burst out laughing. For on re-reading she had to admit she found parts of it quite funny, notably the stuff about the exhibition, and the bricks, and the cups of tea.

She flicked quickly to the bit where he piled on the adjectives - 'ravishing, charming, vivacious and amusing'... what did Disraeli say about dealing with Queen Victoria? 'When it comes to flattery, lay it on with a trowel.' A trowel? This was more like a coal shovel. Well, it might work with a lonely old queen but not with her. Pathetic.

And anyway, she now found herself thinking, what about Paula? If this was as self-evidently a play for her, Ingrid, as it seemed (and not just chaff, as, in extremis, Tom would surely claim) it was hard to imagine how anyone could be more disloyal. Paula had only been away a week! Hadn't she said that, unlike her sexually emancipated friend Friedrich Paul, Tom only believed in one lover at a time? One lover for her perhaps – rather more, self-evidently, for him.

Then she looked once more at the bit about the bricks and found herself chuckling again. How dare Tom suggest she was a rioter? Just because she'd been involved in a punch-up with him and Ernst! Well- that was pretence - if he wanted a real fight she'd give him one.

And on she went on, oscillating between outrage and laughter, but without the slightest doubt of what her answer would be.

That very same day she wrote back.

Dear Tom,

Thankyou so much for your memorable note.

Well, this much you got right - it was certainly a surprise.

I am happy, as last time, to help you with your project, and I agree that an injection of sanity into Advanced Sculpture is as necessary as with Advanced Painting. But in this instance, I think, I should confine myself to.... business. So I shall be more than happy to help sell tickets, and, yes, a little mild accountancy too, but I will leave it at that.

As for making an exhibition of myself, I think that would be most unwise. Did no one ever tell you how little women like being put on a pedestal? Not a mistake I would have expected from *you*. Moreover I suspect you of getting the idea from Oscar Wilde - the time he notoriously exhibited his wife…..on a pedestal …at a charity do …….or is that just coincidence? As for rioting, the only thing that might induce fisticuffs in me are certain kinds of unsolicited, inappropriate compliments lobbed my way from certain very particular kinds of men.

And finally, I know there is a saying among your nation of shopkeepers that 'it's a business doing pleasure with you' but I would remind you that in this instance any such admixture would be combustive, and that business and pleasure should be kept entirely separate, and it is Paula you are supposed to be doing your pleasure with, not me.

Anyway, without getting personal, you remind me of a bull. And if bulls in china shops are tricky, bulls in restaurants are downright dangerous, as you well know. Especially to young women.

For all these reasons, I must decline your kind invitation for Thursday, though thanks so very much for asking.

Somehow, somewhere, I am sure that we will meet.

       Yours very sincerely

        Ingrid.

Ingrid tripped out of her house, popped the envelope in the post box and dismissed the whole episode from her mind. Or tried to. Because, perhaps not so very surprisingly, given the sensual daydreams she had been lately nurturing, the image of Tom Huntingdon kept popping back into her consciousness, as importunate and uninvited as his letter. Now how would HE be in bed, she found herself wondering, absurd and irrelevant as the idea naturally was.

How **would** he be? Well, clearly, less like a bull, in fact - let's be precise about this – more like, perhaps, a rhinoceros; like some antediluvian predator whose onrush would impale her, surely, like a battering ram or the lance of a medieval knight. **Just** like a rhinoceros, indeed.....

And Ingrid laughed again.

The very next day, back winged another letter from Tom.

She opened it upstairs.

'Dear Ingrid,' it read, and then nothing else at all on the first page, except the following :

Poem

Had I your love
Then I would be
As happy as a lark

But as I've not
I think I'll be
As horrid as a shark

YET

Sharks are good, and larks are bad,
To sharklets, and to flies –
How dare we then
So thoughtlessly
Thus anthropo-
Morphise?

She turned the page over; anyone seeing Ingrid's face at the moment would have been struck by her expression, a cross-breed of smile, leer and snarl. She looked, too, deeply tired.

She read on:

…..So there you are, you see; you've done it. Not only have you driven me to tears - as I said you would – I cried this morning – buckets! – but you've driven me to poetry, which is worse. But be not fooled, cruelest Ingrid, by any tone of levity you may detect in the above, which was penned in that Ultima Thule of sadness whence the only possible escape-hatch is a joke. The truth is that the effect you have on me is……. devastating. The real truth, in fact, is anything BUT a joke.

It is this:

Doubt you to whom my muse these notes intendeth
Which now my breast, o'ercharged, to music lendeth?
To you, to you, all song of praise is due:
Only in you my song begins and endeth.

Who hath the eyes which marry state with pleasure?
Who keeps the key of Nature's chiefest treasure?
To you, to you, all song of praise is due
Only for you the heaven forgot all measure.

Who hath the hair which loosest, fastest, tieth?
Who makes a man live then glad, when he dieth?
(Oops, something not quite right with the scanning there)
 To you, to you, all song of praise is due
 Only of you the flatterer never lieth.

'Only of you the flatterer never lieth?' Oh yeah, with bells on, thought Ingrid. Yet she had to admit the poem was rather lovely, and in a way she would never have expected from Tom. How on earth could he have written anything like that?

Well, there *was* something a little old-fashioned about it – at least that was in tune with the conservative Tom.

But the letter carried on:

"…..Which is all there is to say on the matter really. These are my feelings, openly confessed; how you react is for you to say. Now let us turn from Pleasure, which is of course what that was, albeit of a rather melancholy kind, to Business.

You were kind enough to say you would once more help with the money side, if not the rioting. I would very much like to take you up on that. But what I do have to mention, also, is that there is something we have to sort out about your previous bout of accountancy.

Baldly put, the figures don't add up! The takings are higher than they ought to be and the expenditure lower, with the result that we are inappropriately better off. This is remarkable, and an excellent reason for your doing our accounts again, but in fairness to you (you may remember that you, via your employers, provided the initial float - have you/they not involuntarily subsidised us?) we need to sort it out. AND there are further monetary complexities too tedious to mention here.

What it comes to is that, for strictly practical reasons, we really do have to meet; and I repeat my previous invitation, while entirely aware, and respectful of, your earlier reservations: the Cosa Nostra, half way down the Turl, 12.30 on Thursday.

If you don't come I shall not merely cry, I shall weep, gnash teeth, smash windows, riot, and generally behave in such a way that I, after capture, will be the one who will have to be exhibited, as a fine example of that same predatory pantheresque (male version) zeitgeist I alluded to earlier: something along the lines of Male Ugliness (Spirit of the Age) , with flagons of beer, hopefully, replacing the tea.

It is my solemn faith, Ingrid, that it will never come to this.

Your servant, always,

Your slave, alas!,

Your Tom

Mein Gott but he *is* like a battering ram, thought Ingrid - one of those medieval battering rams suspended on ropes, which the moment they have one swipe, however unsuccessful, swing back for another, and then another, and on and on until the city walls….. collapse. Perhaps she might as well have lunch with him and be done with it. Not to mention the fact that she did find him, recurrently, distinctly amusing, albeit against her better judgement.

Although she had another feeling too, and that was how extraordinary it was that Tom of all people could have written that exquisite lyric in the second part of his letter. The first lyric, absolutely, it was just the sort of cynical, clever-dick wordplay she would have expected of him. But the second… that had a singing, pellucid quality, a knight-errantry of the spirit which was about as far from her previous sense of Tom as could be. 'Cantabile', that was the word, and Ingrid was German enough to love anything which felt like a song.

Yet another complex man! On the one hand Tom's leering, beery face. On the other his pure pellucid lyric. How did they fit together? It was weird, it was absurd; it was also………intriguing.

Chapter Thirty-One

Two days later Ingrid was en route for the Turl. Mulling it over had had the predictable result.

Increasingly, these days, the Crosbys seemed happy for her to go out alone - to go out at all, indeed, after being so withdrawn.

Where there *was* a difficulty, however, was with something quite different: of all things, Tom's 'pellucid' lyric.

Because Ingrid had been so struck by it, and so impressed by its potential as a song, that she'd put it to music: composing, however amateur, had been something she'd been encouraged to do when young. So she copied it, placed it on the piano when the Crosbys were out, and plonk plink kerplunkity plonk, gave it a simple melody.

Half-way through a friend of the Crosbys called round, she got distracted, and that evening she was greeted by Mrs. Crosby, poem in hand, saying she'd found it on the piano. Ingrid explained she'd been putting it to music; and Mrs. Crosby looked charmed, and said she was sure Sir Philip Sidney's poem could do with a new setting. A couple more questions and Ingrid realised this poem —famous in England, unheard of in Bavaria - was one of the jewels of English sixteenth century literature and was not, in fact, by Tom Huntingdon at all! Yet again she'd been fooled!

She managed to conceal this from Mrs. Crosby, who assumed Ingrid's embarrassment was caused by being caught in flagrante delicto as a would-be composer. But inwardly Ingrid seethed. Why on earth had she ignored her original instinct, which had insisted this was the last thing Tom would ever write! She felt like cancelling the lunch, until she found herself, yet again, laughing out loud. The whole thing was too ridiculous. Was it Tom's fault she'd reacted in such a starry-eyed way? Of course not. The fault, as ever, was hers - she really must ***grow up.***

Or get her revenge! As she strode into the Casa Nostra, a judicious quarter of an hour late, she treasured the fact that she had, potentially, Tom Huntingdon at her mercy. For *she* knew the real authorship of the poem and he didn't know she knew. Cue, surely, for her to lure him into ever more extravagant claims for his authorship….. then pounce.

And there he was, waving an airy paw, on a table for two discreetly placed at the restaurant's back. Looking quite respectable, for once.

And full of jovial bonhomie, as he slipped her coat off her shoulders (somehow suggestive) and slid her seat under her backside (more suggestive still.)

Not the tone she had intended, by any means. And it was downhill, all the way, thereafter.

The moment they sat down a flagon of red wine arrived. Tom had pre-ordered it. Then, when the waiter came for their order, he chose chops for both of them. His apologies, he said - he knew the menu. Next, he explained, with many guffaws, that the accounting problem which had allegedly brought them together had already sorted itself. There had, it seemed, been a mistake in the maths, ***their*** maths, not Ingrid's after all.

Well, what a surprise, thought Ingrid - I'm here under false pretences.

Then finally, the moment she started on her plan to get Tom to over-egg his authorship, he instantly threw up both hands and admitted everything. Declared, that is, that there was absolutely no question – never had been - of him writing that second poem at all. He'd never claimed any such thing!

"Oh yes you did," cried Ingrid. "Oh no I didn't," retorted Tom. "Oh yes you did!" she cried again, and the pantomime antiphon might have gone on indefinitely had not Ingrid produced Tom's letter from her bag - which Tom snatched from her – and Ingrid snatched back (by now the restaurant was enthralled) - at which Tom grabbed it and held it high above Ingrid's most straining reach, read out the bits concerned, and proved, to Ingrid's furious, spluttering laughter, that while he had indeed claimed authorship of the first poem he'd said no such thing about the second….. though he admitted he'd very much implied it.

"But then I had to," he said. "It's obvious you're the supreme romantic. So the poetry you'd like was equally obvious – something intense. And as I'm congenitally incapable of writing any such thing I had to pinch it. And you've got to admit, judging by your reaction, I was right.

"Sir Philip Sidney! The most parfit gentle knight, the man who gave a drink away – something I'd never do - on his deathbed to a private soldier, with the line: "His need is greater than mine.' Come Ingrid, admit it was the perfect choice- you loved every poignant, pellucid syllable of it, did you not? "

"Well…. yes …." said Ingrid. But she had no intention of letting Tom off.

"Alright then," she said. "If that's the kind of poetry you *can't* write, what's the kind you can?"

Tom looked her straight in the eye.

"Something direct and simple," he said. "Modern message; traditional form. Something like this:

And he delved into a pocket, opened a notebook, and dropped it in front of her.

'The Bankrupt' it said, at the top of the page.

And underneath, just two lines:

"Did sleep bring respite? No. Attend this well:

His days were purgatory, but his nights were Hell."

"Is that based on experience?" grinned Ingrid. "No, seriously…… I quite like it."

"You quite like it. I quite like it, too. Not much, but quite. What about this?"

He turned the page and Ingrid read:

The bride

"Cancer killed her. In ten days alone

She went from girl to crone.

> And yet it wasn't Beth who warmed my tears -
>
> In those ten days her husband aged ten years."

"This I do like," said Ingrid. "It seems more felt. The other, to be honest, feels rather abstract."

"Well, I'm glad you think that, because I wrote the second one, but not the first."

"Here we go again."

"No seriously, it's true; I wrote 'The Bride', and Henry Thornton – you know the chap at Westbury? - wrote 'The bankrupt.' He's a beautiful writer, and we've similar ideas on poetry, but he *can* be rather abstract."

"So what views do you share?" asked Ingrid and they were off and away into poetical theory, for both Tom and Henry, it emerged, wanted to get away from the honeydew romanticism of the Nineteenth century without lurching into the twentieth-century pretentiousness of the Imagists - surely you could combine realism and plain language.

Had not, Tom continued, the best poets been doing that for centuries? Take Shakespeare's 'When icicles hang by the wall'…and right there in the restaurant (by now the chops had arrived and Tom was washing his down with his usual copious swigs of wine) he started singing it:

> "When icicles hang by the wa-all" he caterwauled,
>
> "And Dick the she-e-pherd blow his nails
>
> "And Tom bears logs into the ha-all
>
> "And milk comes frozen home in pail……."

And this was a song that Ingrid knew! Not just the words, either, but the tune: she'd been taught it by her father. So at first she tentatively hummed along, and then, by the time Tom got to the second verse, (Tom, for all Ingrid's maidenly reluctance, had successfully pressed wine on her and had been quietly re-filling her glass) she suddenly came caroling in as well - to Tom's astonishment, let alone her own:

..... "When roasted crabs hiss in the bowl," she roared,

"Then nightly sings the staring owl.."

Then both in unison:

"....Tu-whit! Tu-whoo!

" Tu-whit! Tu-whoo! A merry note!

"While greasy Joan doth keel the pot."

And both collapsed in laughter. But then Shakespeare, Ingrid explained, was hugely popular in Germany. And as for singing in restaurants, she did come from Bavaria. And as for the song - now they'd so noisily reviewed it - she had to admit that Tom was dead right; it *could* have been written by a modern poet, so everyday was its feel.. A shepherd blowing his nails! A servant washing up! She'd known and loved - and sung- the song for years, but never before noticed its mundanity.

"And yet it remains romantic" she said. "I hear nails and pots and grease, but I see trees, frost, logs crackling on the hearth."

"Yes indeed, "said Tom. "Wasn't it Chekhov who said the way to evoke a beauteous moonlit river scene was to eschew the romance and describe the flash of a broken bottle, the dog floating downstream on its back, paws in the air?"

Ingrid took, with relish, another swig of wine. This was the originality she craved – not to mention the simplicity - nor forgetting the humour, nor the singing, nor something else that had also crept up on her, in the last few weeks – a distinct and growing weakness for red wine.

All of which was by no means what she had expected from lunch with Tom. For this was *fun*, loudmouthed, jolly, unpretentious, *fun*, as well as being stimulating. For the first time since she had been in England it was like being back home in Bavaria. Blearily she began to realise one reason, perhaps, why she actually quite liked Tom.

God knows, he certainly enjoyed singing. And now he wanted to sing 'When icicles…' right through again.

But hardly had they started when the restaurant's Maitre D. came over, and suggested, very gently, that perhaps they might see their way clear to quieting down. At which Tom expressed outrage – but the maître D. insisted – still more outrage from Tom - and next thing Tom and Ingrid stormed out, Tom scattering coins to pay their bill. Moments later they were on the pavement, outside.

And still they laughed uproariously.

"Why is it that wherever I go," cried Ingrid, "and whoever I'm with, we always end up on the street?"

"Oh Ingrid," said Tom, coughing with mirth, "You make me laugh so very much."

Which was new to Ingrid. No-one had found her *funny* before. Looks, yes, originality, certainly, eccentricity even, but *funny*? And as they made their uncertain progress down the High every remark Ingrid made set Tom laughing again - but then she found him funny too.

And it was more than that. No-one could accuse Tom of any special talent as a listener, not like Alexey, anyway, but he did take her opinions seriously. Seriously enough to argue with them, which he did robustly and straightforwardly.

A conversation with Tom, in fact, was like a boxing match, blow swapped for blow. And Tom pulled no punches – but then nor did she. In brief she found herself treated as…. an adult.

As the two of them wound their sodden, uncertain way down the High, giggling helplessly at every stumble, it seemed wise to find somewhere suitable to sober up. Ideally as far as possible from anyone they knew.

"Let's go to the Botanical Gardens," said Tom. "That's quiet!"

Now there's a good idea, thought Ingrid - not least because this was one quiet place which was also public, and Ingrid remained distinctly wary of being *a deux* with Tom.

So they walked down to just short of Magdalen bridge, through the garden's entrance arch, and found themselves in an empty, open wilderness of flower beds - a few stray visitors, mainly mothers with young children, their sole companions.

Soon they drew level with a little summer house – or was it a gardener's hut? It looked as if it had begun as one and declined to the other.

As they passed the door, Tom threw his arm around Ingrid's waist, hoicked her inside, lifted her face up with his other hand, and kissed her.

Ingrid was stunned. She'd seen the likelihood in Tom's eyes but had never expected anything like this. His bear-like grip was so strong, so inexorable; his lips so fleshy and hot; his tongue, thrust deep and insistent far into her mouth, wrenched around like a snake. With an effort she thrust him back and ping! slapped him hard on the cheek.

Ping - ping! Like whiplash he slapped her back - pure reflex, plainly, beyond thought. If Ingrid had been stunned before, now she was flabbergasted – no man, anywhere, in all her eighteen years, had ever treated her like that. So shocked was she that she felt weak at the knees, and began to teeter - at which Tom grabbed her again round the waist, lifted her up and back again towards him, and once more thrust his tongue deep into her mouth, this time effectively imprisoning her by thrusting both hands round her shoulders and deep down onto her buttocks.

So now the only escape route was a series of shuffling steps backwards, with Tom locked onto her. So their progress resembled a grotesque, slow-motion two-step - till they cannoned up against the far wall.

At which moment one of the visiting mothers, complete with child, stepped into the doorway, and backed swiftly out. "What is it mummy?" pleaded a little voice, answered by her mother, gently reassuring.

Suddenly, as if on its own volition, Ingrid's mouth swung open; then more remarkably still, **her** tongue came alive too, thrusting deep back into Tom's mouth.

At which he seized her hand and pressed it down between his legs. She tried to pull back but he held it there, so they both froze, for a moment, on the brink of …..what?

Then outrage once more overcame her, and she tried furiously to push him away. His strength prevented her, so just one escape remained.

She suddenly, violently, squeezed his crutch. He squealed with pain and doubled up, she thrust quickly past him, and with swift, furious strides she was out of the hut and away, the mother and child, still outside the hut door, following her exit with wondering eyes.

Chapter Thirty-Two

She heard nothing from Tom for two days.

His 'pounce' had shaken her. It was so sudden, so overwhelming! Yet far more alarming was her reaction. How ever could she have found anything like that *exciting*? True, Tom had proved a jolly lunch companion and she'd enjoyed their conversation beyond anything she'd expected. But never previously had she felt a glimmer of conscious physical attraction. Yet look what had happened.

So where on earth had such feelings come from? Was it really true, as certain psychiatrists said, that the body knew better than the mind?

Not to mention Paula. How would she feel about this? First the betrayal by her man, who makes a play for another woman; then the further betrayal that the woman concerned is her 'best friend'; finally, by far worst of all, her best friend ***responds***.

……Yet it ***was*** intriguing. Of course Tom's pounce was unthinkable in one way, yet in another it was at least simple and direct. Hadn't it taken the soulful Alexey almost three weeks to reach the same point? Nor was Tom that ugly, really – he was actually quite good-looking – when sober – quite a Greek God, even, in his own overblown way.

Indeed, if Tom hadn't been Paula's it could conceivably have been…….quite different.

So it seemed ironic, in all the circumstances, that two days later she got Paula's first letter from Scotland, and enclosed was a ticket for a West End play, J.M Synge's 'The Playboy of the Western World.'

She'd arranged, wrote Paula, to see it with Tom, the week after she came back. But now she'd found she'd have to stay a few days extra – her sister was seeing a consultant in Edinburgh and she felt duty-bound to accompany her. The ticket should not be wasted.

Ingrid would surely love the play – did she know the audience had rioted the first week it was performed in the Abbey Theatre in Dublin? And Tom, who had the other ticket, would look after her – indeed she'd commanded him to do just that before she'd left.

Which Ingrid found extraordinary. So Paula, of all people, is setting me up with Tom - of all people! How little she knows her man! For the first time Ingrid wondered if her friend was quite so worldly-wise as she'd seemed.

So she wrote back and refused - without a hint of the real reason. Instead, she explained how busy she was finding herself these days- she mentioned, inter alia, the mooted London sculpture exhibition - and finished with just that air of frenetic gaiety that had earlier alarmed her friends.

But Paula wrote again. She quite understood, of course. She was glad Ingrid was so busy! Although Ingrid **would** have found the Synge quite fascinating – a whole play built around a man who'd killed his father. A play for the times and for everyone they knew, for weren't they all engaged in killing, if not precisely their fathers, then the world their fathers had made, the tyrannical, puritanical Nineteenth century?

However! Not to bother about that, said Paula. She had another, better idea. This too would involve Tom, plus many others, in a truly improbable concoction that would widen Ingrid's horizons even more, if only her young friend could fit it in.

How would she like to join her, and Tom - and others - on a 'Friday-to-Monday' at Clayton Court, a country house just north of Henley-on Thames, the home of the Honourable Charles Fisher, yet another of the Oxford gang? And if she was wondering who Charles Fisher was, try this.

Did Ingrid recall that first evening in New College when she'd met Tom and the rest? Well, the Hon. Charles was none other than the 'hearty' who Tom had knocked down in the quadrangle before he'd entered Alexey's rooms. Yes, they'd become friends!

"I knew," wrote Pauline, "that Tom had gone round the next day to apologise and I knew they'd begun seeing something of each other, but it was only recently I realised just how friendly they'd become. Quite a romance! It turns out they both have what might be described as a 'Call of the Wild' philosophy – do you know Jack London's books?

"They both feel modern life is too degenerate and soft. They look back to the good old primeval days when men were men, prey was prey and the sole object of any decent self-respecting hunter was to bring back the bacon in record time, preferably after a good chase and a bloody denouement.

"What adds to the fun is the politics. For Tom, as you may know, is a lower-middle-class boy – his father was a Derbyshire shopkeeper who rose to be mayor - and he is as politically conservative as you might expect. Whereas Charles, whose father owns five estates, including one in Scotland, not far from where I am staying, complete with castle, is a rabid socialist, virtually a communist.

"Come to think of it I saw him a couple of times in the audience at the St. Ebbe's Socialist society, but all he ever did was laugh. As he was a toff, I assumed he was a Tory - but it turns out he was laughing because our people weren't socialist *enough*.

"Indeed, he's set up his own socialist society at his college, Balliol, a startling combination of local trades unionists and his aristocratic chums, and the membership is expanding daily – two hundred new members, university-wide, this term alone.

"So the weekend is going to consist of two parallel events, running side by side.

"A) Conventional, aristocratic 'igh-society socialising with his mother's friends from London;

"B) meetings involving the honourable Charles' political chums, including the trades unionists.

"The estate is fortunately very large.

"As for our lot, there will be me and Tom, and you, hopefully, and Ernst and the Germans and the amiable George – who I know you like - and, all in all, the whole thing could be a riot. Just up your street.

"Oh, and if you're wondering how two men of such opposite political persuasions as Tom and Charles get on, remember how Tom, for one, gets on with me. Then add in the Call of the Wild touch that both men are very keen on boxing.

"Indeed, they have some Advanced theory that the two people at a boxing fight best qualified to be friends are the boxers themselves. For all their swapping of blows, they feel, they are the ones, out of the whole crowd, who have most in common.

Come! Come to Clayton! I command you. And let me know very quick."

And this invitation Ingrid did accept, very quick. Good prospects of fun and no compromising tete-a-tete with Tom. And she could hardly ***avoid*** Pauline, whatever had been going on. And George, so easy-going and accommodating, was always a plus.

As for the Crosbys, they'd surely be delighted – for this weekend would be intellectual ***and*** posh.

Chapter Thirty-Three

A week later Ingrid, Paula, Tom, George and the Germans, led by Rudi, arrived at Clayton village station.

The Claytons had laid on five horse-drawn wagons, into which the fifty-odd London guests swiftly packed themselves, with much joshing and hilarity. They all looked under twenty-five, all were dressed in the height of fashion, and, most daunting of all, all seemed to know each other. Ingrid and her friends crept into a corner of the last brake in the row. Even Tom looked abashed.

And so they set off, quite a procession, from the station up to the house. The locals came out of their homes to watch. The women guests, who had travelled down in what looked like ball gowns, were almost all in white; the young men in blazers, with the occasional suit. Add in their hats and hatbands and the colours were dazzling; the whole thing looked like a seething, swarming herbaceous border.

Most striking was their manner. Every tone, every call, every movement of this jeunesse doree proclaimed an absolute ethic of ***play***; the most harmless of poses, seemingly, except that it was acted out in front of those same village spectators whose every tone, call and movement proclaimed the ruthless imperative of ***work***.

So that even in that brief journey up from the station, even before they had entered Clayton's gates, Ingrid sensed a quite new social universe.

But above all Ingrid felt the difference when the brakes rounded a bend in their upward road and the passengers caught the first glimpse of

Clayton Court, louring massively in the brilliant sunlight. The way it stood there, solid and serene, surrounded by its attendant oaks; the flash and gleam of its lawns; the sense it gave of a parallel universe, ineffably secure, in which life became one ordered, restful progress from one ordered, restful community to the next......

While high on a tower flew a mighty banner, embossed with what were presumably the Fisher family arms. And as it furled and unfurled languidly in the breeze, insouciant and calm, it radiated an entire class system's confidence and pride.

Most suggestive of all, for Ingrid, was the moment when the procession entered the gravel oval in front of the house. A bright yellow automobile came scooting along and overtook them; Ingrid felt a thrill of excitement from those in her brake. "Stanbury!" someone gasped; and indeed it was that famous minister of the crown, who waved a cheery paw at them, in a gesture that looked surprisingly young. He wore a straw hat with one side up and the other pulled firmly down – he might have worn it at Monte Carlo. It was smart, racy, even caddish. The last thing one would have expected of a minister.

The column stopped, and as if by droit du seigneur the Stanbury automobile pulled over in front of them. The chauffeur skipped round Stanbury's side and opened the door.

What followed impressed Ingrid most of all. For Stanbury had been carrying a map, a parcel, and a pair of goggles; and he handed them to the chauffeur without even looking at him. With the assumption, clearly, that the world was poised, at any moment, to accommodate his whim.

The chauffeur took them, (he too, clearly, expected no recognition) skipped back to the car, and swished it round to the back of the house. In a moment it was as if neither he nor the car had ever existed.

Stanbury walked into the front porch of Clayton Court, without a backward glance.

A handbell rang.

It came from a liveried footman, placed just outside the front door. Beside him stood what looked like their host, the Marquess of Clayton; tall and broad, with a fine brow, he'd just stepped out of the main entrance, followed by a dozen other adults, presumably guests.

He stepped forward and began a speech. It was charmingly informal.

"Welcome to our home!" he said. Ingrid chuckled - she'd long noticed how the English rich referred to their mansions, however vast, as 'homes.'

"We really are most frightfully pleased to see you – many, of course, we know of old – and we do hope you are going to feel comfortable here, and will have a happy time!"

More graciousness, more understatement. And now Clayton outlined a little of what was planned.

He explained for instance, that the male guests, some of them, anyway, would be sleeping in three large marquees they could see behind them in the park (Cries of 'coo!' and 'Crikey!' from the men, followed by thundering, good- humoured laughter.)

Then, went on Clayton, as well as three dances, the main one on Saturday night, there would be the usual line-up of Clayton events - croquet, tennis, boating, swimming (hopefully unconnected with the boating) even, for the dauntless, a motor car race.

In short, as always at Clayton, there was very little danger of getting bored, and he assumed …..At this moment he was nudged by a slender, sardonic woman at his side. Evidently the Marchioness.

"Trades Unions!" she hissed in a stage whisper.

"Oh! Good gracious yes!......and the Trades Union meetings too, for those whose bent is politics! Most important. Although I should add that these meetings, which started earlier in the week, will be winding up tomorrow. And the whole thing, of course, will be hosted, indeed masterminded, by Charles- where *is* Charles, by the way, my dear?"

A shaking of the head: a theatrical projection of ignorance, arms spread wide, by the Marchioness.

"I do believe he's shooting," she said finally.

"Shooting anything in particular, dear?"

"Rabbits, I believe."

"Trades Unionists!" yelled a voice.

"Oh no 'E ain't!" cried another voice, this one cockney . " 'E *wos* wiv us – but 'e scarpered an hour ago. We don't know where 'e is neiver!"

More thunderous laughter, followed by cheers; while the Marquess explained that he was sure Charles would turn up, like the bad penny he always was; the servants magicked away the luggage as mysteriously as Stanway's chauffeur had vanished the car; while the liveried one - he of the bell - ceremoniously conducted the guests into the garden, where three great tables were laid with iced coffee under the trees.

White dresses, dark blue shadows, shimmering lawns – it was like a Monet painting. But Ingrid failed to appreciate it. Still feeling somewhat phased by all this glitter, she'd hoped to escape to her room for five minutes to repair her face.

But that, evidently, was not to be.

The Oxford group arranged themselves under the cedars. Thus fortified, they tried very hard to hide their social uncertainty behind witticisms about their fellow guests - Tom and Ernst, in particular, excelling themselves.

Yet Ingrid felt they had very little to be unsure about. Both Tom and the Germans looked splendid - Von Leckburg, especially, fitting naturally into this milieu. George, amiable as ever, radiated modesty and good humour; she herself, she knew (and this was confirmed by many intense glances from young men) looked her very best - as well she might, given the effort she had put into her preparation.

But it was Paula, above all, who seemed to have risen to this aristocratic occasion. Surprising in a socialist! Like Ingrid, and like the other women guests, she was wearing something approaching a ball gown. Like Ingrid, again, she had eschewed conventional white for something more colourful. Deep turquoise in her case, in contrast with Ingrid's ultramarine - Ingrid was struck, not for the first time, by how well her friend suited formal clothes. Then she saw Paula smiling.

Ingrid followed her glance. Dimly, she could see a stir amid the guests, a vague eddying, followed wherever it went by laughter and whoops. Peering some more, she saw a short, strutting figure walking towards them through the crowd.

Who was that? Some friend of Paula's? Surely not their host, Charles Fisher! Unconsciously - perhaps because Charles was an Honourable - she'd assumed he would be tall; but now a yell indicated that it was, indeed, Charles, and here he came, short and broad, waddling through the crowd with his gun over his right shoulder. Like a peasant in Tolstoy, thought Ingrid, or a seventeenth century musketeer. Walking with a slight swagger – or was it self-mockery?

And the contradiction was reinforced as he came close. Turning to a friend, Charles' profile looked aristocratic enough – indomitable, even, like a cliff against which ocean waves would break in vain. But turning again - transformation. For from the front his face was full of irony, almost comical. And, as he saw his Oxford friends, it spread over with the most characteristic, *complicitous* grin.

"How *are* you," he cried, ignoring the other guests, and grasping Tom warmly by the hand. "Thank *God* you're here. What a *frightful* bore, all this. I *do* apologise, most frightfully. How long have you been here? I'm surprised you haven't died of tedium already – or old age." He turned to Paula: once more her face lit up and it struck Ingrid how different she looked when she met someone she liked. Her aloofness - the downside of her statuesque hauteur – disappeared.

"Paula, how wonderful to see you," Charles said. "You look terrific – not that *that's* news, naturally. I've just been with your socialist chums. Well, mine actually, but I've a confession to make: the meeting – something about local government, I think - for the life of me I can't remember - was so boring I walked out.

"So I went shooting! And lost track of the time! And me with all these social responsibilities on my *special* weekend! Twenty-one! Who would have thought it? Who would have thought I would last that long?!" Another complicitous grin.

Then he flung his arms round Paula and Tom's shoulders. "Oh Paula, I really think you and Tom could be my salvation - and you!" (addressing Ingrid) "and you!" (the Germans) "all of you! I feel a stirring in my breast. What is it? I know! It's hope!"

And he lay down his gun on the coffee table, upsetting two cups, then picked up the milk jug and took a swig from it direct. With a grin, wiping the cream off his mouth, he offered it to Tom. Tom swigged it too.

Now Charles gazed round almost furtively. "Come on, all of you" he said, with a gesture encompassing the whole New College group. "I'll show you round." And off he led them through the crowd, Ingrid and co stumbling anxiously after him, quips whistling between Charles and his other guests, though he hardly stopped for anyone at all.

What he did do was beckon some to join his train. Remarkably, those singled out did just that. Verily verily, thought Ingrid, the man's a Jesus, put down thy coffee cups, O guests, and follow me! And then - astonishment.

What was it she found familiar about this tall fair haired man Charles called to, the one with the languid good looks? Good God. but it was the Adonis from the bus! Her failed pick-up! Gulping with embarrassment Ingrid swiftly put several yards between them. Yet all was well. Adonis showed not the remotest sign of recognizing her, which was fortunate, if slightly annoying.

Meanwhile Charles and the rest of them - a good dozen, in the end, on top of the Oxford group - were clean out of the crowd and into Clayton Court's rose garden: one of the largest Ingrid had ever seen, surrounded by a weathered redbrick wall, and overflowing with sultry, sagging blooms.

Ingrid gasped at its beauty. She would have loved to linger. But Charles ploughed on regardless, till eventually they reached an area of meadowland between the rose garden and the river. And there he paused, staring out over the steep drop that led down to the bank below.

He beckoned everyone around him and seemed about to make a speech. Mein Gott, thought Ingrid, the Sermon on the Mount.

"Welcome to my twenty-first," said Charles grimly. "Well - I say 'my', but in many ways I seem to be the last person concerned. As I said to Mama, when she showed me the guest list, 'this thing is bigger than both of us.' "

And he described how his mother had chosen most of the invitations, and that they turned out, mainly, to be the children of her friends; in short, effectively, it was *her* guest list.

So he'd put his foot down. He'd told 'mama' his only real interest these days was socialism, so couldn't he have some trades unionists along - even a whole week of progressive politics? "Mama was appalled."

Not, she had explained, that Charles should misunderstand her. Her objections were social, not political. "She allowed I'd hosted socialist meetings here before, without notable catastrophe. Her objection was having her fashionable friends and my unfashionable oiks here *together*."

So after huge argy-bargy and confrontation, Mama and Charles had compromised. The socialist meeting had been arranged for the week before, overlapping by just a couple of days. While as for the " 'igh-society aspect" - Charles had managed to personalise the guest list here as well, which was why there were lots of guests here who *weren't* his mother's friends. Including the New College people, of course.

"What it comes down to is that you represent a party within a party, just like my Labour Party guests, in fact, who all seem to be in the Independent Labour Party, which is by no means the same thing as the proper Labour Party, as they shall certainly tell you should you ask them, possibly at some length. So taking all things all round, all aspects in all ways, all parties to this party would seem to be parties within parties so I call on you to sink your wider differences and come to the aid of the party – *my* party, the one this is about.

"Oh, and something else – my father - in an inexplicable oversight – omitted to tell you that the highlight of the weekend will be a boxing contest. Tom and I will be fighting to the death, or something very near it, tomorrow afternoon! Those present that evening in New College will know why.

"Dear Tom, who has since become my very good friend, knocked me down that night and now – despite discovering that I'm a boxing blue - has offered me my revenge. Which I shall very certainly take. Anyway, two-thirty tomorrow afternoon on the forecourt. Remember.

"And one last thing: I have secretly hired five charming coloured musicians from America called the Chicago Real-Time Stompers, who are here on tour and who will introduce an element of surprise to tomorrow's dance. Is anyone here unfamiliar with ragtime? Not least will it be a surprise for my parents, because, in an inexplicable Freudian slip, I have forgotten to tell them - but why should they, poor things, miss out on that most enviable of modern experiences, the shock of the new?"

Now Charles led his coterie back to join the rest- but as they strolled along the ride above the river, Charles manoeuvred the New College group aside, explaining to his other friends that there was "something you lot are familiar with but these people aren't" that he needed to show them. He would catch up with the rest later.

He walked his Oxford friends to another cliff-top, just fifty yards along, and pointed.

"Down there, in the woods," he said, "just by the river, is where I'd *really* have liked to hold my coming of age. It's a place of pure magic. It's an inlet that forms a little pool, surrounded by banks so high it's like a beach, and you can sit there and be quiet and it is heaven.

"It's remote and wild and utterly beautiful and nothing to do with politics and changing the world, or 'igh society and keeping the world the same, nothing to do with anything at all, in fact, except nature and beauty and truth: it's the resort of Pan.

"Yes, I swear, it *is* the abode of Pan, the most holy place I know, and I defy anyone who goes there not to be infected by it. I'll show it to you later if we get a mo, and perhaps, if we are venturesome, we might engage in Rites."

Delivered of this enigmatic promise Charles led his guests back to the lawns.

En route they ran into the Marquess and Charles' mother, who greeted him rapturously. Charles responded in kind.

"Oh thankyou mama, thankyou popsy, for arranging such a wonderful weekend for your son! Thanks for even *imagining* so many exciting things to do! It really is most frightfully thoughtful of you and I just know that everyone here is going to have the jolliest weekend ever! I know I will!"

And the really remarkable thing, thought Ingrid, was that he seemed to mean it.

An hour and several ices later, Ingrid and Paula finally escaped to their rooms to sort themselves out.

Already Ingrid had more impressions than she could digest. Never before had she been in an environment so sumptuous or so spacious. And the space was a great deal more than physical. It was, equally, the breadth of tastes and opinions prevalent there.

She was used to intellectuals and even socialists; she had rubbed shoulders with gentry. What she had not experienced was such worldviews simultaneously, notably in Charles. It gave one a wonderful sense of richness and of freedom.

And there were, too, the more obvious kinds of space. Ingrid's bedroom, for instance, was the largest she had ever slept in. No less than three Georgian sash windows lined one wall. The chest of drawers, and even the chairs, seemed larger than life; while Ingrid's bed, to her surprise and delight, was a genuine four-poster, also huge, with red silk curtains you could draw and make into a tent. Ingrid duly closed them, then squatted inside her little tepee, chuckling.

She shuddered to think how cold this room might be in winter, but now, in summer, it was anything but. Re-opening the bed's curtains she revelled in the fragrance of the room's chestnut panelling; the periodic crack as the wood expanded in the afternoon sunshine; the way in which the three Georgian windows looked almost like paintings - frames, seemingly, for the landscape you could see beyond. Not forgetting the ivy overhanging outside, gold and emerald in the sun.

And beyond the ivy, once again, more space. A view over the park to a distant ridge, crowned with a viewpoint pillar: huge, stately, imperial. While the ridge itself, swelling up like a wave, was one of those hills beyond which there must surely be the sea.

Chapter Thirty-Four

A tap at the door. It was a young manservant. So young, in fact (he wore a pill-box hat, like a performing monkey) that Ingrid struggled not to laugh. He bowed, and handed Ingrid a letter on a silver salver. She thanked him, dismissed him - for a moment she wondered if she should have tipped him - and opened it. It was from Paula.

"I couldn't resist it" she read. "Isn't he sweet? Do pop over to my room - the 'Clematis' room along the corridor from yours – for a brief jaw. Things to tell."

It was getting late to dress for dinner, but Ingrid was eager to swap first impressions - and get some tips. She padded quickly down the corridor to Paula's room. The 'Clematis' room turned out to be remarkably similar to her own, with noble furniture, three sash windows and the same stupendous views.

"Rather wonderful, isn't it" said Paula, gesturing toward a marquetry chest of drawers, tricked out with cupids and apes. "Amazingly, Lord Clayton actually feels *poor* – the slump in land values – yet *I'd* say he's scraping by. Anyway, I thought you might have been a touch taken aback by Charles Fisher's presentation of himself this afternoon, and could use an explanation."

"Well, yes," said Ingrid, "he did seem pretty much up to the standard of craziness I've come to expect of men. Does he want to hold this party or does he not? Unless I much mistook him he gave three totally conflicting answers in ten minutes."

"Well, he's confused, to put it mildly. He's a dear really - did I tell you I saw him a little while I was in Scotland?" (No, you did not, thought Ingrid.) "He was at their Scottish house up there - Dun Glen - and he talked quite a lot about his family. Tom's told me about it too.

"They really have the strangest relationship. In some ways very close - his mother adores him – in others his parents reject everything Charles stands for. Hence, in part at least, the socialism. Not to mention the further complication of his father. Did you know he's one of the leading athletes of his age? Five Oxford blues, let alone numerous other athletic achievements. He really is a totally overbearing physical presence, something quite impossible to live up to – AND highly successful in business."

His mother overwhelming socially, his father overarching physically – and neither of them remotely interested in the things Charles really liked, which were nature, poetry, and painting. "He ran away to Paris for six months to become a painter, would you believe! – he ran back." So Charles constantly oscillated between their ideas and his and effectively had a whole contrasting range of personalities.

"Less Jekyll and Hyde, in fact, than Jekyll, Hyde, Monet, Manet, C. B. Fry and Nelson all mixed up in one briskly alternating package - and yet, as I said, he really is a dear, he can be incredibly sweet as well as impossible. And, like so many crazy people he is extraordinarily perceptive – real X-ray vision about people – and never, ever, dull.

"Oh, and terribly fond of Tom. Quite fond of me, too, I think, and generally very keen on his 'own' friends as he puts it, which now apparently means us - so fond that he's managed to get us invited onto his parents' table! Yes, tonight!"

"So they've bunged another table onto the end and that's where we'll all be sitting tonight, one great big happy family, 'mama', 'popsy', Charlie, Ernst and all.

"Oh, and the other person Charles has taken a shine to, guess what, is you! Yes, you, miss utterly gorgeous Uberspeer! He told me so himself. Indeed he described you as a 'stunner.' I think we've heard that before? Didn't Tom call you that, the first evening in New College? That's probably where Charles got it from. But then Tom, too, is one of your avid fans - you do *realise* that, I hope?

"Oh no, he doesn't think that at all," said Ingrid, dearly hoping she was not, as she suspected, blushing. "It's just his way."

"Oh yes he does, Ingrid! He thinks you're wonderful! And believe me, that's quite a compliment. He doesn't say that about other women at all."

And Ingrid (a glance in the mirror across the room confirmed she had indeed blushed scarlet) found nothing more to say.

The process of 'arming herself', as Ingrid thought of it, for dinner took nigh on two hours. But the results, as usual with Ingrid, were memorable. Without planning it, any more than she had earlier, her choice of colour reversed those of the other guests.

Where she had worn colours when they wore white, now she wore white where they wore colours. But then white went wonderfully with her fair hair. And as ever she tricked it out with one or two cleverly chosen accessories; an amethyst necklace borrowed from Mrs. Crosby; a bracelet; and, especially, pendant ear-rings, with gold filigree chords, which sat superbly on her long neck.

Others, as Ingrid well knew, might look more expensive; none, lacking her exquisite skin, could match her bloom.

She met Paula and the rest of the Oxford party on the landing. As they went down they were met by Charles Fisher. He shepherded them through a hall which felt like an atrium, three stories high, off which all the main rooms opened.

Ingrid was struck by the fact that all three floors, to a height of forty feet, were embellished by the heads of stags, foxes, and fish. She wondered if hers might not end up there too.

Then Charles shepherded them all into the library, where Lord Clayton's table were assembling before dinner.

And now another novelty. This time a social manner - a way of sitting, even - Ingrid hadn't seen before. Most especially was this striking among the older guests, but how to describe it?

It was as if they ***arranged*** themselves rather than sat; as if they conveyed gentility merely by the way they leaned back in their chairs, each limb, somehow, placed in the most elegant if tenuous position, whether a forefinger stretched high against a temple expressing attentive listening, or a leg stretched out just six inches further than it might have been across the floor.

Lordly indolence! And yet - who was it who said manners are a mere formalisation of natural good behaviour? The chief feeling in the room was one of courtesy, even kindliness. Ingrid was especially struck by the Marquess, Charles' father, as he sat to the left of his wife with his chair toward her. His gaze was one any woman, after thirty years of marriage, would surely die for. A stylisation of the most profound appreciation and approval - the same look, in fact, his wife gave him.

There was a feminine quality to this scene, even among the men, which she had never seen in upper-middle class circles like her father's and Mr. Crosby's.

And most feminine of all was Stanbury, who caught her eye as she came in. Indeed Stanbury, who occupied a prime position beside the Marquess and Marchioness, felt so crafted, polished and embellished a personality that it was as if his whole being - not merely his manner - was a work of art. No doubt this was why he felt it so natural, as with his chauffeur earlier, that people should look after him. Rather as one might cherish some prize exhibit, in the national interest, in the V. and A.

Yet it was this exquisite, if slightly hothouse creature whose smile embraced her and, half rising from his seat, gestured her to sit on a chair that Charles, noting his interest, pushed in beside him.

His welcome, so fulsome and so charming (Ingrid had heard Lord Stanbury 'liked young people') felt nevertheless a bit like being invited by some fathoms-deep sea king into his underwater kingdom. A haunt of exotica in which Ingrid, enfranchised by his approval, was now another ornament.

The room, it turned out, was discussing Germany.

"Now Ingrid, you couldn't have appeared at a better moment," smiled Stanbury. "This nice Von Leckburg here was making the entirely reasonable point - a ***British*** point really – that he could quite understand why we should be concerned about the growth of the German fleet, not because we have anything in the least against their becoming a naval power but because while for Germany naval predominance is an option, for us, given our island situation, it's a necessity. A sine qua non of our survival.

"I must say, Herr Von Leckburg - may I call you Rudi ? I'm overwhelmed by your understanding. Why, you're a great deal more reasonable than many of ***our*** people, let alone yours – is there any way, do you think, Ingrid, you could fit him into your government?"

There was something about Stanbury's manner which made Ingrid lose all shyness.

"I'd be delighted, especially if he'd be considerate enough to marry me. Then I, too, could take part in his career. But I do foresee one problem. I have not yet – not entirely, anyway - got the ear of the Kaiser."

"That, surely, is because he has yet to meet you," said a voice.

"It's just a question of getting her introduced," said another.

"Abso-lootly!" drawled the Marchioness. "That's really all it will take. You know the Kaiser, Henry," she said to Stanbury, "arrange it. In that one act you bring about innumerable benefits. You introduce the Kaiser to a ravishingly pretty girl – a great benefit to him. You introduce Ingrid to the Kaiser – the mainspring of her future influence. You make Rudi's career, get Ingrid married, and secure the peace of Europe – all by that one act."

"REALLY", said Stanbury with a fulsome, amazed air which Ingrid saw was his social pose. "A one-act drama. **Really**. And to think of all those other acts, over the years, I've perpetrated so diligently, including several in the House of Commons, to so little avail."

"Si jeunesse savait, si vieillesse pouvait." said Von Leckburg.

"*Exactly.* Which reminds me of a quite charming but improper joke which I cannot possibly tell" (addressing the Marchoness) "in your company, Kitty, as you are far too young."

"I'll have you know that I'm a great deal older than I look."

"Precisely; you look a great deal younger than you are."

"Is that your point or mine?"

And so the banter continued, like the babbling of a brook, in little rushes, eddies and swirls. Already Ingrid could see how hard it would be for anyone to sustain a serious conversation in such an atmosphere: again, the pre-eminent ethic of *play.*

The butler announced dinner. The Marchioness, noticing how taken Lord Stanbury was by Ingrid, suggested he took her in.

Yet now, at table, more playfulness still. Indeed, it was more like snooker than a meal. Shots, quips, ideas, bon mots, all were fired from all quarters and bounced and cannoned off the guests indiscriminately.

It was absolutely fine, apparently, for someone way down on the left hand end of the table to attempt a long pot into a conversation on the far right; or for anyone to zig-zag their way up and down the table, bursting into five separate intimate conversations – then taking up again, as if quite natural, with the partner they'd just abandoned.

Yet into this most febrile of English atmospheres one of Ingrid's compatriots was trying to inject sobriety. It was little Albert, he of the catlike grin.

Picking up the earlier hints of European war, he tried to develop them.

"No, fighting is a profound truth." he was saying. "My father fought the French in 1870 and he said it was quite fascinating what war told you about human nature.

"How hard it was to know, for instance, which soldiers would be brave and which would not. So often, he said, the bold - ***genuinely*** bold, mark you - people in everyday life collapsed utterly under the stress of battle; while the unsure, self-effacing men - the kind the others instinctively treated with contempt - would turn out, under pressure, to be heroes.

"Strangest of all was that the last people on earth to know would be the men themselves. It makes you wonder! Had the timid ones, perhaps, been playing a psychological game all those years?! Strong characters masquerading as weak? Fooling everyone around them, of course, but above all, remarkably, themselves?"

And Albert gazed round the table with his surprised, cat-like grin. So heartfelt was his monologue that for a moment Clayton's levity, unprecedentedly, stopped dead.

But not for long. For as the table paused, a voice rang out from the other end. One of those random, long-distance pots, butting in unannounced.

"If anyone tried to co-opt *me* into a battle I know exactly what would define *me*. It can be summed up in one phrase: "He who runs away........ lives to run away another day!" That'd be *me*."

It was Ingrid's bus-debacle Adonis! Red-faced in the candle light and presumably drunk. He grinned round at his friends.

The cat-like smile froze on Albert's lips. Physical war, he seemed to be thinking, might or might not happen with these people; cultural war was already fact.

But the marchioness, seeing Albert's discomfiture, intervened. There were other ways to lighten a table up.

"Yes one *does* wonder," she drawled, "but then of course we women will wonder forever, because such experience is unique to men. How will we ever know? Only by comparing it, perhaps, to that other experience which is unique to *women* - childbirth – now *that* certainly defines a woman's character, in ways that are, if anything, more unpredictable still! But the other thing they have in common, of course – both killing and creating – is that they are so often forced on people against their will."

"Absolutely mama," cried Charles who was sitting opposite his parents, with Tom and Paula on either side. "Nothing matters more than autonomy, as I'm sure you'll agree!"

"Yes indeed," cried Ingrid, tongue loosened by wine. "A woman's right to choose!"

"Or as the Americans would put it," chuckled Stanbury, "her right to schmooze!"

"Her right to booze!" This from Tom.

"Her right to shoes!" shrieked the Marchioness, capping them all, and driving the last nail into the coffin of all that inappropriate solemnity. Her sense of triumph included gratitude to Ingrid and Tom: for like footballers sending a pass to one who scores the goal, they'd set up her success.

So that for the rest of the evening they basked in the marchioness' favour.

Indeed, they were eyed in a quite new way by everyone, while Paula, too, as the connection that had brought them there, shared in their glory.

It had been a long day, and shortly afterward she and Paula excused themselves and went to bed.

Not that there was any chance of sleep before chatting. They sat down in Paula's room.

"What especially counts is that you hooked Lord Stanbury," said Paula. "He isn't just the favourite of the old, he's the guru of the young. Mark my words, you'll find everyone treating you quite differently tomorrow."

For no-one should underestimate, she said, the power of a dinner table like this.

The marchioness, for instance, had a penchant for taking promising young men under her wing. One young man in particular, remember the blonde chap sitting two along from Charles' left, the one who'd made the he-who- runs-away joke? Ingrid certainly did. His name, said Paula, was Edward Stourbridge and he'd lately, hot from Oxford, been made assistant managing director of Hemfields, one of the most reputable insurance businesses in the City.

And whence came his recommendation? From the Marchioness , whose protégé he had been these last two years. And how had he achieved this? In essence, socially (though his looks had been no disadvantage.) True, he was gifted intellectually as well, but it was his ability to hold a room that had been crucial.

Edward's clumsiness tonight, incidentally, drink induced, had been out of character, though he'd have to watch it, as the Marchioness could be as swift to demote her favourites as to advance them.

Chapter Thirty-Five

Yet strange as anything, thought Ingrid, after she and Paula parted, was that her friend seemed to feel little jealousy that it was Ingrid and Tom, rather than Tom and Paula, who had thus been singled out. She seemed almost pleased.

What was certain was that Paula's predictions for the next day turned out to be true. Wherever Ingrid went that Saturday, she was greeted by smiling faces.

And what fun she had that morning, in the simplest way! She joined the tennis tournament and reached the final of the mixed doubles. She played golf for the first time ever - even if she did put one drive through the windscreen of Lord Stanbury's car.

But most uproarious of all was the motor race, which took place just before lunch. This time, finally outmanoeuvred by the strange, unspoken peer pressure that had been operating all day, she accepted the partnership of Tom. And of the two races that ensued, one was driven by the men, but the other by women. To add to the chaos, the women were commanded to drive backwards …..at least that meant they didn't have to change gear ……. and Ingrid won! (Driving was something she'd learned a bit, back in Bavaria) And once again, as Tom and she accepted the prizes of an ostrich feather fan, (women) and starting handle (men), they seemed treated, somehow, as a unit, a natural-born duet of stars.

Paula and Charles reappeared at lunch. Paula from her room, Charles from the Trades Unionists whither he had fled after the tennis - overcome, seemingly, by that part of him that found the brainlessness of the weekend too much to bear.

And now, as they rejoined the golden duo of Ingrid and Tom, all four bloomed into a veritable quartet of wit. Perhaps Charles and Paula needed a little light relief after the seriousness of their mornings. Ingrid, in particular, was so carried away by the badinage that she completely forgot, till reminded by George, the main event of the afternoon: that boxing match between Charles and Tom.

Which gave her another reason, and a very heartfelt one, for joining the socialists. For despite the gay expectancy of everyone else at the prospect of a punch-up, Ingrid viewed the Tom-Charles battle with dread. Panther or no panther, she drew the line at physical violence.

Fortunately, she detected a similar reluctance in Paula, who was of course committed elsewhere, anyway - to her scheduled speech. Then Ingrid remembered Charles had said Ernst, too, had been asked to speak in the same session.

So at half past one, she and Paula said goodbye to Charles and Tom as they left for their fight. While a quarter of an hour later she, Paula and the Germans set off in the other direction, for the converted barn where the trade unionists were re-convening at two.

Both Ernst and Paula triumphed, especially Paula: poised, witty and ironic, the trades unionists loved her.

Then as Paula sat down, Ingrid glanced over her shoulder and saw that Charles had joined them. In the split second she could see that the boxing match hadn't hurt him …….. but where was Tom?

"Recovering!" said Charles.

"You look remarkably untarnished. What happened?"

"I won!"

"Is Tom alright?"

"He's fine! Never better. Merely knocked down for a moment, that's all. He lay prone just long enough to lure me over. Then the moment I turned round, he leapt up and kicked me up the bum!"

And when Charles chased after him Tom took a flying leap into a tree - whence he pelted Charles with branches and refused to come down. It took all Edward Stourbridge's charm, for a full ten minutes, to broker peace.

At which Tom sloped off to have a rest.

Now Charles, too, lavished compliments on Paula's speech.

"You're so different, Paula, from the rest. Those…. bureaucrats….. seem constantly stuck in a no-man's-land between extremism and mediocrity. And the one thing they seem *utterly* incapable of is practicality- unless it's wages - they're practical enough about strikes! But launch into any wider sphere - any genuine programme, say, of nationalisation – and they evaporate."

"Perhaps," said George. "But what about health? You could surely sell them that."

"Why so?" asked Charles.

"Because we can actually cure things these days and people's demand for access is going to become unanswerable. There's even support for the idea, can you believe, among the doctors."

"But a National Health Service, or whatever you call it, would be just one timid step toward socialism, hardly the thing itself."

"Isn't that just the kind of millennialism, rejecting anything that it isn't everything, that you're against?"

And Charles fell silent.

Then suddenly, with an almost physical jerk of irritation, Charles said:

"Do you know, I feel the urge coming on me again to flee! Flee from both worlds! Mammon as represented by mama, realism as represented by the trades unions' pension fund.

"Flee away, instead, to *my* world!" he cried. "Flee to that little magic dell I pointed out, and promised to show you if I possibly could!

"Let's go *now*," he hissed, "immediately, while no-one's looking! It really is the most interesting thing around here, far more interesting than toffs, revolution, art, wit, the lot. Indeed, I realise now, this could be my chance of celebrating my birthday the way I want to, if only for two hours! ***You must come!***"

And it was a tribute to Charles' magnetism that his friends agreed.

So now Charles, with much mock-conspiratorial whispering, suggested they met at 'the large lime tree', along the terrace, and proceed from there.

"The lime!" he hissed, "Or as Ingrid's compatriots would say, the linden! The big one! You do know what a linden tree looks like, don't you Ingrid? Think Berlin, think Unter Den Linden!" And once more the complicitous grin.

Ten minutes later, having extricated themselves from the others, they assembled at Charles' tree. And it was indeed a magnificent specimen, the first in a lordly avenue.

The trees merged into each other like a hedge. And as the friends walked forward, it was like processing up the nave of a cathedral; secret, holy, with the feeling that the further you went, the closer you came to something sacred.

Ingrid turned to Paula. "Charles is right - you did speak wonderfully today," she said. "You had them in stiches."

"Yes, it did flow rather nicely," Paula replied. "But, you know, satire has its limits. I only wish I was better at being serious."

"What sort of serious do you mean?"

"Oh, something like that remark of Lenin's: 'communism is socialism plus electricity.' That's as succinct as Oscar Wilde, yet what a world of meaning!"

"It's very good, certainly" said George. "But isn't it still millennialism? Electricity is all very fine but capitalism seems to find it pretty handy, too.. ….."

"Well, I know how electricity would affect *me*," said Paula, " if I lived in Russia."

"How?"

"I'd manage a power station."

"Good God!" cried Charles, "I can just see you like that, Paula, bossing all those men."

"Don't be silly. Seriously, I can't think of anything that would contribute more to a new society than work of that kind - just the kind of mundane, practical contribution people are always on about."

Now Charles turned to Ingrid.

"And how about Ingrid! Ingrid Uberspeer plus electricity, what would *that* produce?!" And he pinched her.

Here we go again, thought Ingrid: in the best traditions of Clayton Court, the seriousness spirals off into jokes.

So now it was Ingrid who was upset. She had no objection to her new-found status as social 'star', but why did everyone find her more trivial than Paula? As for pinching - no wonder Charles got on so well with Tom. What they shared was cheek.

Yet her irritation soon dissolved - overwhelmed, as with them all, by the beauty of their surrounds. For now they had come to the end of the avenue, which opened out into a circle of beech. Sunlight and the shimmer of leaves replaced the gloom.

Charles took them to the circle's edge and pointed, through the undergrowth, to the river bank below. For there, he declared, was his pool.

And so it was. A hundred yards beneath them, a half-moon of sapphire, gleaming, tempting, magical. The path down, Ingrid could see, wound through pine trees and she could smell their scent, reminding her of childhood holidays in Spain. She was filled with sudden longing to go down there – even, crazy thought, to swim!

The idea must have struck all of them simultaneously, for next moment Charles said:

"I say, why don't we take a dip? I've swum there often and it's so wonderfully warm today. Do let's!"

"It would be lovely," said Paula, "but there's just one problem – we've no costumes."

"Oh, don't worry about *that*! We'll swim naked of course; much nicer than being clothed."

A claxon of alarm bells rang in Ingrid's head. There was she and Paula with two men, neither of whom she knew well, and one she hardly knew at all.

"I'm really not too sure about that," she said. But not wishing to be a spoilsport she added: "It would indeed be lovely, if only we had things."

"Well, why don't I go and get them?" offered George. "Surely it will be possible to find something, with the aid of Charles' sturdy retainers? I'm happy to try."

"Yes absolutely," cried Charles," it'll be an absolute cinch, if you can bear it! Just find Holworth, you remember? He of the bell? He'll sort you out in an augenblick - that is the right word, Ingrid, isn't it?" And he pinched her again.

Ingrid, Paula and Charles set off down to the pool. The path was narrow, overgrown and in places blocked – hardly anyone except Charles ever went there. Huge fern fronds curled over them, while brambles tore at their clothes. It felt warm, damp and sultry, and the vegetation smelled both rancid and sweet - jungle-sweet, thought Ingrid. At one stage the path dropped so steeply they had to slide down on their backs.

With one last plunge they reached the bottom.

And here at last was Charles' sanctuary. It was a semi-circular bite of river, ten yards long and thirty wide, a miniature Lulworth Cove. The edges were gravelly sand, and, after a rise of a foot, a bank of grass. This formed a flat, even ledge right round it, of brilliant, almost fluorescent green - as if a fairy band had cut it.

They lay down on the sunny side. Desultorily, Charles began talking again about socialism, and Paula briefly answered him. But they soon subsided. A trout rose with a kerplosh.

"How long have you known this place?" said Ingrid.

"Oh, about fifteen years," grinned Charles. "Ever since I was a boy. I was shown it by one of our gamekeepers - he taught me to swim here. And every time I return I feel six years old."

"I can see that," said Ingrid. "I feel as if I've been here before too."

"In your dreams perhaps," said Paula.

"It's dreamy alright," said Charles.

Prosaically, Ingrid began to worry about her dress, which might stain on the damp ground. Of course, were they to swim they could lie there in their costumes.

"I wonder where George has got to?" she said .

"Maybe Holworth abducted him," said Charles.

"La trade blanche," said Paula.

"It's a clear possibility," said Charles. "He could be on his way out of the country at this moment. Every man has his price - but what would George's be, I wonder?

"Oh, I'd pay at least £100," said Paula. "He's quite lovely, is George."

"I'll up you £5O" said Ingrid. "He's sweet and kind and courteous *and* supremely bright; how rarely do you get these qualities together - above all in a man?"

"Very rarely indeed, " said Charles "Which is what , of course, makes me so special."

The women snorted. Paula lay back on the grass. A moment later she sat up again. "I'm slowly, but effectively, frying," she said, "AND there's flies on my head and a centipede crawling up my leg. Where *is* George?"

"Probably Casablanca by now," said Charles.

"Well," said Paula, "he has no right to get abducted when young women need him. I want my swim!"

"Me too!" said Ingrid.

"There's only one thing for it," cried Charles, " if he doesn't turn up soon……. we'll have to swim nude after all."

"Speak for yourself," said Ingrid.

"I most certainly *will* speak for myself. I'll go naked even if you two won't. Come to think of, it I'll do it now. Carpe diem, mate, tempus fugit; we could be hanging around all afternoon."

And he began unbuttoning his shirt.

"All I ask," he said, "is that you avert your maidenly eyes, especially you, Ingrid, as with young ladies I am particularly shy."

And a moment later he began, with difficulty, working his trousers down his legs.

Nevertheless, soon his short, stubby, heavily muscled body was quite nude – the rounded flesh, despite the muscularity, almost cherubic. Then with a run and a roar, he was in the river, shrieking and squealing at the cold.

Then Paula stood up: "Oh the hell with it," she said, "I'm going in too."

Soon she was tossing her last garment over her shoulder - the emergence of her body from the husk of her clothes, thought Ingrid, was like an almond stripped of its shell. For a moment she stood there, chin up, head back, in that characteristic Paula pose. Then a moment more and she too was in the pool, after a classic bow-curve of a dive.

Now Ingrid was feeling increasingly left out. And the pool looked so delicious, and she was so hot, and the last thing she wanted was to spoil the fun.

In sudden resolution she too, stood up and swiftly, almost violently, tore off her clothes. Yet the moment she was naked she no longer felt the least bit hot and when she dived in (the realisation that George might appear at any moment gave her wings) the shock of the freezing water was so great she had the same sensation she felt every time she swum anywhere except the Mediterranean - for a split second she **knew** it was a mistake.

So after a couple of breast strokes, Ingrid tore up and down in a crawl. While Charles and Paula screamed and squawked and lunged to get out of her way, crying "Sea monster! Shark! Au secours!"

Yet the shock of the water was more than physical - it transformed Ingrid's mood. Gone was her irritability, replaced by pure delight. Paula felt the same. And as for Charles, he had indeed reverted to the age of six. For twenty frenetic minutes they jumped, dived, chased, and splashed about like porpoises. Finally they hauled themselves out of the water and onto the grass. Of course they had no towels: so they lay down together to dry in the sun.

All three were shivering with cold.

"Let's do what eskimos do," said Paula. "Use body heat to warm up!" And she grabbed Ingrid by the shoulder and pulled her roughly against her breasts.

Half reluctantly, Ingrid let her: her friend's body was undeniably comforting, strange though it was to be thrust into such sudden physical intimacy. But then Paula's body seemed to blur, in Ingrid's mind, into the lush and sultry flavour of the cove.

Then Charles snuggled up the other side of Paula.

If Paula's embrace of Ingrid had been a surprise, then Charles' of Paula was more shocking still. What was he thinking? What would Tom have said?

Nor was this all.

"What about George? How will he react if he finds us like this?" she said.

"I'm quite sure he'll undress and join us," said Paula. "He's nothing if not amenable, is George."

And meanwhile the cure was working; they were getting warmer all the time. Soon all three stopped shivering. And then, as they thawed still more, they relaxed. Not a word was spoken; they simply lay there, feeling good.

Soon, a guttural chuckle from Paula. She was gesturing towards Charles. He was snoring. Lying down again, she felt Paula's body twitch into unconsciousness. Then gradually she began to doze herself. Soon she was asleep.

She woke feeling wonderful, a superb combination of warmth and physical satiety. Little prickles of electricity glowed in her muscles. She glanced at her watch – half an hour had passed. They really ought to be thinking about getting back. For tonight, though there was no dinner, there would be a buffet, then a dance.

She turned to Paula.

She'd vanished! And so had Charles! She was alone. Her friends' clothes were still there, so they must be somewhere near; perhaps they'd gone back in the river.

She lay back again, secure in the knowledge that even a host as maverick as Charles must have some plan for later on.

Behind the ash trees, overhanging in huge cascades, was a copper beech, its leaves black and glistening against the blue. Wind stirred its branches, so it threw itself back and forward, as if tossing its head in delight. How beautiful, thought Ingrid; how utterly, utterly beautiful.

She stared across the pool. Some leaves floated motionless in one corner. A red hawk hovered. Then slowly, moving left to right across her vision, she saw a bright yellow twig, seemingly upright in the water.

Now this was remarkable. How could it float, upright? And wasn't it going against the current? Then it turned round, and began floating back the way it came. An eddy, surely?

And then it began to rise out of the water. And reached ever higher! It *was* a reed. And finally, the ultimate apparition on this most surreal of afternoons: attached to the reed's bottom, by his mouth, was Tom Huntingdon.

Ingrid sat speechless, not knowing whether to laugh or scream.

Tom swam into the shallows and stood up, coughing.

"Good afternoon," he said. "You know, this whole thing of breathing through a reed is utter bollocks. Another moment and I would have been drownded, stone dead."

And with big slow steps, stumbling a couple of times on the uneven bottom, he waded toward her. At one stage he fell clean over, but he recovered quickly and scrambled out.

And now, once more, Ingrid didn't know whether to laugh or scream. For Tom, like her, was naked, or nearly so. He wore a pair of long-johns, transparent with wetness. As so often - she had to say - the man looked comical.

"Sorry about the deshabille," he said, as if wearing the wrong hat. "Like you, I imagine, I wanted a swim and had nothing to wear. "

He grinned. "Frightfully cold, isn't it? Do you mind most frightfully if I join you in the sun to warm up?" And he lay down on the grass just a foot or two from Ingrid and stretched out; while Ingrid, even more divided now between outrage and hilarity, grabbed her dress to protect her breasts and eyed Tom with amazement.

"How on earth did you know we were here?"

"Oh, contacts," said Tom, tapping his finger against his nose.

"And I thought you were supposed to be resting!" said Ingrid, "after your fight! You seem to have made a remarkable recovery."

"Well that, my dear, is where you are wrong. I was badly wounded." And he showed Ingrid a lurid black eye. "Not that Charles did this," he said. "It happened when I fell over. I'd had a drink." And he grinned again, and Ingrid laughed too.

"Even so," said Ingrid, " it doesn't look good." And indeed it didn't. In just two hours it had already turned from red to bright green, while below the eye, on the upper cheek, was a small but open wound.

A moment later, almost without thinking, some instinct made Ingrid lean forward to touch it. As she moved, her dress slipped out of her hand; both she and Tom gasped, while her hand shot back to cover herself.

But Tom seized it and held it in a vicelike grip, sitting upright, now, and staring full into her eyes. "Don't do this," he said, his voice breaking. "Don't pull away from me again." And he drew her hand back to his wound. She gently touched it. And he kissed her naked arm. First on the wrist, then up and up, in a series of delicate, butterfly kisses, then suddenly, in a rush, he kissed her full on the lips, wrapping his other arm round her back and drawing her overwhelmingly into his body.

She pushed him away. But he pulled back; and now, like that time in the hut, he thrust his tongue deep into her mouth; and again, as if from nowhere, Ingrid felt a rush of desire. Incredibly she found her own tongue thrusting, writhing around his. Tom rolled her over on her back and lay on top of her, his mouth slipping down to her left breast and sucking it gently – not fiercely, now, but softly, delicately, like the butterfly kisses before.

Ingrid felt the milk run to her breasts; she felt her vagina twitch, opening and closing like a clam. And now, once again, here was Tom's massive, firm erection, pressing down on her like a pole. He wrenched off his long johns. He drew her legs apart; his fingers opened her vagina. Then guided by his other hand, his penis thrust suddenly, swiftly, into her. She cried out in shock, at the shuddering new experience of invasion.

Tom was not inside her long. Gasping and groaning, he pumped like an animal, each stroke more desperate than the last, till finally he exploded into orgasm; then he lay against her, his breathing gradually subsiding. While she gazed over his shoulder at the copper beech beyond, still glittering gloriously, black and silver against the blue.

Soon Tom fell asleep, while a torrent of thoughts rushed through Ingrid's head. So it had happened at last! Her childhood was at an end - even if it hadn't been remotely as she had planned. With Tom, indeed, of all people on God's earth! Already her strange eruption of desire had subsided, and she was wondering what on earth she'd done.

God, look at them, lying naked on a beach! And at any moment Paula and Charles might come back, let alone George! What had she done! And what on earth would Paula think if she found out? Once again, Ingrid felt intensely the betrayal of it all. Tom's betrayal of his lover; her betrayal of her friend.

Then absurdly, she started worrying about time. How long had they been away from Clayton House? She glanced at her watch. Two and a half hours! If they didn't leave now they'd never get back for supper. She turned to Tom. Look at him, lying there, self-satisfied and serene! No wonder he was looking pleased with himself. The bull, indeed, the gross, sated bull - and yet she found herself leaning over and stroking him.

Then swiftly but furtively, lest she wake Tom (she had some vague plan of rushing back on her own) she'd just begun pulling on her clothes when, with a rustle and crack of twigs, Charles and Paula came through the bushes. And yes, they too were still nude.

"Good God!" cried Paula, gazing at Tom, "a beached whale!"

Then as Tom stirred: "What a surprise!"

Was Ingrid imagining it, or was that irony?

Then turning to Ingrid, with a smile: "Well, Ingrid, I hope you slept well! I see you had a visitor. Where did *you* spring from, Tom? What happened to your clothes?"

"What happened to yours?" said Tom.

The situation was absurd; stranger still, no-one seemed remotely bothered. Tom and Ingrid's position spoke for itself, yet Paula, especially, seemed singularly unfazed. Indeed, she looked almost pleased. Not to mention whatever she had just been doing with Charles. What, they'd just been for a stroll? In a flash Ingrid understood what she had been noticing between them, subliminally, all day.

Everyone, in fact, had plainly been having sex, and everyone, in some way, had been betraying someone else. Yet only Ingrid seemed concerned. Tom, it was true, was eyeing Charles with a slight frown. Then Charles sat down, and looking round with a bland smile, said:

"Well, I told you, didn't I, that this place might give rise to Rites!"

Which was when everything crystallised, for Ingrid, in one flash of understanding.

"Did you plan this?" she blurted to Paula.

Charles and Tom smiled uncertainly; both murmured something and then stopped; both looked at Paula. And Paula, grinning more broadly now than ever, replied:

"Yes."

Chapter Thirty-Six

The word seemed to hover, motionless, over the conversation. Ingrid stared fixedly at Paula.

"What do you mean, yes?"

"I mean," said Paula, 'Yes.' Call me strange, but that's what 'Yes' usually means to *me.*"

"But what do you really mean? What are you talking about? **What** did you plan exactly?"

"What a lot of questions! Well, to take them one by one...."

But in the event Paula never addressed any of them because at that moment, with a slither and a bump, George dropped down from the path above - arrived back, finally, from Clayton Court.

"My God," he cried, "Naked as the day they were born ! What happened! Oh, Ingrid, Paula – I do apologise ….."

"Apologise for what?" cried Paula "Being over-dressed? We forgive you. Why not join us?"

"No, it's just that -"

Ingrid dived for her clothes but Charles, utterly unfazed, shot George one of his most comical, complicitous grins.

"We felt hot" he said. "And you never came back with our things. And we wanted our swim - are you *quite* sure you won't join us?

"I'd love to, truly" said George "But even before Tom explains what he's been up to" (Tom, it later emerged, had intercepted George two hours earlier and promised to take the costumes down on George's behalf) "I've a message to deliver. Brace yourself, Charles – it's from your mother. She says come back immediately because there's a horde of buck niggers harassing her who say they are musicians for the dance. And they're Americans, too, so they won't take no for an answer. Something about a contract."

"Oh ***GOD!***" cried Charles. "I knew it – it's a ploy - she wants me back to have fun. Her fun, that is. And here am I having ***my*** fun down here, and now we've got to stop and drag ourselves up there and have her fun instead. Oh God Oh God …. ……"

His look of amusement was replaced by an air of deep depression.

"I'll have to go."

"So must we all, "said Paula, "if we're going to do anything at all, today, beyond behaving badly. Funny how much nicer it is than behaving well."

And so, swiftly dressing themselves and grabbing the swimming things, en route, that it emerged Tom had dumped in the bushes, they made their way up to the house. Charles detached himself and went in search of his mother. Tom and George went off to play croquet. Paula and Ingrid disappeared to dress for the evening's ball - the buffet would be served at ten o-clock.

Although Ingrid decided to lie down first, and see how she felt. She claimed a headache. Paula, still smiling, but now more solicitous, said she would shortly come and see how Ingrid was. And they would talk. Ingrid flopped down on her vast bed, and promptly fell asleep. Within moments, seemingly (in fact it was three quarters of an hour) there was a tapping at her door. It was Paula, already dressed - looking stunning in a floor length white tulle evening gown, tricked off with emerald ear-rings. She'd been helped to dress by one of the Clayton maids.

Except perhaps for the heightened colour in her cheeks you would never have guessed her exploits of the afternoon. She maintained the poise Ingrid envied so much.

"So how are you now?" said Paula. "Is there any chance at all you'll come to the ball? And what did you make of our adventures this afternoon!?"

"What did *you* make of them, more to the point," said Ingrid. "Why did you say 'yes' when I suggested you'd planned it?

"Would you rather I'd say no?" said Paula. "There's always **something** to be said for the truth."

"Then tell me the truth, now, please!"

For like a lot of people who have harboured a slow-growing resentment it was only at the moment of social contact that Ingrid realised it. Above all she felt furious with Tom - how dare he take advantage of her? But with Paula, too, who was clearly in on it... .... whatever 'it' might be..........though above all, truthfully, she felt cross with herself.

Nevertheless, now Paula was all tact, if just a wee bit patronising. She sat her young friend down; she offered her whisky from a hip flask, magicked from her skirts; she even suggested she help Ingrid dress for the dance, just in case, unlikely though it might now seem, Ingrid felt like going along later. After all, she pointed out, "This is hardly the moment we want the company of a maid."

And as they stood in front of the mirror, Paula swiftly and deftly 'hooking Ingrid up', her fingers on Ingrid's shoulders, the story came out.

Yes, said Paula, you could say she'd planned it, in a way. Well, if not exactly planned it - certainly given things a very good shove. Yes, she *had* asked Tom to 'look after' Ingrid while she was in Scotland, and was aware, of course, how Tom would interpret 'looking after' – not least, to be honest, because she had more or less *instructed* him to seduce her! (Ingrid gasped.) Yes, this was true – once again Paula was smiling - but Ingrid must understand it was for her own good.

It really was quite obvious to her, if not to Ingrid, that she had long passed the moment when she needed her first, genuine sexual experience. To be honest, Paula had felt sorry for her - there'd certainly never been any prospect of anything like that with Alexey, as she knew personally, only too well. And to be more honest still, to her sympathy had been added guilt – for it had been plain from the start what would happen, or not happen, with Alexey, and she felt, in many ways, she should have intervened earlier.

And now, here was Tom, this new, highly competent lover, who clearly wanted Ingrid desperately - Paula seemed unabashed by this - and she really felt she ought to share him, for Ingrid's sake, in fact for all their sakes. (Another gasp from Ingrid.) So yes, it was with her blessing that Tom had first sent her those letters. And yes, she had helped plan their lunch. Then when that failed the mooted theatre visit, too, had been meant to further Tom's cause.

And finally, above all, there was the presence of the whole pack of them here at Clayton House! The climax of the 'plot'! ....if plot there were; for today's events, certainly, had largely happened by chance. Mainly because she'd been lucky enough to get a message back to Tom that they'd be in the cove, and he, in turn, had met George as he walked down.

As for the nude swimming, and Ingrid being left alone, well you could call that planned, but it was just as much spontaneous, and as for Tom's refinement of swimming into the cove under a reed, well that was pure Tom, it hadn't been planned at all.

One thing, thought Ingrid, for sure - Paula never lost her capacity to surprise.

"The whole thing's crazy!" she cried. "Inhuman, too! I mean, if you really gave a fig for your relationship with Tom, why would you want to put him on to me?!"

"Precisely *because* I care for him and know his attractiveness as a man, and because I care very much - rather more than you realise - for you; and it was obvious, frankly, if nothing was done, that you would be flaffing around in a state of compulsive virginity forever and that isn't a position I would recommend for anyone!"

"So are you seriously telling me you don't feel jealous? Or is that another emotion you have long since left behind, in your advanced, emancipated way?

"Oh Ingrid," said Paula, and now her tone really was patronising, "Surely you can conceive of *some* relationship which isn't about ownership? The more you give in life, the more you get, surely you can see that? Can't you grasp that the whole thing was above all an act of *generosity* - possibly the purest, most genuinely unselfish act of friendship you'll ever encounter? As Friedrich Paul said....."

"Friedrich Paul again!"

"Yes! As Fri - ..."

"- Oh to hell with Friedrich Paul!"

"And to hell with *you*!" Now Paula snapped as well. "What it comes down to is this - (she slowed, and stressed each word) " – *you really must grow up.* Who's had whose interests at heart in all this? Have you been thinking about me, or me about you? Perhaps we can talk again when you've calmed down."

"You don't seem so calm yourself!" yelled Ingrid back. But it was to Paula's back, for Paula had left the room.

Ingrid flung herself down on the bed, furious, now, with everyone in the world, with Paula, Tom, Charles, the whole Clayton set-up, indeed, the whole corrupt, hypocritical, pretentious pack of them! Grow up indeed! Like all successful insults it was its truth that hurt. Why ever, how ever, had she found herself in such a situation? How had she allowed herself to be so grossly manipulated, violated even, by so many people? And the whole lot of them had known everything all along - or most of the time - had known about what amounted to a conspiracy!

Ingrid was little given to paranoia, but she felt it now. To hell with them all! – well, one thing she would not be doing, that much was sure, was go to their foolish, corrupt, pretentious dance tonight. For one thing she'd got a headache - she *couldn't* go, she wasn't well.

Chapter Thirty-Seven

She woke, an hour later, feeling refreshed and far more jovial. Not least because she'd had another of her caricature dreams - this time about the lovely Edward Stourbridge, the bus Adonis, he of the drunken wisecracks at dinner. You'd have thought she might have dreamed about Tom Huntingdon, large as he had loomed in the last twenty four hours: instead, it was the sweet- faced, broad- shouldered, dissipated-looking Edward - who she imagined making exquisite love to her.

A lovely dream! Though it must be said, as with that dream about Alexey, its chief characteristic had been the tallest, most gargantuan satyr-like penis in the world - which shook her even more. She really was quite startled to find out just how explicit, not to mention repetitive, her subconscious was. Had her fantasies no originality at all?

Not that she was going to get involved with Edward. She'd just dream about him - dreamboat, Adonis, that's Edward, nothing more. No, really, no chance at all! Things were already quite complicated enough. "One fling at a time," she muttered to herself, then made a mental point to deploy this quip later, among her fellow-guests, should the right moment crop up.

At which point she heard music. The ball had begun! She glanced at the clock over the fireplace: it was nine o-clock. Too late to go now for the start. But did that matter, really? This seemed a pretty flexible household, Charles' part of it anyway, and she could always plead her headache. Because what she quickly began to realise, with the evaporation of her anger, was that she *did* want to go, after all.

And all the more she wanted it when she heard what the orchestra were playing: Franz Lehar's Gold and Silver waltz, her favourite dance of all. And as she sprang to the window, she could see the dancers, in the wing to the left, through the ballroom window. The introduction had finished and now, with a slow, sensual swing, the orchestra slid into the opening melody, the suavest, most seductive sound in the world.

She'd heard Lehar had a full length nude painting of a woman in his study, right across one wall. She believed it, you could hear it in the notes.

And now, swinging into vision in Charles Fisher's arms, came Paula, the embodiment, as ever, of aristocratic languor, for all her communism.

That did it. The ball was where Ingrid wanted to be, and she wanted to dance there as beautifully, as languidly, as her friend.

She shot to the dressing table, completed her toilette, grabbed some earrings and a sash, glanced at herself in the full-length mirror and decided she looked acceptable. (In fact she looked spectacular.) Then she galloped down the stairs toward the door that would take her across the courtyard toward the ballroom.

But she never got there. For in front of her, crossing the courtyard, were Paula and Charles, with two steps behind, Tom Huntingdon and a woman she didn't know. George followed them on his own. They hailed Ingrid cheerily.

"Ingrid! So you are coming after all!" said Charles. "How wonderful! Although there's just one thing...."

"We've just left the ball. We're going to see the black men," said Paula. "To hear their 'jass' or whatever it calls itself. Why don't you come?"

"Well..."

"Believe me, the ball can wait," said Charles. "Whereas the jass, I promise you, can't: it's something you'll never hear the likes of again." Ingrid hesitated - she'd been looking forward to her Lehar. But now Tom, too, entered the fray. His manner was gentle, almost suppliant. (As well it might be, thought Ingrid, after this afternoon.)

"Do come, Ingrid," he said. "It won't be the same without you."

His partner eyed Ingrid questioningly.

"Oh, forgive me. Miss Quentin - this is Ingrid Uberspeer. Miss Uberspeer : Miss Quentin."

Miss Quentin extended her hand. "Good to meet you," she said.

"And very good to meet you too," said Ingrid.

Ingrid wondered how obvious her blush was, and whether Miss Quentin noticed it. Not that she cared, of course. Because this newcomer looked pointy-faced and shrewish, not to mention old.

"We've just met," said Tom by way of apology. "We've been dancing."

"Trying to, anyway," said Miss Quentin, grinning, while staring fixedly at Ingrid.

"You've all my sympathy," said Paula. "Tom's dancing is beyond eccentricity – it's dangerous."

"Worse than his boxing," said Charles.

"I should say so," said Miss Quentin, still eyeing Ingrid intently, "but then they say how people dance is how they conduct themselves in bed - eh Tom?" And she nudged him forcefully in the ribs.

What behaviour from a stranger! Even Tom was struck dumb.

Charles rescued him. "All the more reason for trying out this 'jass'," he said. "The whole thing is you don't have to know how to dance it at all, you just improvise."

"Precisely," said Miss Quentin. "That's why they call it ' jass', of course. 'Jass' means sex, don'tcherknow, and sex is nothing if not improvised, ain't it?!"

Mein Gott, thought Ingrid, this munchkin has more to her than meets the eye. She gazed more closely: a neat, tight figure, now she noticed, and sharp, almost petite features......a definite spark......but there was no getting away from it, a great, hooked nose, better suited to a sixteenth century corsair than a belle at a ball.

The five of them went off toward the marquee where Charles' band were playing. The men walked ahead on their own, the women following; and as they went, Ingrid learned a little more about Elspeth, which was what this strange Miss Quentin strangely called herself.

She was, it emerged, one of the feminists who had so rapturously applauded Paula's trades unionists speech earlier. She'd struck up a conversation with Paula afterwards. Her father was the local vicar, so she'd essentially been invited as a favour. But as she knew hardly anyone there, and Paula had taken a shine to her, she'd got Tom to dance with her.

But as they neared the tent Ingrid heard something she didn't expect. *Arab* music! A wailing, howling sound, exactly like a band she'd once heard from Morocco. Yet as they entered the tent she saw it was, indeed, the 'nigger' group - but playing music like she'd never heard before. Ragtime she knew about, from young people's parties in Entlingen, but this was different. The wailing, the shieking, the *pain,* mainly expressed by trumpets! What 'music' was this?

And where was the sex in it, as Elspeth had declared? In all that pain? Then Ingrid realised: the pain was the sex.

Instantly she was interested. For this was the only music she'd ever heard that remotely described the *reality* of sexual experience, certainly hers. And then ....the wailing number suddenly stopped, as it were in mid bar, and the musicians started something extraordinary, the wildest, shrillest bacchanal she'd ever heard.

Trumpeters standing up, and capering about! A bass player dancing with his instrument! Trombonists slithering their slides, so their playing seemed shot through with curves and hills and valleys, and then, most amazing of all, the *dancers*, frenetically leaping about the floor, shrieking, waving their arms, screaming! She watched one woman, in particular, whose dance step looked exactly like someone who'd stepped onto a pool of ice, lost her balance, and was stumbling, slithering, kicking her legs to stop her falling.

"What's *that*?!" she yelled to Charles, above the din, who was eyeing her with amusement.

"It's the Charleston," he said. "D'you fancy a drink?" And Charles drew a flask from his pocket and handed it around.

Ingrid had not drunk brandy before, and it felt like someone had stuck a firebrand down her throat. But she liked it. Moments later Paula delved into her skirts and grabbed the bottle she'd produced in Ingrid's room, and round *that* went too – but this time vodka. And Ingrid liked the vodka even more.

Then servants appeared with wine and champagne, and everyone took some of that too, and within half an hour all five of them, like everyone else in that cacophonous tent, were roaring drunk. While the wine and the spirits and the 'Jass,' and the infernal, devilish dancing (the marquee was lit with dark red oil lamps, making it feel more satanic still) seemed increasingly like a vision, even a dream.

Yet a dream, somehow, which seemed more real than everyday life, with a distinct, if utterly mysterious quality of ***recognition*** - as if Ingrid had known about this strange new world all her life.

Charles asked Paula for a dance, but Paula, unusually, looked shy and refused. And as Tom looked uncertain too, and so did Ingrid, they all stood in a row, looking sheepish.

Till suddenly Elspeth, of all people, leapt up and charged straight into the melee and moments later began charlestoning, with the wildest, most comical movements you ever saw. Like a manic, cocaine-fuelled dwarf! thought Ingrid. Then Elspeth grabbed Ingrid and dragged her onto the floor, and Ingrid, surrendering, copied everyone as best she could, until finally, after three wild minutes, she collapsed helpless onto the floor, laughing.

At which moment the music changed again, and this time slowed into the heaviest, sultriest sound in the world – a 'smooch,' apparently, according to the endlessly knowledgeable Charles - and the dancers intertwined and stood, bodies glued together, hardly moving. And Elspeth grabbed Ingrid again and, before she could stop her, pressed her tight little body into hers, Elspeth's hard round breasts pressing up against Ingrid's bodice like tennis balls.

Which was when Ingrid saw, across the room, Edward Stourbridge, Mr. Dreamboat himself. And a moment later they'd locked eyes – a reprise, almost, of the time on the bus – then next, incredibly, Edward was walking across the room toward her, grinning with delight.

He dodged round two dancers, skidded on some wine, kept coming, till finally....... he walked right past her. Instead he went up to Paula and asked ***her*** to dance - and Paula, perhaps more confident trying something slow, accepted. So now Paula, too, was dancing, glued to the lovely Edward, both murmuring intimacies, Ingrid noted, into each other's ears.

Although it was an unsure vision by now as the alcohol had finally taken over and everything was blurred.

Indeed, all Ingrid remembered, later, was a series of pictures:

She remembered, for instance, dancing briefly with George, and then - when she fell over! - how solicitous he was, and how he sat her down and chatted with her, making sure she was alright.

She remembered - or thought she did – how, come one of the 'smooches', she saw Paula and Elspeth locked deep in each other's arms, oblivious of all around them, which seemed strange till she noticed several other women, all round the room, doing exactly the same.

But above all she remembered how she ended the evening - she never knew how - in the arms of Edward Stourbridge, and this too was a 'smooch' and went on, seemingly, for hours.

And he was tall and warm and gentle and wrapped her in his arms, and she lifted her head - he was a good foot taller than she - and they locked eyes, and he bent over and kissed her softly, very tenderly, on the mouth.

Then once more memory blurred …. though Paula filled in most of it, the next day.

This much was plain. As Charles' 'jass' party broke up they went back to Paula's rooms - the same group she had gone with, minus George, who claimed he was 'tired' - but now plus a quite staggeringly drunk Elspeth Quentin. And there they took still more alcohol, this time champagne; then Tom and Elspeth disappeared; then as Ingrid sat there with Charles and Paula, feeling ever more surplus, there was a knock on the door and lo! it was none other than Edward Stourbridge. And the moment he came in Charles and Paula, too, disappeared. Then Edward took Ingrid by the hand and suggested they once more dance.

"But there's no music," said Ingrid.

"We'll make our own," said Edward, and both laughed at the terrible joke.

Moments later he'd wafted Ingrid back to his room. And there, at last, Ingrid made love with a man she truly desired – though still unclear, in her drunken state, whether this, too, might not be a dream.

Although despite her ardour (or maybe due to the drink) it failed to be quite the rapture she had hoped. But at least - as Ingrid sensibly told herself later - they'd made a start. Or as her mother might have put it, if not usually in quite this context, "No finishing until you first begin."

A point re-emphasised by Paula at the post-mortem next day.

Chatting in a discreet nook in the garden, in the dead hour before the guests' departure, Paula confessed her role in once again advancing her young friend's sexual education - this time with Edward Stourbridge.

The whispering, she explained, as she and Edward danced, had in fact been Edward pleading for an introduction to Ingrid.

For Edward described how he'd seen her that time on the bus and how much he'd been attracted and how certain he'd been what her staring meant. But he had, apparently - most uncharacteristically - held himself back, because if there was one thing Kitty Clayton had imposed on him, as a condition of her continuing favour, it was that he drop his compulsive womanising.

But now, he explained, the situation had changed again. For he was so out of favour, these days, there was little to lose. "I might as well be hung for a sheep as for a goat," he said, which was not, perhaps, the nicest way of putting it.

Nevertheless, Paula had been happy to help – she'd been impressed, and amused, by Edward's eagerness – and she'd sensed an even greater voracity in Ingrid.

"You're a wicked wicked woman," said Ingrid, "and I don't know why I consort with you."

"I do," said Paula. "It's because I make things happen that you don't quite dare yourself. That you want, but won't allow yourself to get."

Chapter Thirty-Eight

Tumultuous though the weekend had been it was only a prelude, it emerged, to a still more hectic period that soon developed among Ingrid's friends.

For she found herself involved in an ever-escalating experiment in 'free love': an anglicisation of everything Friedrich Paul had imagined. The protagonists thought of it as their own 'little club', and it involved Paula, Tom, Charles, Ingrid and Edward. Not to mention, a touch surprisingly, the add-on of Elspeth Quentin, to whom both Tom and Paula seemed to have taken a shine.

Most memorably, a week after the Clayton weekend Edward Stourbridge made contact with Ingrid and asked her if she would have lunch with him at a cottage lent him near Henfield, five miles outside Oxford. And she came and they made love, this time successfully; they met twice more, and each time went better still; but it was the fourth time they met, still in the same pretty cottage, that Ingrid had the experience, she felt, that changed her life.

She was sitting on the couch in the dining room beside Edward. They'd had lunch.

Edward had introduced her to his 'favourite' wine, a green-gold 1897 Moselle, which Ingrid knew well back home but had never drunk in quantity. They'd emptied two bottles. Then they'd feasted on salmon, which Edward had brought in the boot of his car; while for her part Ingrid had brought some specially chosen peaches for dessert - but they never got to eat them, because as she got up to fetch them Edward stood up too, caught her hand, and steered her swiftly into the cottage's only bedroom.

"I'm giving you a present," he said.

He picked up the chair from the dressing table and plonked it down in the middle of the room. Ingrid eyed the chair, and Edward, warily.

"Come here," he said.

Ingrid moved over and stood in front of him.

"Take off your clothes," he said.

"How dare you."

"But I insist."

"You'll have to unhook me."

"Fine."

And now Edward started unlacing the back of her dress; a moment later he tugged at a kind of girdle round Ingrid's waist – and to the surprise of both, the dress instantly fell in a little puddle on the floor. In under a minute, she was naked. Edward remained clothed.

"Turn round," he said.

And Ingrid, still more wary now – what did he have in mind? – turned, nevertheless, presenting her back to him and awaiting his touch; but to tease, he waited too, until, suddenly, silently, delicately, he touched her on the right shoulder, the tiniest remotest feather-touch imaginable, scarce a touch at all.

Then the same touch on the other shoulder; then a sudden, unexpected brush, just as feather-light, on the back of her thigh; then both hands now, once again on her shoulders, but moving now, roving delicately all over her back; still the lightest touch imaginable, more like a breath than contact.

"The lighter the touch, the more the sensuality," he said.

"A paradox," murmured Ingrid.

And now he turned her again, and as she moved, her mouth sought his, but he pushed her back with a breathed 'not yet,' for his lips were on her left breast, his hands still roaming her body but a little more firmly now; then his lips were on her right breast too - and finally, a little awkwardly, he sat down on the chair (so that's why he got it out, thought Ingrid) and she had to admit it *was* the right height, because he was able, now, to slide his fingertips between her thighs, while still sucking her breasts.

At which moment she realised, with a flash of recognition, that something similar had happened with Alexey that time on the walk, but not like this, she said to herself, not like this ....

Because now, unlike those previous times, the moment steadily, ever more thrillingly, began to build, and with Ingrid's body burning, Edward laid her down, still running his hands over every inch of her (Ingrid was especially excited when he would touch, unexpectedly, her feet and toes, which seemed exceptionally sensitive) and then he gently opened up her legs, and slid his mouth down her stomach to her pubic hair, and to her thighs, then back to her stomach again. Little hopping, teasing, fairy kisses, as Ingrid wondered where his mouth would go next.

Then finally, as she had half feared, half hoped, his mouth slid down between her legs, and for the first time she felt his lips on her vagina, then on her clitoris, and he was delicately licking, then sucking, then gently rubbing it with his forefinger, then licking again, then once again caressing her breast, then feather-light- touching her toe.

Until, slowly, deliciously, the waves of pleasure built in her, her pelvic muscles started trembling, the waves built up still more, the muscles rigidified, then went into spasm, then slid sumptuously, delightfully, into the first, true, all-body orgasm Ingrid had ever known. Each wave and pulse of it deliciously reiterating, till finally, still infinitely slowly, it faded into the most gentle and lingering of retreats.

And it happened three times more.

"You're multi-orgasmic," said Edward. "Did you know that?"

"Multi-what? I don't know what that means," said Ingrid. "But multi-grateful, yes. Edward, you're a marvel."

"And you my dear, are a miracle, and a natural, too," and now at last, Edward stripped off his clothes, (so concentrated had he been on Ingrid's pleasure until that moment) revealing, as Ingrid had suspected, an erection rather larger than her dreams.

Then he plunged into her.

And for the rest of the afternoon their sex was a rolling, thrusting, writhing affair, as far removed from that featherlight sensuality as could be.

"I have a name for you" announced Edward, as they prepared to leave. "It expresses your sweetness, and the way I salivate each time I think of you."

"What's that ?"

"Cake".

"What a cheek. Well, I've a name for you too," said Ingrid.

"And what might that be?"

"Crumpet."

"Well, I've never been called *that* before," said Edward.

"Well, you should have been," said Ingrid.

Yet cake or crumpet or whatever else the patisserie might have on offer, the experience unlocked something in Ingrid. For the first time she lived what she'd merely fantasised about before. For what she realised now, for all her earlier daydreaming, was that she'd never really **believed**, till then, that she deserved what she desired. Some unconscious restraint, some sense of unworthiness, had held her back.

And now, it had finally happened! So that all she wanted - and she wanted it right away - was the same experience again, and again and again and again; which was when she remembered a line she'd read once in her father's 'Arabian Nights' – ' ....for that a woman's desire is greater than a man's......' She'd dismissed it then but now she wondered if the Arabs weren't onto something.

And not unnaturally, the more enthusiastic she became the more avid Edward became as well. He was thrilled by Ingrid's ardour and titillated by his role of initiator, introducing Ingrid to all the sexual experiments he'd learned over his years of quite considerable 'debauchery.'

Yet for all this he was most struck by something simple, and in its own way touchingly innocent: the way Ingrid kissed. She would reach her mouth up to his and, as their lips touched, she would relax and spread them wide, in the most searching, rhapsodic abandon. It was this trust, this fearlessness almost, that appealed to him most of all.

Unsurprisingly, such voluptuousness was soon evident to their friends. They got jealous, for all their free-love ideology.

Tom, for a start, as Ingrid's prime initiator who had so rapidly been cast aside. And what made it worse for Tom was that Paula, now, was making love consistently with Charles. Which had, in turn, the predictable effect of making Tom more avid still to make love, whenever possible, with Ingrid - which she, in her lordly way, permitted now and then (when Edward was not around.) Then Charles, too, approached Ingrid - one evening down at the cove - and they made love together too; while Paula and the sparky Elspeth, seemingly, were making love with everyone - so free and easy, so comradely and uninhibited, were they all.

Though what swiftly became evident, for all the sexual camaraderie, was that Ingrid, in particular, was in a position of growing power. The one woman all three men most desired, quite plainly, was she; and while Edward unquestionably was the one *she* wanted most she quickly realised she could pick and choose according to her whim.

Some situation! - however unintended and unplanned. And Ingrid, if she were honest, *was* intrigued. Indeed, she wondered...... *was* she a predator, after all, as Tom had suggested all those weeks ago? A huntress? A veritable Panther??!!

Not that this bold adventurism lacked hiccups. There was the jealousy, for a start, even if it did add piquancy to it all. There were the logistics – Clayton Court was quite some distance away, awkward to get to from Oxford. And as for Ingrid's relationship with her employers..........by now she'd become a veritable expert in the lies, evasions and plain bald whoppers which enabled her regular meetings with her friends.

Despite which, time and again, the Crosbys seemed on the brink of finding out. And one of the dangers, curiously enough, was letter-writing. For Tom, presumably as a kind of compensation for feeling edged out, began sending her streams of self-consciously rude and explicit notes, replete with every Anglo-Saxon word imaginable. And one day the most explicit of them all arrived at the Crosby breakfast table with its corner damaged in the post, so a good couple of lines were clearly visible as it lay there on the plate. Ingrid blushed scarlet and snatched it up, aghast at what might have been seen. But she should not have worried.

For Tom's handwriting, by a stroke of chance, was similar to that of George. So that the Crosbys, it emerged, were merely amused to see how embarrassed Ingrid was feeling at the evidence (they assumed) of a friendship they knew she had long been carrying on with that most rock-solid paragon of charm, good sense - and, from their *in loco parentis* perspective - utter security.

And indeed, she **had** been seeing George, as well as the others - on a strictly platonic basis. More, she'd had the foresight to ensure the Crosbys knew about it. Just in case she needed cover.

Not that she minded seeing him, anyway - she was genuinely fond of George.

Chapter Thirty-Nine

For George had never been part of the Clayton Court shenanigans. Right from the first weekend of the ball he had distanced himself: not in any self-righteous way - his manner had always been, if anything, amused – but he had, when invited to join in , declared he was 'not quite up to it'.

But then there had been, too, recurrent hints that there was a woman back in Cambridge with whom he was involved. The way he talked about her, Ingrid reckoned they were virtually engaged.

And what that meant was that the utterly staunch George, as well as providing cover for other meetings, was her lifeline into the conventional world. There was something so solid and reassuring about his manifest faithfulness; for betrayal was *the* quality of Ingrid's new lifestyle that bothered her most of all, for all the 'freedom' and fine phrases.

Gradually, in fact, George took over something of the role previously occupied by Paula. He became a sounding board, a testing ground, for Ingrid's new ideas, which she could try out on him all the better for his non-involvement.

And as the summer wore on, there was plenty to try out. At least twice a week, the 'Cleopatra' club, as it now called itself (Anthony and Cleopatra had apparently formed such a club among their friends, devoted to hedonism, as disaster approached them during the Republican civil wars) would meet, at Edward's cottage, or in a wood, or in someone' s college rooms. And the 'shenanigans,' as Edward called them, got ever wilder.

Yet gradually Ingrid's sense that she had finally found herself sexually, if hardly spiritually, began to pall. Slowly, but inexorably - more and more she found herself talking about this with George – she felt jaded. Or in the simple phrase which seemed to express it: 'it's not me.' Something, increasingly, was missing, even concretely wrong: a feeling which was exacerbated as the Cleopatra club's indulgence moved up yet another gear, initiated, as so often, by Paula.

For Paula became ever more explicit about a tendency she had erstwhile only hinted at. She became an out-and-out advocate of 'sapphism,' as she put it, 'a love beautiful and pure, passing the love of man.' So that now her enthusiasm for Elspeth Quentin, so long a mystery, was explained. She and Elspeth were lovers - as well as being heterosexual lovers of everyone else as well.

One day, at the cove, Paula began talking about 'bisexuality', as she called it. Surely everyone must agree that in art, especially literature, possessing both female and male sensibility, of which sexuality was merely a symptom, was a huge advantage. Imagine, having not merely half, but *all* the understanding of the world!

Not, she added, that bisexuality should be confused with true homosexuality, whether female or male. That was something else again. Everyone felt some physical attraction for their own sex; what distinguished the genuine homosexual was that it was only in same-sex relationships that they could find true love, their grand amour. Think of Oscar Wilde, with his genuine attraction for his wife Constance, and then .....Bosie! There was no comparison.

A view which was accepted with predictable liberality by Paula's friends. Although Ingrid, privately, felt less sure. Indeed, if she were honest, it came down to something quite simple. Theory was fine, 'Sapphism' undeniably romantic, yet she still found something repulsive, even nauseous, about Elspeth and Paula caressing each other's bodies.

And most especially did she feel this the evening after Paula's bisexuality protestations. For something happened which shed light, Ingrid thought, on why it had taken place just then.

She and Paula, carrying two big bags of picnic things, were the last to leave the cove. Halfway up the hill they put the bags down to admire the view.

Then Ingrid, standing a bit below Paula, suddenly felt her friend's arm snake around her neck. Her head was jerked backward and, almost before she realised what was happening, Paula's firm, sickly-sweet lips were on hers.

But this time, unlike that assault by Tom in the Botanic Gardens, Ingrid failed to respond. She felt a rush yes, but one of pure repulsion - she pushed Paula forcibly back then, thanks to the slope, stumbled herself, and fell over, with difficulty avoiding rolling right down to the cove. But when she stopped and looked up, she saw that Paula's state was even more traumatised than her own.

For Paula, too, was crouched down on her haunches.

She was weeping. Silently, profusely, in utter desolation.

At which moment Ingrid understood.

Or as she put it to Edward, when she saw him alone a couple of days later, (this particular revelation she felt more comfortable sharing with Edward rather than George) she saw, or thought she saw, why Paula had so long and consistently played Pandarus to Ingrid's sexual education.

"It's as if she made love to me vicariously, getting others to sleep with me on her behalf."

"Well, I can understand her starting point," said Edward. "*My* critique is how long it took her to act. Like the philosopher said, 'Live dangerously!' Who'd have thought that Paula, of all people, would be so timid?"

Who indeed, thought Ingrid. Though the more she considered it, the more she wondered whether it was not possible that Paula was herself one of those she had described as a 'true' homosexual, one whose deepest emotions could only engage with those of her own sex And that very depth of feeling – amazingly, directed of all people toward Ingrid herself! - had been what had hamstrung her, making it so hard to express herself.

And now, more than ever, Ingrid felt confused.

Then there was the question, too, of how this latest revelation fitted into her growing disillusionment with the 'Cleopatra' club. Most especially what happened after she and Edward talked.

For despite her protestations, he instantly told Charles, Elspeth and Tom.

And all four of them merely found it more material for laughs. A callousness she had, alas, increasingly come to expect of them.
Indeed, so strongly did she feel this that in the small hours of the morning, when such thoughts would race and re-race through her mind, she would find herself, now, feeling *physically* sick. One time, a fortnight later, she actually vomited.

Then the next morning the same thing happened. Soon the bouts of sickness became routine, while at other times she felt euphoric. She put it down to her familiar volatility until finally, at the instigation of Mrs. Crosby, she saw a doctor. (The Crosbys saw it as "a relapse.")

Which doctor, Dorothy Fenwick, the daughter of one of the Crosbys' friends, and the only woman GP in Oxford, shared, fortunately for Ingrid, the Crosbys' liberalism. She even believed, unusually for those days, in patient confidentiality.

For what she told Ingrid was the one thing she hadn't thought of.

Her diagnosis was simple, and Dr. Fenwick was quite sure.

Ingrid was pregnant.

Chapter Forty

Dr. Fenwick was infinitely kind and assured Ingrid she could talk with her at any time. But Ingrid only wanted to be alone.

The surgery was just off St. Giles, half a mile from where the Crosbys lived. Ingrid began tottering home. She swayed like a drunk. ***Pregnant!*** It was incredible. At a stroke, her life was transformed.

What would people think? What could she do? How would she survive if, say, she were dismissed? Suddenly there was a grand canyon at her feet. And now, once again, the eternal Ingrid response to life's crises: how could she ever, conceivably, have been so ***stupid?***

An especial horror crystalised, in Ingrid's mind, around certain conversations.

Imagine talking about this to Mrs. Crosby! She couldn't conceive of such a moment. Or her friends? A floodtide of bourgeois inhibitions overcame this erstwhile sexual revolutionary.

Then another thought. The first person she would naturally talk to, surely, would be the baby's father - and with a lurch she realised she didn't know who he was. God help her! Most likely, of course, it was Edward. He was the one she had been making love with most, and most avidly, too, if that had anything to do with it. Ingrid suspected it had. But how could she know for sure?

More important, how could she *prove* anything at all? Along with Edward, she'd slept with Tom five times, even Charlie Fisher twice. And how protesting they'd been, she reflected bitterly, about the efficiency of their contraception (manfully dealt with by themselves, of course, though each, she'd noted, had had a different theory. That should have warned her.) Away with the fairies, they'd all been, all the time!

Yet at this very moment, just when Ingrid's mind felt overwhelmed by panic, and every task an Everest of effort, a whole new state of mind broke through.

It started, as so often with Ingrid, with a particular moment. One night-time, as she was bathing the children. Maybe something about the bathroom's womblike warmth, plus the childrens' delight in her attention, brought it on.

It mainly involved four-year-old Jane. Because the time-honoured bath-time tradition had always been, as soon as Ingrid got Jane out of the water, that she would hold her opposite the bathroom mirror, a white towel wrapped round her head to catch the drips. And Jane, gazing at her reflection in the mirror, would cry 'Cakey baba! Cakey baba!' with huge delight. She seemed to feel she looked like the little icing figures of eskimos, in white hoods, that decorated the Crosbys' Christmas cakes.

And it was when Ingrid held her there, always a joyous and intimate moment, that she found herself wondering: suppose the reflection opposite was different, suppose, in three years' time, this was *my* child! Maybe a little girl like Jane, my very own creation who I was cradling in this way - that same minute creature who is already, in some way, germinating in my womb. What would *that* be like, how would *that* feel? She kissed Jane's head and turned quickly away, but the thoughts kept coming.

What might her baby look like? Herself, or Edward? Assuming it *was* Edward's of course. Well, if it was Edward's, it would look fine enough! Although God help her it were Tom's. Once again, the maverick chuckle.

But however it turned out, it would be *hers*: how extraordinary to have her own little Ingrid to cherish (the child's sex, it must be said, seemed as predetermined as her name.) How wonderful, all that warmth and beauty and delight! But then Ingrid had always longed for children - indeed, she remembered telling the amorous Heinrich, back in Germany, prophetically it now seemed, that she was scared of making love because if she did, and got pregnant, 'I would love the baby and not be sorry.' He'd looked puzzled.

And yet…How wonderful to have a child to bring up! How delightful to buy her pretty clothes, to take her for walks in the park, to show her monkeys at the zoo, to buy her Christmas presents, to make a cake for her birthday, with a special picture, in icing, on top. How utterly sweet and tender to..... kiss her goodnight!

At which moment, with another lurch Ingrid would think – 'and the *father*? What about him?' - and the daydream would dissolve, and would be replaced by the return of 'Johnny Panic' as Ingrid called it, those recurrent surges of small-hours terror. For some reason they always broke through at precisely 3.18am.

And she would remember, once more, the starkness of the choice before her. Either she would bring her child into the world, with every imaginable problem, or......... she would kill it: destroy this tiny, kindling creature in her womb, with all its promise and trust.

And back would come the fears.

She must talk to someone.

It would normally, naturally, have been Paula, but how could she possibly talk to her, after what had happened? Or Mrs. Crosby, as Dr. Fenwick had advised? The Dantesque horror of that thought made Ingrid chuckle. But who else? A male friend, like George? Ingrid balked at this - far, far too intimate for that relationship. Anyone else? Hook-nosed Elspeth, maybe? Why not? It sounded as hopeful as anything else.

Indeed, so desperate did she get in her 3.18 am ruminations that she wondered whether she shouldn't take the bull by the horns and go straight to Edward. It made as much sense as anything else. And who knows, it was at least possible that he might be sympathetic ...... indeed surely that was the most likely outcome, yes, surely, for whatever else, he was a gentleman – if a rakish one - and was certainly in a position, if he wished, to help practically. He had money. Although a moment later her mind collided again with that insistent thought: ***she didn't even know if he was the father.*** And she would have to tell him that. Okay, remind him, if you like, because, as a fellow free, untrammelled spirit he pretty much knew already.

Once more the worst thing was imagining the conversation.

At which moment she got a note from Paula, who she'd not seen since their confrontation on the cliff.

Paula wanted to meet her.

And when they did meet, in Christchurch meadows, what quickly emerged was that Paula had heard - God knows how - about the pregnancy. This was why she'd contacted her. More surprising still (her reaction might have been very different) she was gentle and kind.

This astonished Ingrid. Apart from any predictable resentment, the Paula she knew might have launched into one of her evangelical-feminist tirades, told her to get a grip, abort the baby, or have it adopted, or worst of all – because most daunting – defy the world, bring up the baby herself.

But instead, as Paula gently teased out the details, encouraging her to describe the possible reaction of her mother, or Mrs. Crosby, or Ingrid's fears of ignominy and being dismissed, it was as if Ingrid was addressing someone new.

With the result that when Ingrid got on to how hard she would find presenting all this to their mutual friends – the part she dreaded most – she dissolved into tears.

At which Paula got up, took two steps across the grass, and drew her deep into her arms.

And this time, far from rejecting her, Ingrid accepted the embrace. indeed she lent thankfully on her shoulder, while her friend stroked and re-stroked her hair, just like a child.

Which was when Ingrid realised what had transformed her friend.

It was love.

Now Paula was whispering coaxingly, reassuringly, into Ingrid's ear. Fear not, Paula murmured, why didn't SHE talk to people like Edward, as Ingrid naturally found it so hard - why not? She knew him of old and he held no fears for her.

And she would talk to the others, too, to Tom and Charles, if Ingrid would like her to. And force discretion on them, on pain of death. And do other things, as well, if they would help in any way: she would become Ingrid's enabler in all things practical.

Then something struck her.

"I know one person, certainly, you *could* talk to at this moment. Someone who would be utterly sympathetic and discreet."

"Who's that?"

"Why, Mary Thornton," said Paula. It had apparently only just occurred to her. "No, really, she had a very similar experience herself, albeit years ago. Everything you feel now she's felt herself."

Mary Thornton! Yes, Ingrid had heard something about Mary being pregnant before she was married. Though she'd never given it much thought - there was always that kind of gossip flying around the 'Cleopatra Club'. What she *did* know was that she'd always liked Mary's manner – and her evident kindness.

"Well, yes," she said, "I'd like to if you'd care to set it up."

And Paula assured her she would.

A week later Ingrid did go and see Mary Thornton, and she was as sympathetic as Paula said. And they started meeting regularly. So that now, adding Mary to the newly transformed Paula, Ingrid found she had no less than two new 'sisters.'

Less successful were Paula's meetings with the putative fathers. Edward was at least concerned and courteous, and acknowledged his paternity as a 'possibility' - but he wouldn't take responsibility at this stage. Tom, well aware of all that had occurred between Ingrid and Edward, and with more than a hint of schadenfreude, blamed Edward. And as for Charles, he claimed his skills of premature withdrawal made the whole notion of his fatherhood fantastic, and dismissed the suggestion out of hand.

In short, the reaction of these fine, post-Victorian freethinkers was pretty much that of their fathers. All of which Paula, reporting back, edited gently, concerned that Ingrid should feel the minimum of hurt.

Yet one man was destined to behave differently.

Three days later Ingrid was poking around the newspaper section of Smiths, dilatorily pursuing Mrs. Crosby's suggestion that she update herself on Ireland. The rasher commentators were predicting 'civil war.' Then she heard a politely stifled cough, realised it came from a man behind her, and turned to see the smiling face of George.

"George!" she exclaimed, in genuine delight. Indeed, she was surprised how pleased she **did** feel.

"None other. So why are you ferreting around the blatts? I thought newspapers weren't quite your line."

"They're not. But in extreme circumstances I have been known to read them. And things in Ireland are certainly getting extreme."

"They surely are. But I know why - they're my relatives. Did I ever tell you my father came from Northern Ireland? My aunts and uncles spend their entire lives feuding – that's when they're not drinking, or fighting in the streets, or both."

Ingrid laughed.

"Then you must be the black sheep of the family. **You** don't strike me as a fighter - in the brawling sense, I mean."

"That's true. Fisticuffs aren't really me."

"Except, like me, when circumstances get extreme."

"Exactly. Though it would take a lot, I have to say, to get me fighting. It would have to be something **very** extreme - someone impuning your honour say, something unwarranted like that."

Now what on earth did he mean by *that*? Ingrid coloured.

"Then that would be very chivalrous of you, but I hope you'd show restraint. I've had enough aggravation, lately, to last me for life."

"I know, I've heard......." George seemed to falter. "That is to say, I've heard a little. I tell you what - "

"What?"

"Why not take a brief rest from your strife? I could buy you coffee."

"Well yes - perhaps – ....why not?" And now Ingrid felt another rush of pleasure. What was it about George? Surely more than *just* his manner.

And five minutes later they were duly installed, just fifty yards up the road, in the Cadena café – just three tables along from where, months earlier, Ingrid had had that first momentous tea with Alexey.

As they sat down, Ingrid gazed at George with new concentration. Like all who knew him, she adored him. No-one was more considerate or kind. And yet, for some strange reason, she'd never taken him quite seriously as a man. Was it his plunging, coltish manner? That 'sheepdog' thing? Or just that he seemed so young? Well, they were all young, for God's sake, and she was youngest of all. So how did that signify?

Moreover, now she eyed him more carefully, as it were for the first time, he didn't look particularly ingenue at all. Indeed, in one way he looked almost middle-aged; there was a firmness, a pipe-smoking thoughtfulness about him quite different from their other friends. And he was quite handsome, too, with his pale blue eyes and shock of curly, jet-black hair. How strange that she'd only just noticed.

"Do you smoke a pipe?" she asked.

"Eh?"

"Just wondering," grinned Ingrid. "It's merely that you look very much the pipe-smoking sort, but I've never actually seen you smoke one, ever."

"Well, it has been known," said George, "but it's very rare. Why do you ask?"

"Oh, I don't know, said Ingrid, " idle curiosity." But she did know. It was what a pipe seemed to represent. There was something irredeemably domestic about a man who smoked a pipe. Amiable and unthreatening. In short, a brother; not quite a man. Not quite a man?! What did that mean?

Then she realised she knew exactly what she meant. And she realised, too, she had lately had enough of men, in that sense, to last ten years. Right now, in fact, a brother was what she longed for.

They sat in silence. Ingrid glanced around the room.

"Do you smoke?" asked George.

"Eh?"

"I said, do you smoke?"

"Why do you ask?"

"Well, *you* asked *me*."

"A pipe, d'you mean?"

"Come now! Cigarettes."

"Well, it has been known – "

"- But it's very rare!"

And both laughed.

They'd ordered coffee and it duly arrived, rather splendidly presented on a silver salver. The waiter, to Ingrid's relief, was not the one who had so frequently served her and Alexey.

"Alright," said George, "Just one more question. It's this: **why** do we keep asking each other about smoking?"

"It's obvious, surely. It's symbolic."

"Symbolic of what?"

"Well, with pipes, with men, it's the firm, steady pulse

of masculinity....."

"That's me alright. And with cigarettes - with women?"

"It's the – well...."

And at that moment Ingrid realised just precisely what cigarette-smoking in women ***did*** symbolise, to some people anyway, and she stopped dead.

George saw her discomfiture, but just smiled.

"I have a better question still," he said, reaching over his shoulder to lift the sugar bowl from the tray. "It's this, and it's very serious indeed. Milk? No milk? Quite a lot of milk? Or cream?"

Ingrid chose cream.

Despite which Ingrid returned, now, to what was, these days, her regular mood: of sombre introspection. While George just sat there, sipping his coffee.

And continued to say nothing - yet somehow managed to project an intense, mute sympathy. So much so that Ingrid, remembering that vaguely suggestive remark he'd made earlier, the one about her 'honour,' found herself asking to her surprise:

"Tell me George – have you heard .....anything .....about......me?"

And George, who had heard things, looked kindly once more, and said again, "A little."

And in a flash Ingrid knew precisely what she would do: she'd tell George the whole story. She would get his support, and even his advice. And it said everything about the atmosphere between them that she knew such support would indeed be given, and given most graciously.

Above all because, in their talk so far, he had never, for one moment, put her under the slightest pressure. His tact had been absolute – so that now, equally, was Ingrid's trust.

Speaking in a low, but firm voice, periodically gazing around the cafe, she told him everything - well, everything about the pregnancy, anyway; the more complex shenanigans of the 'Cleopatra' club she left out. And above all she avoided the capo di capo of all questions – which man was father of her child.

And still, to her astonishment, George seemed utterly unfazed. Nevertheless, it was a huge confessional she was dropping on him, and she gradually sensed it was having its effect. Though not quite the effect she might have expected.

For when Ingrid paused for a moment, George sighed deeply, looked up at her and said:

"Did I ever tell you anything about my sister?"

"No." Ingrid never even knew he had one.

"Well, yes, my sister Rachel had a very similar experience to yours. Similar in some ways, that is."

And George told her Rachel's story.

At nineteen, apparently, Rachel – who was seven years older than George – had got pregnant by a young man she had met at the Guildhall School of Music in London, where she studied piano. She'd been aghast – George's father was a respected Cambridge academic – but she'd been deeply in love, and quite sure she wanted the baby. Her feelings, seemingly, were matched by her partner's. The sole difficulty, quite a hefty one, was that neither of them wanted to get married. "They were beyond that," said George. "Far too free-spirited. A bit like your Cleopatra-club friends, perhaps."

So, they came up with this clever idea. Rachel was due to go to a summer school the following autumn in France, almost exactly the time when her baby was due. Using this as cover, she would go abroad, have the baby, get it brought back, clandestinely, to England by a Frenchwoman they would pay - then have it fostered. Her friend knew a young woman who was herself childless and would be delighted to help. Especially as she, too, would be well paid. (Rachel's lover was not short of money.)

They would then find some excuse to visit the child regularly till they were ready to settle down. At which moment they would suddenly 'discover' that they too were incapable of having their own children, and would generously take over the fostering of their own child.

"You might think quite a lot could go wrong with this." said George. "You would be right."

For in the event the foster mother, not unpredictably, fell so deeply in love with the child, a little girl, that, when the time came, she balked at giving her up. Then Rachel and her lover fell out. And he went off to America. And the foster mother took his absence as a further, 'respectable' reason for not surrendering the child.

So by the time the girl was three, Rachel, now living on her own, had lost lover, child, respectability - everything.

Now Ingrid saw why George had been so reluctant to embrace the free-love adventures of his friends. He knew where such 'self-expression' could lead.

Nevertheless, as George once more subsided into silence, Ingrid realised he had yet to tell the story's end.

"So what happened?" she said. "How did it all work out?

But she instantly regretted her question. For the answer was evident on George's face.

And now, another silence, while Ingrid indulged her penchant for self-flagellation. How could she have been so crass, so unimaginative, as not to grasp that George's sister had killed herself?

It was George who broke the silence. Now his tone changed again - full of energy and practical suggestions. It was as if he was blaming ***himself*** for where the conversation had gone. What a tale to drop on Ingrid at this time!

So, what, he asked, did Ingrid need? Tell him what he could do, practically. Had she the medical information she required? Had she ......forgive him!...... broached the matter with the father? Ingrid told him what Paula had done. Had she any friends with comparable experiences, who thus might help? Ingrid told him about Mary Thornton. Anyone else?

"Well," said Ingrid, "there is someone....."

"Who's that?"

"Someone I would dearly like to talk to about all this, and who I honestly think *would* understand...."

"Who is it then, Ingrid....... do say...."

"My mother! Pathetic, isn't it? I....I..... just want to be with her. It *is* pathetic, isn't it?"

"I don't think it's pathetic at all, I think it's perfectly natural. Why shouldn't you want your mother in a crisis? The only question I find myself asking, and I really don't know quite how to put this ..... are you quite sure she'll be as sympathetic as you think?"

"Yes. I know it sounds surprising. But I know her. She's strangely liberal about such things. And she's never failed me yet."

"I believe you. And your father?"

Ingrid's mouth tightened. "That I'm *not* quite sure about. I think so. I hope so."

Now George was once again pondering.

"Have you considered – quite simply - going home? To Germany, I mean? This summer?"

"Well no, I hadn't – but I suppose it's a thought...."

"You surely don't have to tell the Crosbys *why* you're going – not at this stage, anyway."

And George expanded his suggestion. He was himself – as was Tom, of all people! - going to Munich for a summer school. And wasn't that quite near Entlingen, Ingrid's home? If she did decide to go, and they got the timing right, he could even escort her there. And maybe help her, later, if required - he'd be that close.

And as for Tom, well - they were going over separately, on different dates, they'd already arranged that, and he could ensure Tom was kept at a good, safe distance from Ingrid throughout their stay, unless she wanted otherwise.

Well, said George, she should at least consider it.

And Ingrid did consider it, long and hard, over the next couple of days. And the more she thought about it, the more she liked the idea. Go home to mother! To Entlingen! Gradually, the idea became an obsession. If she went back promptly, no-one would yet be able to read her pregnancy, physically. Then after arriving home and, hopefully, getting her parents, and their resources, on her side, who knew what else might profitably be done?

So, after two days cogitation, she plunged.

She asked to have a chat with Mrs. Crosby. She'd been in England for nine months now, she said, and recently, especially, she'd really missed her parents. She knew it was very last-minute but was there any possibility at all of her going back to Entlingen that summer? For a brief holiday? She knew, she repeated, how sudden it all was but it went without saying that she would do anything, on her return, to help the Crosbys out.

And though Mrs. Crosby gave her one of her strange looks, she said she'd talk it over with her husband.

By next day she had spoken to him: they were aware, after all, of Ingrid's frailties. So subject to the approval of Ingrid's parents, it was agreed.

And when Mr. Crosby wrote, as he did the same day, to Ingrid's parents, he strongly advised them, if it were at all convenient, to accede to Ingrid's wishes.

Not least because both he and Mrs. Crosby, he said, had become increasingly concerned, over recent weeks, about Ingrid's 'flightiness' and, even more, as Mrs. Crosby put it, her 'secrecy.' There'd been more than one time when they'd strongly suspected she'd fibbed about where she'd been - and when she'd returned from such trips, she'd been noticeably distrait.

Without being melodramatic, they feared 'a relapse.'

Back came an instant response by telegram. The Uberspeers would love her to come. Ingrid's mother, in particular, was rhapsodic at the idea of seeing her daughter.

And so it was arranged. Ingrid would leave for Entlingen on July 6th, in the company, and under the protection, of George. An arrangement with which the Uberspeers were entirely happy, as the Crosbys had vouched wholeheartedly, as everyone who knew George always did, for his utter reliability and honour.

And as for Ingrid - she found herself looking forward enthusiastically, even avariciously, to her return.

Chapter Forty-One

Meanwhile, at Westbury, the Thorntons' regime had entered its golden time. All the old programmes - the horse riding, the gardening, the cricket, continued as before. But now there were new ideas, ideas that had been quietly germinating in Henry's mind. Plans that Henry, ever more self-confident, felt inspired to try.

For Joe Parsons's workers were around more than ever - with the addition, these days, of Joe himself. Time and again he would turn up unannounced, round, jolly and grinning, and would set to work, usually with Ben or Ted, on something practical. Fence-mending, perhaps, or a little light mechanics.

Indeed, Joe only had to look – or so it seemed to Henry - at a mowing machine and it would work. Fortunate really, as with Henry it had always been the opposite: one glance and it would break down.

And it was remarkable how often such days would end with Joe suggesting they round things off at the Roebuck, with 'a sensible drink,' as he put it. 'A sensible drink!' ....how Henry loved that phrase. For behind it lurked the ghost of all those other drinks – wild, raucous, and hugely enjoyable – that **weren't** sensible.

One day Joe came in with a letter he'd written to another farmer, in an attempt to settle a border dispute without solicitors. As might have been expected, its tone was impeccable: easy, friendly and radiating common sense. But its spelling was atrocious. "Could you check it for me, Henry?" asked Joe. "Just want to get it straight."

And this gave Henry his inspiration.

"I'll do more than that," said Henry. "I'll teach you proper spelling and a bit of grammar too, if you'd like me to, then you'd be able to put the whole lot of them to shame."

Henry had seen things Joe had written and it was plain he had enormous problems putting anything on paper.

Joe pushed his hat back on his head, the way he did when limbering up for a laugh.

"Well, oy don't roitly know....."

"But only on one condition - "

"Whassat?"

"That you teach me mechanics. And I assure you, if you take up my offer, the one who'll need the patience will be you."

What Henry was suggesting, in fact, was the first of what he described to himself as 'learning swaps'- one of the new ideas he had been yearning to try. The notion was you matched two people, both experts at one thing and hopeless at another, and 'swapped' their expertise, so each became both teacher and student. Both idiot and expert in the same relationship. Henry thought this could do wonders for anyone's self-confidence and capacity to learn.

Joe gazed at him in silence, a study of surprise, intrigue, and amusement.

"Well! oy....oy...... well, oy don't roitly know.......but.....then...why not?"

And his face flooded into his most genial, jolly grin.

The next day Henry had his first mechanics lesson from Joe, and, in the evening, Joe started spelling lessons with Henry.

Soon Joe was coming three times a week, both for the 'swaps' and for more general work around the camp. And Henry was right - it was Joe who needed the patience.

Nevertheless, Joe spoke so well of Westbury that soon yet more of his workforce were drawn in - his son, Fred, and Harry Pick, and Ben Tennant and Ted Molesley. 'The whole catastrophe' as Joe put it.

So it seemed natural, in turn, that the Westbury boys would help Joe's workforce with the harvesting and as many as a dozen would sometimes work in Joe's fields; which Joe liked because it meant he had less need of the itinerant labour he usually employed in the summer (and never trusted) and which helped compensate, too, for any time spent by his workers at the camp.

So that it was all the stranger, in this happy atmosphere, that gradually, insidiously, Henry began to feel restless.

At first it just showed itself in a need to get away - to go off by himself for an hour or two, and read. The stimulus of socialising - the processing, perhaps, of all that human information - would become too much, and he needed quiet in which to calm down and assimilate.

For which a book, and his genuine love of literature, provided the perfect alibi. But it was more than that. Stumblingly, uncertainly, the way he formulated it to himself was that he seemed to be experiencing 'a form of starvation.' And slowly he realised what he was starved of. Writing.

Writing! This from the permanent possessor of a 'writer's block'; from the man who could sweat anxiously for two hours, write five lines and then flee, walking the hills for hours. (Two sides of the same coin, of course, as Alexey had pointed out.) From the self-flagellating torturer who was not only his own Torquemada but his wife's and family's too.

The victim was missing his own rack! How could this be? When he'd first stopped writing to concentrate on Westbury he'd felt a perverse exhilaration, a sense of freedom he'd not known for years. Yet now, seemingly, this had merely been a reaction. With the economic imperative removed, it was easier, perhaps, for his love of writing to shine through. And make its demands.

Gradually the feeling grew on him, and finding a huge, creamy-paged notebook he'd bought two years before but never used, he began to write short paragraphs, based on the events of the day. It was a kind of writer's notebook. He could say what he liked and stop the moment he got bored – less demanding, even, than writing a letter.

Yet steadily this process escalated until he found himself 'dabbling', as he put it, with the very project he had supposedly put on hold - the two collections commissioned by Cecil Hampton.

Late one evening he was sitting at his desk producing yet another version of the 'Stars' poem when Mary came in.

She peered over his shoulder.

"What are you doing?"

"Just fiddling about."

"Ah, that's the Stars poem, isn't it?" she said.

"Yes."

"It's very good," said Mary.

"Do you think so? Which version do you mean? There are twelve so far, I think."

"Twelve, really? You *have* been fiddling about. My memory is that when you stopped writing to run the camp you had only three."

"Well yes, I did then but as you correctly say, I've been fiddling ever since."

"But I thought you were relieved you could stop writing?"

"Yes I was, but I seem to need to do it anyway."

"You do indeed, "said Mary, and although she was still standing behind him, he could feel her smiling. She walked round in front of him, sat down, rested her head on her arm and gazed deep into his eyes.

"You secret fiddler you," she said. "Fiddling away in the depths of the night, all unbeknownst to me, and I thought you'd given it up. How long has this been going on?"

"Weeks," said Henry. "I've been betraying you for weeks."

"It's that muse again, isn't it.? You've been betraying me to your muse."

"I confess I have; but you know I love you even more than she."

"I'm glad to hear it, although, as you know, your muse is the one rival I'll accept."

And it was true. Mary had always felt the camp work and the literary work could be combined. The financial security the Westbury work gave was wonderful, but it would be a catastrophe, surely, if it took over Henry's life.

Maybe he should consider something like the suggestion made, Henry had said, by Anthony Parsons: camp work in the morning and writing in the afternoon.

Or, countered Henry, writing in the morning then camp work in the afternoon? That way he could use his brain first and body later – to unwind his brain.

Mary moved round behind Henry, massaging his neck.

"Get thee behind me, Satan," said Henry.

"I am behind you," said Mary.

"Seductress! What makes you think you can influence me?"

"Knowing you as long as I have."

In the event, both proved right. Henry did start writing in the morning; slowly at first, but with ever-gathering momentum.

Though the chief glory, for Henry, was what he did in the afternoons, which made such a contrast. Even the back-breaking task of digging stones and weeds from Joe's crops appealed to him. And when the rests came he would lie out with the other workers, and revel in the sun burning off his sweat.

In the mornings, in fact, he was pure mind; in the afternoons, pure body. And the luxury of drifting into both states gradually, without jerking himself forcibly from one to another, delighted him.

And who, typically, had enabled this wonderful state of affairs? Who'd spotted his 'starvation' without his saying a word, and, waiting with her usual tact for the right moment, seen what he needed and quietly enabled it? Who, even now, was amply fulfilling her part of the new arrangement, emerging not merely as his loyalest-ever supporter, but as cook, bill-payer, accountant and even administrator in her own right?

Mary, of course, Mary, naturally and forever; and with that came the inspiration for another poem to counter that constant limitation of Henry's work, its inhuman abstraction.

And the poem, 'Mary' came swiftly and readily. And though its theme, paradoxically, was how no made-up poem could possibly match his real-life wife, it came with force and vigour. And it was good.

As was their life, and that of all around them. One morning Henry woke up with, for him, a quite new feeling. It was a sense of lightness, ease and hopeful expectation. Turning to Mary's sleeping head beside him, Henry realised what this feeling was, that went so well with the fresh green of the trees outside and the promise of dawn.

It was happiness.

Chapter Forty-Two

A week later, at Westbury, Henry woke early. Another lovely day. He lay watching Mary.

There came the sound of the post.

During the hard times, moneywise, he used to dread its coming, with its bills and threats. He would never open anything on a Saturday morning, for instance, so he wouldn't have to worry about it over the weekend.

But now he had dispensed with such ploys. It had become what it had been when he was a boy - a thrill, an adventure, a romance.

He clambered out of bed, moving mouse-like to avoid waking Mary. There was a parcel, and one letter. The parcel was a seed catalogue – he'd been expecting that. He opened the letter. It was from Cecil Hampton, his publisher. He read it with interest. It was probably a response to the latest dollop of material Henry had sent him; work he was confident about. It had included the poem 'Mary', and others he had written about the children.

One reason Henry felt buoyant was that this was the second package he'd sent. And the first had been greeted with something approaching rapture. Cecil had declared the new poems Henry had added (and the old ones he had reworked) a real advance on anything sent before.

In particular Cecil had noted how Henry was humanising his material. 'Less poplars, more people', as Eric Rother, who read it too, had said. So Cecil would surely have liked 'Mary' even better. How good to have a sympathetic publisher!

Henry began reading. Cecil was indeed appreciative. "The vein you so productively opened you have tapped still further," he wrote. "More, you have learned to condense – or as Keats put it, you "load every rift with ore."

Even that most dreaded word 'but', starting the next paragraph, did not disturb Henry. Any praise from Hampton was often qualified, as it should be, and Henry always learned by it.

But this 'but' was different.

For what Cecil said was that he had just come from a meeting of his editorial board where they had decided, to his profound personal regret, not to publish Henry's collections after all.

Henry stared fixedly at the letter, held stiffly in his left hand. Mainly, he felt disbelief. Surely this could not be true! The letter was short, but even so there were a couple of lines of explanation. He scanned them avidly.

"Of course this will be a massive disappointment to you and naturally it begs questions. Suffice to say, at this stage, that it is the decision of the editorial board as a whole - not just mine.

"Yes, they have changed their mind. In essence they seem to feel your work is old-fashioned, and that we should be giving priority to publishing work that is above all ground-breaking and new.

"Typical was their critique of a poem like 'Memory' - the one that seems, however subliminally, (in fairness you said it yourself) to predict a European war.

"European war?" one said. "Everyone knows it's not even a moral question, but a practical impossibility in our interdependent world. Your

Henry Thornton, even though he feels, I'm sure, that he's a pacifist, is really in the same camp as Rudyard Kipling."

"But what you may recall," went on Hampton, "is that our firm's 'democratic' constitution means the board can overrule the publisher, and that is what they have done.

"So there is, I fear, no way their decision can be reversed."

Henry read it again; and again, and again, this time concentrating on the explanations. Even now, his main feeling was incredulity. How could Cecil – oh, alright, Cecil's firm – have changed their minds so dramatically? How could this be? He analysed the letter's every word, for clues.

He felt a stir behind him: Mary had woken up. He turned and faced her. She looked like one who gazes on a corpse.

"What is it Henry," she said. "What have you heard?"

Henry passed the letter to her. She snatched it and read it through. She glanced up.

"Oh, Henry," she said, and there was infinite sorrow in her voice. "The **bastards**. How could they? What does this mean?" She gazed wide eyed at Henry. For a moment, he was what he'd been when they first met: the father who knows all.

"What does it *mean*?" said Henry savagely. "It '*means*' precisely what it says – they aren't going to publish. It's as simple as that."

"But why?" said Mary, still staring. "Why? The reasons just don't add up. What's all this about an editorial board? It's Hampton's firm, surely, and his decision in the end. How could he change his mind so suddenly after such enthusiasm?"

"You ask *me* why?" said Henry. "How should I know? Because he's a publisher and has his own particular priorities and views; because he's not the man we thought he was, and we've been fooled; because something's changed and he isn't going to tell us about it - how would I know?"

"Oh Henry," said Mary, and again there was infinite sympathy in her voice. "I am so very sorry."

"And so am I," said Henry, "So am I."

He turned to her with the old, savage look.

"This much I'm sure you can believe: I'm sorry too."

But – as ever - what to *do*? Mary toyed with the idea of going, once again, to see Eric Rother. Cecil had said he would be writing to him. If there was a hidden human angle Eric would surely know it. "One thing I've noticed," said Mary. "When the reasons given for something are patently absurd, the cause is simple - they aren't the real reasons."

In the event it was Henry who went to see Cecil, in his London office.

And found no 'reasons'. As he reported back to Mary on his return.

"Perhaps," said Henry, "there's something he still isn't saying."

"Perhaps you should have told him how you felt."

"Really?" said Henry. "Really? You know my views on self-control in business. Argue in private, if you must, with people you really care about and with whom you need to clear the air - but not in public. As I've said before, in any such situation one should above all ask oneself 'what would Bismarck do?' That is to say - how would someone act who had passion and genius but self-control, too, so that nothing would be achieved but the most practical, realisable prospect on the table........and then, when you've worked out what that is.....do it," he finished lamely.

At which Mary laughed out loud. This was Henry at his most pontificating and absurd.

"What would **Bismarck** do?!" she said. "Come in Henry, your time is up. This is publishing, not the Congress of Berlin!"

"Is it?" said Henry archly, "is it? D'you know, I do believe you're right. My point was simply that even in these dire circumstances - ***especially*** in such circumstances – it's important to maintain a reasonable self-command and not let fly with one's feelings, however satisfying that may be at the time."

"And let fly with them at home, instead!" cried Mary, "Where it's safe, and where the only people you'll hurt are those who care for you, and won't hit back!"

"Yes! Yes! Alright, if there's no other way! And one might hope, perhaps that 'those who care for you' might realise that such restraint is maintained very much in ***their*** interests, very much for ***them***, and, above all else, not a jot for the comfort of the one who's exercising his self-control!"

"Ah yes," said Mary, "that's you alright. Selfish out of your deep-seated generosity, that's you! How strangely altruistic you are, to be sure, and to think I've mistook you all these years!"

"Go to Hell!" cried Henry, turning away from her; then a moment later he turned back, for he could hear a kind of coughing, snivelling noise he couldn't place.

Was Mary crying? He thought so; but in his savage mood he didn't even care.

Chapter Forty-Three

Meanwhile, there was still Westbury. Not the be-all and end-all of Henry's existence, certainly, but nevertheless a real achievement. As Mary constantly reminded him.

One day in early July Anthony Parsons wrote him a letter: he was returning to England in a week, and wanted to meet. Their 'Westbury experiment' had been a success. Now they must consider the future.

"There you are, you see," said Mary, "It's not all bad. You remember those hints he dropped that he was possibly looking for more than a stop-gap, maybe a successor? In practice he's been auditioning you and you've passed. He probably wants to offer you something permanent."

"Perhaps he does," said Henry, "But that doesn't mean I'll take it."

"It won't harm you to at least consider it."

"Well……. I'll talk to him," said Henry.

As expected, the interview started well, as such talks with Anthony always did. He was profuse in his praise.

"Everyone's amazed" he said, "although I think the person who's most amazed is you. In fairness, didn't I always tell you could do it?

"You certainly did."

"The whole thing has been classic Westbury," went on Anthony. He'd been particularly struck by Henry's 'learning swaps', he said, which Henry had talked about in his letters. "A lovely idea," he said. "Each learner both idiot and expert. No hierarchy. No anxiety. Pure Westbury!"

Nevertheless, said Anthony, with the air of one who reaches his point, what he'd really wanted, as he'd said in his letter, was to address the future.

Henry pricked up his ears. If Anthony wanted him to take over in the long term, he would at least consider it, whatever he'd told Mary

"You see, what I've decided is that for the immediate future I'm going to carry on."

Now *that* Henry had not expected. Why?

"Because I realised while I was away that Westbury was my life, my all, and even though I'm knocking on a bit, I really don't want to be retiring just yet."

Anthony paused for a moment and gazed at Henry, a smile playing around his lips.

"You see," added Anthony, "in a way I've been feeling ….how can I put it……a kind of **starvation**."

Snap! The very word Henry had used to describe his own reaction to being deprived of writing.

"I mulled it over a lot while I was in France. I'll give up eventually, of course, but only when I have to. And not just yet."

"And meanwhile?"

"Frankly, I don't think there'll be a meanwhile. I thought I'd start back right away. Although you'll have to show me the ropes of course. All these changes! And it goes without saying that I'd like you to stay as long as you like - given everything you've achieved it would be a crime to lose you. Oh, and one more thing -"

"What's that?"

"I've asked Robert and Jane Hamblin if they'd like to come back down to help. Remember them?"

What? *Robert and Jane*? Henry's heart lurched. He remembered them alright. For they, and Henry, had a torrid history.

Both in their twenties, they'd long worked, in the past, at Westbury summer camps. And they had, in the view of everyone, been disastrous. Authoritarian and ill-humoured, they hated everyone, and everyone hated them. Worse still, they'd reserved an especial antipathy for Henry.

Robert, especially, had made Henry's life hell in all the areas where Henry was vulnerable - which meant, effectively, anything practical. When he dealt with a flood, for instance, or split a plank while building, or struggled to unjam a lock……. most extraordinary of all was the day it emerged that Robert had removed, and even hidden, the mower's starter motor - all to 'prove' that Henry had lied about mowing when Robert was away in London. (In fact Henry hadn't). Behaviour verging on the criminal.

Yet Anthony, unlike everyone else, had always revered Robert - and Jane too: a source of mystery, given Anthony's acuity, to all who knew them.

"They've been working with me in London," Anthony carried on, "they've been superb. But now I think they could be just the people to take this place to its next level – you know, mechanisation, electrification, all that. Leaving *you* to concentrate on the human aspect, the things you do so well."

But Henry could no longer hear him. Robert and Jane! For setting aside their dire malevolence, there was another reason why they reserved a particular dislike for Henry Thornton.

Henry and Jane – unbeknownst to Anthony - had been lovers.

Unlikely liaison! True, it had been three years earlier, before Robert and Jane had got together, and true, too, the affair had been relatively brief: six months from start to tortuous finish. But lovers they had been, and Robert had known it.

Henry, of course, had been married, seemingly happily, to Mary. While Jane was a seventeen-year-old village lass, buxom, bouncy, much inclined to giggles and torrents of song-like laughter. She worked two days a week as a volunteer at Westbury and was exceptionally good at what she did, especially with the boys aged under eight. Yet she never opened a book, ignored painting, and had never heard of the classical composers Henry so revered. What could she and Henry possibly have in common?

Almost everything, it turned out - everything that counted. For her part, Jane plainly felt there was something special about this sensitive, artistic man, so utterly unlike – this much was true – the men she'd known in Westbury village.

While Henry felt embraced, enfolded, by the first truly unabashed sensuality he had ever known. Soon they were meeting regularly, deep in the forest.

Grinning roguishly, Jane's preferred name for Henry, when alone, was 'Big Prick'. And while prick size, large or small, was the last thing Henry thought about in relation to himself, it was encouraging, nevertheless, to be so called - a crude but flattering acknowledgement.

Quite soon, however, the inevitable supervened. Mary, sensing changes in her husband's manner, realised something was up. Eventually she accused him outright. Henry denied it. But as others, too, had begun to grasp what was going on, Henry decided to end the affair. What possible future could it have? Was he really about to leave Mary and the children – for Jane?

And, like many uncertain men, having made the decision, he made it ruthlessly.

He cut her off in one fraught, half hour interview, deep in the woods.

Jane left the village the same night. She moved in with relatives in London, to the area where the boys from the camp were based, the Hoxton end of Anthony Parsons' operation.

Which was where she hooked up with Robert Hamblin. Within six months they were engaged; in a year they were married. But she never let slip for a moment to Anthony or anyone else, excepting only Robert, what had happened. It remained unsubstantiated rumour, and at Westbury, in particular, everyone pretty much forgot about it.

But not the Hamblins. In the three years that followed they cherished a deep hatred of Henry - and everything that 'toffs' like him represented.

Soon Anthony ended his talk with Henry and went his cheery way, blithely unaware of Henry's reaction.

While Henry plunged yet deeper into despair.

Robert and Jane! On top of his publisher's rejection! On top of the ending of his Westbury regime! Henry knew exactly how it would turn out. Robert would undermine him at every turn, while Jane would stir the boys into resentment and even rebellion. It had happened before! Soon everything he and Mary had built over all these months, all that trust, good humour and camaraderie, would be destroyed.

What a difference a fortnight could make! Two weeks ago, everything promised fine; now, whichever way he looked, disaster.

Chapter Forty-Four

But what could he do about it? Nothing. And soon, as Mary feared the moment she heard the news, the twin debacles – the publishers and the Hamblins - began to destroy the Thorntons' family life.

First Mary, then the children, became the target of Henry's dire vituperation. Indeed, Mary felt she'd never known Henry quite so sick at heart, and therefore so cruel.

Every meal became a row, every chore a cause of huge vindictiveness - in which the event itself would only ever be a starting point, whence Henry would launch into a huge circumnavigation of every fault the other party might ever have had. The unfairness of it was intolerable.

The final trigger was a visit by Paula, brought down by George.

Hesitant at first, Mary gradually unburdened herself to her friend. And the more Paula heard the more furious she became.

She was angry, yes, at the behaviour of Henry's publisher, she was angrier still at Henry's reaction, but she was angriest of all with Mary herself. Above all her 'victimhood' and 'dependency.'

"Why must Henry always take it out on you? What about *your* needs, *your* pain, for Christ's sake? Not to mention the kids'?"

Mary promised to reform, but Paula refused to believe her - and harangued her all the more.

Mary brought out the bully, it seemed, in everyone.

Nevertheless, Paula's ideas turned out to be a time bomb. Again and again, over the following days, Mary found them returning insistently to her mind.

Above all she was sick of her husband's constant, self-absorbed depressions. Surely, if anyone had the right to be depressed it was she: put simply, how many of their difficulties were her doing, and how many his?

So when, around two o'clock one afternoon, after a miserable lunch (the children were in the forest) in which every attempt at conversation with Henry was resolutely rebuffed, she found herself doing something unprecedented in their relationship: she attacked.

"Come now," she found herself saying, "things aren't *that* bad." (Even now she masked her anger in empathy.) "Let's be honest: Westbury was, as you say yourself, only a makeshift - it was never what you really wanted. Which is to write. So at least Anthony's behaviour solves that problem for you. And it solves another, too - it means you'll get some course work done next term."

A latent worry of the golden period had been Henry's lack of academic study, crowded out by everything else.

Henry ignored her.

"What I mean is," said Mary, now with a slight falter in her voice, "There are silver linings, and I think we should recognise them ...."

Now Henry looked up.

"Have you been talking to Paula?" he said.

"Well, yes I have," said Mary, "certainly I have, but not especially about-

"- About what?"

"About us...."

"About us......" repeated Henry, gazing at her with the familiar sardonic air, but now with something new and frightening in his face.

"......Yes," he went on, "I would hope you've not been too heavily involved in discussion, with our mutual friends, about our private affairs – about *us*. "

As so often when she crossed Henry, Mary felt nervous: her voice broke, she even stuttered. How she hated herself at such moments! Gathering courage, she carried on.

"It's not that there isn't everything in the world to worry about," she said, "and the way people have treated you has been desperately unfair, it's just that you never seem to see anything positive in our lives at all! Surely, it's when things are bad, above all, that you should be optimistic – in fairness to me that's what I've always done. I've done it for both of us!"

"Yes, throw that at me too," said Henry in a detached, even tone, looking away from her.

"I'm not throwing anything at you! I'm just trying to be real! I'm just pointing out that even in the most difficult situation there's always a way forward, and you have to grasp that, if only for mere survival, and above all never give in to narcissistic, self-regarding -"

Henry still ignored her.

Mary threw in her last card, the one that never failed.

"Alright, don't think of me, think of the children! Think how it is for them to live in this atmosphere, day after day, week after week! Think how *they* feel!"

And mentioning the children did indeed hit home. Henry turned to her in cold, sober fury.

"Yes, I do think of the children. I think of you, too. I think of all of us! And as for reality, there's one thing you've left out."

"What's that?"

"Money!" almost shrieked Henry, with a violence, contrasted with his earlier icy quietness, that made Mary jump.

"Money!!!" He almost screeched. "You realise we' re going to lose all that ***money*** you so desperately care about, and that got us into this weird, impossible, would-be-managerial situation in the first place! When I stop doing what I'm doing I'll no longer get paid! (Of course, Anthony hadn't said that, but at this moment Henry believed it.) "And think of the effect that'll have on you, and on your ever-beloved children! This much I can tell you, *that* bothers me, indeed it breaks me apart, and I wouldn't call that concern especially narcissistic – though maybe you would!"

Suddenly, Mary was staring into the eyes of a madman.

And for the first time in their relationship, Mary felt physical fear. He could punch her, knife her, do anything at all – she knew it. Yet moments later back came the guilt. Of course, Henry felt the loss of the money – he always did. So far, far more than he admitted.

"Oh, darling," she said, stumbling and sniffling now, reaching her hand forward to caress his face. But Henry caught it and threw it aside - with such force he nearly knocked her over. Mary burst into tears.

Which was, for Henry, the last straw. He advanced on her with hand held high. Mary shrieked with horror, dodged round the table, and rushed out of the room.

But Henry didn't pursue her. Instead, as if felled by a shot, he slumped into a chair: looking back she saw him staring in front of him with the same blank balefulness with which their conversation had begun.

And now an icy silence enwrapped the whole family, and went on for three days.

Till gradually Henry began noticing something new: a cracked, desolate expression on Mary's face, a combination of deep sadness and what seemed, for all her youthfulness, like premature age.

For the first time in their relationship, she looked almost ugly.

And he knew why.

To peer into her sad and battered face was to gaze as into a mirror. His own angst, his own perversities stared straight back at him.

And that realisation, unthinkable and yet undeniable, made him angrier still.

Chapter Forty-Five

Not least because he saw too, in her eyes, something more than sadness. A strange, indefinable resolution, a mood he knew of old but had no idea how to interpret at this time.

Yet he felt it with good reason.

Mary had decided to leave.

The events of the last two weeks; the extraordinary viciousness of Henry's behaviour; the impossibility, as Mary saw it, of things ever improving; and, above all, the 'time bomb' of Paula's intervention, which only worked because it articulated what Mary was already feeling - all coalesced into the certainty, finally, that she must act.

So now the battered vacant look was replaced by the firm, determined knit of her eyebrow, and her walk regained its soldierly resolution.

One day, after yet another spat had propelled Henry out of the house into his beloved forest, Mary sat down and wrote a telegram, followed by a series of short letters. The telegram was to her sister Helen (who, hearing about the latest situation, had insisted Mary come to stay) announcing that she would take up her offer right away.

While of the letters, the first was to George, telling him what had happened, and asking him, as far as humanly possible, to give Henry support. The second was to Paula, letting her know she was finally taking her advice. And the third, a note rather than a letter, was to Henry. "I have left," it declared baldly, "and gone to my sister. I have taken the children. I will be in touch."

She walked quickly into the village, sent the wire and posted the letters. An hour later she went back and picked up her sister's response. All was well. Helen was eager to welcome them. And within two hours of the kids' return from school, before Henry had come back from the forest, they were gone.

Yet when Henry returned, and found what had happened, he was less than astonished. For he had been dreading something like this for days. And from the clipped, matter-of fact tone of Mary's note, he knew she meant it.

She had left, finally, and taken the kids. The last link had fallen into place. Everything he valued had been destroyed.

Yet Mary herself, duly ensconced at her sister's, soon had second thoughts. While outwardly firm, especially with Helen, she noticed things. For a start the children, confused and devastated, immediately missed their father. Little Josephine, especially, was inconsolable. Then there was the question, too, of what would happen to Henry. A couple of letters to friends weren't much provision for someone who would now, presumably, be more depressed than ever, and might, she feared, do anything.

Soon, removed from the constant, carping pressure of Henry's sarcasm, she felt what she had never really lost for a minute: the fundamental, beyond-logic fact that right or wrong, crazy or sane, she loved him.

So after three days in which she felt increasingly aghast at what she had done, especially the speed of it, she arranged with her sister to look after the children, and travelled back to Westbury to see how Henry was. After all, she told herself, there were all manner of things to be sorted out - the food for Henry, the bits and pieces she needed for her stay.

She wired the day before to make sure Henry would be there.

No reply. But she went anyway. Wednesday was a horseriding day and she'd never known Henry, even in his blackest moods, miss one of those.

Yet the shock was destined to be Mary's. For when she entered their cabin - Henry was out, presumably with the horses - she saw, on the table, a note in Henry's writing, addressed to her.

She snatched it up.

'Dearest Mary,' it read,

'I got your telegram. Thanks.

I'm afraid this will be a great shock to you but now I too have decided to go.

On Tuesday morning, just after you left, I got a letter from Alexey inviting me to France. It seems he heard about our difficulties, possibly via Paula.

I thought about it carefully and decided I would accept his offer. By the time you read this I will have gone.

I think it is better thus. To be honest I'm no good to anybody at the moment - neither you, nor the children, nor, frankly, myself – so the best thing I can do, in the interests of all of us, is remove myself from your lives.

To be more honest still, I'm not sure I've ever been any good to anyone ever, especially your dear self, which is why, whatever happens in France, I will not return.

Kiss the children for me and bear up. Both you and they have fine qualities which you will be able to draw on in this awful situation, and I am quite sure you will pull through.

Especially when Henry Thornton is removed from the equation.

God bless you all,

I remain, always,

Your loving

Henry

Dumbly Mary gazed at the page. This had, of course, long been a possibility. But the reality was more devastating than she'd thought. Had not Henry once said, "The one thing madder than the madness of our relationship is the notion that we would ever part?"

Yet now it had happened. Both had walked out, and their relationship was at an end. Though one curiosity struck her. Why, she wondered, had Alexey suddenly been so forthcoming with an invitation, that same Alexey who had been so disinclined to help Henry earlier, notably when Henry had asked him for help with his book? He'd been more than ready to help Mary....

And then she realised. Now, of course, instead of being a success, Henry was in the greatest crisis he and his family had ever known.

And Alexey was nothing if not forthcoming in a crisis.

Chapter Forty-Six

So now everyone seemed to be leaving for the continent. Alexey, of course, had been in France two months. Now Henry was off to join him; while George and Tom had had their Munich summer school pencilled in for weeks, and Ingrid was accompanying them. True, the holidays were looming, and all concerned were accustomed to travelling, but this was quite an exodus. As Mr. Crosby observed, it was as if some strange emotional tempest was in the air, a restlessness affecting everyone. "It's not just Ingrid," he said, "it's all of them."

It was unusual for someone as placid as Mr. Crosby to view the world in this way, yet there was something in it. The Cleopatra Club crew, for instance, looking back in later years, saw the wild shenanigans of that summer – even individual disorientations like Ingrid's – as part of something much wider: a hectic unease that seemed to seize everyone as 1914 unfolded. An enforced gaiety, a dance macabre.

At the end of June crack units of the British fleet made a ceremonial visit to the German port of Kiel, at the mouth of that very Kiel canal whose widening had long alarmed Germany's rivals. The Kaiser hosted them, sailing up the canal in his royal yacht, the Hohenzollern, and there were dinners, dances, sailing races.

On June 28, the Kaiser, competing aboard his racing yacht the Meteor, spotted a German launch in his wake, struggling to catch up.

Aboard was Admiral von Muller, Chief of the German naval cabinet. He bore a brief but eloquent message. Earlier that afternoon, in the Balkan city of Sarajevo, the Archduke Franz Ferdinand, heir to the Austrian imperial throne, had been assassinated.

The menace, so long sensed by Henry, so readily dismissed by everyone else, had become real.

Chapter Forty-Seven

Real enough, indeed, to invade the Crosbys' breakfast table, that noted sounding board of international events.

It was June 30th, two days after the assassination. The first bits of journalistic analysis were appearing.

Mr. Crosby, stuck on his first cup of tea, while studying a piece in the Manchester Guardian, suddenly sat up, put down his newspaper, pulled off his glasses with a dramatic air, and said:

"I wonder if this could be it."

"It, dear?" said Mrs. Crosby.

"What Bismarck said to Ballin all those years ago. "I shall not live to see the World War,' he said, "but you will. And it will start in the East.'

"Ah, that 'it'."

Mr. Crosby looked irritated.

"Ingrid's father told me," he said. "He got it from somebody at Sanssouci."

Ingrid looked up. But she remained preoccupied with Harry and Jane, who'd been squabbling throughout the meal.

"Well, Bismarck was right about one thing," said Mrs. Crosby, "he certainly didn't live to see his war. But what makes you think he predicted what's happening now?"

"Because he was Bismarck!" said Mr. Crosby. "Which sounds ridiculous. But one thing that man was, above all else, was a visionary. He saw things, intuitively, which he could never have logically explained. Although, having said that, there's no shortage of logical arguments as well."

Mr. Crosby settled back in his chair. He's revving up for some periods, thought his wife – she knew the signs.

"The constant instability of Turkey, and the determination of Russia, eager for the Straits, to exploit this; the equally remorseless decline of Austria, and her fear of the 'battering ram,' as it's been called, of Serbia; the endless, shameless feuding of every other state in the Balkans, their betrayals, their constant wars, not to mention the malign influence on them all of Germany, quite as much as Austria and Russia....."

"Germany?" interposed his wife. "Russia, yes, Austria naturally, but why Germany?"

Once more Mr. Crosby looked irritated. But Mrs. Crosby carried on.

"Surely the whole point of German policy, especially your beloved Bismarck's, has always been to keep **out** of the Balkans, that's Austria's affair." She didn't remotely mean it, but she loved to puncture Henry's periods, which she viewed with a mixture of irritation and amusement.

"Well not Germany directly, I grant you," conceded her husband. "But Germany through Austria, certainly. As Germany's last reliable ally in Europe she's forced, whatever Austria does, to back her up."

"Oh, you see the hand of Germany everywhere," said Mrs.Crosby, "Like everyone does these days! Doesn't he Ingrid!" Ingrid looked up again. "You'll be quoting Bernhadi soon, the *drang nach osten,* Greater Germany, Weltmacht, and all that! But it's all so absurdly exaggerated; Bernhadi is only one part of German opinion, and not even a particularly significant part. To be fooled into viewing Germany in this way is to fall hook line and sinker for the Daily Mail. David, I'm surprised at you."

Now Mr. Crosby looked almost angry – yet amused, simultaneously, just like his wife. They were limbering up, Ingrid realised, for one of their sparring matches, an aspect of their relationship she found intriguing. Now, finally, she gave them her full attention.

"Come Lucy, you know I wasn't saying anything of the sort. All I am saying is that *everyone* is involved in Balkan politics, and that's what makes it such a tinder box. Anything could happen there at any time, and when it does, kaboom, the whole thing goes up in a flash! That's what Bismarck meant, and he was right; it's the one place in the world where everyone is involved, yet everything is beyond any individual government's control."

"And what *I'm* saying is what I was saying to Ingrid just the other day- did you get that newspaper, Ingrid?" (Ingrid nodded) " - all this talk about a European war ignores the one thing that's happening right now, right on our doorstep: war over Ireland, and *civil* war at that."

"Well, not quite civil war *yet* dear, although I agree that - "

"Curragh? The British Army mutinies?"

"Well, only the officers, dear, and only resignations - "

"57 out of 70, and the commanding officer too?"

"That's true of course, and yet - "

"And all but two resigned from the Fifth Lancers, and the same as well in the Sixteenth?"

"Where *do* you get you information from, Lucy! My, what a mine of knowledge!"

"Sources, David, sources" said Lucy, subtly smiling.

Then both of them were laughing. And a kind of peace was declared. But then this was the pattern, it seemed to Ingrid, whenever they squabbled. The facts were irrelevant - what counted was some strange, half-humorous, half-sexual battle for power.

Even so, as also always happened, both wanted the last word. This time it fell to Mr. Crosby.

"Nevertheless, I do feel we'll be hearing more about the Balkans. Not least because the Kaiser *will* feel compelled to get involved – whatever you say, Lucy- and he may try anything, almost on a whim. What is it his own subjects call him? 'William the Sudden.' And what did Asquith say? "There's something strangely childish about German diplomacy.' Very true."

Lucy Crosby, mollified by her success, nodded limited assent; but down the table the other adult present, who had up to then been far more interested in the form rather than the content of the dispute, felt suddenly insulted. Germany *childish*? How dare they? By what right did they thus infantilise a great country - *her* country, and in her presence for heaven's sake?

But perhaps it was not so very surprising that this particular insult stirred Ingrid's patriotism. Any imputation of childishness, in her or anyone else, was, for Ingrid, like a red rag to a bull.

And now another telegram from Ingrid's parents. And for the first time a note of urgency. 'Advise come promptly,' it said. 'Developing European situation means possible travel problems." This was a new dimension. So Ingrid steeled herself and talked it over briefly with the Crosbys and they were, predictably, reassuring.

Her parents had undoubtedly meant some kind of manoeuvres, they said, but they would be merely precautionary. It was extraordinarily unlikely anything would happen. "We've seen it all before," said Mr Crosby.

While Mrs. Crosby re-iterated that Sarajevo was an Austrian affair, not German, and would surely be well contained within the Balkans. Like all the other Balkan firestorms of recent years.

With which Ingrid gratefully agreed. After, all without wanting to be callous, this was only an assassination. It wasn't as if anyone was trying to grab another country's land.

No, nothing would happen! God knows, as the Crosbys said, it would be sorted out. This was how it went in politics, there was this huffing and puffing and brinkmanship and in the end there was a deal. The big powers, especially, had too much to lose, and too much experience, to make idiot mistakes.

Nevertheless, this 'war fever', as Ingrid thought of it, joined Ingrid's other anxieties at 3.18 am.

It was less than a week, now, before she was due to go. She and George - Tom was travelling later - were booked to leave Victoria on the morning of July the fifth. Setting off earlier, whatever her parents' nervousness, wasn't really an option. She had plans to make, things to arrange.

And yet.... her parents would have understood such difficulties.....and still they'd sent the telegram........ she wondered what they knew the Crosbys didn't. Nervous as her father often was about other things, he rarely got hysterical about politics.

Added to which, as a German, albeit in many ways a singularly unpolitical one, Ingrid did have an inbuilt, centuries-old sense of insecurity. Her personal paranoia shaded into the national. Especially the thing everybody at home was always on about: 'encirclement' by other hostile powers. Dimly she could see how Austria and Germany might try to keep any conflict limited, but what about their enemies? Weren't they increasingly in league?

It was, potentially, a game of big power dominoes, each counter bringing down the next and the finish could be Armageddon.....no, it was unthinkable! It was a fantasy, not part of the real world. Statesmen were too sane - in their own interests, you didn't have to look for any finer motive - to actually *create* catastrophe. It was, Ingrid decided once again, her own problems inflating her fears.

Time sped on. Three days, two days, then just twenty-four hours before her departure. And then it was the day itself, and Ingrid, accompanied by the whole Crosby family, and her usual improbable collection of bags, found herself on the platform at Victoria station, waiting for George.

The wait was brief. Unpunctuality wasn't George's style. He appeared – and now the Crosby family were grinning as happily as if he had been their own son. While Ingrid, feeling nervous, felt reassured the moment she saw him.

And now everyone dropped into the strange, hectic jollity people reserve for farewells. Two porters helped George and Ingrid hoick their baggage onto the train; the children lost, then found, the chocolates they'd bought to bid Ingrid goodbye; they had a brief row, settled by Ingrid; then she and George got on the train and leant out of the windows, quips whistling between them and the Crosbys.

Till suddenly, through the glass of the station ceiling, Ingrid glimpsed sunshine and blue sky. The day had started dull but was now transformed. And Ingrid felt a flash of her old sense of adventure. She grinned ravishingly at George.

Then the whistles went, the train started moving, and just as they began to roll Ingrid saw, she swore, Mr. Crosby on the verge of tears. She noticed, too, that Mrs. Crosby was staring at him, looking severe.

The Crosby children kept waving, jumping up and down, till the last. Then the travellers moved back into their compartment, flopped down, and suddenly, from nowhere, Ingrid felt a lurch of grief.

Chapter Forty-Eight

Two days later George and Ingrid were rolling steadily toward Munich. There they would part. George heading off for his seminar, Ingrid joining her parents, who were coming up from Entlingen to meet her.

George gazed, as he had so often during this journey, at the crestfallen figure sitting opposite, this Ingrid who had always been so bouncy, cheeky, and resilient. And his heart went out to her - so pale and crushed-looking! The real wonder was how she'd coped as well as she had. It was only in repose, when less able to control herself, that she seemed really deflated.

But there was more than sympathy in George's stare. For whereas Ingrid adored George as a friend, hugely valuing his gentleness and understanding, George felt something more – he was deeply attracted to her.

George, like so many others, had succumbed to Ingrid's charms.

Not that he was about to admit it, least of all to himself. For one thing, there was loyalty - loyalty to Alexey, curiously enough: despite everything that had happened, George still felt Ingrid belonged to his friend.

For another, there was her pregnancy. From his sister's experience he knew too well what that could mean, utterly excluding, in George's view, anything but sympathy at this stage.

Yet there was a third factor too, the one, perhaps, George felt least inclined to admit of all. And that was because for all his reasonableness and maturity, which so impressed all he met, George felt himself, in many ways, only half grown up – through his ignorance of sex.

Like so many middle-class boys, he had spent his adolescence at a boarding school, totally segregated among males. And unlike more moneyed, cosmopolitan friends like Alexey, or the Germans, or, pre-eminently, Charles Fisher, his home couldn't provide him with the social education he lacked at school. His father was a Cambridge academic – and a Northern Irish Unitarian at that. How George envied the likes of Alexey his sophistication! How overshadowed he felt every time a woman entered the room!

What he failed to grasp, of course, was that his very shyness - linked with his self-evident delicacy and warmth - had its own undoubted charm. Especially compared to a blabbermouth like Tom.

Yet what made the present situation poignant was that Ingrid, perversely, seemed an exception to this rule. For despite all her fondness for George she felt, as we have seen, some strange lack in him, some fathomless *je ne sais quoi.* And George knew this.

But soon they were in the outskirts of Munich, and, with the expectation of arrival, George's spirits rose. This was Germany, after all! This was the heart of the new Europe, the place that had thrilled and fascinated George throughout his previous visit, with his parents two years ago, to Berlin.

Germany! The home of Bach, Mozart and Beethoven, the land of Goethe, Schiller, and nowadays, the incomparable Rilke, of higher criticism, moral experiment, of Wagner and Nietzsche! The empire which had come from nothing to become the second greatest industrial power in the world. The land whose army had been the terror of Europe since 1870, and whose navy, ever expanding, had caused a series of naval scares in the UK, from the century's turn.

You could say a lot about Germany, but you could never accuse it of being dull. Nor anything other than the ideal place for a young man in search of adventure.

Moments later they rolled into Munich station, Ingrid leaning half out of the window in her excitement. Suddenly there was a kind of explosion amid the crowd on the platform, a wild, childlike jumping up and down. It was her mother! And behind her, grinning boyishly, her father, patting his hair down in the breeze.

Then Ingrid and George were out of the carriage and, like two arrows, Ingrid and her mother shot into each other's arms.

And Ingrid's bags were unloaded, as ever a complex job, then George's, much simpler, while the travellers sketched in their journey. And Ingrid's parents told Ingrid the Entlingen news, which wasn't much, each story greeted with re-echoing gusts of laughter.

So jolly, in fact, was the meeting and so readily did the Uberspeers take to George that it seemed inevitable they should ask him when he had to be at his seminar, and where he was due to stay. In the hope, clearly, they might have tea together before he went on. And when George explained that though the seminar itself was in Munich proper, he would in fact be staying in lodgings at Frolich, just five miles away, more whoops from the Uberspeers.

George could come back with them, even stay the night! Or a couple of days! Or a week! Because it would be half an hour on the train, perhaps less, for him to get back to Frolich from their house.

The invitation pleased George, but at the same time, warning lights flashed. Was it really politic, in the circumstances, for him to spend that kind of time with Ingrid's parents? Given everything she would shortly have to tell them? Might he not queer her pitch? Nevertheless, meanwhile.... well .....just going to tea - oh yes, alright, maybe overnight too - that would surely be fine.

Entlingen was in the foothills of the Alps, a good seven miles south of Munich. They glowed, an ice-blue enigma, in the distance. Yet even in Entlingen there were considerable hills; and by four o'clock, with the valley in shade and the hills in brilliant sun, they drew into Entlingen station. Twenty minutes later the Uberspeer dog cart, followed by Ingrid's baggage on a separate, hired buggy, drew up at the Uberspeer house.

Inside she let herself be shepherded fussily upstairs by her mother, who then left her alone in her room, to sort herself out.

She flung herself on her bed, exhausted.

Meanwhile, downstairs, George discovered new excitements. Ingrid's father, much encouraged by various neighbours, was suggesting a party to welcome Ingrid back. And it should be soon, no?! As soon as possible! Say, in a couple of days?

George wondered. Was that really such a good idea, given the state Ingrid was in? And he noticed, unless he was very much mistaken, another dissenting spirit in Ingrid's mother, voluble about her daughter's need for rest.

But all such discordant notes were soon swept aside in a floodtide of Teutonic 'heimat' enthusiasm, and within minutes the party was fixed for the following Wednesday – just two days on from then.

Chapter Forty-Nine

So two days later, at three-o'clock in the afternoon, Ingrid found herself amid a roaring cacophony of Uberspeer guests, plus George, all invited to celebrate the return of what Herr Uberspeer called, rackishly, 'the prodigal.'

The Uberspeers, in a remarkable piece of improvisation, had laid on an elaborate buffet *abendessen* of which the centrepiece was a large silver tureen of champagne cup. From this the guests, using a ladle, were taking generous pulls. They poured it into flagon-like glasses. It was already having the predictable effect.

Ingrid, flagon in hand, formed the centre of a rowdy group.

Her first instinct had been to avoid drinking anything at all, or only a very little, but her mood had taken another plunge before the guests arrived and she'd craved alcohol to cheer herself up. For Frau Uberspeer had explained how eager her husband was to 'show Ingrid off', as she put it, (she spoke with the air, it must be said, of one who indulges a little boy.) And Ingrid knew, from long experience, that her mother would in the end do exactly what her father required. This was not a trait in her mother that Ingrid admired.

And most especially did she feel this as she had already had the inevitable first conversation in which Frau Uberspeer, baffled in attempts to pump George, had tried to establish why the Crosbys felt Ingrid was so troubled back in England.

Ingrid hadn't, at this stage, been up to telling her mother the full story, so she'd given a limited truth: a polite version of her misalliance with Alexey. And her mother, as Ingrid expected, had been satisfied. She knew how deeply Ingrid had been thrown by her affair with Heinrich - the very one indeed, which had precipitated Ingrid's 'recuperative' trip to England. No wonder her daughter had returned so shattered.

And yet, thought Ingrid savagely, surveying the surging masses of 'her' party, the fact that her father knew the state she was in hadn't stopped him from fixing this foolish celebration. So she stood and laughed politely, glass in hand, with a gaggle of Frau Uberspeer's friends who had captured her, gazing at the only too familiar assemblage of guests in the room.

There was that old fart of a professor, the spluttery one, and there was the judge, the one she'd challenged, all those years ago, with that 'judge-not-that-ye-be-not-judged' quotation…….. and here, oh dear oh dear, came that best friend of her mother's, Frau Schumacher, bearing down on her like a galleon in full sail.

What was this? Ah yes, she was pumping her about her time in England. Had Ingrid managed many trips to London? Been to the theatre much? Had she got out to Blenheim, that German-sounding palace just outside Oxford, described by some as the British Potsdam……..

By the way – waggish, now - was George *really* just a friend? She doubted it! She'd seen how he looked at Ingrid and she knew that look, it wasn't a friend's look, no! "Confess it, Ingrid you've been up to more in England than you let on!" (Frau Schumacher hadn't stinted on the champagne cup.) "Your whole manner is quite different from when you left. So much more - how can I put it? ……mature! Glowing! Grown up! Something has happened to you, my dear, I just know!"

At which Ingrid, volatile as ever, once more coloured – what had Frau Schumacher seen? Or even heard?

But she covered her tracks as best she could, poking Frau Schumacher in the ribs and giggling, so that the Frau congratulated herself, later, on the subtlety with which she'd flattered her.

"It's the one thing that never fails," she told her friend, Frau Schildinger. "The one compliment a teenager always wants to hear: that she looks older than her years. The exact opposite of us!"

Meanwhile George, across the room, had momentarily shaken off *his* gaggle of female admirers, also middle aged, who had surrounded him for half an hour. He surveyed the room – my, what a din! How unimaginable that any middle-class English party could be like this! But unlike Ingrid, that day, George loved this German 'full-heartedness,' as he called it.

And now, heading his way, was none other than the grand architect of it all, Ingrid's father, Herr Uberspeer.

"Why are you standing like this alone, lieber George?" he said. In fact George had been standing there less than a minute. "I think you are finding our German ways a bit too... what was that word David Crosby used to say of us... ... *hearty*, no? Very different from England, nein?"

"Well, it's different, certainly," said George, "but in many ways I prefer it. The English are too restrained."

"I know this," said Herr Uberspeer. "I have seen it often, on my visits to your country. But tell me George - on a quite different matter -" (some instinct told George this was the real reason Uberspeer had come over) "what is your feeling about the Balkans? Are you in England worried, like us? I have to tell you" - he lowered his voice - "there are many of us, especially people in the know, who are very worried indeed."

George made a point of looking attentive. There were things, clearly, Herr Uberspeer wanted to say.

"You see," said his host, "this situation is far more difficult than Agadir in 1911, let alone Morocco in 1905. They were dangerous, yes, but they were in Africa, the interests involved were not so vital. But this Serbian situation – this is Europe, and I know the Austrians. I know what they can do."

Now Herr Uberspeer looked still more confidential, yet strangely pleased.

"I know people who **really** know, and I can tell you the Austrians are determined on war. Of course, nothing, naturally, is being said in public, but believe me, they are. And if they fight Serbia, and Russia stands nobly by its fellow-Slavs, that will bring in France, too, Russia's ally, and then us, as Austria's ally, and then boom!" Uberspeer threw his arms wide. "You know what old Bismarck said? He said it to Ballin more than twenty years ago: 'I will not live to see the great war, but you will, and it will start in the East."

My God, thought George, is everyone in Europe quoting that remark? Ingrid had said it to him on the train.

But now Herr Uberspeer's manner was becoming more urgent still, and George sensed he was about to say the thing he really intended.

"Tell me," said Herr Uberspeer, "if that situation should arise, what would be the attitude of England?"

And he fixed him with a gimlet eye; and now George realised that he and Uberspeer were surrounded by yet another gaggle, this time of men.

"Well," said George, aware of the eyes on him, "That would be hard to tell. If I know anything about Sir Edward Grey, he would probably say: "Our response will be commensurate with events.""

Herr Uberspeer snorted.

"Yes, that is what Grey would say, but I asked *you*, George - what would *you* say?"

"Me? Well, clearly that would depend -"

"Depend? Depend on what, George?" It was the fattest of the group, cuttting in, looking more agitated still. "Are the German people," he cried, "not England's admirers, your friends, your **relatives**, virtually, after all? On what does loyalty to relatives 'depend'?"

"Well, for my part I love Germany, and I would certainly never -"

"Never what, George? Fight us? Is that what you mean?

"The last thing I would ever -"

"No, I have to tell you! I do not believe you!" Now this was yet another one, some old, spluttery chap with whiskers. Was this the one Ingrid had said had been a judge? "It is not the last thing, it is the very first, and you have been looking for a chance to launch this war since Victoria died! You are *jealous* of us, admit it, you have been jealous of us for years, and you will take any chance that you are offered to beat us down!"

The judge's face, wide-eyed and utterly out of control, was thrust right up against George and to George's amazement, it was more than anger, even, he could see there - it was hate.

"Well, personally, I really don't want to slap anybody down, I truly don't," he said lamely, and took another sip of his drink.

But at that moment George was rescued by.....a cake. There was a stir among the guests. The sitting room door was thrust open. Herr Uberspeer let out a triumphant 'Tarraa!' and there, on the threshold, was a quite enormous cake, at least three feet across, supported by two nervous and overburdened little boys. Shimmering on top were a mass of candles.

"And now Herr George – your song!" cried Uberspeer, turning to George with a sudden, disconcerting switch back to his former warmth. With a lurch, George remembered that he'd promised, earlier – under pressure – to sing 'an English comic song' at the party, and when he'd said the only one he knew was something out of The Gondoliers, which was hardly appropriate, Herr Uberspeer said it really didn't matter at all, anything by Gilbert and Sullivan would be fine. All Germans loved Gilbert and Sullivan, he said - almost as much as they loved Shakespeare.

Wild-eyed, George gazed appealingly at his only possible ally, Frau Uberspeer, but she just grinned and shrugged her shoulders. Beyond her, Ingrid looked more unavailable still – if anything (George saw the glass in her hand) she looked out of control.

But now the whole room, orchestrated by an arm-waving Herr Uberspeer, was clapping and chanting, rhythmically, 'Commeekzong! Commeekzong!' until finally George cracked, lifted his hand – instant silence – and, feeling as foolish as he'd felt in his life, launched into:

"There lived a king as I've been told,
In the wonder-working days of old,
When hearts were twice as good as gold,
And twenty times as mellow....."

And the little boys advanced precariously, plus cake, to the dining room table to the jaunty strains of this grotesquely incongruous Gilbertian song, while Herr Uberspeer raised his hand and called Ingrid over to cut the first slice, come on Ingrid, do us the honours, do please, let us show you just how much we have missed you…

All eyes turned on Ingrid, looking more wild-eyed than ever. But she seemed frozen to the spot. George moved quickly to her side. With his help, she recovered momentarily and mechanically, zombie- like, lurched a few steps forward.

But just as she reached the cake her eyes rolled upward like a pratfall in a play, and, to cries of alarm from the guests around her, she collapsed.

Chapter Fifty

There was a rush of guests to help, but in the event Ingrid came round almost immediately, and was quickly helped up. Her mother said Ingrid must go straight upstairs, so she and George, spurning offers of assistance, helped Ingrid to her bedroom, where they laid her down.

Moments later she was sick. Frau Uberspeer, obviously shaken, yet studiously calm, thanked George effusively but said 'we will look after this ourselves now.' The Uberspeers' housemaid had joined them. George felt it politic to withdraw.

He returned to a concerned and slightly sheepish-looking party downstairs. Ingrid's father, after a brief foray to Ingrid's bedroom, went back down too. But with the central figure of Ingrid thus removed, the party began to wind down, and soon broke up.

The next day a somewhat recovered Ingrid told George what happened next.

When Ingrid's sickness had passed, she'd stayed sitting up in bed, locked in Frau Uberspeer's arms. Her mother had rocked her back and forth, stroking her, caressing her hair, with little pecking kisses on the ear, just as she'd done when Ingrid was a child.

For ten minutes they'd sat like this, in silence. Ingrid had felt, she said, like one who'd just been saved from drowning.

Then finally her mother laid her down and told her to rest. Still nothing had been said; but rather than leave, her mother elected to sit and watch her, as one might watch the terminally ill.

And it was at that moment, inspired by this womb-like sense of security, that on impulse, falteringly, Ingrid found herself telling her mother the real reason why she had come.

She told her, stumblingly, about the pregnancy; she explained a little about the build-up (the 'shenanigans' were hinted at, if edited;) she mentioned her biggest dilemma, now, among the many facing her – her growing sense that *not* having the baby might be even worse than having it.

And her mother, though visibly shocked, was only the more concerned. So she pulled Ingrid yet more fiercely into her arms. And both wept.

All of which, though not intended, was what Ingrid had expected from the mother she knew. Yet even as she lay there, safe in her embrace, she realised the next question involved no certainties at all. What about her father? Now he would have to be told. And if so, when? And by whom?

For instinct made Ingrid far less sure of her father's reaction than her mother's.

So when Frau Uberspeer – no doubt sensing this - suggested that she, rather than Ingrid, speak to him, she acquiesced. Albeit feeling rather cowardly. But then, as her mother pointed out, she knew how her husband's mind worked, and his moods.

Nothing happened that evening. And the next day Ingrid, feeling better, busied herself around the house. Yet all the time she watched her parents' faces. Had anything been said? Did her father look more strained, more angry, or - wild hope! - more tender than usual? He gave little away – meanwhile his manner was as considerate as ever, and jovially hospitable to George.

Come the afternoon Herr Uberspeer left home for 'a couple of hours' to return books to the library. Ingrid was struck by how relieved she felt when he left. Just like the time when, as a child, she had a tooth extraction postponed from morning to afternoon. Two, maybe three hours' reprieve! With nothing changed, still everything to be faced - but oh, the bliss of knowing it wasn't happening right away!

Yet still the mystery of her father's mood. But then he'd always been impossible to read.

At 6.OO pm in the evening, Ingrid's mother appeared in her bedroom. She'd spoken to Ingrid's father, she said, and he wanted to see her. Nor was this so surprising - Ingrid had heard what sounded like a row just after tea.

So finally, here was Der Tag!

With a scarcely breathed "It'll be alright!' Frau Uberspeer motioned Ingrid down the staircase to the hall where, with a hand-clasp and a troubled smile she said: "I'll see you later."

Feeling like one who ascends a scaffold Ingrid trod the ten yards to her father's study, and was called in.

Chapter Fifty-One

And was struck immediately by Herr Uberspeer's friendliness.

He greeted her with a smile, kissed her lightly on the head. He took her hand and led her to the settee.

He looked into her eyes.

"Your mother has spoken to me," he said. "I know it all."

"All?" mumbled Ingrid.

Then her father leant over and hugged her with both arms - a thing he never did. Was it because he could see that she was crying? And as his face touched hers she could feel tears on his cheeks, too.

Then he drew back and seemed to change gear. Talking faster than usual, but otherwise as warmly as before:

"Look, Ingrid," he said, "as I explained, your mother's told me everything, so at least you already know this much, **you** won't have to tell me now. And let me say first of all and above all else, how much I feel for you! These last few weeks must have been a nightmare. And I would like you to know, too, how glad I am, and your mother too, that you have come home. It really is the best possible place for you to be.........

Then suddenly: "Look! Your mother and I have talked and the one thing we're absolutely sure of is this. You've got to have the baby."

Ingrid started. This she had **not** expected. What, he was suggesting she should have the child, and bring it up? With all the ignominy? Such moral courage was remarkable.

Her father carried on.

"Any......alternative.... clearly.....is unthinkable. It is far too physically dangerous, for a start. And we really would not want to risk you...... or your child....whatever the circumstances."

Still her father talked.

"Indeed, not only is there the danger, there is the dreadful cruelty of depriving any human being of life. What right have any of us to play God at such a moment?

"Far better, certainly, to have the baby and then see what can be done. There are all sorts of ways, some of them quite attractive, in which the child could lead a life worth living, even *more* worth living, in certain circumstances, than most."

At which Ingrid blanched. But of course! How could she have been so stupid! Her father was talking of *adoption*, plainly, that was what he meant. I.E. have the baby, but get rid of it, well out of their lives – probably secretly! - so the scandal would be gone. Regardless of any maternal feelings Ingrid might or might not have, and with the decision, to all intents and purposes, made by her parents alone.

So stupefied was Ingrid by this - above all by the manner of its presentation – that she sat tongue-tied for a good ten seconds. So her father, seeing her discomfiture, began again:

"Believe me, Ingrid, I absolutely understand your difficulty with this. The situation is impossible, for all of us!" The first flash of anger.

"And yet, you know, there really is no reason why adoption should be so bad, even bad at all. At least, when a child is with adopted parents, then it will be with people who actively want to look after and cherish this much-desired human being. Very different from innumerable 'natural' upbringings, as we both well know."

But Ingrid continued to stay silent, shoulders hunched, mouth turned firmly down in ways that reminded her father of how she'd been, when cross, at three years old.

So after another minute of silence, her father shook his head, sighed deeply, gazed at Ingrid with strange, intense attention, and said:

"Now, Ingrid, I am going to say something I thought I would never say, and hoped I could avoid saying today. Though I knew I might."

More intensity.

"And I should tell you that I have agreed with your mother that I should say this, if I had to, as ……it ………concerns us all."

Now, finally, Ingrid looked up at him.

"What I have to tell you, Ingrid, is that you are yourself.... adopted. Yes, adopted! Adopted lovingly, openly, with all the joyous expectation that you have surely felt over all these years. But adopted, nevertheless; and I tell you this because I want you to refer, now, to your own experience, so you can see just how attractive such a situation can be.

"This much, Ingrid, you surely cannot deny – how intensely you have felt loved, by both your parents, all these years?"

And this time Ingrid, utterly amazed, could not have said a thing had she been offered ten thousand pounds. More, her father now reverted back to her ***baby's*** adoption, not her own - impervious, seemingly, to the effect on her of his news.

After all, (he continued) he naturally wasn't talking about some abstract impersonal adoption, such as you might do through some kind of agency.

No, nothing like that! Obviously! Rather a proper, planned, considered relationship with a very particular family.

"I mean for instance, Frau Schumacher has this friend, Elly Zollern, who lives in Calberg, just ten miles the other side of Munich, not that far away, who's been longing for children all her life but has not been able to have them..." and as he saw the anger grow on Ingrid's face " ...she really is extraordinarily nice, and well off...." – yet more anger – ".....I mean you can't ignore that aspect! And naturally if any decision was to be taken of this kind, it would be taken by all of us, with your authority, obviously, being paramount ....."

And so he continued talking volubly as ever, while Ingrid's mind went whirling through what really mattered, what mattered above all – that her parents were *strangers*, however loving, and that her mother, especially, this creature she had adored and relied on all her life, was not even her own flesh and blood.

And that had been the one thing, above all, that had brought her all this way to Entlingen! The idea that here, in all her chaotic and uncertain world, was her sure and certain home. The heimat she was connected with instinctively, beyond mind or reason.

And her father was telling her these feelings were unreal! Ingrid was appalled. So distraught did she look that even her father, locked in his own deep self-absorption, could not but notice.

So gradually his tone eased, his advocacy slowed, and the points he made became softer, gentler. Indeed, he almost seemed to regain the sympathetic tone with which he had begun. Until he asked:

"Have you any idea at all, Ingrid, how your baby's father feels about this?"

Ingrid gasped. She'd forgotten that - what on earth to say!

"Clearly," her father pursued, "it is at least arguable that he should be consulted; in certain circumstances, he might even help."

"I..... well, you see...... I don't know....". Ingrid stumbled, and stopped.

At which her father, seeing her distress, said:

"I realise how delicate it must have been even addressing such things with him...."

Ingrid stayed silent.

"Have you talked to him at all about this?"

"I don't know..."

"You don't know? Forgive me" (just the beginnings of strain) "I can see how hard such a conversation must have been, but clearly you must know *if it took place*. What kind of fellow is he?"

Still silent.

Gently again: "Is he sympathetic?"

"I don't know."

And now, finally, understanding.

"Ingrid, who is the father of this child?!"

The longest pause of all.

"I don't know."

At which Ingrid once again dissolved into tears; while Herr Uberspeer, shedding the delicacy he had shown throughout their talk, looked, by turns, first comprehending, then aghast, then, finally, tremulous with wrath.

Moments later, vaguely mumbling, Ingrid tottered out, leaving her father still stuck in his armchair, staring fixedly at the wall.

Chapter Fifty-Two

So now what? For it was her mother's reaction she feared now, after what she'd let slip about her baby's paternity. What on earth would she think, come the moment when she would be told? What could Ingrid say? And she **wanted** to talk to her, even more than before, because all other horrors were now dwarfed by that bombshell of her 'adoption.'

So Ingrid strode off in search of her.

"Mother!" she called, in the sitting room downstairs. No answer. "Mother!" she cried on the upstairs landing. "Mother!" she yelled, finally, in the back garden, and it was there that she finally found her. Secreted on the far side of the shrubbery, part-hidden by the house. As if she'd been hiding.

But this time, unlike their earlier encounters, Ingrid's expectations were unfulfilled. For far from denying her husband's story, as Ingrid had so dearly hoped, all her mother would do, utterly distraught, was keep repeating, over and again, how "none of any of this, in any way, can change our love for you." And she refused, repeatedly, to say anything else at all.

And when Ingrid finally demanded: "Are you or are you not my mother, yes or no?" (only too conscious of the absurdity of any such question) it was Frau Uberspeer who sobbed and ran away.

Her mother rushed upstairs and locked herself in her room. Twenty minutes door-banging by Ingrid was ignored. So now, in a maelstrom of confusion, sorrow, and swiftly escalating anger, Ingrid went in search of her last possible source of sympathy, George.

Yet when she found him - reading in his room - she found it impossible, at first, to say anything at all. And while gradually, haltingly, she began to tell him bits and pieces of what had happened, she found it so hard that George soon realised that if he was going to do anything at all to help this family, he would above all else need time.

So he quickly offered, and he did this very readily, to stay at least three more days.

Off went a telegram to his would-be Frolich landlady, Frau Gross, followed by another to the director of studies at his seminar.

As an excuse, George wheeled out the old chestnut of influenza.

Chapter Fifty-Three

At which moment there came a telegram from Tom, addressed to George. It had been forwarded from Frau Gross. It turned out he'd arrived in Munich, had contacted the address George gave him, but heard he was away. And was wondering, understandably, what George was up to.

"Oh **God**!" cried George, as he opened it. He'd clean forgotten about Tom.

"Oh God," he said again, while Ingrid peered over his shoulder, assuming it was from Frau Gross.

"Oh God," she said, as soon as she saw the sender.

"Yes indeed," said George. "Trust Tom! What timing! In fairness, he's right; I owe him an explanation."

"Well then, you'd better give him one," said Ingrid. "But leave me out of it."

She was not feeling at her most charitable right now.

George fixed to meet Tom in Munich the next day. The sooner he went, he reasoned, the sooner he would be back, and could continue supporting Ingrid.

The Uberspeers were happy for him to go. They knew how much he meant to their daughter, and they realised, too, that if his help was to continue he must carry on with his life. He had to do something, for instance, about the seminar he was supposed to be attending. Tom Huntingdon would know the ropes.

George naturally assumed he'd go to Munich on his own. Yet that evening, when he'd once more fled to find peace in his room, there was a knock on his door.

It was Ingrid.

"I'm coming with you," she said.

"What?"

"To Munich."

"Munich! Really! Are you sure that's a good idea?"

"Quite sure. No, I don't want to see Tom, he's the last person I want to see, so I won't get in the way. Frankly, I just want to get out of the house."

"Well, if you're really.........."

"And I'd like to visit Munich. Entlingen has its virtues, but I've had my fill of small towns just for now."

And so it was agreed.

Chapter Fifty-Four

By ten the next day they were drawing in to Munich's Hauptbahnof station, Ingrid rubbernecking around as energetically as always when she entered the great city.

And there was the Frauenkirche, Munich's cathedral, with its tall twin towers, and their strange, Eastern-looking cupolas. There was the clank and bustle of trams, the clatter of pigeons, the rush of pedestrians, the cafes sprawling across the pavements of Marienplatz. And there, above all! were the fashionably dressed women, so notably more stylish than the locals back in Entlingen.

All of which would normally have been more than enough to raise Ingrid's spirits. Instead she felt a strange, blurred flatness, not depression exactly, more tiredness; this was one of the ways her nervousness took her, especially after a bad night's sleep. And last night had been a very bad night's sleep.

Nevertheless, she still hoped that 'Dr. Munich', as her father called it, would work its magic.

She and George had already agreed, at Ingrid's insistence, that they would part the moment they arrived at the station, to make certain she would avoid Tom and any friends. Not least because another telegram, late last night, had announced that Charles Fisher, no less, had arrived in Munich as well.

"Yet another of his escape jobs, apparently," said George. "Fled to Munich to study painting – he says. 'Fled his mother,' is how **Tom** puts it, and I think he's right."

Yes indeed, thought Ingrid, whatever Charles' motives, he was another huge reason to forgo any reunion. George would handle all that. He was due, it emerged, to meet Tom, and Charles, plus some German student friends, in the Zitronenbaum cafe, just by the Marienkirche, around eleven. Ingrid meanwhile would entertain herself (an art gallery, perhaps?) until around four o'clock, when they would meet at another café, the Eiffel Tower, in Neuhausertrasse. Then they would go home.

"Give my love to Tom and Charles," she said. "Or thereagain, maybe not."

"I think you're right there," said George, kissing her forehead. "Maybe not."

Which left Ingrid on her own. And now again the same, incongruous flatness, as she surveyed the scenes that had previously brought her such joy.

Stranger still, she found herself obsessed by, of all things, the smell and taste of *toast*. She'd dreamed about it the night before. Toast! Her dreams had long been weird, but this was new. And it seemed to involve, too, some vague, warm, enveloping male presence, though who or what this might be, Ingrid had no idea.

Meanwhile her mind was in its latest whirl of speculation. What **was** the story of her adoption? If adoption, that is, there truly had been. (At present, after all, she had only her father's word for it.) Well, WAS it true? And as for her father's anger about the paternity....... she understood his being disturbed .... but *that* disturbed? Reduced, almost to apoplexy? She saw more to this, a great deal more, than met the eye.

So what to do? Every option - exhibition? tram trip? shopping? - felt distasteful. Eventually, in the hope that shopping rarely failed, she made her way to Madam Confrere's, a specialist young ladies' boutique in the Kaufingerstrasse.

And there, as ever, were the latest fashions, selected with Madame Confrere's usual flair - the bias, as ever, towards Paris. There, appropriately, were those wide-brimmed hats - amazing how long they'd stayed in fashion. Ingrid had bought hers two years ago.

But then she noticed another section of the shop. It was in the darkness toward the back, a part that had evidently just been opened. It was for children. And on the shelves, a whole array of toddler clothes - jackets, trousers, frocks - and above all, boots. Red boots!..........Why did red boots, especially, strike her so? Of course..... it was because she herself had worn red boots when she was little ..... they were her mother's favourite...... when she was little…and moments later she was thinking, again, about the louring presence in her belly, and the clothes and sustenance this creature, too, would one day demand. Demand of someone, that is - unlikely, let's be honest, to be she.

She fled into the street.

And headed for the Englischer Garten, then scrapped that for the zoo, then ditched that too and hopped on a tram, getting off in Marienplatz and dropping instantly into her most forceful, determined stride, the better to tell herself how masterly and self-controlled she really was.

Nevertheless it occurred to her that her constant sense, today, of being out of place, out of time, with no connection or purpose....all this had a name. It was called loneliness.

And she found herself remembering something Alexey had said, all those weeks ago, one of a myriad things that seemed so true at the time.

He'd said that however much lonely people are ignored by others, there will always be some part of them, however unconscious, that actually sets up – creates - their isolation. Above all by the simple process of avoidance. And today, clearly, she had been doing that very same thing.

So it was the more perverse when suddenly, a hundred yards away, but distinct as only such a man could be, she saw, of all people in the world.... Alexey! *Alexey*!!! - and with him, or so she thought, *Paula* .... though they instantly vanished into the crowd.

Gott im himmel, what was this?!! She'd now reached the stage, apparently, of seeing visions.

Although it did underline, lonely or no, that if this *was* her state of mind, she must indeed avoid social contact. So she turned away, a good half mile before she reached the street where she knew George, Tom and the others were due to meet.

And found a seat under a fountain. And got involved with a mother and child. And stood up abruptly and went striding off. This time down Kapellenstrasse, also full of cafes, though these were smaller.

But her vision-seeing had not ended. For now, there, right in front of her, was...... Tom! And Charles! And George too! At a café ten yards away– shop windows had distracted her. And, a moment later, a roar of 'Ingriiiiid!' in Tom's crassest, most bumptious style, a vast grin on his face, and Charles looking flabbergasted, and George, in turn, appalled. For this encounter was no vision at all. It was real.

What to do? She had, in fact, no choice. They'd seen her. So she stopped and gazed at them helplessly, finally walking over and mumbling: "What a surprise."

"What a delight, rather!" cried Tom, as if this encounter were perfectly routine. Moments later Ingrid noticed a familiar reason: he was drunk. Wild-eyed, her gaze met George's, demanding explanation.

George continued to look distraught. Indeed, he looked, if anything, rather *more* alarmed than might have been expected. He said:

"We moved. We were at the Zitronenbaum but Tom suggested we came on here, because this was where he was due to meet his fellow-students. I'll introduce you -"

And a ring of bright-eyed, curious, young German faces stared up at her.

Tom did the introductions.

"Please to take a seat!" It was Tomas, fresh-faced and eager: he'd politely given up his seat so Ingrid could sit next to her friends from England. Tomas moved along one, towards the Germans, while Ingrid, determined to be genial, thanked him smilingly.

"So you are German," said another. 'Pitzi', he was apparently called. "But you are friends with all these English?"

George explained how they had all met back at Oxford.

"Ah," said Pitzi, eyes lighting up, " so Ingrid could be just the person to help! We were speculating - you know English politics, what will they do?"

Oh God, not the 'war' again! Was this all anybody talked about? Not that Ingrid needed to say anything, of course. For much like the lawyers at her heimat party, these students were only asking questions so that they, more importantly, could orate what *they* thought.

And off they went, explaining how the whole confrontation had been dreamed up by the British General staff, who wanted an enemy that might be 'reachable,' - unlike the Russians, with their threats to India, on the other side of the world - and how the other thing was Persian oil, and the deal the Russians and British had made to access it, let alone (the eternal mantra) the 'encirclement,' by all Europe, of Germany......

But Ingrid had already screened them out. Ach, young men are the same worldwide, are there any, anywhere, who will listen to anyone but themselves?

Although there had been one man who had been different in that respect, for all his faults.... Alexey........my god! that name again!..........because at that very moment, like a klaxon from heaven, she heard Alexey's name spoken out loud, guffawed and shrieked at Charles by Tom.

The two Englishmen were sitting the other side of George, having their own drunken conversation, and their talk, till now, had been drowned out by the students. But at the explosive word 'Alexey' Ingrid tuned in - and though she only heard bits, she worked out a great deal more.

For they were discussing, with much hilarity, Alexey's life in France. And Henry's too. Well, Ingrid knew that Henry had joined him. And Paula was being talked about as well. For Paula, apparently, had also gone over to visit Alexey - though this was the first Ingrid had heard about it.

But as for Alexey…. it seemed that when he'd reached France he'd got involved with some communist woman (this Ingrid believed) and they'd had an on-off relationship of a kind Ingrid recognised. Then when Henry had gone out to join him this relationship had been derailed.

Why? Because, incredibly, Henry had got involved - physically involved! - with Alexey. (*What? Did she really hear this aright?*) Yes! Tom was saying that everything anyone had ever sensed, subliminally, about Henry's friendship with Alexey had proved correct! (Ingrid had long heard such speculation but had ignored it.) That under the stress of events, and in the two friends' partnerless, new-found loneliness, their long-standing relationship had taken a quantum leap and they'd found their true capacity for love – with each other! They'd had, and still were having, a homosexual affair.

There was more, too, about the reactions of the communist, and more still about Paula's contribution, but Ingrid heard little of that, reeling as she was from the news of Henry and Alexey.

Clearly, it could not be true! Yet even now, mere seconds after first hearing it, some other, maverick voice, deep within her, was saying 'Oh yes it could.' Because for weeks now, come to think of it, she had sensed something of this – the force that drew these two men together.

Their faces would light up the moment the other entered the room. They had this constant absorption with each other's minds. They had this fascination, at any moment, with what the other might be just about to say. Whenever they met, and wherever they were, you felt it – far more than ever happened with their women.

This relationship could be real! Hateful though it was to admit it. Dreadful though it was for Mary, quite as much as she.

Yet Tom and Charles, chattering on, clearly found this yet more hilarity, ideal material for the bitchy gossip they both loved. And now Ingrid, who'd felt tense enough when she sat down, felt a violent rush of anger against men in general, against Tom, Charles, Alexey, the self-centred, insouciant students at her side, her father, George, (why not?), against the whole male world indeed, and got up, muttering something about 'the Ladies', and strode furiously back into the café, leaving her companions on the pavement round-eyed with surprise.

Moments later, George slipped off and followed her. For some reason she'd crossed the road to the café opposite. He caught her just inside its door.

Pouncing on him like a fury, treating him as if he had known everything all along, Ingrid described what she thought she'd heard, and demanded, had she heard aright?! George, looking more miserable than ever, confirmed that in broad terms yes, she certainly had.

Next, under pressure, Ingrid forced out yet more details - including Paula's contribution. Because, said George, when she'd appeared in France - herself disoriented by her earlier debacle with Ingrid - she'd got involved (blessed equity!) with the communist, who'd been smouldering at her rejection by Alexey.

No wonder Tom and Charles looked so delighted. You blink, and someone's changed their sexuality. You blink again, they've changed it back. The more you went into it the more ridiculous it all seemed. However, thought Ingrid, could she have got involved in such a farce?

And yet even as all this came out, and George assured her he knew nothing more about their friends' adventures, Ingrid felt George still had something of the weird, reserved air she'd noticed since they'd first sat down. Unprecedented for George. He looked positively shifty!

There was something else he knew, she sensed it, and it must be serious, or he wouldn't be withholding it. And the crosser she got, the more vehemently George denied any such thing, till finally she sat down, fuming, and declared she absolutely refused to move till George came clean.

But he still wouldn't say. What he did do, however, was make a decision: Ingrid clearly wasn't well, he declared, she needed to go home, and he would be happy to accompany her. So explaining to one of the waiters that she'd had a turn, and could he keep an eye on her, he slipped across the road to tell his friends.

Ingrid saw him, with many gestures, explain what had happened. Tom and Charles, she noted, seemed yet more amused.

But there was yet more to come - the strangest moment of all. Across the road, walking nonchalantly down the pavement toward where George and their friends were sitting, there now came...... Henry Thornton, Paula..... and Alexey! In plain view! In Munich, right in front of her eyes!

Her 'vision', earlier, had been real.

And Ingrid understood. George had known they might appear, without having a clue what to do about it. No wonder his manner had been so strange, and he'd been so keen on taking her home.

And now it became plain that Alexey and the others had seen **her**. It looked so, anyway. They stopped, as if frozen to the spot, and Alexey, especially, gazed hard in her direction.

The moment made quite a tableau. Alexey, astonished, staring over at Ingrid; Henry and Paula looking amazed; Ingrid, quite simply, devastated. The whole bunch of them frozen, jaws agape.

At which moment there came the shrill shriek of an engine whistle, blasting the street. Everyone jumped. George looked round for the cause;

but all he could see, down the end of the road, was a full-dress Bavarian regiment, complete with band.

But that, it turned out, was it. The 'engine whistle' had been a blast from the band's fifes.

All conversation stopped. The whole café, the entire street lay silent. Then another fervent, trilling blast from the fifes. Then the band's percussion started with a crude, thumping, one-two one-two beat on the drums. Then the fifes came back again, with a skeetering riff which started high and slid down low, then repeated itself, the drums lurching and rolling underneath.

And now, sumptuously, stupendously, the band burst into the most splendid military march, and as it did, each soldier lifted his leg in the first movement of the goose step while the whole regiment swung forward as one.

It was electrifying. Every person in the street, whatever they had been doing previously, was overwhelmed by this new and compelling force, as the band and the regiment swung down the street, their colours flying in the wind, dust rising momentously in their wake.

It turned out they were celebrating the mayor's birthday. Yet it felt like so much more. For ten minutes, as the street stood and watched, the regiment filed past, each soldier's face, under his Roman-looking helmet, brim-full of ferocity and determination. Above all, as the rows of goose-stepping legs swung simultaneously past, they expressed utter unity and comradeship. All these varied, diverse men, acting as one.

The German students were plainly enraptured, though they tried hard to hide it. More surprisingly the English, too, were enthralled. It felt like the advent of something new, some utterly different spirit entering their lives, noble and grave.

The coming into their lives, as George later told himself, of the Spirit of War.

All, that is, except Ingrid, still stranded across the road. Her reaction, it must be said, was deeply unpatriotic. All *she* saw was yet more male absurdity.

But then, despite her upbringing, she'd never been one to take the goose step seriously. Those posturing male peacocks, they did protest too much!

How she hated men.

Chapter Fifty-Five

And yet, when she reflected on this later, once more the saving grace of humour. Come now, she could not be serious! At this rate she'd have to break windows with the suffragettes, there'd be no other choice.

But the gleam soon passed. And as George and she sped back to Entlingen, she was thinking constantly. And went on thinking when they got back, when, pleading 'exhaustion', she retired to her room.

Of course, it was the affair between Alexey and Henry that obsessed her. For the moment this bombshell overshadowed even her 'adoption.'

Because the more she considered it the more plausible it seemed. After all, hadn't she always sensed a profound vein of femininity in Alexey - his gentleness, his understanding, his flooding, if sporadic, empathy? Hadn't she valued, from the start, his lack of crass, male coarseness - his sexual reticence, in the best sense of the word? The way he'd seemed to value – again, in a distinctly feminine way - the qualities of spirit and character in a partner far more than the attractions of the flesh?

And she could see too, if anything more vividly still, how Henry would impress Alexey.

Not just as an original, or a musician, or a leader, (however improbable), but as a poet, for heaven's sake, of real, demonstrable quality! A truly separate, independent spirit, quite distinct from all the rest. Indeed, with both of them, you could go through a thousand men to find their like. No wonder each found the other unique - *the* quality, Ingrid remembered, Alexey thought the talisman of love.

Small wonder that Alexey found Henry more attractive than a brainless chit like she!

Although her sanity had to add, too, that these men shared countless faults. Not least their readiness to use, and abuse, their women. Whatever their brilliance, they were both, as partners, impossible.

Meanwhile, Ingrid stayed in her room. While George, once again, did his best to survive, in this increasingly tempestuous house, by retreating to his.

Yet in the days that followed, despite her determined isolation, Ingrid sensed yet another level of angst pervading her home. Was she imagining it, or was there something strange about the servants? Some weird, importunate curiosity, quite beyond the studied sympathy with which they'd treated her since her collapse?

Something similar, in fact, to the way people looked at her when she walked in Entlingen town, meeting friends she'd known for years.

Above all she felt it when she re-joined her melancholy, preoccupied parents for meals. For Doris, a maid who'd had been with the Uberspeers for years, was so constantly stealing covert glances at Ingrid that even Herr Uberspeer, usually meticulously polite to servants, told her to keep her eyes on her work.

Something, undeniably, was up. But what? This new source of tension was too much for Ingrid: she resolved to find out.

And Doris, unsurprisingly, became her source. She'd always been like Ingrid's second mother - and her job meant she heard the local servants' gossip.

Nor did she fail Ingrid now. Ingrid's questioning, ever more forceful and direct, soon established that the word was out that Ingrid was pregnant, that the news had spread from household to household, and had inevitably - this always happened in the end – been passed on to their employers.

At which stage Ingrid became a veritable Grand Inquisitor, quite terrifying to poor Doris. Now she wanted to know in which house the rumour had started. And when Doris said she thought it had been the Volsteins' - Jewish liberal friends - a terrible intuition gripped Ingrid. She asked Doris outright: had it been her father, in his cups, who'd said it? For she knew he'd lunched there three days earlier and how louche he could be when drinking. Doris, by now distraught, denied this. But a remorseless Ingrid finally forced it out of her. It was he.

Boiling with anger, Ingrid stormed off to her room. Where she gradually digested the fact that her father, of all people, had been the one who'd betrayed her to the town.

So she must have it out with him – which meant yet another fraught, hair-trigger confrontation.

But events took over.

Just after tea, for which George had reappeared, (a meal which felt, to all involved, like a picnic on Mount Etna) Ingrid's father requested George to favour him with an interview. Right away, please - and in his study.

In both men went, looking deathly; out they came, an hour later, looking volcanic.

For Uberspeer, it seemed, was furious with George for putting Ingrid back in touch with the English. He plainly thought George had encouraged her trip to Munich; and he believed, too, that he had done it surreptitiously, that he had, as Uberspeer exaggeratedly put it, 'lied.'

Were these not, he said, the very same friends who had caused her so much hurt in England? Above all, this Alexey, the very worst of all? The bush telegraph at Entlingen had evidently been working overtime.

But what really amazed George, outraged him even, was Uberspeer's further insinuation - for Uberspeer got angrier at every moment - that George, of all people, might be.... *the father of Ingrid's child.*

A quite extraordinary suggestion. And yet, declared Herr Uberspeer, why not? True, there was no shortage of candidates! But why not George? For had not Uberspeer and his wife, like so many at Ingrid's party, noticed the *nature* of George's feelings for her? Surely those of a lover, not of a friend?

Clearly her father was losing his judgement. Yet when George protested, Uberspeer repeated again, why not? George had lied about Ingrid's trip to Munich, he'd betrayed the Uberspeers' hospitality, he was utterly shameless and unreliable, why not?

At which moment, utterly out of control, Uberspeer had ordered George out of the house.

And George had agreed to go.

Chapter Fifty-Six

So now Ingrid lost all nervousness and sought out her father out.

Back into his study they trooped. She attacked at once.

"How *dare* you order George out of the house?"

Her father said nothing.

"How dare you, when you know what he has meant to me all this time, how good he is, how kind he has been, how much I depend on him? How dare you call him a liar, when you don't even know the circumstances, which were, it's true, that some of our English friends came to Munich on a visit, but what you didn't know was that he'd taken every step he could to avoid my meeting them, for precisely the reasons you suggest, and meeting them was actually an accident! Not a lie!

"Not a lie! How dare you insinuate – how utterly foolish can you be! - that he is *of all things* my baby's father, when the slightest reading of the situation, the tiniest understanding of his personality or our relationship, would make it plain that that, of all things, is beyond possibility -"

"Ingrid, Ingrid...." her father protested - a how-can-I-put-this sigh - "Look at it from *my* point of view. Yes, I agree, I was wrong in the way I talked to George. I go further: it was unacceptable. But I was angry, and surely that is not so strange! Remember, he could surely have told me and your mother who you were planning to meet in Munich. They were, after all, the people crucial to the whole affair. Come to that, *you* could have told us -"

But Ingrid would not be thus forced onto the defensive.

"Let's get this quite clear," she said. "George has behaved utterly honourably throughout this business. Indeed, he's arguably the only person I know, in the whole world, who has."

The insinuation was not missed.

"Well yes, but naturally you must understand how upset your mother and I have been about all this -"

"Exactly! So why do you make it worse by spreading rumours, no, worse than rumours, to use your own word, lies!"

"Well, let's be honest, Ingrid, it's not that absurd, is it? You admitted yourself - well, pretty much admitted - the father might be anyone at all!"

"How dare you throw that at me! How dare you! Not to mention, as I keep telling you, that if there was one person of my acquaintance of whom that would be utterly impossible, it would be George!"

"So you're agreeing it **would** be possible, in fact, with any of the rest? What does that tell us Ingrid, what does that tell us indeed?"

At which Ingrid screamed aloud, with mingled wrath, outrage, and humiliation.

For a minute, both stayed silent.

Finally, Ingrid spoke. But now she was calm.

"We have not yet talked about the central point," she said.

"I thought we had."

"No, we have *not*."

Ingrid's voice began to quiver. But she mastered herself.

"You lunched with the Volsteins recently. And there, as is sometimes your weakness, you got drunk?"

"Well, yes to the first point, certainly, but no, absolutely, to the second. I took a little wine, yes, but only a little. And I strongly object to your tone."

"My tone! Forget my tone! Quite simply, I have it on clear authority that while in your cups you let slip that I was pregnant."

At which Herr Uberspeer blanched. But he quickly recovered.

"I said no such thing. Why would I?"

"I don't know *why*. All I know is that you did."

"And all I know is I did not." For a moment it looked as if Herr Uberspeer really meant it. "Well, maybe I did hint at something. But in the vaguest possible way...."

"Hint at something? How strong does that kind of hint have to be?

"Ingrid, I object to your tone!"

"My tone, again! Is that all you care about? So how about *your* tone, your substance, indeed, when you broadcast my most intimate details to our friends?!"

"I did nothing of the sort!"

"Oh yes you did! In your cups you told the Volsteins; their servants told ours; now the whole town knows. Have you any idea how people have **stared** at me, let alone anything else, for the last few days? They all know! And it is thanks to you, my own dear father! How do you think that makes me feel?"

"Well, I don't know! I mean, I really...."

"I'm your daughter, for heaven's sake!"

A pause.

"No you are not."

"What? Oh really! Yes! But then of course you have explained! I'm 'adopted'! Forgive me! It's all still so new to me!"

"No, it's more than that."

And there was a seriousness in Herr Uberspeer's tone, quite different from both his anger and his sheepishness, which brought Ingrid up short. She shot him a wild, uncertain look and said:

"What do you mean?"

Chapter Fifty-Seven

For now Herr Uberspeer's manner changed. No longer angry or sheepish, or a man in denial, but sober and straightforward. A mode Ingrid knew of old, which meant he was telling the truth.

And slowly he unfolded his tale. Yes, it was true that Ingrid had been adopted, but only, as you might say, half-adopted: her mother was indeed her biological mother. But what was true..... and here he faltered....was that he, Uberspeer, was not her biological father. That was someone else.

Once again Ingrid was reduced to wide-eyed wonder.

"And who -" she began - but no, her father interjected, he couldn't say. Not now anyway. It was, Ingrid would understand, a complex story. He'd been sworn to secrecy, the circumstances had been impossible. One day perhaps, but it was hard, very hard –

"But papa! -" Yet still he brushed her queries aside, far more eager, evidently, to explain the things which had made him mention this at all. "You see," he said, and his tone was once more becoming urgent, "there are *reasons* why both I and your mother have found this situation especially difficult. "

"So what are these 'reasons' then – go on, tell me!"

"I will, believe me, tell you everything I can."

And so Herr Uberspeer resumed his story, clearly hoping this might exculpate his behaviour.

Twenty years ago, he said, he'd been a student at Jena. There, of course, he had met the young Mr. Crosby, and they'd become friends. And there it was, too, that he had met Ingrid's mother; and for a year – maybe eighteen months - he had courted her and they'd fallen in love. But then, calamity. While he'd been away on a trip to England, a former admirer, 'let's call him Johann' had reappeared, and rekindled an earlier romance. "Your mother was vulnerable. Her father had died, she was utterly disoriented."

And by the time Herr Uberspeer returned, this Johann, totally ruthless, had made her pregnant. More, he'd already found ways of getting rid of her, and out of Jena, by setting her up in a village ten miles away. With some money, sporadic visits, and copious promises of marriage.

Very unwisely, but perhaps understandably, Ingrid's mother had gone along with this. She'd even allowed him to persuade her landlady and the villagers they were married already, and her 'husband's ' comings and goings were due to business. And after six months, Ingrid was born.

Meanwhile, her mother had begged Herr Uberspeer to stay away - she was terrified lest his advent might ruin everything.

For Johann was well capable of behaving charmingly, even lovingly. Frau Uberspeer had described his visits. They'd have tea; they'd eat toast; Ingrid adored him. Quite homely, really.

But after a year, very suddenly, he left them. And what little money Ingrid's mother had swiftly ran out. Worse still, her 'husband's' self - evident disappearance started a rash of rumours among the locals, who began treating her as a pariah.

Finally her landlady, always distant, formally accused of her of having an illegitimate child . And Ingrid's mother, at the end of her tether, admitted this. At which her landlady gave her notice.

She wrote to Ingrid's father, explaining her plight.

With Johann gone, Uberspeer was already subbing her small sums of money.

At this further news he thought carefully about it for twenty- four hours then next day, by first post, he offered to marry her.

Frau Uberspeer accepted. They married secretly in another town, and by the time they moved to Entlingen they were the most exemplary bourgeois couple imaginable.

But what also became clear, added Uberspeer, was that she, Ingrid, had no conscious memory of any of this.

Excepting, (a glimmering smile) a life-long love of toast.

By the time Uberspeer's story reached this stage, the atmosphere between them had changed again. In fairness, he came out of it rather well.

Then a strange thing happened.

Her father said:

"You see, to be honest," - a moment's reflection - "I suppose what I'm telling you explains some of my behaviour. You might even say these late events raise ghosts."

"Ghosts?"

"Well - memories of how it was back then - memories of what happened to your mother. I've been nervous, over the years, lest something similar happen to you, and I've been concerned, too, to be absolutely honest, there might have been some similarity of temperament......"

"Temperament? What do you mean?"

Herr Uberspeer visibly reversed.

"I mean," he said - and Ingrid noticed he was *blushing* - "a certain instability perhaps.....a certain nervousness..... in fairness there was that episode with Heinrich before you went to England......."

Some dread intuition was telling Ingrid what Herr Uberspeer *did* mean.

"Promiscuity?" she suddenly gasped. "Isn't that the word you really want, papa? Isn't promiscuity – as you said, do let's be honest! – the accusation you are levelling against your wife and your daughter, on the very slenderest of evidence? Indeed" – and now, once again, Ingrid was almost in tears – "I can see that you might say that of me, however unkindly, but why are you saying it about my *mother* ? How could anything you have told me suggest anything, for her, but the purest misfortune? How -"

" - Because it wasn't just this one instance! There were other instances, too - "

" - *What?*"

And now once again Herr Uberspeer looked embarrassed.

"Other instances - other affairs. One in particular that I knew about. And many rumours."

"Rumours?"

"Yes, rumours, but they had every sign of substantiation...."

"*Really*? And on the basis of these *rumours*, for which there might even be some form of substantiation, you are happy to malign your wife to your daughter, merely to exculpate yourself for your own bizarre behaviour – no wonder you are happy to chatter about me to your friends! You're clearly quite ready to say anything about anyone at all, depending on your whim!"

"Ingrid, Ingrid, I only meant...."

But Ingrid had already stormed out of the room.

Not that this latest eruption was so very strange. When two people are fundamentally out of sympathy anything can happen, at any moment, emotionally.

So now Ingrid went on yet another search for her mother. Yet when she found her, taking her afternoon rest, their talk was once more inconclusive.

Frau Uberspeer did admit, tearfully and under pressure, the essential truth of her husband's story. But she was as reluctant as he to even hint at Ingrid's true paternity. It was simply 'impossible', she said, for reasons she couldn't divulge, for her to say.

And as for those other suggestions of Herr Uberspeer's – her mother's alleged loucheness, even debauchery, when young - well, Ingrid wasn't about to start in on that.

Chapter Fifty-Eight

By six o-clock George had left the Uberspeer household. It had become impossible to stay.

And now, on top of everything, Ingrid's pregnancy was increasingly making itself evident. She began feeling morning sickness – with the incongruity, strangely, that it happened in the afternoon. She felt ever more tired - though this *was* a morning phenomenon. Not to mention new-found food obsessions, notably a weird passion for lemons, of which Ingrid would eat as many as three at breakfast, eyed beadily, and significantly, by the ever-observant Doris.

Soon Ingrid's parents were making suggestions 'to cheer her up.'

There was talk of another trip to Munich, the theatre maybe, or a concert? The chaperones, this time, would be her parents. A boat trip? A mountain picnic? And when all these fell flat, a likelier thought. Two days after George's departure Ingrid's father saw an advertisement in the Entlingen paper for an open-air production of A Midsummer Night's Dream, performed in the park of Schloss Heidelburg, just five miles down the road toward Munich. Now there, surely, he told Frau Uberspeer excitedly, was something Ingrid would certainly like, something that could really take her out of herself.

Had not Ingrid acted in a school version, years back, playing, of all things, Puck?!

And the whole family had fond memories of that time. Herr Uberspeer, as an enthusiastic father, had helped build the set. Frau Uberspeer designed the costumes. While Ingrid, as Puck, had stolen the show and become a local star. It was symbolic of family togetherness. There were photographs.........

Yet Ingrid greeted this suggestion, too, with disdain. And the contrast between her past enthusiasm and her current resentment only underscored, cruelly, the family decline.

Then one Saturday morning, when the Uberspeers were out visiting friends, there came a knock at the door.

Doris was off that morning. Ingrid opened it.

It was Paula.

"Good God," said Ingrid.

"You don't have to call me that."

"Jesus!"

"Nor that either."

Throughout that week, ever since Munich, Ingrid had wondered what Paula and her English friends were up to - though she'd promptly, then, dismissed them from her mind.

Yet the moment she saw her friend, seemingly full of all her old cheek, she realised Paula, of all people, could tell her what had really been going on.

"You've timed this well," said Ingrid. "Everyone's out."

"I know," said Paula. "I waited till I saw your parents leave."

Ah, Paula the conspirator, thought Ingrid. Back to her old self.

They sat down in the kitchen. Ingrid fetched Paula a beer.

"Now tell me," she said, "What on earth are you doing in Entlingen?"

"Working," said Paula.

"*Working?*"

"Yes - I'm working on a play."

"A play!" said Ingrid. "Since when the thesp?"

And then:

"You know, I was amazed when I realised you and Alexey were here. George never told me. Wanted to protect me, I suppose, in my current condition." Ingrid and Paula had a running joke about the word 'condition'. "I saw you, in Munich, way down the street, before you ever reached the café. I thought I was hallucinating."

"Well, we saw *you*, or thought we did, and Alexey felt he was seeing things too."

"I'm surprised he was bothered."

"Oh no, he was very bothered, because.... naturally....inevitably.... he has heard about your... condition..... and..... he's very angry about it."

"Angry! In what way?"

"He's appalled at the way you've been treated, and what you've had to go through. He's really quite het up."

Which was not in itself such a surprise. Alexey had always been empathic. Yet what did amaze Ingrid was what happened next - how she reacted *physically* to this talk of Alexey.

Baboom! went her heart, and baboom! again, and went on thumping, just as it had done weeks ago when they were lovers. Yet she had long since written off all that. Hadn't she? Nevertheless... for now.... she must control herself - she must find out what had happened in France.

So she nudged the conversation towards Henry and Alexey. "It certainly seems to confirm your theory of homosexuality," she said. "It's the relationship – didn't you say? - in which both partners can allow themselves their deepest feelings. The only one."

But Paula failed to rise. Ingrid tried another tack.

"You haven't told me," she said, "what you're doing with this play."

Better luck. "Ah yes," said Paula. "That's why I'm here."

And Paula described how her communist lover, Mathilde, believed in propagating the revolutionary gospel through theatre - she worked for a group called Le Drapeau Rouge and had co-opted Paula to help with the publicity. "They need someone who speaks English," said Paula. "They even pay me – well, a bit."

Yet for all their progressiveness her group believed in traditional theatre too; three days from now, for instance, they were doing Shakespeare, in the open air, at a wood near the village of Essen, just five miles north of Entlingen.

"So what's the play? said Ingrid, with a looming intuition.

"A Midsummer Night's Dream," said Paula.

"Well, I'll be damned," said Ingrid.

"Really? Well – anyway - I thought of you," said Paula, "and wondered whether you might like to see it. I've got free tickets." She did one of her knowing looks. "Publicity you know, inside job. Assuming, that is, your parents will let you out." For a moment, she looked grave. "I've heard about the fracas. George told me. It sounds terrible."

"Pretty terrible, yes –"

"- which is why I dreamed this up - to be quite honest! - to give you a break. And to give you a way of seeing George. And for George to see you, too, if anything still more vital to him. But in a way which would be acceptable to your parents, given the latest bust-up."

"Well yes, but who else will be there? Not Tom! Not Alexey! I couldn't cope with either..."

"God no! And what's more, in case your parents are worried about who you'll meet, we'll invite them too -"

"But won't that – "

"- then cancel their tickets at the last minute. Sudden shortage, no availability. Sudden rush of demand! Leaving you to come anyway, just with me, lest you'd otherwise be so desperately disappointed."

My God, did Paula ever stop conspiring?

"But that will never work."

"Believe me, Ingrid, I understand these things. It will work."

Chapter Fifty-Nine

And work it did.

The performance was on Friday 24th July. Paula collected her, and the two women left together at 5. OO PM. Her parents had been delighted, despite the cancelation: Ingrid would see the play after all.

True, Paula was one of the English coterie, but they had nothing against her personally. They'd live with it.

Ingrid and Paula took the train from Entlingen station, which brought them, an hour later, within half a mile of the theatre.

"I really can't cope with anyone but George," said Ingrid. "Especially Tom. And as for Alexey, it's unthinkable. You do promise me he won't be there, don't you?

"To my knowledge he won't be, no."

"That's not the same thing."

Nevertheless, Ingrid calmed down.

And the theatregoers they joined were calmer, too.

For the mood of Germany, that night, had been transformed. The war scare that had been louring over everyone for a month now, had disappeared.

True, the day before, July 23rd, the Austrians had sent an ultimatum to the Serbs, so ruthless in tone that it surely meant a Gadarene plunge to conflict.

Yet now, in the last twenty-four hours, had come the extraordinary news that the diktat had been accepted!

It was a miracle. You could see the relief on every face.

And as for George, he was one of the first people they saw, as they walked up from the station. With his frank, open face, his air of graciousness and warmth - the one person in the world Ingrid could utterly rely on. Paula disappeared, tactfully, to collect their tickets. George and Ingrid were alone.

Yet what could they say, at such a time and place, but the conventional how-are-yous? So they ended up saying nothing at all. Not that it mattered, certainly not to Ingrid. For the key thing, as ever with George, was not his words but his manner: utterly sympathetic and enfolding.

Later, perhaps, they could find some privacy, and say more. They arranged to meet, if possible, in the interval.

They parted and left for their separate seats. Ingrid and Paula were on one side of the amphitheatre, George on the other. While Ingrid realised just ten minutes with George had left her calmer than she'd been for days.

Until, that is, she saw, on George's side, just thirty yards along - oh my god, the horrid inevitability of it! - Tom and Charles. Rabid as ever, gazing insolently around. Looking out for George, presumably, or even, God forbid, Ingrid herself.

"Who's THAT," she said to Paula, pointing at them, and aware, as so often in the last few weeks, that her agitation stirred interest in everyone around.

"Who's who? Said Paula, screwing her eyes up and peering where Ingrid was pointing. "Ah. Oh! Oh dear. Yes. That does rather look like Tom and Charles."

"It certainly does. And you swore they were not coming!"

"No, I didn't. I said I *thought* they weren't coming, but to be fair, they're not the sort of people you can control."

"I think you knew."

"I didn't! What *is* true is that I wasn't absolutely certain one way or another. That's why I didn't commit myself."

What is this, thought Ingrid, a court of law? But what was worrying, appalling even, was the prospect of being bearded by such friends at such a time.

A possibility which was underscored by the fact that Charles and Tom had plainly got the attention of George, who'd moved to join them.

Moments later they spotted Ingrid and Paula, and were waving frantically for the women to come over. Paula flagged back a clear and definite 'no' - while Ingrid tried to shrink down and hide.

The families around them looked more fascinated still.

A sudden, sweet orchestral chord broke out. It was Mendelsohn's A Midsummer Night's Dream overture. But much though Ingrid loved the score, she was lost, now, in fury. What was it with Paula, that it always came back to this? Why was there always some agenda, some sleight of hand, some story she was telling one person and another she was telling someone else? It was compulsive.

And now there came the horn entre-act, the loveliest passage in the entire work……. but re-enter the farce. For there, on the other side of the arena, separate from Tom and Charles, yet still more grotesquely, was none other than………..Alexey! Sliding into a seat on his own……unless her eyes deceived her…. but no, beside him was Henry - it *was* Alexey!

Baboom! That irrelevant, ridiculous, banging of the heart, that above all *out of date* reaction! It was six months since she'd even thought of him, and yet… It was absurd, yes, but more than that, it was degrading.

She nudged Paula again and pointed the duo out. Paula screwed her eyes up and gazed where Ingrid was pointing: "Ah yes" she said. "I did wonder about that. Ah well."

Which threw Ingrid straight back into her angry, vituperative mood. So Paula knew! She fumed through the first act; she seethed right up to the interval. All this……nonsense!... was spoiling her play. So she was all the more eager, come the interval, to seek out George - assuming, that is, he'd separated himself from the rest.

Pleading the Ladies, she unglued herself from Paula, and walked with quick, nervous steps over to where she and George had arranged to meet - a beer stall on the fringe of the auditorium.

The bar swarmed with theatregoers, surging, pushing, jostling - everyone in the world, seemingly - except George.

At which moment she spotted still more of the many people, that evening, she would have liked to avoid: the Entlingen lawyers! From her 'welcome home' party! Of all people! So she turned on her heel and shot off in the opposite direction – but they'd seen her.

"Herr Schwarz!" she pre-empted, with her broadest smile. "How lovely to see you! And Herr Hoffman, too!"

"Not so lovely. Not lovely at all! Fraulein Uberspeer, we have heard things, shameful things, I have to tell you…."

"So what's the problem?" Here now at last was George. "Can I help?"

The lawyers turned to look at him; in the gloaming they struggled to realise who he was. But once they did, they got crosser still.

"Ach, George, the unforgettable **George** " said Schwarz, turning to him with contempt. "Ingrid's English guest, the one who befriended her, took advantage of her father's hospitality, then betrayed her!"

"Betrayed her?" cried George, instantly bridling. "What in God's name do you mean? In what possible sense have I betrayed her?"

"I don't know!" yelled Herr Hoffman, "I don't know the details! All I know is that Herr Uberspeer would never have ordered you out of his house without very good reason -"

"You are insulting Ingrid?" Now here was Tom, and also Charles; behind them Paula, too, looking ever more concerned.

"I was insulting no-one!"

"I hope so! I truly hope so – that would be most unwise......."

The lawyers' families, complete with children, rushed up to give support; bystanders joined in; the two young Englishmen loured ominously over all, on the verge, clearly, of unleashing the first blow.

At which Paula said "This is no good, Ingrid, let's leave them to it," snatched her by the arm, and frogmarched her out of the crowd into the wood, leaving the disputants, shouting and shrieking, far behind.

They walked fifty yards away from the auditorium, along a footpath lit by the moon. They sat down, Ingrid cursing, shrieking, laughing - typical Ingrid, thought Paula, she'll soon calm down.

As she shortly did, and the two women sat in silence. In the background they could still hear the rumble of the row, clearly identifiable above the theatregoers' din.

Then suddenly it seemed to escalate. Now they heard Tom, clear as a bell, yelling in English: "Will you please make it clear to this man that if he says that once more I shall kill him?" followed by thumps, a scream, a bump, then a loud re-echoing yell, from both Tom and Charles, of "Paulaaa!!!!!" then more loudly still, PAULAAAAA!!!!!!

"What on earth?" said Ingrid.

"Christ knows," said Paula, " but I'd better find out. I'll be back in a mo. You'll be safe here, won't you?

"As safe as I'd be there," said Ingrid.

Paula hurried away.

"Now the hungry lion roars, and the wolf behowls the moon…." And Ingrid found herself recalling Puck's last speech of the play, overwhelmed, suddenly, by the forest all around her. How very dark it was! A fairyland, yes, but strangely threatening….

And then she heard a thumping and shuffling, plainly nearby, quite distinct from the sounds of the play.

Thump, thump, steady and remorseless, closer and closer, almost like something seeking her out. Thump thump thump, a heavy footfall, ever more recognisable…..then round the corner and into the moonlight, baboom! It was Alexey.

Walking straight towards her, with a strained, uncertain smile, as she could see - or sense - despite the darkness. Walking as if he knew exactly where he was going, and where he'd find her.

"Ingrid," he said, peering down at her. "It *is* Ingrid isn't it?"

"Yes, it is. Hello, Alexey."

A moment's silence.

"What are you doing here?"

"Looking for you."

"How did you know where to find me?"

"Paula told me."

"Did she indeed!"

"Yes, she did – please don't be angry. She knew how very much I wanted to speak with you."

"Do you indeed!"

"Yes I do."

And now, more silence, yet Ingrid's heart was thumping, racing, as if her body, not her mind, was driving her. When she finally spoke, it was to say the last thing she ever would have expected: but the words seemed to well up from the depths.

"Why did you leave me?"

The voice of a child.

Even in the darkness she could tell this threw Alexey.

"I didn't leave you," he said finally. "I went away, I had to. I -

"You **did** leave me, you know you did, whatever you say! You left because you wanted to, whatever the so-called reasons. You knew that I had.....*found you out*.... that's why you left me.... regardless of how I felt, or any meaning there might ever have been in our relationship!"

Strange conversation, in fits and starts, in utter darkness.

Now Alexey was more incredulous still.

"Found me out? What are you saying? Found me out how?"

"Oh, don't play the innocent! You know what I mean!"

"I don't, actually, but what I do know is this: the moment we parted I felt regret."

"Oh really! *Regret*! Why, thankyou - that makes all the difference."

"No truly I did - but I was abroad with my family, and the circumstances meant - "

"- So if you really felt like that, why didn't you write? I wrote to you."

"Did you? I never received anything."

Ingrid snorted.

"No, I say again, honestly, I received not a single letter from you, not one."

Ingrid utterly disbelieved him. Again the silence.

Alexey tried again.

"I'd heard things...."

Again Ingrid snorted.

"No, don't be angry; I'd heard things that made me think you were ....distressed........that you were getting involved in….. things.... which I felt were really, at bottom, to do with what had happened between us. I felt sad."

"Yes, you're good at sympathy," said Ingrid bitterly, "Less good at love."

"I know, I know... I don't know how to put it, Ingrid, except to say that I regretted everything from the moment I left, and all the more so when I heard how things were falling out with you."

"Things again! My word, what a lot of things! So what sort of 'things,' pray, did you have in mind?"

"Well.... your, uh, liaisons, for instance.....your pregnancy...."

"Oh did you indeed! And how did you hear about that?"

"Well, I've heard something involving Tom, nonsense surely, of course -"

"Tom? Tom? Aren't you rather out of date? Haven't you heard anything about Edward, say, or Charles maybe – Edward, especially, actually! Now here's some advice. I really would suggest you think about 'things' relating to Edward, rather than Tom."

"Edward? Who's he?" Alexey's sources, plainly, had their limits.

"A friend of Charles Fisher's, don't you know him? There were 'things' with Edward alright, and no mistake! But there again, there were things with Charles, too, as you may have also heard, and others as well, I can't exactly remember, to be frank, I get confused!"

Ingrid had no idea why she was saying all this - it was wild, insane, but it kept welling up within her. And now, smelling blood, she got louder still:

"Not that that would have bothered you much, as we both know, because actual consummation is not what you do, you leave that to others, and in fairness, they've done a pretty good job! Not that your failure to consummate is anything new of course, it's actually the story of your life, and not merely sexually, but in every way one can possibly imagine, socially, politically, practically, with the exception, of course of the one thing you *have* achieved, or so I hear, which is consummation with a man!

"Yes! I have heard 'things' too! Tell me, Alexey, tell me about *your* 'things', please. Do you actually prefer going to bed with a man rather than with a woman, and, if so, does it give you a fulfilment you can get no other way? Or could it be that this, too, is yet another form of avoidance, something that gives you so little real satisfaction that before you know it you are back again pleading with the very woman you originally left, such is your confusion, your disloyalty, your utter incapacity to make any genuine relationship with anyone at all!"

At which moment Ingrid's voice finally cracked and she started crying, though a moment later, unbelieving she had said such things, she fell silent. While Alexey, who had expected anything but this, was tongue-tied too.

The silence lengthened. But this time neither broke it.

Eventually, hopelessly, Alexey suggested they return to the play. They parted and went back to their seats.

And now Ingrid was churning yet again, though this time her anger was directed at herself. Why did she constantly lose control like this? Why did her heart, time and again, overwhelm her head, so she ended up saying things she hardly even meant?

It was the chaos that frightened her. The way such outbursts seemed to come from some maverick, separate self, a self of which, most of the time, she had no inkling. What was this other self? And what was its cause?

And so Ingrid sat, gazing pensively at the stage, unaware that someone else was staring at her more intensely still. For George, eyeing her from his seat, could not believe how beautiful she looked that night, her sadness transforming prettiness into nobility. An air that went so well with the play's poetry, the lovely music, and the night.

And George felt this the more because he had, en route to the toilets, seen Ingrid and Alexey walking back from the forest, after what looked extraordinarily like a tryst. How had *that* come about?

Their conversation, he could tell, had been intense – the very conversation *he* should have been having with her, the intimacy *he* should have enjoyed, if the evening had worked out as he'd hoped. He'd been looking forward to it all week.

Ah, if only he had Alexey's flair with women!

Chapter Sixty

Yet not one of the questions begged by all this would be resolved.

For now history intervened.

Amazingly, outrageously, for all the seeming relaxation of the previous twenty-four hours, it emerged, come Saturday the 25th July, that Austria had received Serbia's response - and declared it 'inadequate.' Indeed, so determined were they to find it so that the Austrian minister in Belgrade, Baron Giesl, had been waiting for the Serbian reply with his bags packed, ready to leave.

He received their answer at 5.58 PM on Saturday afternoon. Within half an hour he had boarded the regular six-thirty train which left Belgrade and crossed straight into Austrian territory, just over the Danube.

By July 28th, notwithstanding the last-minute reservations of the Germans, Austria declared war on Serbia. The next morning, July 29th, they bombarded Belgrade.

The result, in Germany - even in sleepy Entlingen - was like sparks to a powder keg. Deutschland Erwachen! Forget the fact that the quarrel remained, at this stage, essentially one between Austria and Serbia; forget the Austrians' seeming culpability. They were Germany's allies, her Teutonic brothers in the face of a hostile world, and Germany was in honour bound to stand by her.

Or as the 'National Hymn,' Deutschland uber Alles, proclaimed:

Einigheit und Recht und Freiheit

Fur das deutsche Vaterland!
Danach last uns alle streben
Bruderlich mit Hertz und hand!

Einigheit! Unity! One emotion ran through every German breast - tribal loyalty. All the fears, hesitancies, worries, long-term concerns; all the debates, divisions and disinterested calculations, were blown away, resolved into one overriding emotion: heroic determination.

Even Ingrid got caught up in it. A phrase from Shakespeare re-echoed in her head, 'Now all the youth of England are on fire....' well, German youth, in this case, but one got the drift: the joy of leaping from the uncertain to the sure, from hesitancy to adamantine resolve.

Then to add to the excitement Paula reappeared, once more unannounced. With difficulty she persuaded Ingrid to let her into the house, with still more difficulty she got her to come out and talk. Fleeing the village, they walked up the steeply wooded hill behind Entlingen church and sat on the grass.

And Paula started on her latest exculpation, Ingrid gazing at her with weary eyes.

Yes, said Paula, she'd known Tom and Charles *might* be at Schloss Heidelburg, but, as she'd explained earlier, she hadn't known for sure. Yes, she *had* suspected - only suspected, mind – that Alexey might be there too, but that had seemed unlikelier still.......

And yes, alright, once she realised he was there she *had* directed him to Ingrid, in the wood, but only because she'd become convinced they really had to talk. They both had unfinished business. Especially, she stressed, Ingrid – she should have seen how she'd been reacting to the mere mention of Alexey's name.

And as Ingrid exploded into rage - how could Paula possibly think any such ridiculous thing! - Paula said, well maybe she wa*s* wrong to have set up the meeting in this way – though maybe, just conceivably, she was right. Believe her –

Believe her! That was the last thing, these days, Ingrid would ever do. What was plain was that Paula would tell anything to anyone in the world, to suit her purposes. Different things to different people, different things at different times, the literal translation, indeed, of the Greek word, diplo-mat, two faces, two versions, virtually a spy!

And now, a flash of realisation - Paula would undoubtedly make an excellent spy. Perhaps that was a career move she should consider. She had the looks, the talents, and most crucial of all - the faults.

But soon Paula announced all this was academic anyway, now, as everything had changed. "Because we really do seem to be on the brink of an old-fashioned, fully-fledged European war."

"Oh God, yes...... yes, indeed," said Ingrid.

"Quite simply, everyone we know is going home. All these wonderful schemes everyone had! Charles with his art studies, George with his seminar, Tom with *his* seminar, me even, with my theatricals – we're all going home. We'll be stuck here if war does break out. God knows, we could be incarcerated – we'd be enemy aliens."

"Enemy aliens?" Ingrid found it impossible to think of her friends in any such terms. She liked them – well, most of the time - so they were *hers*, they were *on her side*. How could they possibly, whatever people said, be enemies?

But Tom, it emerged, had already booked his passage. Alexey was accompanying him, and so was Charles. Charles was even talking about volunteering for the British army, so convinced was he the British would join in. Henry was teetering; Paula herself, as she'd already said, was leaving; and as for George - his father had ordered him home, at once, without reservations.

"George's father knows people at Berlin university," said Paula, "They're convinced that England can't possibly stay out of it."

"But why?" said Ingrid. "I thought there was every chance that England would do just that."

"They know the plans of the German General staff" said Paula, "and they know that if Germany attacks France – and Germany will attack France, as Russia's ally – they'll go in via Belgium. And that will involve us."

"Ah yes, said Ingrid, "the Schlieffen plan...." Little fragments of history floated into her mind.

"Yes indeed," said Paula. "Germany cuts through Belgium to outflank France's forts, and that's what brings England in, as guarantors of Belgium's security. By the treaty of 1839."

"Oh God yes," said Ingrid, "Oh God."

It was inconceivable, it was nightmarish and impossible........ yet it was happening. Seemingly inevitably, step by step. And now another thoughtful, reverberate silence.

But as the women resumed talking Ingrid sensed there was something else behind all this – by dint, as ever, of Paula's hints and implications. There was much mention, for instance, of the relative *security* England offered........

If Ingrid was right in what she sensed then Paula's agenda was, even by her standards, extraordinary. So extraordinary that Ingrid felt impelled to ask:

"Paula, are you suggesting that I, too, go to England?"

"No, I'm not exactly *suggesting* it but I do feel it's something you should consider. After all - realistically - what is there now, for you, in Germany, given everything that has happened? It's obvious why you came originally, and I've every sympathy – I'd have done the same at your age -" Ingrid grimaced - "but the main things I think you came for, if I am not very much mistaken, I mean help, understanding, and, let's be honest, parental nurturance, don't seem to have been forthcoming at all..... realistically. Rather the reverse."

At which Ingrid, wound up like a clock, once more got cross. Not least because there are few things more annoying than being presented, gratuitously, with the truth.

"My mother has been very supportive." she said. "And my father -" her voice began that irritating quiver.

"......Well, my father is my father.... he means well......"

"I'm sure he does, but again, realistically, I have seen what he has done to you, Ingrid, and I'm just saying there are alternatives, improbable though they may seem right now. There are people who want to help you. People with resources –

"Resources?"

"Well, people like Charles..."

"Charles!"

"Well, he *could* help, should he wish to....and Mary - you know that Henry is probably going back as well? That's not just the war scare, it's that she and Henry have been in touch lately, rather close touch actually, letters flying back and forth, and a big thing she's stressed is that you'd be more than welcome to stay at Westbury, as long as you liked, should you ever so wish.... there's even Alexey........"

"*Alexey!*"

"Yes, Alexey. I know how you feel, and I absolutely understand, but he really is quite genuinely anxious to help as well, and he too has relatives...... with still more resources...."

But Alexey was a name too far.

"I want to make one thing absolutely plain, Paula. I will have no dealings with Alexey in any shape or form. No dealings at all! Do I make myself clear?!"

Paula gave her a sideways look.

"You most certainly do," said Paula. "Very clear indeed."

But now Paula's predictions looked ever more plausible. On the afternoon of the 29th, the day Austria started bombarding Belgrade, Tsar Nicholas of Russia ordered partial mobilisation. The next day, the Austrians mobilised too. At which the Russians mobilised in full. Then on the thirty-first, the Kaiser sent an ultimatum to Russia demanding demobilisation within twelve hours. There was no reply, and on Saturday the first of August the ultimatum expired.

At seven-ten pm Count Portales, the German ambassador in St. Petersburg handed Sazonov, the Russian foreign minister, the German declaration of war.

Chapter Sixty-One

The result, for Ingrid, was to concentrate her mind.

Her friends, both English and German, had proved wanting; her family, downright perverse; her country had committed itself to an adventure which seemed, the more she thought about it, *utterly* insane.

And in all this confusion only one thing seemed sure. Her baby! Solid and real, placed square and warm within her belly. Her baby....... the sole reality in all this chaos. Her baby, and the love she would bear it, and the future she would build for them both, somewhere, somehow, unlikely though the prospect might seem right now.

This, she decided, more surely all the time, was what she knew and what she believed in. And on this she would act.

So when Paula returned to see her the next day, trying ever more vehemently to persuade Ingrid to go to England, she was already near-persuaded.

Not only, said Paula, had Mary already found rooms that Ingrid could use – the rooms previously lived in by Anthony Parsons - but there'd been an intervention, as Paula had thought there might be, by Charles' father.

Though strictly unofficially, he'd said he might very well offer Ingrid (his generosity only matched by his anxiety to head off any scandal involving Charles) an initial sum of no less than £500, to be followed by further amounts to be negotiated. Not to mention – although Paula hardly dared mention it – Alexey's uncle ……

To which Paula added one final argument, one that had only arisen, really, in the last twenty-four hours.

Whatever some said, and whatever happened in Europe, England would stay neutral. A message, apparently, had just gone from King George to the Kaiser, guaranteeing it. This too she'd heard via Charles' parents. What wild, survival-at-any-cost convolutions politics consisted in, to be sure!

If England did remain neutral, what better berth for Ingrid and her baby than the one safe haven in a Europe engulfed in flames?

Nevertheless, the moment that clinched it wasn't logical at all. It involved her mother. On August the first, a Sunday, on her return from church, Frau Uberspeer had retired to her bedroom. At which moment Ingrid knocked on her door, intending one last push to get the truth of her mother's history.

And found her on her knees, praying! And as Ingrid, half diffident, half irritated, started asking the familiar family-history questions, it was religion, in its most intense form, with which her mother blocked her.

For not only did Frau Uberspeer refuse, once more, to answer the crucial question of paternity, but her latest diversion – the war crisis – took the form of a strange new chauvinism: an attack, of all things, on England's *jewishness*.

Taking wing into metaphysics, she arraigned England for its obsession with the *spirituality* of wealth. The idea that you were better morally if you were rich. A notion, she declared, that English Puritanism had picked up through its love of the Old Testament. Hence the "Jewishness."

Mein Gott, but this was madness indeed! Where on earth had mother got hold of this? From her church friends? From those Entlingen lawyers? Yet even the thoughts themselves palled, in their effect, beside her mother's expression: her face contorted, her red-rimmed eyes screwed up narrowly as a ferret's; the precise opposite of the warm, fat smiles of old. The mother she knew had disappeared.

Ingrid, stood there, open-mouthed, saying nothing at all. So this, thought Ingrid, is the other side of my mother's unreasoning, tribal love - tribal hatred. And at a moment like this – judging by her looks! - she plainly includes *me* in this attack on Jewishness. Whatever "Jewishness" means - surely nothing other than a blank cheque on which one can write anything at all in terms of crazy, paranoid fear.

But worst of all was the extent to which she saw her mother, at this moment, as above all *small* – a petty, vindictive creature, impossible to respect.

She turned abruptly and strode out of the room. She would go to England. She would leave her mad, obsessive homeland, and her strange, tormented family, so incapable at this moment of any parental succour, and take up the one sane option seemingly on offer: asylum in England, however worldly and imperfect that offer might be.

Though that was consciously. Half-consciously Ingrid was aware, too, that yet another, still more powerful force was drawing her back toward England; but this she thrust determinedly from her mind.

Chapter Sixty-Two

Not that there was any shortage of distractions. For now the situation escalated further still.

Germany was already at war with Russia. By August the third she had declared war on Russia's ally, France; on Tuesday the fourth, in accordance with the Schlieffen plan, the German army invaded Belgium.

A wave of outrage swept Great Britain and talk of British neutrality began to look wildly misplaced.

Her government sent Berlin an ultimatum, demanding the Germans' withdrawal, to expire that night. Berlin ignored it. By midnight German time (eleven o'clock English time) England and Germany were at war. The catastrophe was complete.

Just four short days had transformed the now rather fanciful-looking plans of Ingrid and her friends. Indeed, Paula's earlier concern, that they might be 'incarcerated' as enemies of the state, looked ever more real. At which stage it became plain what was meant by Paula's much-trumpeted 'resources.' Notably, of course, those of Charles Fisher's parents, but not forgetting too the lesser, yet significant, pull of Alexey's uncle, still in France. (Paula kept this from Ingrid.) Contacts were made, favours called in, and within twenty-four hours the British party (all of them, including Henry) found themselves whisked, by sympathetic German officials, from Munich up to the neutral Dutch frontier and thence to Hamburg.

There they were booked on a rough-and-ready cargo boat which arrived in Harwich, after traversing Mediterranean-blue seas, just six hours later.

Part Three: War

Chapter Sixty-Three

As they approached the English coast, the idyllic weather vanished. The sky became dull and rainy. "Typical British welcome", thought Ingrid, eyeing the scudding clouds morosely.

There was no-one in the harbour to greet them; in fact there was no-one *at all* in the area behind the docks – no carts, cars or pedestrians to be seen. Only – on more careful glance - what looked like *soldiers* lining the streets. Was this the war? Yet the soldiers looked ceremonial. A departing general perhaps? A royal visit? Ingrid's party stood on the gunwale and gazed, speculating noisily on what was going on.

At which moment a bright yellow limousine appeared, nosing carefully down Harwich's main street. Ingrid vaguely recognized it. Out of the front got the chauffeur; he swung round the back and opened the door. There emerged a tall, impressive man in a tweed suit and cap, followed by what was presumably his wife, dressed fashionably in a green travelling coat and hat, held in place with a long scarf. This couple looked familiar. Next two little girls, both dressed in blue, skipped down after them.

Finally, from the seat beside the driver, came a yet older man. This one was more than dignified, he was stately - and in a flash, Ingrid *did* recognize him. He was Lord Stanbury, the very same minister who Ingrid had sat next to at dinner on her first visit to Clayton Court. At which moment she recognized his companions. They were Charlie Fisher's parents. "Mama!" cried Charles, profusely waving.

And now another car appeared, and then another: then a convoy.

And as they passed in front of Ingrid, a further surprise. The cars' occupants were Germans! The first had what looked like officers in it; the next, civilians - but well-dressed civilians, perhaps diplomats? The next, another figure Ingrid vaguely recognized, once again plus wife, but this time accompanied by an English admiral. Now who was he?

As the cars passed, the soldiers presented arms.

When they stopped two soldiers rushed up and opened the doors of the third car, the one with the English admiral. Out got a slim, hunched figure in a top hat and suit.

Now Ingrid understood. This was Prince Lichnowsky, the German ambassador to London. Ingrid had seen him when he came to Oxford to receive a doctorate.

And how different he looked today! For all his dignified mien the man looked shattered.

The ship on which Lichnowsky's party, at least two hundred strong, would embark was just along the quay. And as the Germans debouched from their cars Ingrid and her friends walked down the gang plank to join them.

They'd just started talking to the buzzing crowd, wondering where and how to access their luggage, when they heard a shout. It was Von Leckburg, from New College! He was one of the German travellers.

He walked up with his hand held out in greeting, and soon it was plain that pretty much the whole German New College crew were there. Ernst Hoffman and little Albert and at least two others no-one recognized, maybe students from other colleges.

The two youthful groups, English and German, greeted each other, at first, with the same jokes and laughter they might have done a month previously; moments later, recollecting the obvious, they subsided into sobriety. Though their manner remained friendly.

"A sad moment," said Von Leckburg.

"Very sad," Ingrid replied.

"So you are coming back here?" said Von Leckburg. "I heard something to that effect."

"Yes I am," said Ingrid, "There are, as you can imagine, compelling reasons,".

"Yes, I know," said Von Leckburg. "That is, I know a little."

Ernst Hoffman and Albert, meanwhile, were eying Ingrid less sympathetically.

"The reasons would have to be very good," muttered Albert, " to leave your homeland at such a time."

"The reasons *are* very good," interceded Charles, "as I'm sure you'll have the courtesy to understand."

"They most certainly would have to be."

"They most certainly are."

So soon! The crisis, with a life of its own, had already interposed itself between the friends. They eyed each other sourly.

At which moment the band started playing "Ich hatt' einen Kameraden", one of the noblest of German military songs. A piece about friendship – lost friendship - and surely chosen for just that reason.

And as the group turned, they saw Lichnowsky shaking hands with local dignitaries, including what looked like Harwich's mayor. Until, that is, Lichnowsky spotted Stanbury and the Claytons.

With his characteristic grace Lichnowsky detached himself and walked over to greet them, while the band went on playing. How remarkably, thought Ingrid, did 'Ich hatt' fit the scene before them!

Indeed it had a curious effect. It was as if Lichnowsky's manner, and the spirit of the music, created a floodtide of amiability which overwhelmed all confrontation.

Von Leckburg once again held out his hand, gazing deep into Alexey's eyes, and said:

"Friends in past and friends forever."

And Alexey mumbled a reply.

An hour later the Germans were on the boat.

"Friends in past and friends forever." This was, in fact the last signal sent by the Germans to the visiting English fleet when they'd left the Kiel regatta six weeks earlier. Von Leckburg had clearly been impressed. Ingrid could not but chuckle, even so, that he had borrowed it.

Nevertheless, the British admiralty had arranged the steamship St. Petersburg, on which the Germans were travelling, and it was as if the boat, too, was imbued with the dignity that infected everything else.

With its sturdy, upright posture and its backward-sloping funnels, it looked almost human; and as it glided out into the ocean, (the band, now, was playing Auld Lang Syne), Ingrid felt it took with it everything she knew and understood: a nobler, kinder, and more chivalrous world.

Chapter Sixty-Four

And so Licknowsky sped off to Germany, where he was promptly blamed for Britain's entry into the war. (In fact he had been one of the most earnest advocates of peace.)

But then the catastrophe was so great, and the disorientation so profound, that everyone in Europe was behaving strangely.

Ingrid encountered the English version of this the moment she reached Westbury village, en route to the camp, where the men wanted to say hello to Mary before carrying on to Oxford.

For as soon as they arrived Ingrid sensed the same spying, staring hostility she'd felt in Entlingen. How on earth did these villagers even know who she was? But she felt, instinctively, they somehow knew she was German – and therefore hated her - just as the Entlingers had hated her for being 'English'.

What became plain, over the next few days, was that this 'mental illness,' as Ingrid thought of it, was affecting everyone.

There was Charles Fisher, for instance - whose socialist protestations had always been at war with his conservatism. The moment war was declared, he'd put in for the Honourable Artillery Company. And thus re-established himself in his parents' approval, for the first time in years.

Then there was Alexey. Gone, in a flash, was the communism he had picked up in France. He had a new creed now, knightly advocacy of the weak: the defence of small nations against the bullying of the strong. Of Belgium, naturally, but above all that of Serbia, the rackish, unstable kingdom where all this chaos had begun.

But most startling of all was Paula. For it was she – Paula the communist, Paula the feminist, Paula the pacifist-internationalist par excellence – who became, overnight, the most patriotic of them all.

Her ardour for things British was unlimited, her hatred for things Teutonic unassuageable. (Of course, she excepted Ingrid personally.)

While she hedged, too, her new belief-system with further get-out clauses. Not least the notion that this was, as H. G Wells put it, 'the war to end wars.' So that fighting itself became a kind of pacifism.

Meanwhile :

"Aux Armes, Citoyens !
  Formez vos bataillons!"

More than once, Ingrid caught Paula singing the Marseillaise.

Meanwhile, despite the hostility of the locals – some of them at least - Ingrid began to settle in at Westbury. Above all, she was delighted by the welcome of Mary Thornton.

For Mary had prepared meticulously for Ingrid's coming.

When Ingrid walked into her new rooms the bedcover was turned down, there were flowers beside the bed, and a copy, even, of Pride and Prejudice, Ingrid's favourite English novel.

And as Ingrid sank down on the bed, inhaling the sweet aroma of the cabin's wooden walls, plus the coffee Mary had brought, it felt like that first evening back in Entlingen, when she'd smelled the scent her mother had sprinkled on her pillows. She felt, in fact, that she'd found what she'd been seeking for weeks, throughout Europe ....a home.

She'd telegraphed the Crosbys, but only to put them on hold. She was back in England, she said, but recalled that before the catastrophe she'd been on holiday. Well, here was a way to continue the holiday she'd cut short. She explained the Thorntons' invitation; she said she would be coming back to Oxford 'shortly.'

In fact, she intended no such thing. Not least because the news of her pregnancy would sooner or later reach the Crosbys, and she had no idea how to handle it.

Meanwhile she hoped to create a little oasis, however temporary, of calm. How deeply she needed it! And, rather surprisingly, that seemed possible. For there turned out to be at least some of the Westbury village circle, not just the Thorntons, who were quite friendly.

Because as well as those who hated her and all she symbolised – all things, that is, lewd, licentious and Teutonic - there were others, too, who retained their loyalty to Henry. And through Henry, to Ingrid also.

These friendlier folk - who included, from the village, Ben Tennent and Fred Parsons, not forgetting, of course, Henry's gardening 'pupil', John Croome, had even managed a welcoming banner over the camp entrance. Quite a contrast to the village generally. So that in the camp, certainly, the atmosphere quickly became almost as cheery as before Henry left.

The war, however threatening, failed to engulf them. The landscape remained the same. The harvest fields smiled on as usual; the beech grove, where Ingrid regularly walked, embraced her as ever. At times it seemed quite hard to grasp there *was* a war on.

All of which was further helped by the absence of Anthony Parsons. He'd been in France, apparently, rescuing that same sister he'd helped earlier, the one who'd been bereaved. He'd wanted to get her out before the Germans came.

And when they'd successfully fled - by the skin of their teeth – they'd gone back to Anthony's base in London.

Which led to Anthony's being much more accepting of Henry's return than he might otherwise have been, given Henry's earlier bolt for France.

For Anthony decided to stay in London for the present, to help settle his sister in. Meanwhile, someone, said Anthony, had to hold things together at Westbury – because there'd been another, huge development. Robert and Jane weren't coming to Westbury after all!

Robert, apparently, had joined the army, and Jane had moved to Islington to live with her friend.

The whole, louring threat of their return had disappeared.

A miracle! Henry was delighted.

Chapter Sixty-Five

Crucial to this newly resurrected Westbury was the reconciliation of the Thorntons. Mary was delighted to have Henry back, and Henry was glad too. Although it was the children he appreciated most.

They were the ones he unequivocally loved. For Mary, when things were going well, he felt all manner of delightful things, warmth, humour, companionship, and notably sex; but, in the end, it was the sweetest, tenderest friendship he felt for her, not love. But for his daughters….

And he was, as he had always been, aware of this. How often had he told Mary, to her palpable distress, that he was 'incapable of love!' But what he meant, of course, was….. 'love for you.'

Conceivably he might have loved another woman. Undoubtedly he loved his daughters. But now, since France, a whole new factor had emerged.

What he had found in France, and what had shaken him to the core, was his capacity to love - unequivocally, fully, sensually - another man. He loved Alexey. True, he'd always known he 'loved' him in the conventional sense of deep male friendship. But what astonished and overwhelmed him was the realisation that this could be translated, as it had been for one heady fortnight, into the intensest expression of sex.

The experience of which had been so new, so utterly subversive of every idea he had about himself, that he recoiled as from an electric shock. While Alexey too, though less alarmed than he, had likewise jumped back from such an extraordinary escalation of their earlier, years-old friendship.

Indeed, Alexey's retreat had been one of many reasons why he'd started thinking longingly, again, of Ingrid. Maybe she, after all, and in some way, could prove his heterosexuality?

While Henry's reaction was comparable. For on his return, Mary's sexual ardour, in her delight at getting him back, was extreme. And his response - almost as ardent, and certainly a very great deal more eager than before - was avid enough to go some way toward confirming his own sense of himself as above all else a red-blooded male.

Which pleased Mary very much. But maybe misled her.

Despite all this, little was said. Little was said between Alexey and Henry: they were far too disoriented to sort out what they really felt, let alone discuss it.

Nor was much said between the partners - Alexey and Ingrid, Henry and Mary. After their brief flurry in Germany at the play Ingrid, especially, was floundering as to how to take the subject further with Alexey.

But those around them were talking of little else.

So this cacophony among their friends, of which all four were only too aware, made it stranger still that the only people *not* talking about it were the main protagonists.

One day Mary Thornton decided to change this.

"Perhaps you can guess what this is about," she said one morning, having asked Ingrid if she could face 'a little discussion.'

"It's about Henry," Mary said.

"Yes."

"And Alexey."

"Yes."

A pause. A darting glance.

"What have you heard?"

Ingrid mumbled something, but Mary interrupted her.

"Whatever you've heard," said Mary, "It isn't true."

"Oh! Oh yes. Well, I must say, I thought myself that -"

Now Mary was vehement.

"- No, it's *not* true, because if it were, Henry would not be as he is. I mean, setting aside whether or not he could have any such proclivities - setting aside Alexey, indeed - Henry's behaviour towards me, since he's come back, shows he absolutely does not."

Another pause.

"Have any such proclivities."

Once again Ingrid began murmuring. Once more Mary interrupted.

"You see," continued Mary, "if he did, then, frankly, he wouldn't want me, physically, as he has done, and since he's come back he's..... wanted me.... very much." Ingrid was touched by her older friend's sexual reticence, a reserve she herself had long lost. "I'm not just talking physically, though he has been very ardent" (a nervous smile) "I'm talking as much about his attentiveness generally, which has been as loving and considerate as I've known."

Was that a break in Mary's voice?

"I'm very glad to hear it, "said Ingrid. "But I still think we ought to ….."

"- You see, I know Henry. I know his moods. I know him up, I know him down. I know him roundabout! At his worst he can be savage, but at his best he can be the loveliest fellow in the world." Ingrid looked quizzical. "Oh yes, he can, you see, and that's the thing - his moods are variable. Indeed they swing"- Ingrid nodded - " alarmingly, but that's because he never hides them. Henry can be impossible, horrible even, but one thing he never does is dissemble."

"Yes."

"He's hopelessly committed to the truth."

"Yes."

"And that's the thing, his mind and feelings are inseparable and so are his mind and body, likewise. If he expresses himself sexually with me, now, then that is an expression of how he feels spiritually, and by the same token" Ingrid saw Mary was reaching her bull point "unless he had those spiritual feelings for someone else, he wouldn't be able to express them physically, either. And as he doesn't, he won't."

Ingrid was beginning to feel dizzy.

"That's how I know," rounded off Mary, "*for certain,* he's never slept with Alexey."

"I'm sure – well I certainly hope - that's true, but isn't it just
 possible that -"

"– Look, I think you really should pay attention to what I'm saying because, to state the obvious, if Henry's not sleeping with Alexey, then Alexey's not sleeping with Henry."

That, certainly, was undeniable.

"No, neither of them are homosexual," continued Mary, "I'm sure of it, and as for the gossip, well frankly, it's just nonsense. For the reasons I've just given you."

And indeed, throughout their following discussion, Mary was implacable. Her argument came back, again and again, to the same point, which could be boiled down to: "Henry can't be homosexual, he's too keen on having sex with me."

Which Ingrid could see sounded plausible enough, and yet......... if Mary was so sure of it, why wouldn't she allow Ingrid even the slightest word of dissent?

But it was the only argument Mary would entertain, and it continued until Ingrid, despairing of getting anywhere at all, excused herself to play with Mary's children.

For the truth was, Ingrid didn't buy Mary's argument at all. She entirely believed in the Thorntons' sexual relationship; it was just that she didn't think it proved anything about Henry's other, deeper, 'proclivities.' Didn't Paula have sex with men, innumerable men, yet also women? Even unto hook-nosed Elspeth? There was such a thing as bisexuality; and that, she believed, was Henry's story, much like Paula's.

Homosexuality was where Henry's deepest feelings expressed themselves, in Paula's mantra. Indeed, Henry's very heterosexual ardour, properly understood, could well be the expression of its opposite. In sex, as in so many things, one can protest too much.

As for Alexey, she could only too readily see how HE could be homosexual, if only because any reservations about his heterosexuality, unlike Henry's, were surely plain.

His heterosexuality, quite simply, didn't exist. His homosexuality, on the other hand, fitted the facts; it was the final reason why Ingrid was never going to get involved with, or hurt by him again, despite his recently rediscovered interest.

Not that Alexey's sexuality didn't disturb her, ravage her, obsess her even, however much she thrust it from her mind.

And the particular form this irritation took was always the same. Above all else, (embarrassed though she was to admit it) it was her ***physical*** disgust at homosexual love-making. She hated the idea of Henry's hands moving over Alexey's body, of them kissing each other on the mouth! How utterly grotesque and unnatural! For all Ingrid's late adventurousness she remained, in the end, the daughter of the bourgeoisie.

And yet......was this physical antipathy ***really*** the heart of it?

Might it not - and Mary, observing Ingrid, wondered this - be a kind of mask? One that distracted Ingrid - one that she ***wanted*** to distract her - from her real anxiety: that Alexey's 'proclivities' meant she was being denied the one thing she needed more than anything else in the world: deep, fulfilling, heterosexual love.

Something infinitely beyond the sensuality with which she had toyed.

Chapter Sixty-Six

Meanwhile, European events began to quicken. The Germans swarmed into Belgium. The British expeditionary force left England on August the ninth and was in Amiens five days later. The Germans invested the forts at Liege – and then, a surprise.

On August 12th, at Haelen, the Belgian general De Witte employed the new cavalry techniques of dismounted riflemen to roundly defeat the German Uhlans. Momentarily it seemed the German tide might be stemmed. Some allied generals even saw themselves in Berlin.

Not, however, Britain's new Secretary of State for War, Lord Kitchener.

In a council of war on August the fifth he astounded his colleagues by saying "we must put armies of millions in the field and maintain them for several years." Seventy divisions, he declared, would be required – an army to match the seventy-division continental armies of Germany and France. He further pointed out that even with massive volunteer recruitment, such totals would be unreachable before the war's third year.

Third year? What could the man be thinking? Gradually the British were grasping the immensity of the task before them. And the realisation put ever-increasing pressure on Ingrid's friends. Lord Kitchener's famous poster, with its pointing finger, could have been aimed at them. What ***would*** their contribution be?

Charles Fisher, of course, had already volunteered. Edward Stourbridge, too, was on the verge of getting in. Alexey had tried to volunteer, but had so far failed to find a regiment. And as for Henry, the military agnosticism he started out with had only increased since the declaration. Unimpressed by the patriots, he was equally unenthused by the 'flimsy pacifism' as he put it, of the war's opponents.

Notably the teachers at Greenfields, the progressive local school where Mary taught part-time. "They are far too taken by the beauty of their moral stand," he said. "I don't trust them."

But Mary disagreed - not least because she needed her colleagues' moral support. After all, having finally got Henry back home, she was terrified of losing him. There was the very real possibility, should he enlist, that Rosemary and Josephine's father could be killed.

For a day or two, as the military situation unfolded ever more catastrophically, the world of Westbury stood still. Until, that is, word came that Joe Parsons, of all people, had got involved.

For Joe, like most of the villagers, belonged to the instinctive, 'blood and soil' school of politics. He was determined, pretty much regardless of right and wrong, that England should be defended. And aware that

Henry's friends were eager to join up, but were faced with the same problem as all the other eager volunteers countrywide - too many recruits for places available - he'd had a thought.

Why not make use of the Westbury Camp horses, plus those from his farm, and offer them, with as many of Henry's friends as wished to ride them, to the Oxfordshire Yeomanry? They'd been on their summer camp when war was declared so they were de facto mobilised, not far away, at Northbourne. Here was a fine way, surely, of circumventing any delay. Such regiments, nationally, were desperate for recruits with mounts.

The advantage, of course, would be the speed with which they could join. The drawback, that they would have to join as troopers, i.e., ordinary soldiers, not officers. (Though promotion, surely, would be fast and sure.) Meanwhile, Joe would be making the same offer to his farmworkers. "So you might fetch up beside Ben Tennant," cackled Joe. "Rather worse than facing down Von Kluck."

The idea swiftly gained momentum. Henry, very naturally, liked the connection with horses. Alexey, too, loved horses and rode well. Charles and Tom leapt at the idea, while there was the further advantage, for Henry, that any training, for the next few months, would surely take place at Northbourne - just five miles away. There'd be no need to leave home.

As for lining up beside Ben Tennant – well, weren't they all socialists? What did rank matter if they were serving king and country? Let's rephrase that: "King and community."

Within a week they had all signed up and within ten days they were camping at Northbourne.

They had brought their horses. There were no less than twelve Westbury recruits, including both Oxford students and Westbury villagers. They joined several hundred other 'yeomen' and the vague plan was that the students could combine their training, in the early stages at least, with their studies at Oxford, so close by.

The Germans had based their whole campaign on beating the French in forty days. Well, should any such quick result happen – hardly, true, the outcome they looked for - that would be a clear month, plainly, before the Michaelmas term started in October!

Meanwhile, it emerged that the yeomanry commander, Colonel Tucker, to boost morale, had arranged a grand review of all recruits, on August the eighteenth. Which news enlivened Ingrid and Mary, for they were invited. Not just for their connections of family and friendship, but to acknowledge their own special contribution to the cause.

For within days of the declaration the women of Westbury, corralled by the vicar, had started classes in First Aid and Home Nursing. More remarkably still, someone had found some nearly-new nurses' uniforms.

With the result that Mary and Ingrid were shortly to be seen in bright white dresses with big red crosses on the front: which further helped their reputation with the more sceptical villagers. To such an extent that not only did a growing faction of Westbury villagers declare Ingrid to be 'lovely' but there were those who further declared that she couldn't possibly be German, or from Bavaria, wherever *that* was, at all.

So by the bright and sunny morning of the eighteenth, the day of the review, Ingrid, Mary, Paula and even Elspeth (she'd demanded she come too - she had a constant sense, these days, of being left out) arrived at the Yeomanry camp.

It was in a broad green valley with a stream running down one side, overlooked by downs. Vaguely, Ingrid recognized it. Then she remembered: was it not the identical valley, or one very near it, where she and the others had gone that memorable walk in early spring? Henry later confirmed this: its very remoteness made it ideal for manoeuvres.

The women decanted from the taxi. There were, it turned out, no trains they could take that day. They were late - the taxi driver had got lost amidst the remote and empty fields.

Rows of off-white, canvas tents filled the meadows; beyond them, long lines of tethered horses, working their usual magic on the landscape.

As the women paid off the taxi, then hovered uncertainly, a group of blue-clad soldiers rushed over.

It was Alexey, Henry, and Tom, here to welcome them! But dressed like never before. Their blue uniforms - there were not, as yet, khaki uniforms available - made them look like sailors, even prison guards, more than soldiers. More striking still, they'd got regulation haircuts, transforming their looks. Henry in particular, who'd normally a great mane of sandy hair, was transformed.

Chatting cheerily, the friends walked over to the other guests.

Near a marquee there were cars parked, including a familiar yellow Rolls Royce. Ingrid quickly recognised Lord Stanbury and the Claytons.

And now Colonel Tucker, the Oxfordshire's commanding officer, strolled over to meet them, walking with a gentle, swinging motion, carefully contrived, Ingrid felt, to convey courtesy and ease.

"Hello!" he said, with that familiar English informality. "How good of you to come. I'm surprised you found it, actually. Some people never get here at all."

"We reduced the taxi driver to despair," said Mary. "He said: 'I can find a village, even a farm, but I draw the line at a field!'"

Everyone laughed.

Due to the taxi-driver's 'mild disorientation', it was explained - more laughter – they would go straight in to lunch.

The young and old ate in different tents, for which Ingrid was grateful. This was only the second time she'd met the Claytons since her return, and she knew they knew about the pregnancy. They'd offered that money..... who knows what had been said ......she preferred them separate.

Meanwhile the mood of jollity was sustained, with many wisecracks about where the food had come from (answer, predictably, Charles Fisher's parents - notably the champagne and smoked salmon.) But soon the talk moved to the latest news from France. It was alarming, and by no means what had been expected.

Charles was the authority. He'd heard the latest from Stanbury, who'd got it from Downing Street.

The Belgian forts at Liege, Charles said, had been utterly smashed, by the heaviest artillery the world had ever seen: Skoda 305 mortars and Krupp 420s, the mightiest of them all. And now the German infantry were swarming on toward France. The word was at least 7OO, OOO soldiers were on the move. Some thought their numbers as high as 2, OOO, OOO.

"But that's impossible, they haven't the troops."

"Yes they have, they're using reserves."

"What reserves? They haven't got any."

"Yes they have - they're putting territorials in the front line."

Suddenly the conversation was being monopolised by the men.

"It's the Schlieffen plan," said Charles, in his deepest voice. "They pour down west of Paris, make a U-turn south and then drive East again back toward the German frontier. And they take the main French armies, advancing on the Rhine, in the rear."

"Unless the French, as *they* plan, push through the Rhine so fast they lop off the invading arm, as it were, at the shoulder. That's *their* plan – they call it Plan Seventeen."

"L'audace, l'audace....."

"Or envelopment, if you like – everybody's trying to take everyone else in the rear. Like a revolving door."

"Or like Hannibal enveloping the Romans at Cannae." Here was Charles again. "That's where Schlieffen got his ideas from. It's still, two thousand years later, THE classic of military strategy and it continues to dominate the thinking on both sides."

This brought silence. No-one felt they had the authority to reply.

Except Ingrid. Her days of reticence, in the face of male conversational monopoly, were long gone.

"Tell me something," she said. "I've heard this kind of thing often, back at home. And I've heard, too, how the Kaiser read this book by some American admiral, Admiral Mahan, 'The Influence of Sea Power on History," or some such? And how Mahan's starting point was this same conflict, the Punic Wars, and how Hannibal's lack of a fleet was why he attacked Rome from Spain. Sending those elephants over the Alps! And how this was what convinced the Kaiser that he had to build a fleet and challenge the British....... ......which turned out rather badly, I'd say..... well............ I just wonder this: why are these modern people basing their ideas on such very ancient history, copying wars and battles fought before Christ? Couldn't they find something a bit more up to date?"

If Charles' remarks produced silence, this produced a conversational black hole. Rarely had there been a better example of Ingrid's capacity to state the obvious.

Finally, Tom laughed out loud. "Good question Ingrid!"

While Henry, looking at his most pensive, picked up her thought:

"Yes: and there *are* ideas around surely far more relevant to our times. There's a passage in HG Wells 'Anticipations', for instance, where he says the next war will be one long stalemate, with both sides permanently entrenched. There'll be a front line, a second line and a support line, the troops supplied by railways, and there won't be any advance or retreat or envelopment at all, the whole thing will be stuck."

And this produced the longest silence of all.

Nevertheless, with lunch finished the squadrons formed up, and the inspection began. Then Colonel Tucker had an inspiration.

He feared the ladies' visit, so far, might have been a bit dull. Would they care to ride?

Surprisingly, nearly all agreed. Ingrid had ridden from childhood; Mary, Paula and Kitty Clayton were all good riders too. Only Elspeth, who couldn't ride, was once again left out.

Four horses magically appeared, and with a little help from the men, the women mounted.

And Colonel Tucker suggested they canter down the lines.

After a moment's hesitation - Ingrid especially was concerned about her 'condition' - they accepted.

And off they galloped, the regiment's standard bearer, at a nod from Colonel Tucker, joining them, as a low cheer broke out among the ranks and swelled into a roar.

To the women, the regiment felt like a bulwark no enemy could subdue - especially the officers, posted like breakwaters ten yards in front of their platoons. Who could defeat, or even challenge, such men?

While to the soldiers, these young, romantic-looking women - the standard flying so bravely at their side - seemed like the embodiment of everything they were fighting for: their wives, their children, their aged parents.

The heart, the very essence, of Old England.

Chapter Sixty-Seven

Few felt this more than Alexey, though his vision was above all focussed on an individual - his newly rediscovered love, the lovely Ingrid.

Which was curious, really, given that a big reason he felt this way was sympathy for her pregnancy. For if there was one thing, he knew about *that*, it was that he, for sure, was not the father.

Nevertheless, ever since the friends had landed at Harwich, he'd made it his first priority to care for her.

For his reawakened feelings were above all nurturant. He wanted to help her, in practical, everyday ways. To that end he booked in at the Lamb and Flag, the poshest of the Westbury village inns, to be close at hand. He could afford it, as he was still receiving his uncle's allowance – and he felt it better not to stay up at the camp.

Nor did physical separation, if only by half a mile, prove any barrier. Every morning, for the first few days after their return, he made the twenty-minute walk up to Ingrid's rooms, as regularly as going to work. And when he got there he *did* work – prima facie at the practical tasks with which he routinely helped Henry, but actually in the hope of helping Ingrid.

And all the while he and Henry were scrupulously polite to each other, while studiously avoiding the least mention of the events of six weeks earlier.

That first day Alexey shifted furniture - there were a number of pieces, including a big wooden chest to put washing in, which he carried bodily into Ingrid's bedroom and plonked down by her bed. Then there were bookcases to be moved, plus a good fifty of Henry's books, which Mary persuaded Henry to lend her friend.

But most importantly, before Alexey ever walked up to Westbury, there were the phone calls he'd made on Ingrid's behalf from the Lamb and Flag. First to Charles Fisher, and then, at Charles' prompting, to the

Claytons' steward, to enable the first dollop of money - £50 - that the Claytons had promised Ingrid, and which meant she could now start her new life.

And this carried on in the days that followed. One of the most useful, if simple, things Alexey did was buy Ingrid a huge steel bucket, so fresh water could be brought down daily from the well. And whenever Alexey was there, he'd carry it personally down the slope, delighted to do at least something Ingrid could not.

Yet all these attentions, however lovingly carried out, cut very little ice with Ingrid. However she felt inside, outwardly she maintained her refusal to have any emotional truck with Alexey whatsoever. Not that she was in any way unpleasant. It might have been easier for him if she were. Rather she maintained a detached, steely politeness, a manner that reminded Alexey of an exceptionally well-trained assistant at Fortnum and Mason.

And if Ingrid's detachment was intended, however unconsciously, to be more hurtful than overt sarcasm it succeeded. Every time Alexey spent a day at Westbury, and she responded in this way, he went home more depressed.

But then he was still in the same state he'd been when circumstances had forced him – or seemed to force him - to leave Ingrid earlier that summer, and go to France.

For the moment he'd got there all the feelings he'd suppressed in England came rushing back. Out of touch, he'd felt unthreatened. Soon he felt more in love with her, at a distance of three hundred miles, than when they were just three inches away, in bed.

Yet there were limits to this. Slowly, inexorably, given Ingrid's utter discouragement, he began to back off. Eventually he found his own way of putting distance between them, though his mode of doing so was very different from hers.

The heady influence of the times took over. His love took on a pining, poetic quality reminiscent of the medieval Roman De La Rose (that ardent, dream-like poem whose heroines were so unassailable) and Ingrid soared, in Alexey's mind, to the remotest of pedestals.

For there was something else about the 'Roman's' flavour which especially suited Alexey. The 'Roman', sexually, is about one thing above all else...... non-consummation.

Meanwhile Ingrid, by contrast, was ever more obsessed by the war. How impossible, she thought, to imagine that just three weeks ago the whole of Europe had been at peace - in England's case, less than a fortnight.

Peace! All those Europeans who had now been thrown into such different, chaotic lives, doing the ordinary things that ordinary people do. The Munichers she'd seen on the day of their visit: the bus conductors, policemen, office managers hurrying to work, young men drinking in beer gardens, old women selling vegetables and flowers! All conducting their lives at that sedate, unhurried peacetime pace, with ample time for jokes, squabbles, flirts, procrastination.

And where were the same people now, above all the men? In uniform, engulfed, all individuality destroyed. Their days a horror of wounds and marches, their nights a torment of sleeplessness and shells! How could you connect these two existences?

The one thing certain was the vastness of the 'casualties' - as the military men called them - on every front. (The French alone had 14O, OOO 'casualties' in the four days of the so-called 'Battle of the Frontiers' in mid-August.)

'Casualties', indeed! What did that *mean*?

'War', a friend of Ingrid's mother had once said - a woman who'd been at Sedan in 1870 – is "one long street accident." Ingrid had seen a couple of such accidents in her time and the thing that struck her was how infinitely more horrid they were than ever she had been told.

There was one especially, involving the eight-year-old brother of her friend Madeleine. She and Ingrid had been walking into town to buy éclairs, and the brother, Tomas, who'd been cheeking them all the way, yelled one last piece of lip then skipped briefly off the pavement, just one foot on the road, and instantly – so suddenly it was unreal - was hit by an automobile and hurled across the pavement in front of them and plunged, head first, into a brick wall.

Ingrid never forgot the crack of it. Then out from his nose and mouth came these great, glutinous gobs of blood - not patters, not streams, but gobs, splattering around the pavement like cream. Yet Tomas' reaction had above all else been fear: "Help, help me" he kept crying, "mama, help!" Far more terrible than cries of pain.

Well, that was just one minor 'street accident.' Tomas recovered within a month. If something so insignificant could be so dreadful, what would war be like, with its 'street accidents' multiplied tenfold, thousandfold, with men losing arms, feet, stomachs blown to smithereens?

Was battle as horrendous she imagined? If so, why hadn't she been told? If not, why was she imagining it? Some said such things 'felt different on a battlefield', you were expecting horrors, you were keyed up for them. Maybe it *was* different – or in some other way. Surely it was! It must be! She would have heard, *surely*, otherwise.

Wouldn't she?

The truth, of course, was that it was infinitely worse - beyond imagination, indeed, for minds raised in the quietude of the early twentieth century. Little wonder, as one French officer put it, during the Franco-German 'Battle of the Frontiers', "two or three men go mad every day."

Yet this was, of course, precisely why such euphemisms as 'casualties' were employed. Reality had to be dissembled and reduced - how else could anyone act?

Ingrid shuddered for anyone going out to France. She shuddered, above all, for anyone she knew.

So she shuddered profoundly, when, on August the twentieth, just two days after the review, she heard from Henry that Alexey – summoned, seemingly by his uncle, who was still in France and was 'trapped,' apparently, by the German invasion – had rushed out to rescue him.

Not that she knew any more than this. Alexey had left so quickly - without the chance, even, to say his goodbyes - that by the time Ingrid heard about it, he'd already left the country.

Chapter Sixty-Eight

It had come as an even greater shock to Alexey. The first he'd known had been a telegram to the Lamb and Flag redirected from Oxford, which confined itself to saying he should come to France 'immediately' and then 'need urgent help – will explain.'

Alexey knew this much about his uncle. He never exaggerated. And he knew, too, that his uncle realised Alexey understood this, so there was no more to be said. Alexey would act.

And he must leave quickly, within forty-eight hours at the most. So his life became a vortex of last-minute preparations, a chaotic whirl.

Not least because his freneticism masked deeper anxieties still.

If anyone had asked Alexey how he might react in such a situation, he might have predicted nervousness, even fear: what he actually felt was dread. He felt a sudden steepling terror for what could happen to his uncle and aunt, the couple who had, for so many years, effectively been his parents They'd taken him in when his real parents had disappeared, they'd loved him, nourished him, advanced his interests in every way; how could he now abandon them? While rolling in on the back of his fears came a rush of love he hadn't felt since a child.

But he got help. When Charlie Fisher heard Alexey's news it was the work of a moment for him to suggest, as ever, the intervention of his parents, and therefore the still more powerful intervention of their friend Lord Stanbury.

That very night, a special messenger arrived at the Lamb and Flag by motor-bicycle. He brought tickets, a travel permit, (signed by Stanbury himself - Alexey was now, apparently, Lord Stanbury's 'special representative'), and even, from the Claytons, no less than £80 in cash.

So the thing was fixed in record time.

And so to France. By four o'clock the next day - Wednesday 19th August – Alexey was gazing at the receding cliffs of Dover, from the rear deck of the troopship Firefly, surrounded by 300 Territorials, early reinforcements.

How lovely those fabled cliffs in the late afternoon sunshine, the downs moving from shadow to palest green, a light wind fanning the clouds! How wonderfully they evoked the poets' 'Albion'! It was as if the country, parental, felt obliged to rise to its off-springs' departure, duly presenting itself in its best light.

So vivid was the image, so striking the symbolism, that it plainly infected the solders around him, who'd been rowdy earlier on. Now nearly every face, gazing back at England, looked thoughtful; one of the most striking being that of a young man Alexey had noticed earlier – but as an example of just the kind of person you don't expect to see, but always do, at such a moment.

This oleaginous teenager had a bent nose and a leer – for a weird moment Alexey found himself wondering if he were not some kind of mistake. He was a shopkeeper, surely, not a soldier! Certainly, Alexey had never seen a face like that in one of those heroic paintings you see in history books.

Yet now, if only momentarily, the young man was transformed. For Alexey saw him leaning against an aeration funnel quite alone, his mobile, rueful face frozen into thoughtfulness.

The situation had worked its magic. He too looked fine.

And then, as they docked at Boulogne, another change. No longer heroism, poetic or doleful, but something far more English - which Alexey, as a foreigner, recognised at once.

For here was the nation of shopkeepers in the mode it understood – business. It was like market day. Long lines of carts crammed full of provisions; neat rows of guns, with energetic corporals ticking forms; limbers packed with shells, automobiles stacked in lines, khaki-clad soldiers, with packs and rifles, falling in to march, presumably, to their holding camp. And in the distance, long lines of troops winding up the cliffs above the harbour, their progress throwing up great clouds of chalk-dust. Alexey could see what looked like tents at the very top.

Yells, shouts, commands, the neighs of horses, the roar of cars, and everywhere the sense of *bustle,* of eager, energetic action. England, clearly, felt this 'national emergency' could be handled the way she coped with everything else: with hard-nosed organisation and practicality. What a hive of industry this harbour was! Now Alexey knew what was meant by 'sinews of war'.

While at the back of his mind he had to admit, however ruefully, that a Russian army, similarly placed, would hardly look like that.

Yet even the English couldn't quite quash the heroic. As the cranes swung cannon up from the ships' holds, each gun spinning dizzily as it went, the process looked venturesome, triumphant, a victory in itself. Even the shrieks of the horses, winched up by the same technique (some died, Alexey heard later, from heart attacks) didn't spoil it.

While the guns themselves, once landed, their barrels straining ardently heavenward, made the heart soar.

Half an hour later he was on the quay. What next? He'd left England too quickly to make plans.

He fingered the wallet in his jacket. His best guarantee, surely, was that eighty pounds. It gave him every option, especially when added to his other ace, the 'letter of assignment' from Lord Stanbury. Nevertheless, he still had to make decisions – choices he'd decided he'd better leave till France, once he'd seen what was happening on the ground.

One thing for sure, he wouldn't be travelling by road. He'd go by train, the first hundred miles at least. But where? His uncle's house was in the little village of Frieres, just ten miles from Maubeuge, right up by the Belgian border. And the whole point of his journey was that the Germans were, or were just about to be, pouring into precisely that part of Northern France. Almost certainly the *end* of his journey, therefore, would have to be by road; it seemed unlikely that he would arrive at his uncle's local station, to be waved in by the Prussian Guard.

Would there be a civilian service at all, or would his only option be a military train - if he could get it?

He decided to seek advice from the people who'd know – the British Expeditionary Force Boulogne HQ. So after a few enquiries, and a few wrong turnings, Alexey found his way there, not at all sure, as he approached, of his welcome.

The HQ was in a nondescript brick building on the edge of the main square. Above the door was a somewhat weary-looking Union Jack; each side, sentries with fixed bayonets.

And yet despite the mustiness, Alexey felt a thrill of patriotism. He felt almost English, indeed, at the sight of the national banner out here in France, abroad and at bay. The lion had left its holt to meet its challengers - let them come on! England was ready for them, if they dared.

Adopting his most seigneurial air Alexey walked straight in, vaguely brandishing the letter from Lord Stanbury. His manner seemed to work; the sentries ignored him. Inside, he saw a desk down the end of the corridor, piled high with files. Behind was what looked like an NCO, writing something. Alexey walked up, still clutching his letter. After a brief upward glance the NCO ignored him.

Another union flag hung behind him on the wall. One corner, unattached, dangled precariously.

Eventually the NCO again looked up.

"Yes?" More a statement than a question.

"My name is Alexander Smolensky. I would like, if possible, to see your commanding officer."

This certainly got the NCO's attention. He swore quietly, then, with an air of astonishment which seemed, to Alexey, strangely studied, leant back in his chair, put down his pen and stared Alexey insolently in the face.

"Rank?"

"Private."

"Regiment?"

"Oxfordshire Yeomanry."

"Name?"

"Alexander Smolensky, as I mentioned before."

The NCO gave him a fish-eyed glare.

"What makes you think, Private Alexander Smolkensky" (the NCO made a meal of the pronunciation) "the C.O. wants to see *you*?"

For answer Alexey handed him Lord Stanbury's letter.

Transformation!

"Wait here," said the NCO.

He disappeared down the corridor and knocked at a door: moments later there was a whoop, a crash, and a short, tubby officer bounded out, grinning.

"Welcome, dear boy, welcome!" He had his hand out. "Macdonald's the name. Toby Macdonald. We've been expecting you.

"Heard all about you from two sources, actually – the chief" (General Armstrong, it emerged, in charge of the port) "and Charlie Fisher, who I've known for years. At school with him, indeed, for my sins."

And Alexey began to understand.

Macdonald shepherded Alexey into an office.

"Sit yourself down. Cup-a-char? Tell you what," he said, looking at his watch, "I've got a better idea. Why don't we have proper tea, it's about time?"

And he waved his arm at the same NCO Alexey had confronted earlier.

Moments later this same soldier - his manners transformed - reappeared with sandwiches, cakes, and a pot of tea. He even smiled.

There seemed a remarkable amount of sandwiches, but tea here was clearly a ritual. Two other young officers drifted over from the opposite side of the room. Then Toby Macdonald loped to the door, yelled "Tea!" and four more came.

"So what can we do for you?" said Toby. "I understand you're here to find a relative – your uncle, isn't it? Something about helping him get out of the North? Rather D. of you, I'd say, in all the circs."

He offered Alexey a sandwich, seized one himself and munched energetically.

"*Where* did you say your uncle lives?" Still grinning.

"Near Maubeuge, on the Belgian border - if he's still there, that is. I wired him before I left and heard nothing."

"Hmmm, you could try phoning him from here, if you like – amazing who you CAN get through to, these days, quite as much as who you can't. But the real problem, I'm afraid, is that nobody has a clue where *anybody* is at present or what the hell's happening anywhere, really, and that applies to everyone, Germans, French, Belgians, the lot - even, if I'm absolutely honest, ourselves."

"Talk about fog of war," said a voice.

"Well, we know *we're* attacking – that much is for sure." This from a young, tanned officer with beautifully brushed fair hair, waving a sandwich as if in triumph.

"Yes! We're attacking all right," cried Macdonald, "the French are attacking, the Germans are attacking, the Austrians too, the Russians are attacking in the East - "

"- Everyone's attacking, in fact, except the Belgians - "

Guffaws and shrieks.

"But where?" cried Macdonald. "And who? And why? That's what no-one knows, whatever they pretend, and that's why it's so hard to make plans."

More guffaws still. The levity of it all astonished Alexey. It was only gradually he grasped that these ingénue young officers, so new to war, were trying very hard to laugh, as they felt demanded of them, in the face of fear.

Now Macdonald looked at his watch. "The next troop train leaves in just twenty minutes, if they get off on time.

"It will take you towards Le Cateau, which is currently the BEF HQ, and once there you can decide what to do next.

"I really think you should go right away, if you possibly can."

Yet still the levity:

"The worst of it is you still haven't had proper tea!"

Chapter Sixty-Nine

An hour later Alexey was on the train.

In the event, Captain Macdonald joined him. HQ had heard an encounter was looming that would almost certainly involve the BEF. This could mean huge casualties, which Boulogne would have to deal with. And so, despairing of official channels, they'd sent Macdonald along as their 'spy'. "Only a day trip, hopefully," said Macdonald, "They want me back."

Eventually they found a compartment overflowing with territorials. And Alexey recognised three from the boat - not least he of the leer.

"Wherejew spring from? he said, whose name turned out to be Emsworth. "We thought we'd lost you!" But he humped his bag off the seat and made room.

The train moved off. As Alexey sat down, stacking his case on top of the soldiers' bags, he stowed an introductory note from General Armstrong – brought along by Macdonald - in his wallet, in the same pocket where he'd put the letter from Stanbury, which had had such a remarkable effect. Such personal contacts were clearly crucial.

Come to that, everything in the world, thought Alexey, was personal: who you knew, how you felt about them, how they felt about you, how you placed each other, in the light of such connections, in your value system. And when you extended such thinking to clans and nations, you had the tribalism which precipitated wars.

Worse still, the only people who seemed immune from such infection, for all Alexey had seen, were crazier still. Such outliers were sane indeed on things like nationalism but only because they were 'egregious', in the literal sense of the word – 'out of the flock'. Innocent of the groupthink and susceptibilities of the herd. But simultaneously separated off, emotionally, from all everyday connection: neurotic, chaotic, impossible to live with. Unfit for ordinary human intercourse.

People, if he were honest, like Henry Thornton and himself.

The train roared out of Boulogne and was soon tearing along with unholy eagerness, seemingly, to speed them to their fate.

Nevertheless, at railway crossings and villages there were cheering crowds, all wildly enthusiastic, with much waving of flags and flowers. One woman, at a village just out of Boulogne lifted her baby and cried "He too, like you, will do his duty when he grows up!"

The result was a further upswing of mood. Toward triumph and festivity now - virtually of picnic. Quite literally picnic, it emerged, as Macdonald had brought along a hamper which he proceeded to share with everyone in their compartment.

All of which was the merry tale till two hours out of Boulogne. Then the train slowed down, pottered cautiously, and stopped.

It stood there, panting heavily in the August sunshine. Eventually it moved forward again, but more slowly. Then it stopped again, this time for fifteen minutes; then, with a crash, it started moving backwards.

"Blimey! We're retreating!"

"Mummy mummy, save me!"

"Abandon ship!"

"Women and children last!"

Then the train stopped again, this time for good.

Macdonald investigated; soon he was back.

"Bit of a delay, I'm afraid," he said. "Everybody out!"

No problem about *that*. With a delighted rush Alexey's carriage emptied, as did all the others, and the men swarmed out over the meadow, into a foot deep of lush green grass. There were peasants harvesting in the next field, but they seemed oblivious.

It was a sultry, sticky day. The men disposed themselves around the meadow. Most took off their shirts. There was a wonderful, unexpected sense of freedom.

Then Alexey noticed a stir the other side of the field. Half a dozen peasant women were swapping banter with the troops.

"Bonjour madame" called a tall soldier, addressing a brown, full-bosomed woman in a peasant top. "Comment allez-vous?"

Shrieks of mirth from the other women, who nevertheless pushed the brown one closer.

"Souvenir," she said, with a wicked smile, pointing downward, seemingly, to her breasts.

Now it was the soldiers who were shrieking.

"Souvenir? I'll give her something to remember me by."

"I'll give her something she'll remember all her life."

Then Emsworth walked up to her. He seemed to peer down her breasts, then turned, grinning, to his friends.

"She's got a collection. Of souvenirs. Pinned to her dress. She wants another one."

Routine wisecracks.

Emsworth leered acknowledgement. "No, she wants a genuine souvenir, cap badge or something. She's got loads of them."

And the others, crowding up, saw what he meant. The young woman (her name, she said pertly, was Cecile) had indeed a row of 'souvenirs' stretched right along her dress, just above her breasts. Two cap badges, various buttons, even a belt buckle, in pride of place at the centre of her cleavage.

"I wonder how she got those."

"I wonder."

"Je pense que vous etes tres mechants" said Cecile, dimpling, then something else, in broken English, that no-one heard.

"What did she say?

"She says there's something behind that hedge," said Emsworth, leering some more. "She wants to show me."

More wisecracks, and Emsworth went off with Cecile. Moments later they reappeared.

"That was quick!"

"No, come with us!"

And a dozen soldiers, including Alexey, went off with Emsworth and Cecile beyond the hedge and there, in a slight dip, out of sight of the railway, they found an orchard, overflowing with apples and plums. "Voila !" cried Cecile, with a florid gesture. "C'est tout... pour vous !" (The farmer's view on this was unclear.) And beyond the orchard, a large, dark pond – cool and inviting. Doubtless the water source for both orchard and cattle.

Gestures conveyed the nature of a deal: souvenirs, please, for fruit! Or even - "voulez vous?" - a swim? Or even (intense glances, more giggling still) ...... des baisers?!

"Tell'er to try my breast stroke!"

"Or my back stroke!"

"I seenk," flashed Cecile, showing a greater facility for English than expected, "your natural stroke would be ze crayawl!"

More cheers.

Then suddenly, a roll of thunder, distant but distinct. Less than remarkable, perhaps, given the sultriness of the day. And then some more. And this time the rolling went on and on, so that slowly (and you could see the realisation dawning on each face) everyone realised it wasn't thunder, it was guns.

"Ah, c'est la guerre," said Cecile, with comic-opera mournfulness, as the war, which had permitted this brief interlude of repose, once more engulfed them.

For now, "Everyone back on the train!" shouted Captain Macdonald, appearing, plus two other officers, round the hedge. "The line's cleared, we're leaving. Jump to it!"

A minute later they were back in their compartment, leaving a disconsolate Cecile, and her friends, to stand, open mouthed, as the soldiers waved goodbye. Two waved back. They never did get their souvenirs.

"Now we 'ave our siesta," shouted Cecile, with a shrug.

"I wouldn't mind' avin 'er siesta."

"Stop it!"

Two hours later they arrived at Douai, their dropping-off place for the front.

Chapter Seventy

The moment they reached Douai they were overwhelmed by the most thunderous cannonade imaginable. The shuddering, remorseless, ear-numbing din soon felt like the sole reality in the world.

The concussion of it, the sense it gave of reverberating upward, from the ground, just as much as down; the way it made everything in the world tremble and jump, houses, windows, walls, trees, telephone wires, let alone people.......and yet for all its wild cacophony, it would ebb and flow, for a moment softer, then louder, then sometimes, for a second or two.....quite silent...... but this was worst of all. For you would be waiting, teetering, for the inevitable, cataclysmic resumption, the threat looming over you like a wave - then crash! Down it would come with its monstrous cacophony, and the pounding, throbbing horror would resume, as if the whole world were in pain.

You could see the thought on every face - what *is* this? Where has this weird, inexplicable thing come from? Incomprehension was everywhere, but beyond that, incredulity.

Some battle, clearly, was raging very close – but where? The word was the British were not engaged. But who exactly was fighting who, whether it was the Germans, the French, or even the Belgians, no-one seemed to know.

In front of the station, with this din as backdrop, milled a mass of carts, cars, lorries, packing cases, soldiers and civilians - still relatively orderly, in the British way, but without the spruceness of Boulogne, and with an undertow of urgency, even fear. To Alexey's right his soldier companions were loading themselves into lorries and he was waving goodbye when he saw Toby Macdonald hurrying across the square. He came up to Alexey, looking harassed, and herded him into a nearby estaminet, and thence into a back room, where there was at least a chance to hear each other speak.

"Jesus wept!" said Macdonald, "unbelievable, isn't it? Look, there's no car, I'm afraid. Gone AWOL. I've spoken to brigade and they're trying to find a replacement right now."

Alexey nodded, then asked the obvious question.

"What's the row?"

"Not a clue, "said Toby. "Probably the French - they're supposed to be attacking in the North - but it could be the Germans - they're attacking all the time. Or maybe both. Or even us! Who knows?"

"So where *is* the BEF?"

"Last heard, still advancing, like the French. North of le Cateau. Or so we're told. But nobody really knows."

"Fair enough. So now, ... what's best to do?" Alexey felt he'd better, for the moment, put himself in Macdonald's hands.

"Hang on a bit, I suppose. The car may yet materialise. If it hasn't come in half an hour, we'll think again."

"I'll tell you what," said Alexey. "I could seize the moment to phone my uncle. Any idea where I might find a phone?"

"Try Brigade," said Toby." They're very kind. I'll introduce you. I'm sure they'll let you use theirs."

They headed towards Brigade headquarters, just across the square. But as they walked they were pounced on by a swarm of French women who informed them they had a 'chambre' right close by, where they would be delighted to accommodate them cheaply. A black-haired crone, with warts, a scar, and three missing front teeth, laid especial stress on the lowness of her price.

"I'm not sure it's board and lodging she's offering," said Toby.

"That's what worries me," said Alexey.

Nevertheless, Brigade were most helpful. They led Alexey into a back room where two operators tried to connect him. Fortunately, the walls were thick: it was just possible to hear, with earphones on.

But the lines were chaos. It took fifteen minutes even to get through to the local exchange; five more and they got cut off. Then when they tried again, their own equipment failed; then, by mistake, and most mysteriously, they got BEF headquarters at Le Cateau. Finally, after a good half hour's trying, they reached what the French operators swore was Alexey's uncle's number, but all they got was a ringing tone. Then the line went dead.

So out they went again, plunging, once more into the deadly, pulverising, din.

And now they were assailed by yet another mob, this time of boys.

"Come weeth me!" said their leader, a dark-haired boy of twelve with thick pink lips.

"You make jugalug with my seester! Just round corner, vair' easy!"

Convenience, it seemed, was everything in Douai.

"I best of all!" This was another boy, slim, almost elfin, with an air so innocent he could have been a choir boy - yet his was the most explicit offer of all.

"I deeferent !" he said. "You choose me, you get **me**!" he said. "Beautiful me! You like make jugalug with me you prefer boys to seestairs, no, eh?"

"Piss off you filthy bastard," yelled Toby, aiming a blow, yet the boy remained unfazed.

"You capitan, no, so you are, 'ow you say, Eenglish publeec schoolboy, yes? Then you like jugalug with boys! We know what publeec schoolboys like!"

At which Toby aimed another, heftier blow, and this one landed, sending the 'choirboy' spinning into the dust. And at this the boys vanished, as swiftly as they had come; to reveal behind them a statuesque, middle-aged lady, dressed in black.

She made Alexey and Macdonald yet another offer, this time more sober. Accommodation for the night (genuine), should they wish it, at the very reasonable rate of three francs, including breakfast. Not bad at all and yes, thought Alexey and Toby, if the car never came, they might indeed need somewhere to stay.

So they quickly made terms.

In the event the car ***did*** come, but hopelessly late. It had driven down from Lille, and refugees, apparently, had blocked its way.

So they cut their losses, ate Madame Muireville's supper, and after advice and the loan of a map from Brigade HQ, fixed to leave at dawn.

Soon after supper Toby Macdonald, who'd had a busy day, went to bed. Alexey, his mind still buzzing, took a walk.

Surprisingly, this was now an option, as the bombardment had died down. All that remained were a few isolated, irritable, explosions, much like the 'thunder' they'd first heard during the train's halt. Ominous and suggestive, but utterly diminished.

There was a blessed sense of reawakening. He heard profound relief in the 'bonsoir' of the locals, while the local dogs, who'd earlier looked terrified, were once more chirpy.

He turned down a side street whose eighteenth-century facades seemed tempting. And found himself, suddenly, in a field of sunflowers. Their beauty amazed him. Though dusk had nearly fallen, there was still sun enough for the flowers to be turning, in their sunflower way, toward the light.

The silence of the place, after the preceding cacophony, seemed to shout. He found a low stone wall and sat on it quietly, drinking in the rich, warm light. The sky had deepened to cobalt, streaked voluptuously with red; the sunflowers glowed in the liquid air. It felt incredible, now, that there had ever been the earlier pandemonium - as impossible as calm had felt back then.

And it was just as hard to grasp that he had started the day in England. It felt a century ago. And how many more such days would there be before he got home? Assuming he did get home, that is – wars had a way of being dangerous.

After twenty minutes he felt tired and set off back. As he re-entered the square he saw a cart parked that had lately arrived. It had a white cloth, on hoops, stretched over it to form a tent, like a wild west wagon. At the open end, a family was sitting, finishing their evening meal. There were the parents, what looked like grandparents, and four young children, who would evidently be sleeping there that night.

In a flash Alexey knew they were refugees. It was their eyes – strained and old-looking but with one other quality, too, which Alexey had not yet seen in France.

This was grief - grief in every face – grief for everything, plainly, they had left behind. And while the adults' faces looked dire, starkest of all were those of the children, notably the very youngest, a boy of around eight. It wasn't that he was crying, it was that he was frozen, motionless, staring fixedly at the ground.

And Alexey thought of the boys who had assailed him and Toby earlier. And he saw what may have lain behind it. Who knew what straits their families had been reduced to, after just two weeks of war? What husbands, lovers, sons, had left them stranded?

Behind every story, in this new life, would lie another, and the last thing one could ever do was judge.

Chapter Seventy-One

Alexey woke next morning feeling transformed. What wonders can be achieved by eight hours sleep! And now, with the arrival of the car - a Rolls-Royce - they were poised to set off. (Being granted a Rolls was not in itself so remarkable - they were widely used by the BEF at this stage).

It came with a chauffeur - French Cavalry Chasseur Alphonse Theophile Dupont, moustachioed, weather-beaten, and an expert, apparently, on the driving and servicing of Rolls-Royces. The British chauffeur who had brought the car down from the north had apparently been co-opted by Douai HQ.

Dupont, it emerged, had been separated three days ago from his regiment, and was desperate to rejoin them. This trip might help. And he came with his own advantages.

First, he was local, so he knew the geography; second, there was that expertise with Rolls-Royces - he'd worked for a French count with a fleet of three before the outbreak. And third, and this was stressed with some solemnity, he had his French chasseur's uniform, complete with helmet, which could be crucial in any encounters with 'GVCs."

"GVCs? What are they?" Alexey asked Toby.

" 'Gardes des voies et communications' ", said Toby, grinning. "Guards of the roads and communications, old boy. Antique gents sans uniforms, whose job is to make sure no-one does any unauthorised travelling. And who are half-deaf, half blind, and above all else, trigger-happy. They're a peril to everyone, not least to themselves, but above all to anyone who seems remotely suspicious, like us."

"Wouldn't they recognise their allies?"

"Christ no, they've no idea what a British uniform looks like. They'd probably mistake us for Germans. Hence our chasseur chauffeur, and his gorgeous helmet."

"Well, good old Alphonse, that's all I can say."

"Yes, hurray for Alphonse, he could yet be our salvation."

After a glance at the map they decided to drive South-East, towards Cambrai then on to Le Cateau – which was reckoned, last heard, to be the British army HQ. The staff there would know everything. And they should go immediately - given the predicament of Alexey's uncle there was not a minute to lose.

By eight o'clock, they were speeding on their way.

The two Englishmen had felt mildly tempted to change out of their uniforms and travel as civilians, given that GVC trigger happiness. But then they thought mufti might be harder still to explain.

What they did do, after a brief visit to the local shop, was place a Union Jack on the little flagpole on one mudguard, a French flag on the other, and finally, to cover themselves, two Belgian flags on the boot. Indeed, suggested Alphonse, who was shaping up as a wag, given that there were at least thirty governments fighting the Germans maybe they should put on *all* the allied flags, festooning the car. "Confusing, oui, but how wonderful for morale!"

And if their mood was cheery the weather helped. Forgotten was last night's tranquil calm; today was all about sunshine and splendour, and its spirit infected everything they saw. Three peasant women came swinging down the road toward their car: the very set of their shoulders, the roll of their hips, looked triumphant.

Yet despite their precautions, they had a near miss with the GVCs. Ten miles out of Douai they met this group of sclerotic-looking old men, one with his arm raised - and when Alphonse ignored him the man let fly with a blunderbuss, peppering the Rolls' off-side wing. At which Alphonse accelerated and just managed to escape - while his passengers thanked God they had not fallen victim, in their first few hours, to their own allies.

Until, that is, they reached the village of Caudry, just beyond the regional capital of Cambrai.

And there, as they rounded a bend, they nearly drove straight into a far more formidable obstacle: a six-foot barricade made up of chairs, mattresses and old clothes, stretched clean across the road. More GVCs? Please God no. Alphonse slammed on the brakes.

There came a quiet, rather fruity English voice:

"Thanks *frightfully* for stopping. ***Do*** hope you were not too taken aback. Would it be *awfully* rude to ask you step out of your car with your hands up and stand over by that gate?"

And as they looked around, it was as if a hundred guns had magicked from the sky, all pointing at them. But they were British.

The voice resolved itself into a tall, curly haired young officer, with a craggy, jutting face, curiously at odds with his languid manner. He advanced out of the shadows, gazing at them appraisingly.

"What happened to your car?"

"We were in a fight."

"Who with?"

"The French."

"How *frightful*. Aren't they meant to be on our side?"

"They thought we were German."

"How *ghastly*! I hope you won. But then we, too, thought you were German - we supposed the French uniform was a ruse. There's a lot of that going on these days. It was the helmet that did it. It just seemed a bit O.T.T. .... "

But the spell had been broken. Cheery banter, then drinks, soon established that Toby and Major 'Tom' Salisbury, as he introduced himself, were near contemporaries at Eton and even knew Charlie Fisher, so now everyone knew everyone else .... more drinks.

The travellers explained their mission. For his part Tom Salisbury said his role, and that of other units around, was to help protect the British HQ at Le Cateau, just thirty miles down the road.

"Because anything might happen at any moment," said Salisbury, "if only a cavalry raid."

For no-one really knew where anyone was, let alone the Germans.

"Even so, the biggest problem, in my view" said Salisbury, sipping his wine, "is the utter lack of sympathy between the Allies. We had a chap in here just the other day, young fellow by the name of Spears, some kind of liaison officer between the British and French, God help him. And he described the first meeting of General Lanrezac – the French Fifth Army commander, and our closest neighbour on the right - with the British commander, Sir John French." (French's surname was one of the war's stranger coincidences.)

Sir John, apparently, had moved over to a map, pointed to a place on it, and said to Lanrezac: "Mon General, est-ce-que........" at which point his French gave out.

"How do you say," he asked one of his aides, "cross the river' in French?"

Enlightened, he tried again : "Mon General, est-ce que les Allemands vont traverser la Meuse.....a…a...." he got stuck again; for the place he wished to pronounce was ' Huy', one of the hardest words in the French language. More a whistle than a word. Undaunted, he took a shot: 'Hoy!' he shouted, as if hailing a cab.

Now Lanrezac was stumped; and by the time the interpreters rescued them General Lanrezac (not known for his patience) was so irritated that his answer had apparently been:

"Tell the Marshal that in my opinion the Germans have gone to the Meuse to fish."

Anglo-French liaison, said Salisbury, hadn't exactly flourished since.

Yet joking apart, the question now arose, as ever, what to *do*? And in all the confusion, on this at least Tom Salisbury was clear.

"You should contact Spears," said Salisbury. "Contact him personally. He's a linguist, he's in touch with both armies. But above all he's an individual, with his own judgment, and he's probably the only person, in either the French or British armies, who's really got a clue what's going on."

"He does indeed sound interesting, "said Alexey, "but how would we find him?"

"Well, that can be a problem. He moves around. Liaising! But a good start would be French Fifth Army headquarters, at Rethel. About forty miles from here. If you can get over there – or in that general direction - Spears will sort you out. Or know who can.

"Believe me," said Salisbury, his enthusiasm visibly growing "Spears is your man."

Chapter Seventy-Two

They were soon on their way. Determined, if at all possible, to find Spears before dark.

And now, for the first time, casualties. An endless, faltering, miserable stream, some in carts and lorries, some on foot, some parked temporarily on stretchers just off the road. Alexey was struck by the pale, almost melodramatic look of those he saw – more like a baroque painting than anything modern.

Stranger still were the refugees. So many were covered with white dust – presumably the roads - in ways that made them look almost sepulchral. Especially those in carts. They sat immobile, pale as corpses.

Strangest of all was the utter, ghost-like silence which pervaded everything. Sometimes the soldiers would shout something, there was a vague murmur of moans and cries, but, in the main, the refugees maintained a stupefied stillness, stranger even than their pallor.

So that now, aware that his uncle and aunt must be enveloped in all this, Alexey became ever more alarmed. Soon he began to panic.

He explained his fears to Toby. If only he could try again to just *speak* to them, get through on the phone! But how? Alphonse had an idea.

"Try a railway station. They'll have a phone."

A long shot, seemingly, given their failure to get through back at Douai; nevertheless, worth a try.

And very soon they did find one, persuaded the station master and this time – the mysteries of war! - got straight through.

But the voice that answered was German.

Oberleutnant Karl Von Kant, courteous and pleasant, explained that the Smolensky's house had been occupied by the German army – specifically the ninth German cavalry corps.

Alexey's relatives, he said, had left. His uncle had gone north, of all directions! "To help a friend."

While his aunt, despairing at such quixotry, had declared him 'mad', and fled for the channel ports.

As for their whereabouts now, Von Kant had, alas, no idea.

Then the line went dead.

Now Alexey was more frightened still. He bullied the others back into the car.

Forward they ploughed through a mix of main and side roads. Side roads especially, for the further they got into the French zone the more impossible, on the main roads, became the jams.

And now, when stuck, they tried something new - they avoided the side roads too and drove clean away into the fields, advancing in parallel, as best they could, with the roads. In the pious hope, come the moment when they wished to rejoin, that they would manage it.

And they usually did, helped on by the huge size of the French fields. These went on for miles, sometimes, without encountering a hedge. Only once did they utterly fail to find the gate they needed, and had to drive all the way back, across the same dusty, bumpy terrain, to the entrance whence they had set out.

And it was after just such a manoeuvre that they finally found Spears.

Hopelessly embedded in a jam, pale and exhausted looking, he looked ten years older than his twenty-six years. But he greeted them courteously and invited them to a local estaminet. Luckily, they were in a village.

Even so Alexey sensed, from the start, that this offer was more than mere graciousness. For even this soon Spears had clearly seen something he could use.

And promptly, over drinks, this something emerged. Or as Spears quaintly put it: they were all, he said, in their different ways, "seekers."

He explained. "My job is to find out what the Germans are doing, and communicate it to the British and French. Yours is to do the same – well, leave out the French. Yours, Alexey, is to find your uncle, and if possible your aunt, and yours, Alphonse, is to find your regiment, which means first finding General Sordet's cavalry corps of fifteen thousand, of which three thousand have temporarily vanished – which includes, supposedly, you," (he chuckled) "but what you have to find out is, where are the other twelve thousand? Wherever the Germans are, we'd hope. So you, too, are seeking the same thing."

And now came the suggestion: collaboration.

"My proposition is this. I help you in any way I can - logistically, contacts, even money; while you, in turn, report back to me, whenever possible, and help *me* by reducing my ignorance.

"And who knows, between us, we might even get some working thesis on the facts."

"Is your ignorance, as you put it," asked Alexey, smiling deferentially, "really so great?"

"Christ yes, gargantuan. Though where I differ from the allied commands is that I know it. They're *certain* they know everything about the plans and movements of the enemy."

And in the last few days, he said, especially the last twenty-four hours, this insouciance had reached a whole new, perilous level.

For both British and French had continued to advance - in the blind faith that the Germans were not, in fact, overlapping them, in vast numbers, in the West.

"Yet they surely are. And given that the British are on the very edge of the French left, there's every chance they could be out on a limb. Indeed, the last I heard the British had been ordered to Soignies, that's *North* of where the French are, and if they go there, they will, quite simply, be cut off and destroyed.

"And we'll have lost the war."

The group sat stunned. Now Alexey understood why Spears was so urgent for information.

And yet, however horrendous the situation, Spears' suggestion, they realised, fitted perfectly with their plans. So, swiftly recovering, they agreed at once.

"But there's still one thing that mystifies me," said Alexey. "Why are the hierarchy so utterly determined to ignore all evidence on the ground, when it's so crucial not merely to success, but to their armies' plain survival?"

"Ah, yes! Why indeed! That truly is the strangest question of all. How often have I asked it myself! Yes, ...why......"

But now a flash of humour.
"Try this. I have, in the last few days, been several times commissioned, by the French command, to go searching for the *British* – yes, the *British* - because there's a strong French school that says they aren't actually in France at all!"

"*What*?!" cried Alexey. "When we've been disembarking at Boulogne for days and when, God help us, Sir John French has actually visited Lanrezac in his own HQ?! Don't they believe the evidence of their own eyes?!"

Now Spears was grinning.

"Evidently not! Indeed, they go further: the same adventurous school say that while Sir John and his staff may indeed be in France themselves, they're without their armies - i.e., they're a decoy, a blind, the troops behind them simply don't exist!"

"Well maybe *we're* a blind, maybe *we* don't exist!"

"Especially Toby!"

"Above all Alphonse!"

And everyone laughed.

Chapter Seventy-Three

The next day, the twenty-first of August, they were on the road by 5.00 am. They determined to make headway before either refugees or military got going. And for the first hour or so it worked.

With Alphonse at the wheel there were moments when they drove as fast as ten miles an hour. Indeed, it looked at first as if they might get up to Maubeuge, or even the front line, before lunch.

But soon, both military and civilians began to flood back again onto the roads. With the difference, now, that anxiety had turned to panic.

Not least because the guns, which had not been evident since the 'inexplicable' bombardment at Douai, were sounding once again. A constant backdrop to every aspect of the day, a ground bass colouring all.

After two slow miles Alexey and his companions thought they would get something to eat.

They turned east, hoping this would move them, momentarily, away from the German onslaught – and toward, with any luck, some unscathed village. Soon they left the refugees behind.

But now another roadblock - this time French.

A large, blonde major, who could have passed for a German, held up his hand. The familiar routine: documents, explanations, with the add-on, now, of a letter they were able to present signed by Spears. Then French apologies. Then acceptance.

The troupe were, it emerged, several hundred French cavalry who had been separated from their main body for two days. While trying to find their comrades, they were simultaneously tracking the Germans - though they'd had, as yet, little success.

Meanwhile they were making the best of things, in this little town of Senieres, hour to hour. And as the hour was now that of dejeuner, and their foragers had found some excellent chicken and vegetables, maybe Alexey and his friends would like to join them?

Few offers could have been more readily accepted. More, it emerged that Alphonse's own unit, the Third Cavalry Division, had been seen by locals just three miles away that morning. There was an excellent chance they might find them within the hour.

Not to mention the chicken. Things promised well.

But nothing was straightforward in this war.

Just as Alphonse began backing the Rolls into a yard opposite, they heard a sudden, rackety, buzzing noise. They glanced up: it was an aircraft with the German cross, a Taube.

It banked, then vanished. Or did it? Because three minutes later, it re-appeared. Though this time five hundred feet high. And it looked like something had been thrown out. The French cavalrymen thought so, excitedly pointing.

Alexey realised what they had seen. There was no bomb, nothing like that. Merely a cluster of black specks which burst into a cascade of lights. Just like fireworks! But it seemed to panic the French, who dived for cover, joined by Alphonse.

Somewhat gallic, surely – was it *that* threatening? Then someone grabbed Alexey from behind and hurled him into the canteen, presumably feeling the building offered some protection. But from what? Moments later he and Toby, who'd been thrown in as well, were picking themselves up off the floor, half angry, half amused, when a sudden, rushing, shrieking sound – precisely the sound of an express train in full flight - bore down on them from above. It was followed by the most frightful explosion Alexey had ever heard, shaking not just the houses but the earth beneath their feet.

Seconds later there came another cataclysmic crash as a second shell landed, and then, incredibly, unfairly, a third …….and Alexey understood. These were the heavy howitzer shells that the French talked of and so dreaded, the ones they called 'Marmites.' They named them because the smoke, when they exploded, looked like a giant, nightmare marmite pot. And the Taube they'd seen had thrown the lights out as signals, which had zeroed in the guns.

As the French, from previous experience, had known only too well.

Nothing in Alexey's life had prepared him for what followed. At least two of the shells landed relatively safely in gardens, but one hit a house. And as Alexey rushed over to look, his mind froze. Plaster, floorboards, linen, were scattered around the road, what looked like a leg was sticking out of a window, there were nightdresses, pictures, towels, a tie...... then a child's football landed with a thump, just across the road, bouncing and rolling toward him.

But it wasn't a football. It was a human head. So surreal was the sight that Alexey simply stared, transfixed. But there, on the pavement, was the trunk the head belonged to, that of a woman, fat and middle aged, a chaos of dirty, billowing skirts, pouring more blood from her severed neck than seemed possible. While all around, more like a wind than anything human, shrieks of terror and pain - utterly beyond the control of those producing them.

Never never had Alexey seen anything like it: he simply couldn't take it in. It was the setting, above all, which was so obscene - its everyday domesticity. How could this have happened in this quiet little town? Moments later more shattering explosions hit them, then another, then another three. These landed in the fields behind the houses, so the village was spared, but instead – Alexey realised - the carnage must have struck the horses. Not to mention the cavalrymen who'd been tending them. Alexey didn't dare look.

Surely there would not be more! It was too terrible! It would be stopped! And yet, unthinkingly, appallingly, here, once again, came that horrendous, express train roar, and with it the sense, wherever you were, that it was heading for *you*. These too landed square amid the horses, as they surged like water from end to end of the field.

Most especially was this true of half-a-dozen horses who for some reason were tethered separately from the rest and who the French cavalrymen, who'd ran to help, seemed to ignore.

Suddenly Alexey saw that Alphonse, of all people, had rushed over to this group and was releasing them from their ropes. And then - Alexey never knew why - he found himself following. Moments later he realised Toby was following **him,** and now all three were setting out to rescue the horses, these desperate, terrified fellow-creatures, so innocent and yet so vulnerable.

They reached them, grabbed their ropes, then rushed them, shrieking and screaming, from the field's edge to the woods.

So this was what being 'under fire' meant! So this what was meant by 'casualties!' It was a thousand times worse than he'd imagined. How had he lived all these years and never known? Never never never would he go anywhere near such scenes again.

As arbitrarily as it started, the shelling stopped. But unlike the bombardment at Douai, this brought no relief. Rather realisation, as the villagers grasped the enormity of what had occurred. Their cries of despair re-echoed: one overwhelming wail of desolation.

Yet this was only a short five-minute bombardment, thought Alexey. Just fifteen shells! What would it be like if it went on all afternoon? Or all day? Or all week?

His instinct, now, was to join those who'd rushed back to the village but that would have meant leaving the horses, which would surely create mayhem. And as others had already gone back to help, his first duty, surely, was to stay and calm the animals - which was what the French cavalry were doing with the other horses anyway.

So in the end he, Toby and Alphonse stayed in the wood, calming their charges, stroking them, nuzzling them, so that gradually, with much patting and whispering, the horses subsided.

Alexey, for one, had learned a lot about such things from Henry Thornton.

Meanwhile, mysteriously, the French soldiers seemed transformed.

The blonde officer re-appeared. His sure, authoritative voice rang out - and soon began converting the event, from the catastrophe of five minutes earlier, into the routine vocabulary of war.

Two civilians killed and eighteen injured – unfortunate. One soldier killed, three wounded – relatively fortunate. Ten horses killed and thirty injured - most unfortunate. The disaster reduced to mathematics. Manageable.

And already the stretcher-bearers were at work, the horses were being looked at, and the first ambulance was loading up to take the injured back down the line - including those who'd been in the casualty clearing station next to the café.

For Senieres, which till twenty minutes ago seemed relatively safe, was safe no more.

The civilians, certainly, took this view. One cart was already loading in the main street, its occupants abandoning the family home. What a transformation wrought by twenty minutes!

And soon it was plain that the troops, too, would shortly be on the move.

Even so one of the French NCOs found a moment to compliment Alexey and Toby on their work with the horses. "Incroyable!" he said. For these six horses, it emerged, were strays they'd picked up five days previously, with a view to using them later in the campaign. Up until today no-one had been able to manage them - and that was *before* the bombardment. Yet now, look, they seemed utterly calm!

At which the blonde major joined in, and said had they not been driving, they could as well have joined the regiment, riding! They could have taken charge of those six! After all, their objectives – linking up with the allied cavalry, tracking the Germans – were pretty much the same. But this was hardly the time.....

Or was it? For now a corporal came running over from the village, saluted, and explained how he was 'desole' but had bad news about 'la voiture Anglaise'.

They ran to look. The Rolls was on its back with its chassis bent, at forty-five degrees. It would never drive again. As for the front drawer where their papers had been kept, it had been blown to smithereens. So much for all those letters of accreditation - thank God the money, at least, was safe in Alexey's pocket!

Suddenly the notion of their riding with the French looked less a joke and more like a stratagem, perhaps the only one.

They were introduced to the troop's commander, Colonel D'Aubert. He was charming. And after a brief talk they were co-opted, in the lightning way of war, into the French cavalry.

Within the hour, riding three of 'their' horses and leading the other three on a leash, they joined the French troops as they left the village. But where to? This they didn't know - though Alexey could tell, from the position of the sun, they'd turned north.

Chapter Seventy-Four

The troop moved mostly in column, five abreast, using side roads to avoid the jams.

But now, four hours into their ride, another aircraft. As earlier, it appeared from nowhere, swooped over them, vanished, reappeared, turned tightly, then came lower and lower until ... ...it landed!

More surprising still, it was British. Out got the pilot, off he went to meet Colonel D'Aubert, and five minutes later D'Aubert called a conference.

The aircraftman's news, it turned out, had been dramatic. He'd seen a whole German army corps, that is to say no less than three divisions, or sixty thousand men, all streaming westwards, just ten miles away, having crossed the Meuse. And now they had turned south, so they were within two days of outflanking the allies. And of all the armies, the most vulnerable were the British, on the tip of the allied left.

Yet Spears, remembered Alexey, had said the British might be ordered **North** to Soignies! So this meant the Germans could, potentially, not merely outflank them but come at them from behind. They could perform, on a smaller scale, the very 'revolving door' encirclement which was the Germans' Schlieffen plan.

Yet in all this catalogue of alarm one factor was worst of all. While there were those *at the front* who could accept this heretical thesis, there was no-one in the high commands who could grasp it at all. The pilot had tried unceasingly, and no-one would listen.

He'd had the same problem as Spears.

Which was why, he explained, he'd 'dropped in' as he had. What he needed was on-the-ground corroboration. Cavalry, especially, were in a position to provide it.

And Colonel D'Aubert had agreed to help.

So now the troop sped on more urgently still, heading broadly north, towards the sound of the guns.

They encountered ever more French wounded, some in ambulances, some spilling over in carts, some tottering, wild-eyed and dishevelled, on foot.

All were exhausted, but one thing they shared, and it loomed horribly in their eyes: a chattering terror of the invaders pursuing them. Plus, now, a sardonic sense of the **absurdity** of opposing such an all-enveloping host, its numbers immeasurable, its artillery beyond belief.

It was getting late and would soon be dark. So the squadron stopped and another conference was called. They decided to split up, with one advanced squadron of a dozen, including Alexey and his friends, roaming at speed in front of the rest.

And this new, small squad would sweep towards the northwest at an angle of forty-five degrees to the route they had been following previously.

So this little band soon left behind both refugees and soldiers, and rode, increasingly, through untouched countryside. And what countryside!

Great swathes of sea-green forest, vast sweeps of meadow, distant glimmers, amid the hills, of what looked like fairy glades; tiny villages lost in the forest depths, marked only by columns of pale blue smoke as the inhabitants prepared their evening meal.

Finally, at sunset, they reached a wooded ridge that reared in front of them, and as they threaded their way up, through the dank-smelling paths, it flattened into a plateau. They were on its rim. And facing them, white and placid, was a lake – utterly empty; while the last gleam of sunlight caught the high ridge opposite, brilliant against the darkness below.

For a moment the war was banished, inconceivable. Only the evening light was real; while its reflection glimmered on the lake so mysteriously that Alexey felt he could touch it, hear it even, quite as much as see it.

"Vraiment, c'est belle," said Alphonse, and there was no more to be said. So after a full minute in which the troop, by mute agreement, reined in their horses and gazed, they galloped off to the ridge opposite, the one touched by the sun.

And when they reached it they reined in again.

Because there below, on the twilit plain, as far as eye could see, was the swarming, murmuring mass of the German army.

Chapter Seventy-Five

Round went the field glasses, from hand to hand.

The Germans, it seemed, had stopped for the night. Tents were being raised, rifles stacked, field kitchens lit.

Soon followed muttered comments from Alexey's troop as they pointed out the guns, the horses, the uniforms - as best they could in the near-darkness - in an attempt to gauge which regiments were involved.

There emerged a working thesis.

Three front-line divisions were before them, probably more, comprising a rounded striking force of all arms: infantry mainly, but also cavalry, artillery, cyclists, and row after row of machine guns.

It was exactly what they had been looking for, and what the aircraftman had told them they would see. And given the Germans' location, with its orientation due southwest, their enemies were indeed well placed for the envelopment all feared.

While to Alexey, only too aware of what such forces could unleash, they felt like locusts, contaminated, unclean.

So the troop's duty was plain. They must disengage from the ridge, get back to the main body in their rear, and above all ensure word got back to allied headquarters.

So now they turned and sped back down the slope, round the lake, up the hill the other side, and down again to where, according to their most recent information, the main troop should be.

And found no-one.

Out again with the field glasses. Eventually it was Alphonse who spotted a gleam and a flash of light: the helmets of their troop - on a wooded hill to their left. Why there? No matter, off he and his comrades rode, and three minutes later they had struggled up the ridge and joined them.

And all was explained. Just half an hour earlier the main troop's right wing - riding across the meadows – had sensed enemy masses on their flank. And the searchers sent out to investigate had seen the very same thing, from another angle, as those with Alexey.

So they had hidden themselves in the woods high on the hill, to gain the advantage of both height and concealment. (Perhaps, thought Alexey, they'd have done better to cover their helmets.) Meanwhile they'd sent out yet another dozen-strong troop to their left – who'd reported back yet more alarming news. For here, too, were Germans, advancing en masse.

So the decision, if you can call it that, made itself. The sole possibility was retreat, due south.

Nevertheless, it was clearly wise, before moving en masse, to check this route as well. So now Alphonse, Alexey and Toby formed yet another scout group, and off they rode.

And returned in record time. For the moment they reached the first rise, overlooking the meadows they'd crossed just two hours earlier, they saw before them yet more hordes of German soldiers.

The diagnosis was plain. They were surrounded.

Once more the decision made itself. For the only possible course now was to hunker down, dig in, and hope desperately that the Germans would never know they were there.

So trenches were dug, tents put up, sentries posted, and, as evening slid into night, the beleaguered band settled down to an uncertain supper, much limited by the prohibition of fires.

Fortunately, there was enough bread, cheese and fruit to make something edible, though few would have chosen this as their last supper, if that was what it was destined to be.

But the profound hope, in every heart, was that they might manage, if the Germans moved on, to slip away come morning.

Chapter Seventy-Six

So the waiting began. And Alexey began to realise how anxious he felt.

Increasingly this took a physical form. His limbs, especially his legs, felt heavy and tingled strangely. Throughout his body ran a kind of mobile ache, washing around in waves. Above all these feelings clustered in his stomach, which seemed permanently full of wind, even inflamed. He understood why soldiers called nervous comrades 'windy.'

But worse still was a strange new mournfulness of the soul, as he found himself confronting, for the first time in his life, his own mortality. *I don't want to die!* It was less material than a sense of absolute estrangement, of banishment from everything he knew. From warmth and colour and friends and light, from Henry and Mary and Tom and Ingrid – from his uncle and aunt - from everything and everyone he cherished. And exchanging this for what felt like a voyage to the remotest star, cold, dark, and implacable.......

Then he shook himself and chuckled. What a self-pitying weltschmerz fear could induce in one, to be sure.

He looked across at Toby and Alphonse, who he could just about pick out in the dark. Did they feel any such fears? If so, they didn't show it.

Then Alexey's heart jumped, as he saw Alphonse freeze. What had he seen? Turning, he saw shadows approaching, and when they stepped into the moonlight he saw they were French. He recognised D'Aubert, the colonel he'd met earlier, plus an entourage of half a dozen officers. They'd been talking to the group on their left; now they were coming to talk to them.

That flash of moonlight had been enough for Alexey to glimpse the colonel's face, which looked more impressive, even, than during the day. Colonel D'Aubert was young - no more than thirty-five - but there was a gravitas about him, as well as the charm Alexey had seen, which made Alexey say to himself: 'A king!' And the officers surrounding him, who plainly revered him, looked like his court.

D'Aubert greeted Alexey and his friends graciously. And when he asked them about themselves his interest felt real. How had Alphonse ended up here? And Toby, and Alexey? And when they told him their story he found it 'splendid' - again, the conviction. The officers beamed.

Alexey mentioned their 'commissions' from General Armstrong and from Spears. D'Aubert's interest quickened. "Spears?" he said. "Would that be ***Edward*** Spears, the young English lieutenant?" And when Alexey confirmed this, D'Aubert gasped. Then after a pause –

"I have an idea," said D'Aubert. "Will you permit?"

D'Aubert took a bag from one of his officers, clicked open a metal fastener and got something out.

"If I wrote him a message, "said D'Aubert, "would you deliver it?"

He scribbled something. He signed it, put it in an envelope, and gave it to Alexey.

"It is sufficiently simple," he said. "But it sends my greetings and tells Spears everything he needs to know about the German dispositions. And it goes with my authority, which will help, as we are friends." Another pause. "Edward Spears is a fine man," he said, "N'est ce pas? I knew him well in Paris, before the war."

"He certainly seems so to me," said Alexey. "And all who know him seem to think so too."

"As they certainly should."

With a final handshake D'Aubert was on his way, and as Toby and Alphonse had gone to fetch food, Alexey reflected yet again. What was it this episode reminded him of? Ah yes, that scene in Shakespeare's Henry V, the night before Agincourt! What were those lines about King Henry?......

"For forth he goes, and visits all his host.
Bids them good morrow with a modest smile,
And calls them brothers, friends, and countrymen......"

What sustenance true leadership could give! D'Aubert had even made Alexey feel different *physically.* His sense of burden, his bodily pain, had disappeared.

Chapter Seventy-Seven

By nine o-clock, as it was late August, dusk melted into night. People tried to sleep.

Alexey, Toby, and Alphonse were forward from the line and had made themselves a little nest, mildly camouflaged by bracken and grass. Below was a steepish meadow, a good half mile long. It was flooded with moonlight, dark forest beyond.

By ten it really began to look as if the Germans, too, had settled down for the night.

Then around eleven o' clock - Alexey remembered the time because a distant clock had chimed each hour, and he had counted – there came a cracking and rustling from the woods below.

They peered into the ill-lit view. Alexey swept it back and forth with his binoculars. Still nothing, nothing at all. An owl soared. And once more silence.

Then moments later, just as they'd decided they must have been imagining it, another stirring, cracking and rustling - and then, incredibly, clear out of the gloom, a thousand male throats gave vent to a slow, deep-voiced chorus of 'Deutschland uber alles'. Sung more like a hymn than an anthem. Then yet more silence.

Alexey's flesh crept. So the Germans *were* there! Right in front of them, inside those woods! How could they possibly not know the French were above them? And now the slow, majestic chorus re-started, this time running right through to its end, like some grave outpouring of the German soul.

And once again the rustling, scrabbling and crackling, and then–

A wild skirling of flute and drums, shrill, devilish, yet jaunty! It was a band! A series of thumps, bumps and crashes, now, from where the crackling had been.......and out of the wood came a line of heavily armed Prussian troops, rifles at hip, bayonets fixed, heading straight toward them up the hill. Then another line following, and then another, as this vast, ever-expanding phalanx emerged into the moonlight, which lit them up like floodlight on parade.

They seemed inexhaustible. For now more ranks, and yet still more, came striding on behind them, the moonlight flashing on their helmets, still far off at this moment, but more all the time, coming closer, steadily, inexorably closer........

And Alexey saw that in the front ranks the soldiers were arm in arm, rifle in the right hand, left arm over the shoulder of the next man along. An act, presumably, of comradely support. He glanced to the right and saw the faces of Alphonse and Toby, glassy-eyed, transfixed, under the same spell.

At which moment an order rang out from one of the French officers.

Select your target, hold your fire……. five endless seconds…..then the officer's command…..hoarse, rasping…. and a murderous fusillade was unleashed right down the line, far louder and explosive than seemed possible.

The whole front line of the Germans, including most of the band, keeled over like trees in the wind, scythed down, yet still men behind them came on, with the second line, still arm in arm, now to the front. But the French fired again, then again and again, until the shooting became non-stop. And the attack collapsed into catastrophe, arms flailing, legs kicking near-comically in the air, a chorus, now, not of singing, but of shrill, hysterical screams.

Screams of terror as much as pain. And all Alexey could think about was the phrase he'd heard from Ingrid - herself the fellow-countrywoman of those mangled, tortured men - that war was 'one long street accident.' Indeed it was.

Now there was another voice behind them, also shouting commands. It was D'Aubert, pistol in hand, right there amidst his troops. He strode energetically about, ordering, encouraging, threatening, and the very sight of him gave Alexey confidence. Then something swiped D'Aubert clean over backwards. His fall, like so many of the Germans', looked cartoon-like, comical, hardly to be believed. But he lay there prone and motionless. Surely, he'd not been hit?

Alexey gaped but D'Aubert was just one, it emerged, of ever more casualties among the French, as the Germans fought ever closer, despite their losses. Yet they took advantage even of these, for their bodies, now, were stacked up, one on top of the other, into a wall just twenty yards from the French line. This ghastly earthwork was now being used as cover, as more and more Germans shot from behind it, while the rest swarmed on. And ever more Frenchmen were hit.

How grotesquely horrible were these injuries! Some fell shrieking, as if burned; some, puff! without a sound; some with a soft thud, as the bullet hit the flesh. A man to Alexey's right, shot in the wrist, let out an 'ugh!' that sounded more like disgust than pain.

And still the Germans came, and now they'd smashed right into the French lines and the fighting became hand to hand.

And Alexey saw that 'hand to hand' was yet another fairy euphemism. Sickening, appalling, unimaginable, that was the reality, with the Germans now using their rifles as clubs rather than bayonets, the butts hitting the Frenchmen's' heads with heart-stopping crunches, so the blood flew out of their mouths, a good three feet ahead, like projectile vomit.

Then the most dreamlike moment of all. For suddenly, in front of him he saw Toby, grinning, having just run a German boy clean through with his sword.

Yet even as Alexey stared, a look of surprise came over Toby's face and he keeled slowly to his right, a bright red fountain pouring from his temple. It rose in an arc, a good eighteen inches high, like water from a hose.

He'd been shot from the opposite direction to the main assault – from the south. With a stab of panic Alexey realised what this meant: they were being attacked from two sides. The same thought must have struck the whole troop because the word, now, shouted everywhere, was to get back to the top of the knoll, to gather there, to make a stand.

Pausing to pick up Toby's sword, Alexey scrambled upwards - and panicked still more. Because what became clear was that they weren't just being attacked from both sides, but from all sides at once.

So now surrender, "Je me rends!" was on every lip, as the cavalrymen, aghast, tossed away their rifles and threw up their hands.

But the Germans only butchered them the more.

Somehow, Alexey made it to the top. He'd just decided, whatever else, to sell his life dearly, when he felt a rough hand on his collar, presumably German. Turning he saw Alphonse, gesticulating frantically toward the horses, where half a dozen cavalrymen were already saddled up. "Allez allez allez!" Alphonse cried, leaping onto the nearest horse, and almost throwing Alexey onto the horse beside it. Instantly they tore off, joining the other six, and Alexey realised these cavalrymen intended to cut their way through.

They charged so furiously that at first they seemed to manage it. Then two horses fell. Moments later Alexey saw, out of the corner of his eye, that Alphonse, too, had keeled over, as if wounded, rolling further and further over in his saddle, and soon he was almost off, dragged along by one foot caught in a stirrup, shrieking with pain. And now he was being set upon by Germans.

On impulse Alexey turned his horse to try a rescue. But now more Germans pounced, swinging their rifle butts, and he felt yet another thrill of horror. *They could kill me now.* So he turned again and raced off down the slope, frantically cutting at them with Toby's sword.

Moments later he was through and reached the hill's bottom. Riding like the wind, helped on by his horse's terror, he sped across a wide, moonlit meadow, on and on with no plan at all except an instinct to flee south.

Soon he'd lost even the survivors of his troop – he never did find out their fate. All but one, that is, who seemed to be following him. For a moment he feared he might German. But no, he saw that he was, indeed, French, and was plainly sticking to him as closely as he could.

Together they galloped ever further south. Finally, they found a road, where they went faster still.

And the sound of battle faded from their ears.

Chapter Seventy-Eight

After an hour they reached a wood, buried themselves in the middle, and stopped.

Alexey, shattered in mind and body, slid off his horse and slumped to the ground. Then his new companion joined him. They sat in silence.

Finally, "Mon dieu, mon dieu, " muttered his friend, and this simple appeal to God seemed all that was needed.

The same mood dictated Alexey's answer.

"Jesus."

But there were two more words, nevertheless, that made sense.

"Fabrice," said the Frenchman, stretching out his hand.

"Alexey."

And Alexey took a moment to size his companion up. He was small, dark, and almost gnome-like. But when he smiled - as he did at this moment - he radiated kindness.

The Frenchman offered Alexey a cigarette. Alexey thanked him and they smoked, for two minutes, in utter silence.

"Your head" said Fabrice, leaning forward and touching the left side of Alexey's scalp. At which Alexey felt a stinging pain; he too touched the place, and his fingers were smeared with blood. Then he realised the whole left side of his tunic was bloody too.

Fabrice lit another match and looked more carefully. "Sabre cut," he said. "Je crois."

He delved into his knapsack and applied a field dressing. And then "Une autre': for there was, as well, a nasty wound on Alexey's thigh. This too he dressed. Alexey winced as Fabrice tightened the knot. "Pardon" said Fabrice, and again the smile, his rough face giving off its nurturing light.

Which Alexey appreciated, as he had never been more in need of such sustenance. His mind kept spinning, jumping back and forth with the horror of what he had seen. The crass, brutal use of rifle butts and even spades; the grotesque wounds; above all the weird horror of Toby's shooting - that look of surprise. Yet worse, even, than Toby's death had been Alphonse's - attacked, as he dangled from his horse, from all sides.

Though the true horror of Alphonse's killing, what had finally traumatised Alexey, had been his own...... he hesitated to admit it.......cowardice. His flight, regardless of his friend! How had this happened? Had people seen it? Surely, he'd done no such thing! And yet he had….

With all this revolving in Alexey's head they stayed silent.

But now, again, the crash of guns. They must get on, get away! At any moment the Germans might be onto them.

Alexey hauled himself towards his horse. At first he failed to mount. Then he tried and tried again, and still he couldn't get on. On his fourth attempt Fabrice helped him, and he succeeded. Their horses limped away, as fast as their riders could manage.

Then a moment later, in a kind of delayed recall, Alexey realised he'd seen Fabrice, too, had had difficulty mounting. Though he'd finally managed it. And he grasped why. Fabrice had also been wounded. There were evil-looking bloodstains on his leg. But he hadn't mentioned it.

An hour later they stopped again to rest. They slept for three hours. When they woke they set off immediately, heading south.

Yet gradually they worried less about pursuit, and Alexey, for one, regained his chief priority: delivering the message about Von Kluck's envelopment. They must get it to Spears, and the British High Command, before the allies' advance! This above all! Or their armies would be engulfed.

Another reason for Alexey's eagerness, it must be said, was that he felt this might in some way redeem his earlier cowardice. And it helped that Fabrice, to whom he'd explained everything, was as eager as he.

For, reckoned Fabrice, as soon as their warning was delivered to the British, it would surely be passed on to the French. With the added authority of the British high command. And Fabrice would be a hero!

It had not been often, in Fabrice's humdrum life, that he'd had such hopes.

They hurried on. True, they were heading in precisely the opposite direction from Alexey's uncle and aunt. But what else could they do? The only possible outcome of going north would be to be taken prisoner, if not killed.

Fortunately, the roads seemed clearer all the time and speed was possible. And now, on the rare occasions they were stopped, they had the art of presenting themselves to a tee. They got through any outposts, all British now, like lightning.

Then finally, Le Cateau. A classic northern French valley. A plunge down from the grand sweep of the downs. Then up the steep, cobbled street, the Mairie on the left, the church on the hill, the market square.

And there, among the busy, bustling British, the Union Jack, draped over the entrance of a small-town chateau.

The BEF HQ.

Chapter Seventy-Nine

Something about their wild, careering approach must have impressed those who saw them. Because everyone stepped aside, while the sentries promptly waved them through.

Fabrice, at Alexey's insistence, went off to get his wound checked. Alexey started the routine row with the desk-sergeant.

Then a door opened and in walked Spears.

His face lit up at the sight of Alexey, then fell. For Alexey looked dreadful.

His face was streaked with blood from his head wound, his uniform was in shreds and there was horror in his eyes. A horror which was compounded, now, by seeing Spears.

For Spears looked shattered too.

Nevertheless: "Dear boy," said Spears, holding his hand held out and grasping Alexey by the shoulder. "Where the devil did you spring from? And what happened?" He nodded toward the sergeant with an 'I'll take care of this' air, leading Alexey back to the room he'd left.

It was full of officers. Spears shepherded Alexey to a sofa in the corner, sat him down and gently touched his wound. "What's this? Shouldn't you get it looked at? I say, stay here a moment." He bounded up from his seat and disappeared. When he returned it was with a first aid kit and a half bottle of red wine, which Alexey swigged gratefully.

"Are you quite sure you don't need looking at?" Spears repeated, but Alexey assured him his wounds could wait and far more urgent was what he'd seen: confirmation of the very worst they'd feared.

"I've got this letter from Colonel D'Aubert," he said, brandishing D'Aubert's note.

"From D'Aubert?" said Spears, his eyes lighting up. "The French cavalry officer?"

"The very same."

"That's wonderful. I know him. He's very good."

Spears studied the letter carefully.

"This letter identifies at least two corps of six divisions, at least 120,000 men, and says that after moving west they have now turned south. Did you see them yourself?"

"I did," said Alexey, "Although my understanding was rather less professional than D'Aubert's. But yes, I saw them."

"Good God," muttered Spears, largely to himself, then gazed once more at Alexey with watery, troubled eyes. "When I add this to everything else the situation really is dire."

Alexey didn't dare tell him that D'Aubert was dead.

At this moment they were joined by a short, avuncular-looking man who Spears introduced as the British Intelligence chief, Colonel Macdonogh.

He had his own information. Not only, it emerged, were the Germans enveloping in the way Alexey had seen but their overall numbers, in the West, were growing all the time - as many as nine Divisions, already, three times previous estimates.

Then add to this yet further information, said Spears, that he had gathered in the last forty-eight hours, travelling around the French lines. The French left, it seemed, was in full-blown retreat - which meant the BEF could find itself not merely separated from Lanrezac's forces, but as much as nine miles *ahead* of them; a plum ripe for the German picking.

But even that was not the worst of it. "Look at this' said Spears, gesturing around the room. "Can you guess what these officers are doing?" Alexey shook his head. "In the dire circumstances we know about they're planning to **attack** - to **advance,** God help us, so they could be yet further ahead again!"

"So what's to be done?"

"What we've done already. But we'll try again. We'll increase the pressure on Sir John French - especially the news about the French retreat. Plus what you've seen and told me. And hope against every damned hope that for once in this bloody war someone listens."

And Spears shepherded Alexey and Macdonogh back into the Chateau's drawing room, which was where, apparently, they'd been told to wait.

Shortly afterward a door opened and in strode a short, rubicund general with a bustling air and, beside him, another general of middle height, with noble, haunted eyes. 'French and Murray,' muttered Spears. Bristling with gold braid, they looked, to Alexey, quite wonderfully authoritative: like fearsome, flamboyant tropical fish.

French greeted Spears warmly, with a shake of the hand, while Spears introduced Alexey, explaining why he was there. French cocked his head like a parrot, listening intently; then, noticing the blood on Alexey's head, asked, was he alright? Spears said Alexey would be fine but that he had, like Spears, come straight from the front. Meanwhile, he wondered if Alexey might stay with them while they spoke, in case he could add something?

"Certainly" said French. "Just make sure you get that seen to" - indicating Alexey's wound - "the moment we're done."

And Alexey saw why French was popular with his men, and why they felt, as they put it, he was 'on their side.'

The conversation was succinct. Macdonogh made his contribution. Spears reiterated what he had just told Alexey. Then Alexey put in his own eyewitness confirmation, based on his experiences of the last two days.

Spears' summing-up pulled no punches. If the British advanced as planned, he said, they would be 'annihilated.'

Both French and Murray said very little - just a couple of questions. But they looked grimmer by the minute. Sir John glanced now and then at a map. Finally, they called a halt and said they must talk.

Spears, Macdonogh and Alexey returned to the dining room where they'd been earlier, where the other officers were still preparing for what they cheerily called 'the advance.' Strange moment! Or as Spears put it in his memoirs:

"Round the table, the empty coffee cups pushed out of the way to make room for maps.... representatives of neighbouring units were perfecting details, arranging communications, fixing timetables, making notes in field service books......keenness, suppressed excitement, joy and confidence, sparkled through the ordinary technical conversation of these men who already saw themselves marching to victory on the morrow."

Spears had felt all the worse, he said, because, as a lowly subaltern, he doubted his own judgement. Suppose the information he'd given French was wrong! He thought of Captain Nolan who had brought the order for the Charge of the Light Brigade.

"Then the door opened suddenly and General Murray stood framed against the dark hall. Looking at the officers sitting round the table he said – "You are to come in now and see the Chief. He is going to tell you that there will be no advance. But remember there are to be no questions. Don't ask why. There is no time and it would be useless. You are to take your orders, that's all."

Spears' advice had been heeded, Alexey's mission fulfilled, and the British army saved.

Chapter Eighty

So now another respite. With Spears' help, Alexey went off to get his wounds treated, which turned out to be straightforward enough.

Next, also thanks to Spears, who then had to leave, Alexey was served an excellent supper. The lamp chops, especially, seemed unmatched in all his twenty-three years.

At least, he reflected, as he lit a cigarette, the madness of the preceding days had shown some purpose. Despite all fears, despite all horrors and absurdities, he'd stuck it out. His message had been delivered, the British army saved. He felt somewhat, if not wholly, rehabilitated.

Then he started. Except for his uncle! God help him, he still had no idea where he was, or his aunt, or dear old Clotilde, either! But what on earth could be done, beyond what he'd done already? Precisely nothing.

He sat there for half an hour, quietly smoking. In the next room he heard the intermittent ring of a telephone, as had happened throughout his meal. Then suddenly, after another ring, gasps of astonishment; cries of *"What?"* - and an NCO walked swiftly into the dining room, caught his eye, and said:

"Mr. Smolensky?"

"Yes?"

"Telephone, sir."

"What?"

"It's a German. He's asking for you."

"What?"

Nevertheless, Alexey followed the NCO into the next room, tracked by goggling eyes, and there was the phone, on the table, off its hook. Alexey gazed at the senior officer present: he nodded. And when Alexey picked up the phone it was indeed a German. And now, more astonishment still: the caller was none other than Von Leckburg, he of New College, phoning from Koblenz - the Kaiser's HQ. Von Leckburg of all people! He was an aide, apparently, to the high command.

The Germans, he said, had long known the number of Sir John French's HQ. But this was the first time anyone had used it. Then Rudi explained why *he* had: he'd stumbled across important news, he said, news which could be crucial, he was sure, to Alexey. Even so the last thing he'd expected was to get through, let alone reach Alexey himself, the whole thing was bizarre, but he'd thought he'd give it a try..............

"So what's the news?" asked Alexey.

Very good indeed! Did Alexey remember the time he chatted with that German officer on the phone - the Von Kant who'd occupied his uncle's house? Well, it so happened he was one of Rudi's oldest friends – they'd studied together – no, not at Oxford! - and when they'd run into each other a couple of days back Von Kant had mentioned the phone call and more particularly - he'd just heard - what had happened to Alexey's uncle.

He had, it seemed, reached Hook of Holland and was already - Rudi had confirmed this through Swiss contacts - back safely in England. He was staying, apparently, with the Claytons. Who they both knew. And Alexey's aunt, his wife, was with him and she was fine too. And their maid too, one Clotilde, nein? She was well also, if a little shaken.

Even as Von Leckburg was talking, Alexey's tears began. He couldn't speak. Finally, with great difficulty, he stumbled a heartfelt thanks and, apologising, put the phone down. Somehow, sometime, they would talk properly.

Thank God, thank God, he muttered to himself, through the tears. Yet the tears, unlike so many lately, were tears of joy.

He staggered from the room, wandered into the corridor, bumping and stumbling into passing officers, then found what looked like a passage into the garden. All he wanted now was time to himself. Time to digest at least some of the tumultuous events, tumbling one on top of another, that had overwhelmed the last few days.

It had been the worst and best of life, simultaneously. The cruel, tragic deaths of so many around him; the loss of Toby, Alphonse, and all those young men on the hill, so full of joy and humour and hope …..men who above all *deserved to live*.

And then - within the same two days! - those other, wonderful things: Fabrice and his kindness; the devotion of D'Aubert and Spears; most remarkable of all, the way Von Leckburg – a so-called 'enemy!' - had taken the trouble, surely involving significant risk, to make this contact.

And Alexey's head began spinning so that he was smiling, then laughing, then obsessively shaking his head, and then more tears. Yes, all he wanted now was to get away on his own, to find some respite, some escape - above all else, from *people.*

He found his way to the chateau rose garden, full of sagging, sultry blooms – lovely as he'd seen in France.

Yet even this was not right. For what he really wanted was something more informal, less contrived. And he headed through a gate into a broad green meadow, and then, beyond, into a field. And there, remarkably, was everything he had hoped.

Another sunflower field, just like Douai.

Sunflowers! They perfectly suited his mood. And as he gazed at them, silent and sumptuous, he realised why.

They were as far from the frantic doings of men as could be. They made their own universe: their glowing faces turning endlessly, unanimously, toward the sun, with this strange telepathy between them and the orb above.

And now, even as the sun set, there came the moon, pale silver amidst the flawless evening blue: all part of the same separate, unearthly communion, watching over all.

And Alexey sat in silence, drinking it up.

Then gradually he realised that all the time he'd been there, the war, his inexorable companion, had been rumbling on in the background. Was he imagining it, or was the bombardment getting closer? If so that would make sense, as the Germans were heading southward all the time.

Then moments later, the impossible. Suddenly, incredibly, that deadly whooshing sound of a heavy shell, heading his way. How could this be, so far from the line? Seconds later it erupted, in another of those ear-cracking explosions, an earthquake of debris and earth, in the very next field. Then another and another then a fourth, its shattering concussion closer still…….. then yet another, shrieking toward him, this one feeling as if it truly were aimed at Alexey alone.

So strongly did he feel this that he threw himself to the ground, clawing at the earth as if his nails could dig him deeper. And in came the shell with a moan that was almost human, less a sound, somehow, than a *personality*, like some drear malevolent ghost.

And that was all he knew. He never heard the explosion. Only a sudden blankness, as if swallowed up by fog.

Chapter Eighty-One

It had been less than a week since Alexey left England, yet Ingrid was experiencing her own Gethsemane.

She felt disproportionately anxious about him – disproportionately, that is, given how very little she cared for him these days. For all the obvious and sensible reasons. Yet suddenly, out of nowhere, would come these great rushes of fear. And she would remind herself that this was in one way quite natural, given the way the war was shaping up. But there really was no possibility of feeling more, not in the old way, anyway....for all the obvious and sensible reasons.

It wasn't as if there weren't other things to think about. There was, above all, her pregnancy. At least she'd moved beyond morning sickness. Nevertheless, sooner or later, her 'condition' would become plain to all, notably the inhabitants of the village. It would be unlikely to increase her popularity.

Then there were the reverberations from her trip home. She was still, weeks later, in the same shock she'd felt initially, plus a soaring, seething anger at her parents, notably her father. Then add to this, as if it were not enough, her new status, thanks to the war, of 'Hun', as the villagers called her, some of them at least. She daren't imagine how that might develop.

Yet sometimes, when Henry was in one of his better moods or Mary and the children had been unusually loving, she'd dismiss all this and feel sudden rushes of joy - above all, in her coming motherhood.

This remained the one thing she was sure of. And she especially felt this when she spent time with Rosemary and Josephine. For given her experience as governess with the Crosbys, it seemed natural for Ingrid to give them lessons. The children loved these and adored her - as she did them.

Then one day she got a letter from her father, forwarded from the Crosbys. It came via neutral Switzerland.

He was, it emerged, quite as angry as she, especially, he stressed, 'due to the effect all this is having on your mother.' He simply could not credit Ingrid's selfishness; not merely in 'indulging' herself so carelessly as to get pregnant, but in ' achieving' this in such a thoughtless, irresponsible way. Did she *really* not know who her baby's father was? And then she ups and flees – at such a world-historic moment, she certainly knew how to time things! Etc etc..... and so the letter rambled on, till Ingrid spotted the line which appalled her most.

Her father had felt obliged, he said – though deeply embarrassed - to tell the Crosbys the whole story. So he had written to them. Surely Ingrid could see, given the trust and hospitality they had extended her, they had the right to know?

And this new information upset Ingrid most of all. She had, of course, been half-expecting it. But what disturbed her was its vindictiveness. It was the one thing her father could have done to make her life harder. And he had done it.

And still no news from Alexey. (Not, of course, that she thought about him, for all the obvious and sensible reasons.) Rather, her attention was seized - tentatively at first, but soon with enthusiasm - by a new project of Mary's.

And this was the idea that they should use the Westbury buildings to create a cottage hospital. Such facilities were springing up, said Mary, all over the country, so that any wounded – and it looked like there would be a veritable cataract of wounded - could be tended locally, and stay in touch more easily with their families. And the Westbury camp buildings, surely, could be readily adapted to just such a purpose. Henry, a touch surprisingly, was also an earnest advocate of the scheme and had, in turn, converted Anthony Parsons.

Then add in a further, unexpected factor. The day after Mary described the scheme news reached the village that Ben Tennant's twin brothers, both in the BEF, had been wounded in the opening battles in France. They would soon be coming home. Wouldn't they be ideal for just such a hospital as this? Their wounds were relatively minor, so they'd be well within the remit of Ingrid and Mary.

It could be wonderfully convenient for all. Indeed, as word spread locally, the villagers increasingly got behind this bold new venture.

Yet there were further motives, too, in Mary's mind, that woman so constantly tuned to the thoughts and needs of others. Especially apropos Henry. For equivocal though he was about the war - notably lacking, that is, in the more volatile forms of patriotism – she knew that there was more to his concern for Alexey, often expressed, than met the eye.

Henry felt, she sensed, distinctly emasculated by Alexey's example. Alexey had gone, quixotically, to France, he'd set out to rescue his relatives, he'd faced every possible peril - Alexey of all people, who never committed himself to anything - whereas he, Henry, had merely joined the local yeomanry. And might, especially if the war did end by Christmas, never get to France at all.

So, reasoned Mary, a project like this might give Henry a new, very different, source of self-respect. Which could only help their relationship.

For she was becoming less and less sure, lately, of Henry's devotion. The initial flurry of sexual interest she'd so eloquently described to Ingrid had long tailed off; and with Henry, as Mary so often said, desire and love were one.

Back had come Henry's old, familiar irritability, the sniping, the rows, the sudden storming departures for the woods. Whatever Mary's head told her, her heart knew otherwise. And she felt sad.

So that gradually, almost obsessively, she began telling herself that this hospital project would help. Strange logic, of course, but to Mary's practical mind anything active had its own, near-mystic power.

So she and Henry set about it, with their familiar division of labour - he devising the strategy, Mary the tactics.

Henry saw how suited Westbury was for convalescence - its woodland site, its views, its slumberous quietude. Mary earmarked the rooms - four in particular, store rooms up until then, but with the familiar over-arching Westbury views. And furnished them.

Henry it was who raised the broad question of nursing – they'd need professionals, of course, but how many, and how much should they pay? Mary started the search for them - putting ads in the local paper, then seeking out the beds, the cutlery, the drugs.

But the crucial question, both agreed, was money. Without it, all else was meaningless - but where to find it?

The answer, they realised, was simple: Eric Rother. Eric knew everyone, he knew the Claytons, the Smolenskys, London society - he would be their channel to every source. Especially because he surely felt so guilty over Henry's poetry-publishing debacle that he was ripe for the plucking, as Mary rather ashamedly put it to herself. Unlike that earlier disaster, when things were clearly out of his hands, he could help.

And when Mary wrote to him, she proved right. Rother's reply was swift and enthusiastic. He would come to visit her, at Westbury, and bring with him a small party that would include Colonel Tucker, the Oxfordshire Yeomanry commander who had presided at the review.

So two days later, down they came, and there were three other officers as well as Colonel Tucker. And with them came Charlie Fisher, Paula, Anthony Parsons, Tom Huntingdon even - plus one other couple who had just got back from the continent: none other than Alexey's uncle, complete with wife.

And what was clear from the start, from the manner of all present, was that one way or another the resources would be found. All details would be sorted later.

None of which was hindered by the fact that Ingrid and Mary shrewdly wore their Voluntary Aid Detachment uniforms, red crosses dramatically to the fore, nor by the mildly surprising sight of Paula, too, in V.A.D uniform, an outfit she'd become entitled to after a course she'd done in Oxford. She'd never looked so fine.

So that there was, among the men, a re-kindling of that crusader-like protectiveness that had characterised the review. More than protectiveness, indeed - a sense of real comradeship with these red-crossed heroines, in this most noble and epoch-making of fights.

But all this was eclipsed, within the first ten minutes, when Alexey's uncle suddenly declared he had 'something of an announcement.' He had news of Alexey! After a week of uncertainty, the Smolenskys had received a telegram. Alexey had been wounded. Only slightly, fortunately - he'd been blown up by a mortar shell, but he'd been extraordinarily lucky. There was little wrong beyond mild concussion and the loss of a few teeth. All eminently fixable.

Right now he was in hospital outside Boulogne and would soon be home.

Which was greeted with delight, quite as much as concern, by all present. At least he hadn't vanished, as they'd feared till then.

By all, that is, except Ingrid. She was reeling. She'd thought he might be hurt but had not really expected it; worse, the moment she heard the news, baboom! That old, familiar reaction. And then she *blushed*, of all things, then excused herself and walked away.

She reappeared a moment later looking transformed. She'd seemed quite jolly, earlier. Now she felt remote.

Not that this over-bothered the others. They were touched – especially the Smolenskys – to see how the news affected her.

While Eric Rother was most impressed of all. What especially struck him was Ingrid's empathy. He knew enough of Ingrid's story, via the Claytons, to know of her pregnancy. He also knew that whoever the father was it certainly wasn't Alexey.

So any feelings Ingrid had for him, reckoned Eric, must be pure altruism.

So when might Alexey return? The Smolenskys had it on good authority, they said, that he should be over within a week.

He would hopefully be sent to a hospital in London - but later, suggested Colonel Tucker, half-laughing, wouldn't he make an ideal convalescent patient for the camp? A notion which was received with predictable jollity by all - except, Eric noticed, by Ingrid. Indeed, if he did not utterly mistake her, she even looked ***alarmed*** at the idea.

But then she was very young, thought Eric, and no doubt found the responsibility, even in prospect, daunting. She needed encouragement.

Ah, in the right circumstances he could have been just the man to give it her. How he loved to nurture the young!

Shortly after, the meeting ended. Three cabs took the visitors down to the station, while the officers drove off in their Army car.

Ingrid fled to her room. She stretched out on the bed. The news about Alexey had been one thing; stranger still had been her reaction.

She'd felt a sudden, violent rush of love. It was as if her feelings had sped straight back to where they'd been six months ago. No longer the concern she'd felt throughout his various absences: rather pure, plain, adolescent romance. How could this be?

The answer was clear: those feelings had been there all along, submerged but still alive. The shock had triggered them.

Chapter Eighty-Two

Alexey landed at Folkestone within a week, and was duly assigned to 1st London General hospital, Ashbury Ward, at Camberwell.

The fact that it was London, the centre of the transport system, made it easier for his friends to visit him. It was even possible for George to come from Cambridge. He was insistent, when he heard the news, that he would be there.

So on the second of September, they duly met in the hospital's grey, sparse foyer. The exterior, as they walked up, seemed gloomier still: its centrepiece a huge black tower, coked thick with London soot, louring ominously over them as their train drew up to Denmark Hill station. It seemed, thought Ingrid, less a hospital, more a sarcophagus from ancient Egypt.

Not that anyone would have known this from her manner. For Ingrid and her friends coped in their usual wartime way, with an excess, if anything, of jollity.

And their merriment survived their entry into the hospital - for all its tense, almost studied, air of crisis. Heroic sisters strode the corridors; trolleys followed them, saline bottles flying high; there was a weird, omnipresent smell of gas and antiseptic, mingling strangely with the smell of eggs.

Then there were the patients, white-faced and crumpled, or cheeky and jolly, for the other striking feature of the place was the all-encompassing warmth with which everyone treated everyone else. Indeed, declared George, it would not be too strong to say that the word which best described the atmosphere there was..........happiness.

In short it was like every other hospital on earth, its inhabitants overwhelmed to find that human nature can, after all, be generous.

So even though they got lost and lost again in the corridors, they still maintained their jollity till suddenly, rounding a corner, and thinking they'd gone wrong, there, emblazoned above a door, was 'Ashbury Ward': Alexey's.

A stab of alarm for all of them, but especially Ingrid. She let the others go in before her. And when she followed she gazed round gently, tentatively, as if she could harm Alexey merely by looking at him.

Ten yards away, at a table bright with flowers, sat the slender figure of a V.A.D. nurse. She was about the same age, Ingrid guessed, as herself. The nurse half-rose to greet them.; thick black curls, poking out from her head-dress, framed a wonderfully gentle, pretty face. She smiled sweetly and for a moment Ingrid thought, perversely, how sad that she should have to wear such dull, unflattering clothes, so much less attractive than the uniforms she and Mary had managed to acquire!

Ingrid glanced up and down the ward, scanning each face for the one she knew so well. All the patients were looking in the visitors' direction – here, at last, was something interesting. The nurse, who must be new, was nervously scanning a list, running her fingers up and down, till finally she found the 'S'es. "Ah! Smolensky!" she cried, and gestured, not down the ward, but just behind them: the visitors had walked straight past him.

It was obvious why. Alexey was unrecognisable. His head and shoulders were swathed in bandages, to such an extent that they gave him an almost cartoon air - too many bandages, too much drama, disaster *a outrance*. With the sole exception of his face, most of which had been left open. And as his mouth was open too Ingrid could see a wound that truly shook her: as well as scars and strange, black bruises round his chin there were three large gaps in his front teeth. Some dire, uncaring force had ripped that hallowed face apart.

The others, instinctively assuming her priority, let her through. Alexey looked up, recognised her, and, with a visible effort, smiled.

And Ingrid's jollity was overwhelmed by the most flooding tenderness she had ever known. That dear, dear face, how could anybody have done this to him? To somebody so precious and so dear? It was mad, unimaginable, but now, starting this moment, she would do the very opposite. She would help him, tend him, nurture him, with all the strength she could feel welling up within her. Such a force as would cocoon and cherish him forever.

Mary gestured Ingrid to sit beside the bed. The others dropped back and watched. Alexey continued to fix Ingrid with his strange smile, as from another galaxy. She reached for his hand and held it. She said nothing, but simply stared. And he stared back.

And so they stayed, scarcely speaking, for nearly half an hour, while their friends mirrored their expressions. Even Tom - George had never seen him like this - was transformed.

Till finally the ward sister, who'd been out when they arrived and was now back, said Alexey looked tired, and they should end the visit for now.

With one last gaze and a squeeze of Alexey's hand Ingrid got up and left, the others following her. And Alexey watched them disappear, still with his ghostly smile.

For Ingrid, this was the watershed. First, there'd been the shock of Alexey's departure. Next, his swift return - but wounded. Now, the gross reality of those wounds in the flesh. Each stage had moved Ingrid's feelings closer to consciousness from the depths where they'd been buried. Now finally, with the touch of Alexey's hand, with her overwhelming reaction to his plight, Ingrid became fully aware of her love.

And with that realisation came a clarity and vigour which, linked with the practicality of Mary, was irresistible.

They should - she knew now – take up Colonel Tucker's half-humorous suggestion. Alexey should be Westbury's first patient! They should bring him there and nurture him. Who better?

This might have seemed unlikely given his appearance at the hospital but his progress, after the visit - Ingrid and Mary saw him twice a week for a fortnight – was exceptional. Indeed, it emerged that his disorientation that first time had been largely due to morphia, a point the young V.A.D. had omitted to make clear.

So the offer was made, and readily accepted by Alexey.

Soon a start was made doing up his Westbury room; Ingrid and Mary found curtains, towels, bedding; and on September the fourteenth, just over three weeks from his initial wounding, Tom and Charles fetched Alexey down by train.

Feted by the locals as a hero, he moved in.

Chapter Eighty-Three

And was struck immediately by Ingrid's aloofness. For now, much like that period when he'd made his altruistic attempts to 'serve' her, before he went to France, she felt remote.

She was welcoming, she was kind, she gave him practical help unstintingly: she was the soul of quiet professionalism. The difference - the surprise - lay in just that: her professionalism. It was as if a thin, but implacable veil of abstraction had once more fallen between them, and the naked warmth he'd felt so intensely at the hospital had disappeared.

God knows, he'd become inured to it before. But he'd hoped for more now he was a returning 'hero.'

Not least from the way he'd been treated by her and Mary, on their follow-up visits. Especially the day Ingrid asked him - how sweetly, how delicately she'd put it, how different from her remoteness before he'd left! – to come to Westbury and be their patient.

But above all, he still remembered her manner that very first time, when she'd come with their friends. Despite the crowd, she'd been dominant from the start, and ended up sitting right next to him.

How vividly he remembered her holding his hand! Never had he been looked at like that in his life. Never had he felt so cherished, enfolded, by a power of which Ingrid seemed merely the embodiment.

What, must he tell himself these feelings were a fantasy, a drug-induced hallucination? He didn't think so.

And Alexey was right on both counts – both the warmth and the withdrawal.

For Ingrid had been terrified by the strength of her feelings. Not least the way she'd felt - strangest of all - as if they were hardly her own, as if they existed somehow independently, a separate, mighty force. Blowing through her like a wind! Where had they come from? Where might they take her? With what result? All love had ever meant to her, certainly in adulthood, was complexity and hurt. This pain could be worst of all.

Not to mention the other, obvious factor, forever present in her mind. How could she equate the resurrection of her romance with that other profound commitment, the one she had so recently and resolutely reaffirmed - her baby? Remorselessly growing, every day, within her womb. How could she get involved with Alexey when she was with child? A child fathered by someone else, and she didn't even know who?

And so, albeit with a mighty effort, she had beaten down these reborn feelings, and grafted them over with just such a smooth dispassionate veneer as might conceal the truth. She still felt intense sympathy for Alexey and all his sufferings; but it was a sympathy, she'd decided, she would control.

"How's the invalid," she asked, a touch too breezily, bustling into Alexey's bedroom one morning soon after he arrived. He'd long had his gross, theatrical bandages removed and was reduced to a couple of plasters.

"Alright," he said, leaning forward so Ingrid could plump the pillows. He'd been in bed since he arrived, at her insistence.

She thumped them energetically. He winced. This brisk professionalism was not what he desired. He craved warmth. He'd been trying, for a while, every trick he could dream up to get it.

Today his ploy was to exaggerate his condition. He'd been reading when he heard Ingrid coming, but as she approached he dropped his book and feigned sleep. He tried his very hardest to look vulnerable.

She punched the pillows harder. She felt mildly irritated. There'd been something unreal, she felt, about Alexey's manner when she came in – almost contrived. One arm thrown back over the pillow, like something out of the Wreck of the Medusa. She bashed his pillows again, taking out on them an anger she felt hard to place.

"Would you like some tea?" she asked.

"No thank you," he said, though actually he'd have liked some. But saying so might have made him seem better than he wished.

"You should get some sleep," said Ingrid, vaguely reproving.

She dusted mildly round his table, removed his water, and vanished into the kitchen.

At which Alexey retrieved his book, which he'd secreted under the counterpane, and re-started reading.

Nevertheless, their new-found relationship gradually found its rhythm. Ingrid, with ever-increasing verve, cooked Alexey meals, found him books, read to him, and performed the small tasks of nursing and of care.

Alexey, showing evident appreciation, thanked her graciously, and bore up well, but with a hard-to-pin-down air of wanting more. Which Ingrid resented.

Even so, very soon – however hard Alexey tried to disguise it – he plainly got much better, and they would walk together round the camp, or in the woods.

And talk about the war. How Alexey loved to talk about the war! Above all, over and over again, about the men he'd met: rakish Alphonse, strange little Fabrice, Toby Macdonald, Edward Spears. Ingrid wondered, sometimes, if talking about the characters was his way of avoiding the violence.

Not that he pulled any punches when he did describe it. Nor forgetting, either, the rape of the French landscape, nor the nightmare of the refugees, the utter devastation of their lives.

Indeed, the main thing he wanted to convey, evidently, was the very same as Ingrid had worked out from the start: that war was an utterly different state of being from any they'd ever known. Or something even worse: that it was the foundation of the world they'd always lived in – yet they'd not realised it. This was the most hateful idea of all. That for all the security of their lives till then, they had been living, for years, on the lip of a volcano. All that comfort a miasma, all that safety a dream! The reality was in France.

Reality. That was what Alexey felt he had seen and was at such pains to convey. Starting with Ingrid. So he pitched into her day after day until she, in turn, grew as weary of his harangues as he was desperate at her insouciance. Which for him clearly symbolised the callousness of the whole human race.

It was the look in Alexey's eyes that bothered Ingrid. A gaping, wide-eyed extremism she'd never previously seen, linked with an utterly new tone - rasping, strident, shrill. The look and manner of an evangelist. An evangelist for the reality of war.

One moment was plain weird. She was preparing tea on the stove just off Alexey's room, when she saw him, through the window, striding across the grass from Henry and Mary's room where he'd gone to borrow plates.

And she knew immediately there was something wrong. His lips were set, his eyes were glowing, and his walk, always stooped, was bent over more than ever. Like a whipped cur, she told herself.

She blurted:

"What happened?"

Alexey shot her a haunted, resentful look.

"Nothing 'happened'. I've broken something. That's all."

"Broken what?"

"A clock."

"A clock?" Ingrid felt a stab of alarm. "Not that china clock of Mary's, the special one?" Mary had few possessions, and fewer still she cherished, but she did love her eighteenth-century clock in high rococo, decorated with shepherds and groves. It had been given her by her father.

"The very same."

"Oh, Alexey! What happened?"

"I destroyed it because it had no right to live."

"What?"

"I destroyed it because it had no right to exist," said Alexey, still more whipped-curish, "in its weird, over-embellished cocoon of *safety*," - Alexey almost spat the word - "when everything else in the world is being smashed. Everything, that is, except the remote, the contrived, the unreal– everything and everyone, in fact, that surrounds us here in England!"

This surely was the wildest idea of all.

"But where's the sense in taking it out on a *clock?*

"Where's the sense in any of it?"

To which, in fairness, there was no answer.

Even so, Ingrid had a strange feeling that for all Alexy's highfalutin arguments, the whole thing was somehow personal. In destroying the clock he was attacking her.

Now she too got angry: "It's ridiculous to blame a clock! You'll be blaming the ironing board next!"

And Alexey put his face up against hers, wide-eyed:

"I don't care! I smashed it anyway! I told you, it had no right to exist...." And suddenly he was crying. Then Ingrid was crying too.

"Oh Alexey!" she said, and flung her arms around his neck - at which Alexey gasped. She'd hit his wound.

She jumped back.

"I'm sorry!"

But now he was laughing.

"Watch out! You might break *me*!"

"Oh, I would never do that!"

Now once again morose:

"You already have."

At which Ingrid cried still more, and again threw her arms around him. And this time, suddenly, Alexey kissed her, and she almost responded. Then she broke away and ran back into the kitchen.

Nevertheless, with the clock incident, the tone between them changed. While Ingrid still fended off any lumbering attempts Alexey made to approach her physically, it became ever plainer, to both of them, that the old feelings were still there. More powerful than ever, perhaps, for their long repression.

And yet there remained that huge obstacle between them - Ingrid's pregnancy. How could she reconcile this with her feelings for Alexey? How could she honour both allegiances? And, as so often, she wavered.

And now came the dreams – but very different from those cartoon, libidinous affairs months earlier. These were nightmares.

There were, for instance, what Ingrid called her 'homeless' dreams. She was in her parents' house, but the furniture was wrong, the decoration changed, and no-one was living there she knew. Just strangers.

Worse still were her 'journey' dreams.

She was travelling and had lost her suitcase. Everything she owned was in it (it was a magic suitcase, appropriate to dreams) and she spent the whole night pursuing it, mainly going round and round on the London underground. She never found it.

Some dreams combined both elements, homelessness and loss. She was en route to Entlingen and had lost her money – not her suitcase merely but her *money,* and thus all hope of getting anywhere at all. So throughout the night, as she slipped in and out of consciousness, the keynote of this dream was its insolubility. This was the worst, and most virulent dream of all.

One morning, when she and Alexey were due to take a walk, she'd had just such a dream. Her discomfort was plain: she had a furtive, preoccupied look, and was pale as the moon.

"What is it? Alexey asked, gently. Both were infinitely careful with each other these days.

"I - oh – it's just that I've not been sleeping well lately."

"You've a lot on your mind."

Ingrid shot him a grateful glance. "That's true. It does seem, sometimes, that it's really all too much."

And she began telling him about her nightmares. While in all his old way Alexey, the perfect listener, encouraged her.

Soon, falteringly, with many a stumble and blush, she began telling him just how anxious she was feeling about her baby; then described something of the angst she'd felt since the very first days of the pregnancy; the shock, the sense of scandal, the bizarre reaction of her parents. Till finally, tentatively, drawn on by Alexey's sympathy, she broached something new.

Was it possible (this most faltering of all) that Alexey could still care for her if she had the child? Even though the one thing he knew for sure was that he was not the father? Even though it would make him the partner of what the world called an 'unmarried mother'? Unless, of course............ but she balked at the pragmatic solution, put so baldly.

They had walked to the beech grove at the top of the hill, that very same glade they'd sat in when Ingrid first visited Westbury. They reached the summit; they even settled on the same log. Around them swayed the beech trees, tinged by autumn.

"I love this place, "said Ingrid. "It feels almost.... holy."

"Perhaps it is, for us," said Alexey.

And maybe the grove did work some magic or sweeten their mood. Because the more they talked, the more their spirits seemed to lean towards each other and unite.

Finally, and it felt so natural, Alexey put his arm round Ingrid and kissed her tenderly on the mouth. This time she didn't push him away.

It was spontaneous, but it was also due to something he'd just said. For what he'd told her was not only that he loved her, deeply, devotedly, but that he would indeed accept her child. And he would cherish them both, without restraint or reservation, throughout their lives. Until the end.

And now a great peace descended on them, especially Ingrid, for the first time for many months.

For at last she had a solution. She would fulfil both loves! She would cherish her baby and live her life with Alexey too. She would have both. So much was made possible by what Alexey had said. His experiences, plainly, had transformed him.

How strange that this had coincided with the revival of her love for him, likewise activated, however differently, by the war. Plainly, even the worst of life could be creative.

And now the unveiling of their souls went further still. First Alexey talked about the effects on him of his parents' disappearance, which had been huge. Then he drew *her* out about her childhood. To the extent that time and again she stumbled on things that were quite new, accompanied by tears.

And another shift took place in their relationship. Every day she became a little less the nurse, and Alexey more the mentor.

So when, just three days after their mutual pledge at the beech grove, Ingrid went to see Dr. Fenwick for her latest check-up, it was with none of the nervousness, and even shame, with which she'd been before. Rather it was with a new, calm confidence, surely good for her child.

Thus she was the more amazed when Dr. Fenwick, after careful examination, told Ingrid the results of her latest tests.

She was, said Fenwick, no longer pregnant.

Chapter Eighty-Four

If Fenwick had been kind months earlier, when she'd told Ingrid she was pregnant, she was even kinder, now, when she said that she was not. Yet Ingrid was, if anything, more devastated still. How could Fenwick explain the morning sickness, the swollen breasts, her swollen stomach even, her loss of periods? By now Dr. Fenwick was looking more than sympathetic, she was looking distraught.

Because the only person to blame, said Fenwick, was herself. She should have spotted Ingrid's real condition from the start.

"So what was it?" asked Ingrid.

"There's only one possible scenario," said Dr. Fenwick. "Your body imagined you were pregnant and mimicked the symptoms."

"You mean…what they call…. I think… ….. a phantom pregnancy?"

"Yes, some people call it that. That's rather strong. But something along those lines, I think, yes.

"I made assumptions. The mistake was mine. But then such a condition is very rare - I've only come across one other example, myself, in all my years in practice."

"Oh my God," said Ingrid, and sank down in her chair.

Dr. Fenwick, deeply moved, put her arm round Ingrid's shoulders. "There, there," she said. "It's extraordinary what the body can do sometimes - when influenced by the mind."

She paused. Then, diffidently:

"One thing that can cause this is stress. Would you say you were worried at all, when the symptoms first cropped up?"

That didn't take much thinking about. "I certainly was," said Ingrid. "Very worried indeed."

"Well," said Dr. Fenwick. "That may have been it."

There seemed little more to be said. Thanking Dr. Fenwick for her concern, brushing aside her renewed apologies, Ingrid left the surgery.

She staggered off down the street. Now, yet again, she must rebuild her life.

For the first few hours, back at Westbury, she vanished into her room, avoiding everyone, lying flat on her back. Then late in the afternoon she stumblingly told Mary – though she hated doing it: she was more and more embarrassed by her constant victimhood.

Mary, warmly sympathetic, sent her back to bed.

At six Mary cooked her a light supper. Fortunately, Alexey was out with Anthony Parsons so she wouldn't be seeing him that night, which was a blessing. For all the sympathy he'd surely show she didn't feel up to much right now.

And Alexey was indeed sympathetic, when, the next day, she wound herself up to tell him. And he went on being sympathetic in the days that followed. He said little, he avoided the dreaded pitfall of advice, and above all else he listened, as wonderfully as ever.

So Ingrid's trust in him once more took wing. She even, finally, broached the hardest stuff from Germany, including her mother's own, unmarried pregnancy. He was utterly understanding.

The sole difficulty came when their feelings led them to the brink of making love. (So swift had been Alexey's recovery.) Twice, indeed, they ended up in bed together and tried hard to consummate, as they'd tried so often before. But still they failed. Which patently disturbed Alexey very much.

Not that it worried Ingrid. Her 'shenanigans' that summer had given her sexual confidence, if nothing else. What mattered far more was the emotional connection they were building together and which she so badly needed, and hugely cherished, at this time.

And she realised something else, too. Encouraged by Alexey's warmth, she began to see one obvious advantage in this 'phantom pregnancy' or whatever you called it.

She and Alexey no longer had anything separating them! No angst, no scandals, no generation-long responsibilities. Instead, after all the endless complications of recent months, they could, quite simply, be lovers.

The more she thought about it, the happier she felt; and she resolved to share this realisation with him the first moment they met.

She tried the next day.

They were in the kitchen, they'd finished breakfast, and the time felt good.

Gaily she told him.

And he didn't look happy at all. Not upset, exactly - he even smiled. But he stayed quiet. For a moment she could have sworn he flashed one of those strange looks of his, of angst and alarm, that had struck her from the start.

"What is it, dear?" said Ingrid. "You look concerned."

"No, I'm fine," he said. "You're right. It's true, it does introduce a completely new situation."

And he looked more thoughtful still.

So Ingrid, after a moment, said:

"Are you *quite* sure it's all right -"

"Yes, quite."

"- I mean, I'll be honest - I was expecting you might be a bit more enthusiastic. After all it does offer us - especially me – real freedom for the first time .... "

"Freedom?" A flash of anger. "How can anyone be free in the nightmare of this war?"

Ingrid gasped.

"Oh, no, of course that's true, I meant freedom between ourselves..... "

But now Alexey picked up the war theme and began to run with it.

"Trust you to raise the war again. Are you *incapable* of leaving it alone? The next thing you'll ask me is why I smashed that clock. But then you never have, and never will, be able to realise how warfare, *real* warfare, can affect someone - just what it makes you see, in terms of human nature, about the extraordinary world in which we live."

Alexey paused for a moment, then added thoughtfully, and with due deliberation: "There are, quite simply, some things some people will never understand."

Another pause.

"And it's not in any way their fault."

Another gasp from Ingrid. How had they lurched into this? Yet it was plain enough who these 'people' were! Two outrageous assumptions heaped high upon each other. She had thought they were talking about their relationship; perhaps they were.

"If that is what you think," she said, "if I really suffer from the limitations, you so kindly explain, then I was surely wrong in what I said about our future. How could we ever have the remotest, real connection, free or unfree, war or no war..."

Alexey interrupted her.

"You are," he said, "quite right. We *should,* now you mention it, think hard about our future. Certainly, I've been doing so, I'll be honest about that.

"Right or wrong has nothing to do with it. It's merely that we are different. Okay, there is our difference, clearly, over the war." (Is there, thought Ingrid? I thought we both agreed it was obscene). "But that difference is down to experience, really, you would have to be a superman, or superwoman, an imaginative genius - far more than I could ever be! - to grasp any of it without being there. No, what I am talking about is something much more personal - something specifically between me and you, just the plain, unaccountable difference between two very different people."

Ingrid had no idea what he was talking about.

"We've never got on better since we met!"

"Yes, I know that. I *do* know that. But what I'm talking about is something deeper."

More furrowing of Alexey's brow.

"H. G. Wells..." (H.G. *what*? thought Ingrid) "...said somewhere that couples are constantly berating themselves for not getting on, for not behaving better, when it's actually just a question of different interests. His first wife was a classic - utterly charming, very taken with her at first, but the two of them had nothing in common really. She wasn't, for instance, remotely interested in the kinds of things he was so fascinated by – science, atomic power, the moon" (the *moon*?) "so it got to the stage, eventually, when the only thing that could bring them together was something trivial like.... the arrival of a new kitten...."

Trust Alexey to try and dress it all up as more than it was! But he was still coming; indeed, he was now in some strange full spate –

"It's something similar I'm trying to talk about here; like I said, the differences between us. Not right, not wrong, no blame attached at all. I mean, how interested are you in politics?" (I'm certainly interested when politics leads to war, thought Ingrid.) "Or history? Or chamber music?

"......Whereas you - and Mary- actually enjoy making curtains."

That did it. Till now Ingrid had been reticent under this assault, not least because the absurdity of it struck her dumb. Each blow hurt more, and tears spung to her eyes; but she controlled herself - a pressure cooker confronting the steamroller that was Alexey.

Now she let fly.

"Never, never have I heard such nonsense in my life!" she cried. "Of all the pompous, pretentious rubbish! H. G. Wells indeed! Chamber music! The moon!" Now Ingrid was laughing, almost gay. "The moon! It's all nonsense and nothing to do with anything, really, except your desperate attempt to make yourself feel better by finding fault with me, your oldest trick. Any fault will do. The moon!"

"But I only - "

"You what? Don't try to justify yourself - don't breathe a word! I'm beyond being fooled. Let's be honest: how I am or am not has absolutely nothing to do with any of it. I'm irrelevant in every way. All that matters, and it matters very much to you, is your absolute determination, yet again, to avoid our getting close - an alarm understandable in the light of the last few days, when your guard slipped and we began getting seriously connected, despite everything that has happened, which inevitably, of course, scares the daylights out of you, you poor poor tender little darling, you!"

Now again that look of abject terror on Alexey's face - come and gone in a flash, but plainly there. Followed instantly by his own explosion. Utter abandonment, now, of all pretentions to rationality, replaced by such a raging, incontinent anger as Ingrid had never seen.

"How dare you talk to me like that, you stupid bitch! How dare you! What makes you think you know anything at all about what I feel or why – you bitch, you stupid, ignorant, unthinking bitch, how dare you!"

"How dare you talk to *me* like that, you cretin!".

"Bitch!"

"Arsehole!"

"Bastard!"

"Whore!"

Now both were screaming like fishwives, their voices searing and grating in ways neither had ever heard before, both more appalled, even, by their own hysteria than that of the other.

Indeed, there was a wild electric moment when they could, quite literally, have killed each other. It was in their eyes. And it was true.

Ingrid picked a knife up, Alexey grabbed a vase, and they froze, for a moment, on the brink of calamity.

Then they dropped their weapons, rushed forward and fell into each other's arms.

Both shook uncontrollably.

"Oh God, I'm so sorry! I love you!"

"Oh God, I love you too!"

"I love you, love you, love you!"

"I love you, love you, too!"

And as they felt the crude ferocity of each other's clasp, they knew – with a certainty unmatchable by words - their love was real.

Chapter Eighty-Five

And in the rush of certainty they once more tore off their clothes, ran to the bedroom and made love on Alexey's bed, with none of the tentativeness of before.

Alexey climaxed early, and Ingrid didn't climax at all, but for the first time Alexey entered her and, however clumsily, their bodies were one. They lay there quietly for five minutes and then Alexey slowly, stumblingly, started talking again.

"The truth is.... there is...... something in what you say."

Ingrid stayed silent.

"I have been... avoiding.... real connection...... all my life. All my life." The phrases came jerkily; the effort was intense.

And now his tears, flowing silently, unlike so noisily moments before, took over.

"I....." he stopped and shook his head. "I....... had some difficult experiences......... in my past...."

Ingrid put her arm round his shoulder and cradled his head. With her right hand she stroked his forehead, over and over, like a child.

Alexey mastered himself.

"I'm not Russian at all: I'm Polish." Not such a great confession, surely, but Alexey carried on. "My parents were indeed revolutionaries, but Polish revolutionaries, against the Russian Empire, not against capitalism, or whatever you choose to call it. And my father is not in the United States, nor a political refugee, really - though he was involved in politics – but, quite simply, he vanished. Gone for years - I can't remember him.

"But the real.... the biggest.... difficulty.... was my mother. She was shattered by my father's disappearance. She loved him very much. For my first five years she brought me up, on her own. In Swanage! Of all places! In Dorset, by the sea. And for five years she waited for my father, desperately hoping he would come back. Because at that stage he was still in touch, he wrote.

"And then ..... the letters stopped. I remember how my mother would watch the post. Then gradually......she gave up. I remember how she changed She became…so sad…"

And now the part Alexey evidently found hardest of all. He took two or three runs at it and failed each time. Eventually, in a little rush, it came.

"One day I walked home from school and there was a crowd at our front door. And there was a policeman."

"Oh, Alexey."

"They buried her in a week. Not many people came."

To Ingrid, the moment felt sacred. And now, once again, that intense, overwhelming love as she spread her arms wide, pulling Alexey deep into her breasts.

Tout comprendre c'est tout pardonner. Or as Alexey had so often said himself: true understanding and love are the same thing.

She cradled him in her arms. She caressed him, she wept. She hugged him like a wounded dog. And he kissed her hands, her shoulders, and said nothing at all.

And slowly a new warmth crept into their caresses and they slid once more into making love. But differently, now: hardly sensual at all, delicately though they touched each other, ardently though they drank in each other's physical beauty. Their bodies were mere instruments. The connection was between their souls.

Ingrid, by some instinct, got Alexey to lie down and sat on top of his thighs, talking, now, about their times together, about their walks, about the beech grove, and how those memories would never die; and as she talked, she sweetly, gently, eased his penis, fully erect now, inside her vagina and leaned forward to kiss him on the lips, with that full, wide generous kiss of hers, giving her all. Then she leaned back, murmuring something, then leant forward and kissed him again; and he gazed at her like a little child.

With my body I thee worship. And slowly, but ever more surely, he worked his penis within her, while she smiled, and chuckled, distracting his anxieties by a constant flow of gentle chatter. It was as if she were his mother: and now, for the first time ever with a woman, Alexey felt sure enough utterly to forget himself, thinking only of her, and his pleasure in her.

And so they made love for five minutes, ten minutes, longer still, then Ingrid came, and came again. And still they carried on, with Alexey lost in her, swimming in her, oblivious to everything in the world except this healing, all-enveloping love. So when he finally had his own climax, he came richly, deeply, wonderfully, yet there was a way in which it hardly felt like sex at all: pure spirituality.

Afterward they lay there speechless, their bodies naked, their souls more naked still.

Later, something else struck Ingrid. It was that Alexey's present warmth and gentleness were everything she'd sensed in him from the start. Everything that had seemed, when she knew him better, so cruelly disproved by his behaviour.

Yet now she knew differently. Beneath the game-playing, the posturing and the avoidance, the spiritual beauty had always been there, and had been real.

She'd been right all along.

Chapter Eighty-Six

So now their relationship blossomed into the simple, joyous thing it might have been from the start, had not their emotional histories been so complicated. It became the honeymoon most couples dream of.

They made love with increasing assurance and fulfilment. They talked endlessly: frankly, warmly, with that playful intelligence that had marked their conversations from the start. They took the deepest delight in simple things: in the taste of scrambled eggs, in the beauty of the dawn, in games with Mary's children, who seemed, instinctively, to know something wonderful had taken place.

One of their greatest joys was simplest of all: taking baths together. And here, more than anywhere else, they talked - so that these baths went on for hours, constantly replenished by great flagons of hot water. Whether bathing, walking, eating, or talking, they found that what the poet says is true: life really can have 'the glory and the freshness of a dream.'

Especially was it true of their sexuality, which lay, of course, at the bottom of this delight. Their joy in each other's bodies was so deep, so full of surprise, that it was almost virginal, like a child at the mother's breast. Or as Alexey put it, trying to describe his own sense of physical – and spiritual - radiance: he felt, he said, 'surrounded by velvet air.'

Although the childlike quality of this love, however radiant, was not what everyone would have thought appropriate between adults.

Their friends certainly felt this - which surprised Alexey and Ingrid very much. Surely they, above all others, would take *joy* in their friends' fulfilment? Not least because they knew how difficult life had been for them till then.

But perhaps that expectation, too, was a kind of childishness – the notion that the whole world would be behind them, motherly and nurturant, devoid of any predilections - or jealousies - of its own.

The worst offenders, predictably, were 'exes' of Ingrid's like Tom and Edward. Tom was loudly contemptuous of this 'lovey-doveyness' and Edward was worse still.

None of this, he declared, in one drunken rant – none of the 'sexual emancipation' of either Ingrid or Alexey - would remotely have happened without the 'pioneering efforts' of himself and Tom. Tom, he said, had opened Ingrid up, he, Edward, had made her bloom: between them they'd taken a child and made a woman.

And as for the phantom pregnancy, most bizarre of all, was that not that the purest, plain attention-seeking?

Yet two other friends reacted differently. One was George, still staying with his family in Cambridge, though making the occasional foray elsewhere.

He might, surely, have been most jealous of all; in the event he was - or appeared to be - delighted.

The other was Paula. She too seemed overwhelmed that her friend – both friends – had found happiness, and rigorously defended them. Indeed it soon became plain that anyone who attacked them risked her enmity too.

Quite why this difference from the others should have emerged was unclear, but one possibility, perhaps, was that unlike them, the motivation of both Paula and George was not lust, but love.

These two loved Ingrid. However, Henry, who loved Alexey, was different again. He harboured no such generous feelings toward his friend. In Henry, however unconsciously, jealousy ruled.

Yet he was never one to bitch or gossip. He held himself aloof, sinking into yet another of his self-lacerating desponds, the whole thing made worse by his ever-increasing alienation from his wife, both physical and emotional.

At least his enthusiasm for the hospital project sustained itself and helped a bit. But finally something emerged that made a real difference. And its source, curiously, was Alexey himself.

For now, despite the horrors of France, despite the trauma from which he was only now beginning to recover, Alexey had found himself yearning to get back to the war.

It was as if, having learned now to commit himself in one way - romantically - he'd grown sufficiently to want to commit himself in another: militarily. Certainly, throughout his time in France, despite its rigours, he'd been a spectator. Now, it seemed, he wanted to engage.

For the very trauma that had so shattered him, had had a dual effect. In one way it made him want to avoid any battlefield, at any cost, for the rest of his life; in another it seemed to demand he protect war's victims. The Germans, if they weren't stopped, could do what they'd done to Belgium in the UK.

Others, in their hundreds of thousands, were accepting the challenge. Why not he?

A factor, certainly, was the final arrival, at Camp Holmbury, of the Tennant twins, plus three other comrades, all casualties of Mons and Le Cateau, the battles fought by the BEF after Alexey left France. Alexey talked with the new arrivals at length and saw how crucial a force like the BEF could be (however tiny in continental terms) in a real battle as opposed to the virtual skirmish that he'd experienced.

The extraordinary quality of the British shooting - fifteen aimed rounds a minute from their Lee-Enfield rifles - had convinced the Germans, especially at Le Cateau, that they were being shot at by machine guns. Indeed Smith-Dorrien's Second Corps had virtually stopped Von Kluck's forces in their tracks, however temporarily, at odds of three to one.

This was what determination and commitment could achieve. Alexey wanted part of it.

So that soon, despite their estrangement, Alexey found himself arguing this view to Henry. And Henry, for reasons similar to Alexey, was likewise impressed. Within days, both men were thinking of enlisting. Though for the time being they took no action.

Then chance intervened.

One morning, Charles Fisher paid Westbury a visit, along with Tom. He'd come on his parents' behalf, to check details of the hospital's staffing.

Henry had fixed the meeting. He liked to discuss such matters face to face.

Yet soon the visitors' conversation moved from the hospital to something they plainly felt more compelling: the scheme they'd heard about in London for a brand-new military creation, a 'Royal Naval Division', which would be a hybrid of soldiers and marines. This clearly thrilled them. It was being put together by none other than Winston Churchill and it would be his own special baby, an offshoot of his role as First Lord of the Admiralty.

The particular raison d'etre of this creation, as Charles and Tom told it, being the urgent need for forces which could be used along the coasts. Forces that could occupy, and protect, those French and Belgian ports the Germans were threatening. Because the moment the invaders controlled a Channel harbour, it would be "a pistol" (in a well-known phrase) "aimed at England's heart."

So now it had become intensely, fashionable - especially among the brighter sparks in London - to join 'Churchill's Little Army' as it was being called. Yes, Charles and Tom had volunteered, and had already, provisionally, been accepted. They were joining the likes of the poet Rupert Brooke (one of the very brightest sparks) and would shortly be transferring from the local Yeomanry to London: for the Naval Division was training at Crystal Palace. Though they would soon move down to Kent.

They were truly sad that Henry couldn't join them. Because they'd heard that as well as poets, there were musicians, too, among the recruits - a brilliant young composer called Denis Browne, for instance, a friend of Brooke's. Not to mention an Australian called Cleg Kelly, not only a musician, Oxford-trained, but a rower. Three times winner, no less, of Henley's Diamond Sculls! Well, Kelly hadn't joined yet, but the word was he soon would. So the whole thing, with its marriage of aesthetics and athleticism, was shaping up like a higher Artists' Rifles.

"Compleat Men," said Henry. "Very sixteenth century."

"Iron hands in velvet gloves," said Charles.

"Tears in his eyes and a ramrod in her hands," said Tom.

Yet for all such extravagances, Tom and Charles' regret that Henry couldn't join them was real. For both agreed that for Henry this was impossible. He had too much to lose: his work, his wife, his children. It was beyond him.

So that Tom, especially, was surprised, as the conversation developed, to notice ever more interest on Henry's face, plus ever more penetrating questions. My God, thought Tom, Henry's seriously thinking of joining us. He must be mad!

Not that Henry was moved by his friends' strategic arguments. What counted with Henry, as ever, was the personal.

For a start, Henry thought, however unconsciously, this might be a form of revenge on Alexey, whose 'betrayal' with Ingrid rankled more than he dared admit. If Henry joined the RND he'd be a real soldier, not just a tourist, as his friend had been. What a put-down for Alexey!

Then add on another, linked motivation, more personal still. The RND, for the very reasons Charles and Tom had said, might be sent abroad. What else could solve, anything like as effectively, the overriding problem of his life - his growing estrangement from his wife? In particular her ever-escalating need - he thought - to bully him? (She'd learned autonomy in the months he'd been away; Henry interpreted this as bossiness.) Abroad he would be free - yet beyond any kind of blame. The situation would be out of his hands.

So within ten minutes of the topic first being mooted, despite all his friends' warnings, he announced:

"I'm joining too."

"No you're not!" cried Tom and Charles in unison. "You're insane!"

"I'm going to join," Henry repeated, with absolute certainty.

And despite every argument his friends could muster, practical, personal, and political, that certainty remained, till Tom and Charles left.

They returned to London on the five o'clock train.

"What have we done?" said Charles. "He's abandoning his family!"

"Oh, it's not just us, "said Tom, "there are hidden depths to Henry. Think of his tastes. It's not just landscape poetry he admires, you know. He loves the patriotism in Shakespeare and he identifies with it too.

"To look at him you might not credit it but in the right mood, I swear, he forgets he's Henry Thornton, he thinks he's a military hero. He thinks he's Henry the Fifth!"

Soon after Henry told Mary, provoking the inevitable outrage, so that she, in turn, told an incredulous Ingrid. Who told Alexey.

Which did it. So Henry was enlisting - despite, Alexey noted, all the emotional ties that should have made him stay. Much stronger ties, on the face of it, than those confronting him. And above all else *committing* himself, as well.

So now that pushed Alexey over the brink and he told Ingrid that he, too, wanted to join the Royal Naval Division.

And if her reaction to Henry's news had been disbelief, her response to Alexey's was incandescent. **What** was he telling her? How could he even conceive of such a thing? When they both had found, after all the horrors, this oasis, finally, of security and of love?

So now there developed a plain split between the women and the men, with the natural alliance between Ingrid and Mary swiftly mirrored by the less predictable line-up of Henry and Alexey.

Indeed all four, with ever-increasing anger, bitched and argued right up to the last days of September, when gradually there emerged a compromise.

For the more the men learned about the mooted Royal Naval Division, the more it seemed that joining it would not, after all, mean leaving right away. Rather, as it involved specialist training, they would probably go into action later, rather than earlier, than other units.

So Ingrid and Mary calmed down. Soon they were prepared at least to entertain this new commitment, as it really seemed impossible their men would be sent out before the New Year. And lately, since the battle of the Marne, there were those who were saying, once again, that the war would be over by Christmas.

And so, with the usual wire-pulling from Lord and Lady Clayton, Henry and Alexey found themselves duly enrolled as officers in the Anson Battalion of the Royal Naval Division's Second Brigade.

On September 28th they reported to that same RND training site at Crystal Palace as Tom and Charles.

What's more - with further wire-pulling - it was wangled that they would be back for a week's leave immediately afterward, so that even this first absence would be very short indeed.

But above all else, what seemed certain, to everyone concerned, was that the prospect of their being in any real danger was remote.

Chapter Eighty-Seven

In the event, the very next day they went off to the Royal Naval Division's country camp at Betteshanger in Kent.

And settled into the routine schedule of parades, marches, sham fights, and shooting practice; not to mention football, cricket, and boxing – which had already attracted Tom and Charles, who were already there. More surprising was the presence of Ben Tennant, as well as Fred Parsons, Joe Parsons' son. Even young John Croome, Henry's gardening pupil back at Westbury camp. And two or three others, all Westbury villagers, and all, before now, in the Oxfordshire Yeomanry like them.

For it emerged that the example of Alexey and his friends had inspired them to get transferred. It was virtually an act of imitation – which was gratifying to say the least. So now, even more than in the Oxfordshires, everyone felt the warm, happy glow of comradeship, and the feeling spread, naturally enough, among the Westbury contingent's fellow-recruits.

Soon further pleasures emerged. For Henry and his friends quickly got to know the Rupert Brooke group – known to their comrades as the 'Latin Circle' for their tendency to talk rather more eruditely than others at meals. They had their own, separate table, a little aside.

True, there was undoubtedly resentment, if leavened with humour, among those who observed them. A resentment shared by Henry, as he eyed this fellow poet, so much better known than he, surrounded by his court. Brooke's looks were so striking, his movements so assured, his reddish-auburn hair swept back so dashingly in such a lush, fulsome scoop - if a trifle long. (Which was another thing. How had he avoided having it cut?)

Nevertheless, one supper time Charles introduced Henry to Brooke, explaining that Brooke had asked most particularly, as a fellow poet, to meet him.

Which ended Henry's resentment instantly. Brooke's geniality as they shook hands was heartwarming, his smile ready and radiant. But what charmed Henry most of all was Brooke's attention. Not only, as they talked, did he fix his gaze on Henry unwaveringly, never glancing left or right, but he seemed absorbed, enraptured even, by everything Henry said.

Which climaxed, finally, in Brooke declaring he would very much like to see Henry's poems. Would he lend him some? And Henry, delighted, was only too ready to oblige.

He dropped a selection round to Brooke's tent that very evening.

Altogether, then, this Royal Naval Division business was shaping up rather wonderfully. Henry could scarce believe his luck.

So when, a couple of days later, as his company was dismissed after morning parade, his battalion commander, Major Leveson, beckoned him over for a brief word, he thought little of it.

Until, that is, he saw – just behind Leveson, with the incongruous grin he knew so well – none other than …. Robert Hamblin!! Robert Hamblin, of all people in the world! His tormentor of old, from all those years ago at Westbury.

Henry was staggered.

"You know each other," smiled Leveson, with the air of one who reintroduces old friends.

"We do indeed," said Alexey.

"I've got good news for you. Lance-corporal Hamblin's joining us. Better still, I'm assigning him to your platoon."

This bombshell, landing without warning, was one of the most devastating moments of Henry's life. He shot a glance at Robert - still standing there, impassive, grinning.

"Really?" said Henry, just managing to stifle the instinctive "**whaaat**??!!!!"

"Yes, really," smiled Leveson. "From what I've heard, I'll be doing you both a favour. You'll be able to help each other. And anyway," (Leveson sneaked Robert a conspiratorial grin) Hamblin asked to join you specially. Didn't you, corporal Hamblin?"

For a moment, Robert looked taken aback, then resumed his grinning. Though just for a second, unless Henry was very much mistaken, he shot him a look that wasn't genial at all.

Leveson seemed to notice this fleeting exchange, plainly not quite what he had expected. He frowned slightly, then looked humorously perplexed - then carried on.

"Yes," he said, "I've heard a bit about you both and the things you've achieved together. You're very different, plainly, with very different talents - but mutually reinforcing. So you can do things that are more than the sum of your parts."

He must have sensed more uncertainty because he added: "We'll talk about it later."

Then finally:

"Corporal Hamblin will join you right away. You're tent- building this afternoon, aren't you? Which should mean just the sort of co-operation I've got in mind."

It's just the sort of thing I have problems with, thought Henry, that's true. But Robert Hamblin, helpful? Come now.

Shortly afterwards they were dismissed. Henry strode quickly back to his tent. He was aghast. How could this happen? How had Robert become a corporal? And been sent, of all things, to join him here? Someone somewhere must have planned it; there was no way it could have come about by chance.

But who? That didn't take much pondering. There only seemed one possible candidate, and everything pointed his way: Anthony Parsons.

Not least because Leveson's talk had been stamped throughout, like the mark of Cain, with that strange misreading of the Robert-Henry relationship that had been Anthony's from the start.

All that talk about 'mutual reinforcement'! That was Anthony all right. Hadn't their last conversation stressed precisely that? Yes, Anthony was the source; yet none of this explained why he would have set it up. Why would he do this? Whatever could have been his motivation?

Henry hadn't a clue. True, Robert's manner made it plain that the situation, however incongruous, suited him. Yet why would Robert want any of this anyway, given their mutual history? Why not stay safely, once enlisted, at the other end of the BEF? This new arrangement surely looked quite as stressful for him, as ever it might be for Henry.

But the moment Henry stopped speculating about causes, his mind hit him with the effects. His idyll, truly, had turned into a nightmare! The whole benign structure, so serendipitous and charming, would collapse.

Now, plainly, with Robert as his corporal - *Robert, of all people in this living world!* - every day, inevitably, would be a crisis.

Trivialities would become tyrannies, molehills would erupt into Alps.

With a flash of alarm, Henry remembered the tent project he was working on, the one Major Leveson had mentioned. More of a marquee than a tent, it would be used as a mess, its building blocks the usual canvases, poles and ropes.

How trivial! Yet even this, like all such tasks, would require a certain expertise; where exactly to place the ropes, the precise depth of the pegs, which panels to put up first to prevent the whole thing collapsing. Given all of which the presence of Robert would be enough, more than enough, to ruin everything. Damn it, damn it, damn it all to perdition!

He stepped out of his tent and walked toward the latrines. As he went, round a corner came John Croome, the Westbury gardener. With the slight irony of their new relationship John Croome saluted.

"I see Robert's joining us," he said.

"Yes."

"Going to be our Corporal."

"Yes."

"That'll be nice for you, won't it?" said John.

"Yes. And for you too," said Henry.

"Yes.".

Just a ghost of a smile from both. But the time and the moment were against them, and they left it there.

As it turned out, the tent episode was quite as dire as Henry suspected. At one stage a whole wall *did* collapse, bringing the roof down. And somehow Robert managed to present it, if only by implication, as Henry's fault.

But then setting Henry up to fail, especially with the practical tasks he found so hard, had always been Robert's ploy. How well had he learned to exploit Henry's weaknesses!

So that in the days that followed there were further debacles, or what seemed like debacles once Robert had got hold of them. There was the machine-gun training episode, when they ended up in the wrong valley; there was the night attack fiasco, when they got captured by their own side; worst of all was the Lee-Enfield training incident, which could have put paid to Henry's army career.

Each platoon had been assigned a quota of blanks. Henry collected and signed for them and passed them on to Robert. Henry had instructed the men himself (using knowledge two days old, learned on a course) and the first two soldiers duly fired away.

As they were firing blanks there was no need for a range. But the moment the first volley went off there were yells of alarm from the nearby wood – the rounds were live! There were soldiers there who'd almost been shot! Someone, somewhere, had given Henry's platoon the wrong cartridges.

Henry stared at Robert, appalled, suspecting a trick; Robert stared back, disingenuous, insisting the mistake was Henry's.

In the event no harm was done but the whole thing turned into the usual bureaucratic nightmare as forms were produced, Henry was arraigned, and Major Leveson and others expressed their shock and disappointment. True to form, Henry felt all the angst and anger he'd ever known at Westbury.

Although in this, as in other crises, Henry's salvation was the Westbury villagers. They supported him unstintingly - they loathed Robert even more than he.

So when Henry was approached by Rupert Brooke, that very same evening, and Brooke said he'd read Henry's poems, and would like to talk about them, Henry leapt at the encouragement.

And their talk was excellent. For Brooke, it turned out, loved Henry's work, notably 'England,' the one describing his patriotic vision of a cathedral, and 'Memory' – though Brooke confessed to being somewhat in two minds about that.

On the one hand he agreed with everything Henry said about war's horrors – Henry's sensibility reminded him of his own iconoclasm in poems he'd written before the war.

On the other, he found himself, these days, wondering whether just those same horrors, when wantonly perpetrated by the likes of the Prussian Guard, didn't impose on everyone a whole new moral imperative: to stop, whatever it took, such bullying in its tracks.

So what did Henry think? Had he worked anything out? Or was he as unsure as Brooke himself? And this was the moment Henry valued above all – for though he had no answers he was impressed Brooke even asked.

And he continued to be so treated, in the days that followed, by Brooke and his entourage. So while there were moments, inspired by Robert, when Henry would have cheerfully walked straight out of the camp, there were others, occasioned by Brooke, when he felt as happy as he'd been in his life.

A strange combination, in that lovely autumnal landscape, beneath the soft September sky.

True, most of the tricky moments were easy to read, for good or ill. But some were more obscure. One such was when Henry, on a sunny afternoon, supervised a swimming session in a pond just down from the camp.

All thirty of his platoon were there, splashing naked in the water, and they'd been joined by Alexey's platoon as well. Sixty rowdy, sun-tanned young animals, roaring with delight.

The afternoon was sultry, the pond was in a coomb under a hill, the water glittered as the soldiers floundered about. The scene was idyllic. Yet as Henry gazed on these raucous, cheery bodies, he was struck by the *poignancy* of their nakedness - the terrible vulnerability of their flesh. How much of it would be lacerated, torn apart, just months, even weeks, from now? And Alexey looked thoughtful too. But then he, of course, knew this all too well, from recent experience.

Then Brooke joined them. And after a minute he got a notebook out and wrote something down - then caught Henry's eye and showed him what he had put. It read:

"....like swimmers into cleanness leaping..."

"Just that line," Brooke grinned, "Nothing else. But I quite like it, don't you? Do you ever write down just a single line? I do. It's weird how it can sometimes be the starting point for a whole poem, even weeks later."

Again that comforting sense of equality. Now all three of them – Henry, Alexey and Brooke - were standing in a line, gazing thoughtfully on the men; till suddenly Henry spotted Robert standing on the bank opposite, gazing as intently as they. But he wasn't looking at the swimmers; he was looking at Henry, Alexey and Brooke. And he had the weirdest expression. Spooky as hell.

And the memory stayed with Henry throughout the following night.

Yet all such uncertainties vanished the very next day, October the first. For suddenly the news came that they were to be thrown in – instantly! - to defend Antwerp, in Belgium. The port was, apparently, under dire threat. The 'pistol aimed at England's heart,' was about go off. For the Belgian government, which had made Antwerp its last redoubt, had decided to abandon it, and retreat down the coast. And this meant instant, deadly threat to the UK.

Only furious intervention from London (notably by Winston Churchill, who had gone over there in person to stiffen the Belgians up) had persuaded them to stay their hand. Even so, a key condition had been the commitment of British troops……. which raised the question of which troops exactly ….. until by a predictable process, and you could see how it evolved…..why not Churchill's very own creation, the RND? Despite being mere beginners?

For they were indeed Churchill's babies. And so it was done.

Or as Tom put it "One thing for sure, they must be desperate. Why call on *us* - we're not even trained!"

Frantic, chaotic preparations. Hysteria, anger, panic. Equipment packed, carts loaded, horses hitched up; troops marching away singing 'Hello! Hello! Who's your lady friend?' to the thump of bands.

Then a rapt, delirious welcome at Dover, the whole town cheering, apples thrust into soldiers' hands, young girls walking beside them linking arms.

Then onto the troopship, away into the channel, hooking up with two destroyers. Followed by a wild, windblown night voyage to the Belgian coast. By morning they were anchored off Dunkirk.

The Westbury contingent had just enough time, before they left, to telegram Ingrid and Mary cancelling a planned visit that Sunday. But no time for proper explanations.

Not that that they knew much anyway, beyond the fact that they would, unquestionably, be in the front line.

Chapter Eighty-Eight

The unexpectedness of which was daunting. Especially for Henry and Alexey – their whole notion in joining the RND, as they had assured their women, was its relative safety.

So why was Antwerp so crucial? In all the drama so far it had scarce been mentioned.

The four friends discussed it on the train going down to Dover; they debated it on the ship; they talked about it unceasingly when they landed at Dunkirk, where their sources of news expanded hugely.

And gradually they came to understand.

The threat to the English - the cocked pistol - was obvious. The threat to the Belgians was subtler; *their* fear was that the Germans, swarming round the south-west of Antwerp, might cut them off from the Allies.

And as for the invaders – they were spooked by what might be going on behind their backs. Six Belgian divisions, they knew, were dug in at Antwerp, and the British had landed there too - or so the Germans thought. The British, after all, linking their sea power to Belgian control of the coast, could land pretty much where they liked. Why, the Royal Navy might even ferry an army over from Russia!

For both sides it was dread of the unknown.

On September 28th the Germans had opened fire on Antwerp's forts with 17-inch mortars, hurling projectiles weighing over a ton.

Nevertheless, thought the aghast English, faced with the Belgians' prospective flight, would their retreat really be necessary? They had more troops at Antwerp than the Germans! Somehow, they must be emboldened to maintain Antwerp's defence.

Hence the allied reinforcements, including the RND; hence the despatch of Winston Churchill; and hence, finally, the Belgian decision, at a dawn meeting on October the third, to suspend – in the light of such support - their evacuation.

Yet for all the panic- stricken British preparations, their deployment was grotesquely slow.

At Dunkirk harbour, for instance, the troops spent eight hours playing cards on board ship before they could get off.

Then the next day, when the force finally entrained, their journey to Antwerp took them, at snail's pace, another tedious, wasteful, thirty-six hours.

While slowest of all was Henry's unit, including the Rupert Brooke contingent. They went on foot, marching due north to Vieux-Dieu, one of Antwerp's suburbs. And to chaos, now, was added the surreal: for they advanced through rows of magnificent villas and gardens, utterly peaceful, stretching luxuriantly around.

Strangest of all was how the day ended. Late that night they were led, through an armorial gateway, into a chateau. They'd been billeted in its gardens.

"Little pools glimmered through the trees," wrote Rupert Brooke later, "and deserted fountains: and round corners one saw, faintly, occasional cupids and Venuses – a scattered company of rather bad statues – gleaming quietly...... it seemed infinitely peaceful and remote."

They ate in the chateau dining room. The Anson officers, including Brooke, Arthur Asquith (the prime minister's son) Alexey, Henry and Tom, sat at a baronial table, lit by a single candle.

The light flickered on the surrounding tapestries; they drank coffee out of jugs and tumblers; they ate in silence, as they were with a commanding officer they increasingly disliked. With very good reason: one of his first pronouncements, when they'd set off, was that they would all, almost certainly, die.

And they ate with their fingers, as the cutlery had disappeared.

Next day, they reached Antwerp at breakfast, and found a cafe in the main square. The locals greeted them delightedly, smothering them with everything they had, chocolates and beer and apples and kisses. They plainly regarded the British as saviours. 'Vivent les Anglais!' they cried, and 'Heep! Heep! Heep!' Mysteriously they omitted the 'hurray'.

Henry's troupe resumed their march. They'd been posted to trenches in the second line of Antwerp's defences, the first having already been abandoned. The usual crowds streamed the other way, dominated this time by retreating Belgian soldiers.

Many were wounded, some dreadfully so. But the real shock was worse: they didn't look like soldiers at all. So dishevelled were their uniforms, so utterly dissolved did they seem as human beings, that whenever they stopped it looked like they'd merged with the earth, indistinguishable from the mud and potholes all around.

So that the Ansons, most of whom had never previously been near a battlefield, found such sights – forget the enemy! - quite terrifying. While meanwhile, pervading all, there was the most thunderous, ear-shattering artillery barrage imaginable. Including, for the first time, not just howitzers, but those monstrous 350 and 405 mortars that had been the allies' nemesis from the start.

At last the Ansons reached their post. This turned out to be a line of shallow, messy trenches which looked like they'd just been evacuated. Worse still was the artillery. The Germans, it became plain, were using two different calibres. Shells and shrapnel on the trenches; giant mortars on the forts.

It was these giants, monstrous one-ton shells, landing once every half hour, which were the worst. Just six of these behemoths could annihilate a fort's defences within a day. With their steepling upwards arc then their lift-like, vertical plunge, they could smash though the densest concrete and explode *inside* their targets, hugely multiplying their impact.

These eruptions seemed not of this earth. More like cataclysms in deep space.

Then add in the conventional shells, endless, remorseless, as also the machine guns and snipers, and the effect on the Ansons was disastrous.

Everywhere there were white, aghast faces. Men shivered like dogs. Ben Tennant, driven by some strange atavistic instinct, hid his head a foot deep in his trench, his backside sticking up like an ostrich.

Periodically someone got hit, the screams, as ever, expressing fear far more than pain. This was the first time they'd been under fire, and it had to be this.

Yet worse still was the Ansons' sense of uselessness. Half the shells weren't even aimed at them. They soared straight over to Antwerp, doing God knows what to the very civilians who'd cheered them. What in Heaven's name was the British role, except some delusionary tokenism, while their allies were being pulverised in their rear?

So Henry was the more surprised when he saw the unlikely figure of Winston Churchill, of all people, ten yards in front of the line. Henry recognised him from the photographs. He stood quite upright, cigar in one hand, binoculars in the other, looking for all the world as if he were on Brighton beach.

So dangerous was the man's position that Henry wondered if he weren't imagining it. Till suddenly Churchill turned, shouted something to the man next to him, wrote a line in a notebook, and *grinned* (Henry never forgot that baby-faced grin.) And Henry realised Churchill's aim: he was, meticulously, checking the Antwerp situation on the ground – a key reason why he was there at all.

And he saw, too, that the rumours he'd heard about Churchill were correct. He was fearless - to the extent that Henry now found himself wondering whether he was quite right in the head.

But Churchill moved on, and after half an hour during which everyone, infected by his mood, felt braver, the terror returned. The worst thing, especially for the recruits, was the sheer *physical* trauma of the explosions: each separate concussion making the body jump, involuntarily, as if leaping off a red-hot stove. Bad enough if it happens once, beyond imagination if it happens all day.

And it did happen all day - and the days following too. Yet despite this and innumerable other horrors, Henry gradually realised, to his astonishment, that for him personally his biggest problem was something an outsider would have found unimaginable: it was Robert Hamblin! Just like in peaceful Betteshanger! That endless, insidious, undermining presence….

For the incidents between them accrued, just as they had in England, constant, incongruous, remorseless.

Why did they affect him like this? It was absurd. Yet the fact remained that Henry was more traumatised by Robert's behaviour - near-comical as that might seem - than by the war.

The only thing he could tell himself, in mitigation, was that everyone around him seemed susceptible in similar ways.

For despite the unthinkable physical trauma, what most bothered them, he could tell, was what they felt about *each other*.

They reacted, in fact like everyone does, in every human situation – office, prison, factory, sports team ……even this.

Chapter Eighty-Nine

Of course, Henry got support from Alexey, Tom, and Charles. But most of the time they were away with their own platoons. And while his own men stood up for him too, above all those from Westbury, Henry began to sense, nevertheless, a shift of sympathy.

It was less that anyone *disliked* him, more that they were becoming visibly thrown by his incompetence. Modern war, after all, was quite as much about everyday, practical tasks, often mechanical, as anything else. If his men couldn't rely on him in these, how could they trust him with anything else?

The climax came the day after they arrived. John Croome – the youngest in the platoon, who was already looking unsteady - was crouching under the lip of their far-too-shallow trench when Henry, who was carrying a loaded pistol, began crawling toward him.

Just as Henry got up to him the predictable happened. Henry slipped on the waterlogged ground, thrust out his hand, and inadvertently fired. He missed John by rather less than an inch. John screamed with fear - he somehow got scratched on his wrist - while his comrades stared at Henry, aghast. It was with real difficulty that Henry and the others calmed John down, who now looked more nervous than ever.

But the incident's worst casualty was Henry himself. The first moment possible he went off to the officers' toilet and sat there, alone, head in hands. And gradually found himself praying, of all things, for some form of action – even combat – however horrific.

At least it would involve things he could do! Charging, shooting, throwing himself around physically - almost like cricket! (For a moment he laughed.) He would rather rush across no-man's land, risking the traversing German machine guns, than endure a moment more of his nagging, hopeless incompetence in this bizarre trench life as he knew it.

And the prospect of such an outcome seemed likelier by the hour. Throughout the afternoon the German bombardment got closer, the shells hurtled more thickly overhead, and the machine guns swept more ruthlessly across their tiny, two-foot-deep trenches.

Steadily, too, the casualties mounted. None killed yet in Henry's platoon, but at 3.30 young Cottle, crawling back from his position to get tea, shrieked loud and fell, flapping like a fish. He'd been shot in the backside, a great, tearing wound that looked more like it had been made by a hacksaw than by a bullet.

Now John Croome looked more anxious still, staring fixedly as Cottle's friends rushed to his aid. They got a field dressing on and had the stretcher bearers up in minutes, but after Cottle had gone John still sat there staring, google-eyed.

And yet, and yet - still, no sign of a German attack. Though surely one must come soon.

Then a message. Lieutenant Thornton to see Major Leveson, presumably about the attack. Henry crawled his way to the communication trench and found Major Leveson in his own dugout - this at least was deeper, in a haven of dry ground –and there he had fifteen minutes tete a tete with his commander. In which it promptly became clear that the reason for the meeting was that Leveson wanted to tick Henry off for his mistakes.

Yet Leveson tried hard to be fair. So Henry was contrite. And the conversation became quite amiable. Soon, after asking a couple of questions about German intentions (Major Leveson had no news at all) Henry crawled his way back to his platoon.

Though he quickly noticed someone missing: John Croome.

A stab of alarm. He called Corporal Rose.

"Where's Croome?"

"Gone with Corporal Hamblin, sir."

"Gone where?"

"Gone to Fort Six, sir."

"Whaaat?!"

"Gone to Fort Six, Sir. Something about a message."

Fort Six?! The closest Belgian fort to their position?! Gone to the one place more likely, even, than the trench they were in to tip poor John over the edge? Where the Germans had been dropping mortar shells all day?

"Corporal Hamblin thought it might be better if Croome withdrew for a moment from the line."

Well, that made a little more sense. To get to Fort Six they would first have to go back, away from the line. Then further back, much further, before they would have turned right toward the fort then looped back up. Maybe Robert was intending to leave John Croome en route and pick him up on his return.

Yet all such speculation became irrelevant when Robert and Croome suddenly reappeared.

For now Croome looked worse than ever.

His glassy-eyed opacity was compounded by an almost epileptic drooling from the mouth. He was plainly on the very verge - Robert supporting his every movement.

"What the hell has happened?" Henry shouted. "Where have you been?"

And the story unfolded. They had indeed headed back from the line, and Henry had guessed right, Robert had meant to drop John off and go on to the fort, on a commission given him by Major Leveson. But they never arrived. After a hundred yards they heard the fort had surrendered.

Moments later they met troops from the fort's garrison. They had somehow got out. They were beyond shock, in a kind of madness.

They were burbling about the shelling. How the pauses between explosions had been bad enough, with their slow-building, nerve-grinding anticipation – till the moment the round was fired and they awaited, terrified, its arrival.

Yet worst of all, they said, in those final seconds before the shells actually struck, they found themselves involuntarily screaming - not through fear, but because the air, as the shells came in, *was sucked up out of their lungs;* and it was this they found most nightmarish of all, the unwonted rape of their bodies.

And it was hearing them tell of this, chattering, incoherent, that had finally done for John Croome.

For now John was more hysterical still, shivering rhythmically, uncontrollably, and no-one had a clue how to help him.

Another shell exploded, just in front of their trench. Then another on the right; then one on the left, then another, twenty yards behind. Usual pattern, four shells straddling.

And the dread, familiar screams came from the right, where the second shell had landed. Henry peered over there, looking for who had been hit.

At which moment, his back turned, he heard Corporal Rose call out, in a strange, almost routine voice, "He's off."

And Henry turned to see John Croome legging it out into no-man's land. Unbelievably he'd jumped from the trench, sprinted away, and was fleeing blindly toward the Germans.

What was he doing! This was certain death - even though Croome was swerving around as if trying to avoid bullets. Surely, thought Henry, the Germans would see he was just a kid, they would hold their fire, give his comrades a chance to rescue him – but no: a machine gun opened up immediately, remorseless, implacable, and Croome, hit once, twice, a dozen times, started spinning still more, veering wildly to left and right, at one stage jumping, grotesquely, straight up in the air, then vanishing as he tumbled into a shell hole forty yards from the line.

"Fuck, fuck, FUCK! Stupid little bastard! Stupid cunt!" yelled Rose and burst, incredibly, into tears.

As did Henry himself. It was impossible to grasp. How could this happen? Above all to John? As the youngest man in the platoon, they'd all thought of him, half-consciously, as their son.

"Poor little sod," said Ted Molesey.

And now silence. The guns, momentarily, had stopped firing.

Then a thin, reedy wail, more like a bird than a man. Followed by a grating, screaming groan. It came from the shell-hole where John Croome had disappeared. Then moments later - did Henry really see it? – a hand, waving, just visible above the crater's rim. Then another wail.

"Christ," said Corporal Rose. "He's alive."

He was. Though the bird-like cries followed each other so regularly they seemed almost orchestrated. First a scream; then a groan; then silence.

Then another scream, another groan….. and more silence. Till suddenly, John's voice crying "Help! Help! Help!" in ever increasing fear, as if he'd suddenly grasped the catastrophe that had engulfed him.

That was enough for Henry.

A feeling of intense, almost maternal compassion overwhelmed him. It had been building since John first ran out but now seemed to fuse with all the other feelings that had been swirling around inside him for days: his horror at the fighting, his pity for the refugees, his sense of personal incompetence and desperate longing to do something, anything, that might just for once be useful….. all ballooned into a wild desire to act.

Moments later he was out and over the top of the trench, yelling: "I'm bringing him in!" Followed by "Anyone coming?"

But all he got was startled looks. So he rushed alone, straight out into no-man's land, arms thrashing, legs pumping, though he stumbled constantly and at one stage nearly collapsed. A manic, staggering progress which ended almost before it began, as he hurled himself into the shell hole beside John. At which moment he realised he'd not, miraculously, been hit – nor even fired upon. Where were the German gunners? Had they taken pity, however belatedly?

What was certain was that Henry had got safely across; and there, tumbled grotesquely just under the crater's rim, was John Croome, white as a sheet and pouring blood, especially from the stomach. And staring at Henry with stark, pleading eyes.

Chapter Ninety

Now what? thought Henry, as he tumbled down beside him. What do I do *now*? Come to that, what have I *done*? For in the past few minutes, unique in his life, he'd felt as if possessed by some separate, alien force, nothing to do with his real self at all.

His heart beat wildly, he panted like a dog, then he saw blood on his arm – he'd been hit after all. Or was it his fall? He looked again at John and the poor kid looked ghastly; he was bleeding from at least six places, each wound making a thin spindly stream which joined up with the others, at the bottom of the shell hole, in a puddle of black blood, swiftly spreading.

Clearly if John were not got back to the British line he would die. But how? There wasn't a prayer without a stretcher - how crazy, thought Henry, that he had rushed across no-man's-land like that, how utterly insane, when to shift John you'd need at least two people, maybe more, and above all else a stretcher! Crazy, crazy, crazy, what he had done!

He reached over to John, infinitely careful to keep under cover, then put his arm under his shoulders, to get some idea whether he could lift him - at which John let out a wild, unearthly scream and Henry started back. He subsided to the other side of the shell hole and stared fixedly, with absolutely no idea what to do.

Well, one thing could be to look around, get the lie of the land. If he raised his head fast enough, then ducked down swiftly enough, he'd surely get away with it. He rose - and saw a chaos of mud and bricks, nothing else. Above all he saw no life in the British line. But what did he expect? The same German fire that was pinning him down had imprisoned them too; their heads were resolutely submerged.

They needed to be. The moment he'd raised *his* there'd been a vicious 'ping!' - a sniper had marked him already. Ten seconds later came a hurtling, express-train whoosh! as a shell came in – a shattering explosion - then another - then two more...... and then, like a musical accompaniment, the starting up of the German machine guns, traversing and sweeping the ground.

He realised he could look backwards without raising his head, as the shell hole had a kind of slope to it, with a ridge raised on the German side. He was aghast at what he saw. The machine gun fire came in gusts, rather than bursts, more like wind than bullets, scattering and raking the earth. What human being could survive it? Anyone who ran into that lot would be scythed down like wheat.

And he grasped, in a fearsome slam of understanding, just how desperate their plight was. Above all, of course, for John, but fear made him selfish. His whole long slow life, with its joys and griefs and complications and absurdities could end *at once, right now* ....so weak with fear he felt, he could scarcely move.

He lurched once more toward John, struggling to get his field dressing out, intending to bind at least one of his wounds. But he couldn't even do that. He had no strength. His body had betrayed him! And even if he'd been able, how would he start? This was just the sort of thing he was bad at and he was terrified his clumsiness would make John worse.

There were thin lines of blood running out of John's mouth down onto his neck and Henry was fascinated by their ruler-like precision, so narrow and so controlled, two perfect parallel lines. Like beautifully cut strips of tape. Bleeding from the mouth, he vaguely remembered, meant internal injuries….and at that moment, as his face hovered up against John's, he realised John was trying to talk.

What was he saying? Was it 'water'? Or 'hurt'? Or even 'drink'?

He listened more closely.

It wasn't 'water', or 'drink', or anything like it.

It was "mummy, mummy, mummy," breathed over and over again.

Chapter Ninety-One

And so the hours passed, with John slipping in and out of consciousness, the machine guns slaking the ground, the shells bursting fearfully around them, and the hard, mean 'ping' of sniper bullets as they ricocheted off the crater's rim.

And Henry felt more helpless by the hour.

He did make one more attempt to bind John's wounds, but this time the result was even more bizarre than before. At first he made headway, and pretty much got the dressing on – till suddenly John erupted, with extraordinary force. He pushed Henry away, then somehow fell on top of him, the two rolling down the crater in a wrestling match, to end up at the bottom in the mud.

Amazingly, John survived this too. But Henry decided he must make no more such attempts.

And John began, once more, those strange, rising and falling, bird-like wails; followed, as earlier, by the groaning....... and then silence. Then the same again....and the silence.... and on and on, till night fell. At which stage John started a mantra that was new: 'Oh dear, oh dear' he muttered, at intervals, for half an hour. Said with the intonation of an old man; said over and over again, rather calmly, in a tone that sounded almost apologetic.

Yet stranger things were shortly to unfold. Around seven o-clock, as the autumn night drew in and got ever colder, Henry spotted ten Germans crawling past their crater, heading for the British line. My God, at last, the German attack! He raised himself, and was about to yell a warning, regardless of consequences ....but they were gone. He must have imagined it.

Then something *really* weird. There were Mary and Rosemary and Josephine, clear as a bell, walking toward him from the British lines, carrying flowers and fruit. They must be crazy, they would be killed! Then they too vanished.

And he understood. He was seeing things, he was hallucinating under the stress.

So that half an hour later, when it had long been completely dark, and both he and John were once more fitfully dozing, he knew he was once more fantasising when Alexey's face appeared over the rim of the crater, having crawled over, seemingly, from the British lines. And Ben Tennant's and Fred Parsons' faces too.

Which seemed crazier still. Until he realised – they were real! As whispers confirmed. Quite why it should have been Alexey (who was, of course, with another platoon) and not someone from Henry's own outfit, remained unclear; but it was, indeed, his comrades and his friend.

And they were saved.

Saved? Well, that's how it felt, for a full five seconds - till Henry remembered they had to get back.

Meanwhile Alexey's little party swarmed swiftly and silently into the shell hole, manhandling two stretchers. *Two* stretchers? Breathless whispers established they'd assumed Henry was wounded too - otherwise he would have tried to get John back. And the guilt which Henry felt already was compounded.

There were, it turned out, five of them. As well as Ben and Fred there were two from Alexey's platoon. And they immediately began binding John's wounds, Alexey taking the lead. Here again were Alexey's deft, efficient movements, that physical certainty Henry envied so much.

They had, it seemed, no fear of making mistakes. Nor was John Croome nervous. He submitted quietly to what they did, and soon the bleeding seemed staunched. Henry's dressing had not, said Alexey, been as bad as he had feared. Indeed, it looked very much as if John would live.

So when to move? They had come over when the sky was temporarily dark, in a night partly cloudy and part bright. The clouds had temporarily hidden the moon. To return, said Alexey, they should wait for another such pitch-black moment. They would gear up, get everything absolutely ready, and then - 'give it a go.'

"Give it a go!" How the language creaked and staggered, thought Henry, under the strain.

And so they crouched and waited, as Alexey explained why he, of all people, had appeared.

When Henry had made his dash Alexey hadn't seen him. His platoon was fifty yards to Henry's right. But gradually he'd grasped what had occurred – and the way he'd heard it, Henry's actions sounded heroic. Albeit mad.

More, he'd got the sense that Henry's comrades - despite Henry's 'heroism' - seemed distinctly reluctant to help, certainly while it was light. But this was wrong! Surely Henry must be rescued, whatever the cost. Maybe, said Alexey, he'd been infected by Henry's craziness – but he couldn't leave his friend, he'd thought, in such a predicament, whatever others did.

So he called for volunteers from his platoon. Remarkably, two offered, despite the fact that Henry wasn't even their officer.

Together they crawled to Henry's platoon and explained their plan. Which shamed two of Henry's platoon into volunteering as well.

And thus the presence of Ben Tennant and Fred Parsons.

Now Alexey pointed. The moon was coursing swiftly in and out of the clouds. At any moment it would disappear.

He alerted the others. No words were needed. They grasped the four corners of John's stretcher. Alexey took one, Ben and Fred two more, while Henry took the fourth. But still they eyed the sky.

And the moon whirled on, while all knew what its disappearance would mean. Then it darkened – and no-man's-land went black – and they surged forward, panting and slithering through the mud.

It was extraordinarily hard. By unspoken consensus they lifted John's stretcher just an inch or two above the ground, shifted it forward, then put it down again. Then slid it a bit, then paused; then lifted it again; then slid it some more, then put it down again - then once again paused; they did this for what seemed like five minutes (it was probably little more than one) yet still, when they looked forward, they seemed no nearer the British line.

Absurdly carefully, they moved again. The weight seemed terrible; stones scraped their knees. Even breathing was difficult. Yet still they fixed on this haven of hope, the British trench.

The trench! The route to home, wives, children, fifty years of life ....then suddenly - Alexey's hand was pointing upwards, toward the moon, and signing halt.

For the moon was once more changing, scudding from dark back into light, to brighter and brighter light, shining, sheer, implacable, as it finally sailed out into the sky alone.

They froze - nerves tingling at the prospect, at any moment, of bullets, shells, every kind of annihilating blow. While obliviously, infinitely slow, the moon crept on and on and disappeared once more behind the clouds.

Again they were off. Grasp, lift, inch forward, skid….. grasp, lift, inch forward, down…..then this time, as they lifted...... Henry's foot slipped. It slid into a hole - and he fell! And the stretcher lurched over! And John Croome shrieked, uncontrollably.

A dreadful, frozen pause: then a German flare flew up and then another, and instantly the landscape was as bright as day.

And cruelly, implacably, the machine guns started firing, the bullets scything into them like hail, thousands upon thousands of them. At which the British, from the trench behind, responded and now fire came from both sides. Ben Tennant was hit and Fred Parsons was hit then suddenly, incredibly, Alexey jumped up and was dancing, leaping, just as John Croome had done earlier. Till he too fell huddled and motionless on the ground.

The flares died down and there was silence. Then the moon came out again and there were corpses everywhere.

Now Henry and the two men from Alexey's platoon, miraculously unhurt, stood up, grabbed John's stretcher, and rushed for the British trenches. And somehow got there.

They skidded into a heap, John Croome sliding chaotically half off the stretcher as they fell.

Incredibly, they were safe.

And Henry was still unscathed. And now, to his amazement, he was surrounded by soldiers applauding him. Then he realised – for them he was still the hero Alexey had set out to save.

But John Croome was dead. That last fall did for him, unless he'd died already from the bullets. And Ben Tennant and Fred Parsons were dead too, out in no man's land. But most terrible of all, Alexey, Henry's friend of years, the one living creature on this planet, for all their differences, rows and arguments, he truly loved, was dead as well.

Tom Smith and Peter Jessop, on the other hand, the volunteers from Alexey's platoon, had survived. They sat stunned, ten yards away, heads cradled in their hands.

Henry sat in silence. For a good two minutes no-one spoke to him (he was near-invisible in the gloom) but when someone finally did, he realised his initial sense was right – his platoon thought his initial rush had been wonderful, extraordinarily brave. And if they knew the truth?! Not that Henry thought about that: he just sat there shivering and weeping, asking no more than to be left alone.

But even that minimal blessing seemed impossible. For here, in the darkness, a looming figure. Major Leveson. Was Henry okay? Asked with concern.

But Henry found the question absurd, and didn't answer. Well, said Leveson, more sharply, there really couldn't be any more 'stunts' like this, conditions wouldn't allow it. Bloody tragic about Smolensky and the other two, of course, let alone young Croome. "Dreadful, really." A pause. "Not least because we're going to have to leave them there, I'm afraid. We're pulling back."

"Pulling back?" cried Henry. "We only just got here!"

"Ours not to reason why," said Leveson, "Apparently we've been outflanked. Anyway" - he tried hard to sound sympathetic - "We've leaving right away: the order says, 'with maximum speed.'"

And Leveson bustled off.

And indeed, despite the incongruity of the decision, within minutes the Ansons were gone. Though not without difficulty – some, outraged at their precipitate 'retreat', refused to obey, while others had to be pulled out of their trenches bodily.

So now began the nadir of Henry's life. They marched north-west – he thought; heading for some town called Saint-Gilles. Where they would entrain.

All were shattered. They were exhausted, thirsty – Antwerp's water supply had been cut off - and aghast at leaving the city to the Germans. But while each of them felt failures, Henry was worst of all, from what he saw as his cowardice. Made all the harder by this fantasy of him being a hero.

Meanwhile they slogged on through the night, while the scene became more hellish by the hour. There were the retreating, exhausted troops, some horribly wounded. There were the columns of refugees. There were donkeys, dogcarts, even oxen – while here and there, mysteriously, a cart would block the street, often without horses.

Yet even this Dantesque tableau was outmatched by what greeted them in the Antwerp suburb of Hoboken, where the German bombardment had set the city's oil tanks on fire. Unavoidably (there was no other road) they marched within yards of the inferno. 'Hills and spires of flame', was how Rupert Brooke later described it - while the blaze, spasmodically, surged clean across their way.

So loath to cross such fireballs were the Ansons, their officers ordered them to run though at the double – at pistol point.

Once every ten seconds a German shell would land smack in this conflagration, throwing gusts of flame up to 200 feet. Just after Henry's platoon got through two shells landed just behind them, plumb amid the troops following. And like dragons' breath, the fire surged over them all.

Henry tried very hard indeed, in the weeks that followed, to forget what he saw then.

Nevertheless, his platoon carried on. An hour later they reached a pontoon bridge which had been erected over the river Scheldt and, once over, they felt, irrationally, more secure. And so they continued, until in the small hours a military policeman herded them into a village church. It was packed, from porch to altar, with snoring forms. They joined them.

And when they woke, six hours later, they found a train, reached Bruges, and got through to Ostend.

From where they sailed for Dover, landing in the early morning of October the ninth.

They had been away five days.

Although it turned out they were in some ways fortunate. For the clownishness which had dogged the Belgian adventure from the start, reserved one final throw.

Through a mistake in orders, at least two trains went off without their full complement of soldiers. Through this and other misinformation (at one stage the British thought the Germans were advancing along the very railway line they meant to use) Commodore Henderson, a key British commander, decided the retreat was blocked. With the result that he crossed over the nearby, neutral, Dutch border - and had his men interned.

Which was reflected, on the RND's return, in one of the more bizarre casualty lists of the war. It went like this:

Killed	5
Wounded	64
Missing (including interned)	2, 040

Which grotesquerie was quickly noted at home. Most notably by the enemies of Churchill, who promptly blamed him.

And yet, from the point of view of Henry and his friends, there was yet another postscript, and that wasn't farcical at all.

For two of those RND casualties, it emerged, were Tom Huntingdon and Charles Fisher. They'd been part of that column behind Henry's, engulfed by the Hoboken fires.

Tom Huntingdon had suffered 'burns', though how serious was unclear.

But there was no uncertainty about Charles.

He was dead.

Chapter Ninety-Two

All of which was, of course, unknown to Ingrid and Mary, and everyone else they'd so precipitately left behind at Westbury.

But then the Ansons' departure had already been shocking enough. Especially for Ingrid, for whom it mirrored Alexey's earlier exit to France, way back in August.

Yet again life had betrayed her! The whole point of her friends' joining the Royal Naval Division - the way it had been sold to her and Mary - was the notion that they would be staying in England, at least for the time being. And now - the news came via the Claytons - they'd been sent to the front, to Antwerp. And Antwerp, clearly, was in the thick of it! Why else the rush?

How crazy, how utterly perverse of Alexey even to entertain the thought of joining up in such circumstances! Why had she let him? Why had she listened to him? Why hadn't *he* listened to *her?*

It was just too terrible, too absurdly unfair that he might be taken from her at such a time.

Mary, fortunately for both her and Ingrid, reacted differently. Her instinct, as ever, was for action, her concern, as always, for others. So she busied herself with the patients in the new-fledged hospital - the Tennant twins, who were improving daily, Tom Hickman, another villager, still bad, and three newcomers, army regulars wounded at Mons. And she persuaded Ingrid to get involved as well.

They could both, hopefully, find relief the classic way: by helping those with greater problems than themselves.

And it worked. Mary dropped smoothly into her nurturant gear, Ingrid thrived visibly on the human contact, and their ward of six moved quickly from therapy to something more like music-hall: the banter, ever more risqué and rude (one of the new patients was Australian) suited Ingrid, especially the repartee. While the patients' biggest problem was too much laughter – it could hurt.

Soon this activism spread into other areas of their lives. With Ingrid it took the surprising form of housework. The gay insouciance of her days with Alexey were replaced by a mania for orderliness and putting things in rows.

So now Mary activated yet further forms of 'Ingrid-therapy' by encouraging her, when not nursing or 'hausfrauing', to get ever more involved with the Thornton children. And this worked too, wonderfully well. Ingrid, as ever, loved playing with the girls; they loved being with her; while Mary benefited, as always, from the harmony of those around her.

There were many delightful moments between Ingrid and the children, but one especially, not long after the RND had left.

It was the day George came visiting from Cambridge. For George's deep love for Ingrid, still formally unacknowledged, meant he constantly sought ways to cherish her.

Which was why he quickly passed on news he'd heard via friends of his father: that the regular army's Fourth Division would shortly be leaving for Antwerp. And that this, in turn, would almost certainly mean half-trained units like the Royal Naval Division would be pulled back.

"Of course, it's not certain but it's very likely," he said. "At the least it means they'll put the regulars into the hotspots, rather than the RND. It should make things easier for those we know."

Yet Mary saw the grimace on Ingrid's face. Because she and Ingrid had agreed that they would never – not even positively - mention Antwerp, or anything like it, in any circumstance at all.

And what she noticed, too, was that moments later Ingrid got Rosemary and Josephine to help her make cakes. For baking, Mary knew, was something Ingrid only ever did when she felt upset.

So out came the eggs, the butter, the sugar and the flour, and the great round ceramic stirring bowl, while Rosemary and Josephine began their routine fight over who should stir.

Mary popped out for a moment and the kids, still more excited by her absence (they found Ingrid easier to play up than their mother) started flicking great gobs of mixture at each other. Next, turning the cakes into missiles, they hurled them around the room. Then George, asked by Ingrid to carry the prepared cakes to the oven, took three steps across the floor, skidded on a puddle of cake mix, and dropped the lot.

They fell right at the feet of Ingrid, a mini volcano of eggs, flour and sugar, engulfing her skirt. Yet she laughed uproariously, bent down, grabbed two great handfuls and started hurling them back at George; who threw them back again; at which the kids pitched in once more, with redskin whoops.

Soon everyone was throwing everything at everyone and the four of them were shrieking and cackling like the children they'd all become.

At which moment, re-enter Mary. But no longer alone. For now, standing beside her – exhausted, haggard, but nevertheless standing there - was none other than ....Henry Thornton.

Henry! Back from the war. Returned, resurrected, with no warning at all! The kids froze, transfixed - then erupted into barbarous delight.

But Ingrid felt a terrible fear. For Mary and Henry didn't look right at all. Mary, especially, was having difficulty meeting Ingrid's eyes. And when she finally managed it, there was a distraught look Ingrid instantly understood.

With a shamefaced gesture Mary motioned Ingrid out into the yard.

And there, falteringly, guiltily, Mary told her about Alexey, and the catastrophe of which he had been part.

And Ingrid, very slowly and silently, slid to the ground.

And knelt there, head between hands, rocking back and forth, while Mary cradled her, and George and Henry hovered in the background, looking helpless.

Ingrid stayed like this a full minute, Mary glancing now and then up at the men, with eyes that said, 'leave her alone.' Till suddenly Ingrid erupted, sprang to her feet and knocked Mary flying, simultaneously letting out an unearthly scream. Followed by a torrent of tears, yet more screams and then a furious flaying and punching so that Mary grabbed her as if she'd gone mad.

The men leapt forward; but now Ingrid collapsed again, and lay stretched out flat, feet kicking, arms pummelling, her wrists smashing again and again onto the ground.

Mary cradled her, holding her head whenever she could catch it, and muttering sweet, motherly imprecations in her ear, calling her 'darling, darling, my poor sweetest dear' - then looked up to see her children staring, having run out from inside.

"What's happened to Ingrid?" cried Rosemary, "Is she ill? Will she be better soon?" and stood there white-faced, still bespattered with the cake mix of minutes earlier.

Then Ingrid once more erupted.

"No, no, it can't be true!" she cried, "it just can't, it's too unfair, he can't be dead, he mustn't, it's too cruel, oh Alexey, no, no, no!" then grabbing at Henry, "say it's not true Henry, say it, please, it can't be, oh God, please help me, someone help me, please!"

And she launched into great streams of rhetoric, of blame for herself, of curses against God, of wild, disconnected memories of Alexey, some of them extraordinarily beautiful: momentarily George thought: 'Christ, Shakespeare was right; people *do* talk like this at such a time.'

Then once again, utter silence. Ingrid seemed to compose herself, sat up, and walked slowly back into the sitting room. She sat down on a chair. Seconds later, she got up again, strode over to the mixing bowl, lifted it high above her head, and smashed it.

Chapter Ninety-Three

And this strange oscillation between quietude and grief became Ingrid's pattern, in the days that followed. For here was the consummation of all her fears, from the moment she and Alexey had first met. Stretching back years beyond him, indeed, to her remotest childhood.

Her mood swings terrified her. One day she would clear out every cupboard in her room, the next put everything back again; the next, move the furniture and rehang the pictures; the next, think better of it and put everything back where it started. Then would come two days' nursing (she alarmed the patients), a day's cooking – with all the utensils left for someone else, usually Mary, to clear up - then gardening, and then a sudden, urgent need to shop in Oxford. Then another day of utter silence, conducted from morn to eve in bed.

There were dreams, nightmares, as well as times when she stayed awake all night. Other times she got off quite well then woke up, bolt upright, at 3.18 AM: that earlier numerical mantra of anxiety re-entered her life.

And always her mind returned to one simple, overwhelming fact: the *uniqueness* of Alexey. There was no one like him in the world, nor could there be. She remembered him once saying that the sense of someone's uniqueness was as good a definition as he knew of love.

The simple phrase would roll round her head, day after day, until it became still another obsession. "There will never," she kept repeating, "never be another Alexey.'

All the news she heard seemed bad, everything in the world seemed sad. The Claytons, she understood via George, were devastated by the loss of Charles; then she heard of yet another death, this one especially grotesque.

For Robert, the chap she knew had long tormented Henry, had been killed in a motor accident in the UK. On the docks, of all places, just half an hour after he got off the boat from Antwerp! Thought he was still in France, looked the wrong way as he crossed the road, and bang! knocked down by a lorry. Took him a day or two to die, and his wife was terribly upset. As was Henry too, remarkably - no doubt the randomness of it underscored the whole Europe-wide calamity.

Yet the thing that disturbed Ingrid most, if truth were told, was not, in fact, a death, but an injury. Yet an injury so horrible that in some ways it was worse than being killed.

And that was the burns suffered by Tom, who had been engulfed in the same fire as did for Charles. Not that the burns were especially deep. He'd been lucky, unlike so many around him. But the simple fact of it had seared his soul.

He'd come down to Westbury with George, just after he'd been released from hospital. George had hoped the trip might cheer him up. Though as Tom was frail, they'd stayed only a couple of hours.

But that was enough for Ingrid to get the most vivid sense of what had happened to her friend.

He was transformed. It wasn't his injuries – you couldn't even see them. They were on his chest, and already healing. It was his manner. His jokes, his jauntiness, had vanished. Instead, he scarcely spoke, and spent most of the visit looking vacantly round the camp, cadging George for cigarettes.

He was alive in body but the Tom she'd known was dead.

Chapter Ninety-Four

Henry and Mary, meanwhile, were going through their own misery. Mary had never seen Henry so depressed.

He felt horribly responsible for what had happened - and, as so often, hopelessly incompetent. Had he not rushed to 'rescue' John Croome in the foolish way he had, Alexey, quite simply, might not have died.

What added to the absurdity was that there were still people – including many in the village – who thought his actions heroic. All this despite his constant attempts to correct them. (They put this down to modesty.) Gradually he realised people believed what they wanted to believe. Faced with the unbelievable horror of this war, its utter inhumanity, they craved something that might compensate, if only to retrieve their faith in human nature.

And remarkably, absurdly, their material, in this case, was Henry Thornton. He, of all people, given the truth! It was bad enough feeling guilty. Now he felt a fraud.

He had plenty of time to think. Two days after his return he went down with a mystery illness, running a fever. His diagnosis remained obscure, but he was given sick leave from the army - quickly extended, when he failed to recover, to two months' convalescence.

During which he reacted to his depression in his usual way - by withdrawal. By solitary walks; by long, lonely sessions of violin playing; by poetry writing. All failed. Even work with his beloved horses, engineered by Mary, let him down. The sole constant was his permanent, rumbling irritability, exploding intermittently into rows, which matched even Ingrid's capacity to alienate everyone he knew.

And the worst of it was that he and Ingrid bounced their depressions off each other. At first he felt nothing but sympathy for her, but soon she began to annoy him, not least because each time he saw her desperate, shell-shocked face he felt that he personally, quite as much as the Germans, had caused it.

Worse still, Ingrid felt the same about him. His gaunt features only reminded her, if she ever for a moment forgot, of the catastrophe they'd both endured. Did he really have to look quite so down, so defeated, every hour of the day? After all, God knows, wasn't everyone calling him a hero?

Which was more than they were calling *her*, for heaven's sake. For they - certain of the villagers, anyway – were now calling her an alien, an enemy, a despicable Hun! He should try *that* for size, and see how it felt to suffer everything he suffered and yet remain a rank outsider, bereft of all sustenance, friendship, and above all, family.

Chapter Ninety-Five

Yet now, into the fraught provincial world of Westbury, there blew a breath of fashion.

A letter came for Ingrid from Kitty Clayton. That she should think of Ingrid, so soon after her own bereavement, was typical of her fabled empathy.

And the letter was charming; the first part, especially, moving Ingrid very much. But later, something different: for Kitty raised the possibility – only the possibility, at this stage – of a joint memorial service for both Charles and Alexey. Extraordinary! Yet Kitty explained: they both had been, as she put it, 'such comrades in the fight' and they had something else in common, too: their bodies remained unfound.

"But that does not mean their achievement should go unhymned. Indeed their sacrifice, the noblest men can make, should resound throughout the world. Above all their brotherhood.

"For who can deny that oldest and simplest of truths - that there is nothing nobler a man can do than lay down his life for his friend? For that is what Alexey did, did he not? Lay down his life so Henry Thornton could live; while Henry in turn, risked his to save John Croome, albeit unsuccessfully."

And so the letter wandered on for several pages.

But the more Ingrid read, the angrier she felt.

The reality was the deaths were meaningless - so the Marchioness invested them with huge, exalted meaning.

The reality was they were ugly, squalidly so; she called them beautiful.

But above all else, and this was the part that turned Ingrid's anguish into wrath, was Kitty's fantasy that these deaths were some kind of triumph, the triumph of heroes, rather than plain, unmitigated disaster.

For Ingrid, unlike the Marchioness, had no use for heroism in any form. What she wanted was not a dead hero, but a live lover. Instead, she had a corpse! Ah, poor, dear, Alexey….

What especially upset Ingrid was the letter's end. By way of rounding things off, the Marchioness reminded Ingrid how profoundly impressed everyone had been by Ingrid that first weekend they'd met at Clayton. Notably, of course, Lord Stanbury……dear oh dear, thought Ingrid, does she really feel she has to pour her socialite's balm onto every contact she makes?

For what it underscored was Ingrid's growing sense that the funeral, for all the Claytons' genuine grief, would essentially be about that other, over-arching priority of their lives - social competitiveness.

What Kitty intended, clearly, was the funereal equivalent of a society wedding. And that same elaborate, county-and-metropolitan guest list she'd put together for Charles' twenty-first weekend, which had so angered him then, would be repeated here.

Stanbury would be coming, and Eric Rother too, plus a hefty scoop of society families including the Manners, the Charterises, the Horners and the Asquiths (Arthur Asquith, one of the prime minister's sons, had, of course been at Antwerp.)

And while there were invitations to Charles and Alexey's real friends, like Henry, Mary and Paula, there were also a healthy sprinkling of more star-spangled comrades like the young New Zealander who had made such a stir in London lately, Bernard Freyberg. To say nothing of Rupert Brooke. And Rupert Brooke, it turned out, was a friend of Eddie Marsh, Churchill's private secretary who would be coming with the de facto guest of honour, Churchill himself.

So the circle was complete. Although the Churchill connection, at least, was real. The RND *was* his creation. Thus Alexey and Charles were, in a sense, his babes.

The proposed venue was New College chapel. So the service would surely be dignified, and Alexey would get a send-off unimaginable otherwise.

But it was the last thing Ingrid wanted. She'd have preferred something simple and quiet. And she was certain this would have been Alexey's wish, too.

Yet what could she do? She could hardly refuse. For one thing it wasn't her choice: if anyone should decide it was the direct relatives of the deceased. And if the Smolenskys had any objections they'd yet to voice them. Added to which the flood tide of preparations, it emerged, was already in full swing. Opposing them, even if she could find a way of doing so, would take more energy than she could conceive of right now.

And so, for days, she drifted on. Until there came, out of the blue, another letter; this time from Rudi Von Leckburg, that most gentlemanly of the German New College Rhodes scholars.

It came from a prison camp in England. He was a prisoner of war.

Chapter Ninety-Six

She'd last seen him when he'd left Harwich that time with the German ambassador. And last heard of him through Alexey, when Rudi, Alexey told her, had telephoned Sir John French's headquarters. Both times his contribution had been characterised by the chivalry which was his hallmark.

He'd been captured, it emerged, by English cavalry on a visit to the front. As an adjutant to the German Crown Prince, he'd gone forward to reconnoitre.

More remarkable still, she read, Albert, that other New College Rhodes scholar, he of the catlike grin, had been captured too, quite separately, and was in the same camp. While most extraordinary of all, so was Ernst Hoffman, the Bavarian who'd courted her so floridly when Alexey first disappeared. But the news of Ernst was grave - he'd been wounded, was in the camp hospital, and might die.

Could she possibly visit them, Von Leckburg asked? It would be so encouraging to see a German face, especially hers. More, Ernst was asking for her. She seemed to symbolise something for him, presumably home. If she could come, it would be wonderful for them all, especially Ernst.

For all the difficulties, Ingrid was stirred. For one thing this was real. Here was war in fact, not fantasy, so different from Kitty Clayton's high-flown histrionics. For another it offered Ingrid the opportunity of doing, for these sorely taxed men, what she would so dearly have loved to do for Alexey. And they were Germans, fellow countrymen, marooned in a foreign land like her!

So she wrote back and agreed. And while it took some fixing, she managed it. Suffice to say it took tact, Eric Rother, the marchioness, and finally even Churchill to make it happen; but it was done.

So a week later off she went, with both Paula and Mary, to a newly erected prison camp at Brotwell, just south of Oxford. And there, reluctantly assisted by two distinctly shirty guards, the three women distributed chocolate, cigarettes, and war news of uncertain provenance. While they accepted heartfelt condolences for the deaths of Charles and Alexey. Their German friends, plainly, were genuinely shocked.

And how tragic was this meeting, compared with those light-hearted times back in Oxford! Yet Ingrid was struck, too, by her compatriots' stoicism, as also that of their fellow-prisoners – there must have been five hundred of them, mainly from Prussian regiments - and above all by their lack of chauvinism. No-one seemed to blame anyone for what had occurred.

Nor did anybody blame Ingrid personally for being in England. They accepted it as her circumstance, for which there must be some very good reason, as they had theirs.

What especially impressed her was the attitude of Albert, who had been so aggressive that time they'd met at Harwich. Now he was quiet and even humble; nor did Ingrid feel this was merely the deflation of prison life. Rather she felt that he, like she, like everyone around them, had been transformed by recent events.

They were so vast, so superhuman, that all pettiness shrank away. Ashamed, and above all *irrelevant*, under their glare.

But it was above all when she found Ernst - in the camp hospital, where he had been given his own ward - that such thoughts struck her most. She went without Mary and Paula, guided by an orderly, as Ernst had most urgently asked to see her alone.

She and her escort poked their way along a paltry, dust-strewn corridor, strangely still after the hubbub elsewhere in the camp. And there was Ernst, in a little room with just a wardrobe and a chair. He was curled asleep in a half-moon, like a dog. He looked smaller.

With a start he woke up and stared at Ingrid, uncomprehending.

Then his face lit up.

"Ingrid," he breathed. "How wonderful! I can't believe it."

Yet the first thing she thought was: my God, he's just like Tom. He's wraith-like, a ghost. The man I knew has disappeared.

Except that Ernst seemed worse still. His face had a cardboard sallowness; his skin looked paper-thin. Even turning in bed exhausted him.

And yet in seconds, as he more clearly grasped her presence, he started to change. More and more, he stared at her fixated. A look of reverence lit up his face - of hero-worship even.

"Ingrid," he breathed again, "How marvellous."

My God, thought Ingrid, caught between compassion and alarm, who does he think I am – his mother ?

"How are you?" she said.

"Bad, pretty bad. They tell me I might die."

"Surely not."

"No, it's so, I'm afraid. The stomach. The doctors told me. This can be very bad."

And indeed, his bandages were wound beneath his waist. Ingrid didn't dare look.

"I have a day perhaps, two days. They have told me, and I am prepared."

"Oh, Ernst."

"No, they have told me."

A sudden look of surprise came over his face and Ingrid realised it was pain. Stay silent, she thought, if at all possible. She reached for his hand and held it. But now he was once more talking.

"I asked for you to come."

"Yes."

"I wanted to see you, very much."

"Yes"

"I wanted to give you these" (he handed her a packet of papers, from his bedside table - were they letters, diaries?) "and I wanted to tell you something -"

"What's that?"

"I love you."

What ? – And here he was staring at her again with the same, glowing, adulatory gaze.

"I love you Ingrid, I always have and always will."

Oh my God, thought Ingrid, the poor fellow *is* hallucinating, what I thought is right, he does think I'm his mother. He's become a child: Ernst, the grand radical, the charismatic winder-up of audiences against property and power, has been reduced to something infinitely *less*, rather than more, than other men.

And now Ernst was talking again, asking her something else -

"I want you to sing, please, that song I sang to you once - you know, 'Bist du bei mir', that song of Bach? Sing it to me now? Please?"

Which once more panicked Ingrid. Come to think of it, she did remember Ernst singing something like that, all those weeks ago - to the great hilarity of their friends, and her own embarrassment.

Nevertheless, the melody was one of her favourites and she could see why Ernst would have wanted it. For it was, in fact, more appropriate to a deathbed than to love. She remembered the start:

"Bist du bei Mir, Geh ich mit freuden
"Zum Sterben und zu meiner Ruh........

 - "With you beside me, I will go with joy
    "To death and to my rest.......

But *sing* it? In a situation like this? And she could scarce remember it anyway….

So Ingrid hummed it - the best she could do - till the orderly came back again and she stopped.

A day later she heard Ernst was dead.

Chapter Ninety-Seven

All of which set her wondering.

Yes, of course Ernst had been fantasising – but that was the form his reality took. Better, certainly, than the daydreams of Kitty Clayton, or those who thought they were involved in some modern-day Roman de la Rose.

At which there arose, in Ingrid's mind, the first glimmer of a plan. And from the beginning, it must be said, it contained a clear element of malice.

Her starting point was the strange dualism of Kitty Clayton's mind. Because for all Kitty's patriotism she was, just as vigorously, utterly dismissive of all vulgar anti-Germanism, constantly stressing how Charles, especially, had been beyond any such limitations.

Well, why not get the Marchioness to make good on her pretensions? Express them, somehow, at the funeral? Why not add Ernst's coffin to the flag-draped coffins of Charles and Alexey, as she'd heard was the current scheme? Why not turn the service into *real* mourning for the war?

Add a German corpse, in fact, to the English debacle of young men dumped like garbage. A true camaraderie this time. A camaraderie of death.

So she wrote to Kitty Clayton. She suggested that the 'chauvinism' of the service be toned down; that any priestly eulogy should embrace the Germans too; and finally, the real shocker, that Kitty should include Ernst Hoffman's coffin in the same remembrance service.

And back, by return, came Kitty's reply. It was kind, it was sympathetic, it was impeccably polite. It said no. Words like 'appropriate' and 'inappropriate' were much used.

So off sped a follow-up from Ingrid, rather firmer; and back came a reply from Kitty, firmer still.....then Ingrid, through Henry, recruited Rupert Brooke and Eddie Marsh; at which Kitty wheeled out her full artillery of contacts in London society.

Soon the row became the season's cause celebre. Indeed it got so each protagonist, on either side, was refusing even to speak to the other party. The service was on the brink of cancellation.

And like that it might have stayed had news of the dispute not filtered down to the remoteness of the Brotwell POW camp. From where Von Leckburg, appalled at what he'd heard, wrote quietly charming letters to both Kitty and Ingrid declaring that the last thing he and the other Germans – and above all Ernst - would have wanted was anything that might cause more anguish to people who had already suffered so much.

And a compromise was brokered by Eddie Marsh.

Kitty agreed that Ernst's name should be read out, at the climax of the service, with the briefest of eulogies by Lord Stanbury.

While Ingrid backed off her demand for Hoffman's coffin.

Though she extracted one last concession when the form of service was being planned, a concession whose significance was plainer to her than to Kitty.

Which was that a solitary piece of German music should be played: that most moving of Bach arias: 'Bist du bei Mir."

Chapter Ninety-Eight

Three weeks later, the funeral took place.

It was indeed a sumptuous affair, with over two hundred guests, the New College choir, and Alexey's and Charles' coffins, draped in Union Jacks, side by side at the chancel rail.

Kitty was there, and Stanbury - Churchill had failed to show at the last minute – but most of Ingrid's friends had come, excepting only Edward Stourbridge, who was in France. While the expected dollop of Kitty's society friends stood well to the fore, notably Rupert Brooke, heading a young and glamorous RND contingent.

Ingrid, who had started out fiercely intending to suborn the ceremony, felt differently as it loomed near. Now her hope was the opposite - that it should above all else go right. Or, more honestly, that she would get through it without breaking down. It would be dreadful to give way in front of all these people.

For as she entered the chapel, she felt on the verge not merely of emotional, but of *physical* collapse; she was supported, like an old lady, by Mary on one side, Paula on the other, as they shuffled to their places just half-way up the aisle behind the choir.

Yet for all the fraught build-up, as guests arrived the centuries-old beauty of the chapel overtook such lesser feelings, elevating the mood.

As did the coffins. For there they stood, at the climax of the nave, abstract, inhuman, implacable.

So that each guest felt a solemnity unimaginable previously. How can I do anything, everyone thought, but act appropriately in the face of this? All trivia falls away.

And then, just as gravitas had palpably settled on all present, there came the clear, pellucid notes of Jeremiah Clarke's trumpet voluntary, a piece more normally used for brides' entries at weddings. This was how Kitty chose to start a funeral!

It was her triumphalism: the polar opposite of anything that might have been thought of by Ingrid. The philosophical war between them was still being fought - but now through music.

Yet as the service got under way, it was Ingrid, perhaps inevitably, who caught everyone's attention. She seemed the quintessence of youthful tragedy. Pale, blonde and Anglo-Saxon looking, she looked - ironically enough- emblematic of England's suffering.

Though for Ingrid herself, each hymn, each prayer, was another bridge to cross, another step toward her primary goal of getting through the service without imploding. And she performed heroically, right up to when the priest made his invocation.

For the priest took his text from Matthew Sixteen: 'For whosoever will save his life shall lose it; and whosoever will lose his life, for my sake, shall find it.' The very same idea as Kitty's: that such deaths could be a *triumph* – something for which their loved ones should be grateful, rather than sad.

Yet even this grotesquerie Ingrid managed, by a whisper, to accept, repressing her profound desire to stand up and shout that any such notion was surreal, wicked, and above all, mad, mad, mad! And she even survived the brief - albeit more temperate – eulogy of Ernst that followed; though that, patently, gave as much difficulty to other congregational members – a eulogy for a Hun! - as the moral phantasms had to her.

No, what finally made her crack was the last anthem of all, Bist Du Bei Mir.

".... Ach, wie vergnuht war' so mein Ende...."

The words pierced her to the heart; soon she was trembling. Somehow, some way, she just managed to keep control.

Not that she was the only one so moved. The whole congregation felt something similar - notably George. To him it seemed as if the choir, as it sang, became one sensitive, sensual organism, each breath a lover's gasp. And as he gazed on Ingrid's melancholy, preoccupied face he found himself longing for each favourite phrase so he could match it to her looks. In George's imagination, Ingrid and the anthem became one.

Which was when, for the first time ever, he discovered an ambition he'd never even thought about till then.

He would marry her.

Marry Ingrid! Make her his wife. Regardless of all difficulties, ignoring all rivals, to hell with every problem of culture and creed, oblivious of the fact that given the innumerable other options open to her, she would never think of marrying a man as uninspiring as he.

He would marry her, protect her, defend her in her distress; he would cherish her…..not least, in part, out of loyalty to Alexey.

This new imperative would override all.

Chapter Ninety-Nine

Yet for all such intensities, in the days that followed the most profound anti-climax was felt by everyone. Especially Ingrid. Not sadness exactly - that would imply something too active, too energetically aware - just a grey opaque nothingness, grey as the November clouds which filled the skies.

It reminded Ingrid of a winter's day, years previously, when she had sat on a cliff on the North German coast overlooking the Baltic. A cliff so high, and a day so misty, that there was nothing to be seen, no sky above, no sea below, just this hanging, floating stillness. The sirens, warning passing ships, hooted periodically in the gloom. Mournful they were, unseen, adding still more to the sense of threat.

Nothing could bring back Alexey now. Those two coffins, sitting there in the chapel side by side, had been only too eloquent. She and Alexey would never speak, ever again. Nor would there be any resolution of the pain. Just nullity. Dead. Nothing at all.

Meanwhile the funeral continued to reverberate socially, but in a different way. The squabbling ceased to be about who had been invited; rather it was about who had not. The event had been widely reported.

Typical was a letter received by Henry, just three days afterward, from his father. Not only did it fail to offer the mildest succour for Henry in his distress, but its main concern was that the Thorntons had not been asked to the funeral, whereas the Crosbys had. After all, as Mr. Thornton pointed out, the Crosbys were 'hardly relatives.' Worse still, the letter was full of complaints about the war's ever-escalating pressure on his father's business and finally, as a rider, the usual hints that the least Henry could do was lend a hand.

Despite the long-standing resentment between them, had the circumstances been different, Henry would have done just that. But as it stood, his father's insouciance – his utter inability to comprehend, let alone sympathise with, the pain of anyone else - made Henry angrier than ever. He left the letter unanswered. And grew still more depressed.

The sole advantage of all this was that, combined with a letter now received by Ingrid, it helped bring she and Henry together. For Ingrid had heard from her parents, too, via neutral Switzerland. And Ingrid's letter, just like Henry's, showed utter incomprehension of any problems other than their own - and was full, too, of hectoring criticism. Above all of Ingrid's flight to 'Germany's principal enemy'; they hated England, apparently, even more than France. Her father, especially, seemed to link this 'betrayal', in a confused way, with that other 'betrayal', her pregnancy.

Of course, her parents were ignorant of the pregnancy's extraordinary end. But why on earth, wondered Ingrid, was her father *so* vituperative? She could only imagine it was guilt. If Ingrid - he maybe thought - , were not deceitful, licentious, and now traitorous, to boot, why then – given her father's present anger, and his behaviour in Germany before she left......*what was he*? The answer being unthinkable, she must be damned.

And Herr Uberspeer regaled her with the local war news. He mentioned several young men they knew, among whom was Karl-Gustav, Frau Schumacker's son, who had ' fur das vaterland gefallen' in recent weeks. The way Ingrid's father wrote it, he blamed his daughter for this too. Indeed, the sense she got was that casualties, in his mind, were only real if they were German. Ah, had he but known about Alexey!... and yet she wondered, savagely, if that would have made a blind bit of difference.

A brief, diffident letter from her mother, also enclosed, only disturbed her more. Ingrid could feel the love in the first two lines: her mother prayed for her, she said, every night, and Ingrid knew it was true. She kept Ingrid's bedroom ready for her, she added, and Ingrid believed this too - but then she also - even in this tiny letter! - launched into that same vituperative attack on the 'Jewish English' that had been the last straw before she left.

Ach, her mother, too, had died, yet another casualty of the war. What a couple her parents made! How *small* they felt at this moment -   just when events demanded real breadth of spirit. And Ingrid wept .... then stopped and cursed them both to Hell. Gott im himmel, what was happening to her?

Nevertheless, these parental letters, hers and Henry's, brought about the first sympathetic conversation between them for weeks. For both felt utterly isolated; both felt the same, ill-nurtured loneliness; both bemoaned the insouciance of the old. Such lack of imagination was clearly much the same throughout Europe.

Perhaps events like this were just too large for the average citizen to grasp, unless experienced directly.

Nevertheless, one representative of the older generation did manage to get through to Ingrid, even if it involved little connection with the war as such.

A week after the funeral Ingrid got yet another letter, postmarked Oxford, in a handwriting she recognised. Was not that...Mr. Crosby's writing? A nervous thrill ran through her, given what he'd presumably heard about the baby. Although he too, of course, knew nothing about the upshot.

A pause, and then she ripped it open and there was the familiar Holywell address at the top of the page, in its curious dark green print. As with that very different letter from Alexey, months back, after their first argument, she flipped quickly to the end - to get the flavour of the whole, from how it finished. It sounded alright:

"......So look after yourself, dear Ingrid, and, remember, Lucy and I have always held you in the highest possible regard. And let us know, again, *please,* if there is anything at all that we can do to help, in what must be the most exceptionally trying circumstances.

With deep love from us both,

David and Lucy Crosby

And both signed their names, Lucy adding a chaste little cluster of kisses.

Yes, that certainly sounded amiable – rather more so than she'd expected. So now she read the letter through properly. It was quite short, but what struck her was its tone.

Mr. Crosby explained how he had been moved to write because he and Mary had been so impressed, at the funeral, by Ingrid's looks. "It was plain you had suffered so very much, and our hearts went out to you."

There were other phrases that touched her too, like "the children still talk about you, every day" though there was little, specifically, to put her finger on. It was the overall feel, somehow, shining through the words.

It felt parental. Parental in a way she'd never known from the Crosbys before. (She suspected Mr. Crosby, who'd written the letter, was its source.) And such nurturance was something Ingrid dearly needed at this time. Indeed, in some way it seemed to make up, at least a little, for the disappearance of her mother.

The Crosbys left her 'pregnancy' unmentioned, probably out of tact.

So here, in its own small way, was something to feel good about. And there was more to come. For the day after she got that letter, after much heart-searching, Ingrid joined Henry, Mary, and a large congregation of locals at a very different memorial service from Alexey's, this time in Westbury village.

It took place in the little parish church, with its Saxon tower, whence flew the cross of St. George, while union flags draped the nave. Yet there was very little chauvinism about it. The flags felt more like poignant attempts to find meaning in meaninglessness than anything else.

Overall, the service, attended by around a hundred villagers, was notable for its simplicity and grace. Most gratifying of all, for Ingrid, was the warmth of the locals' reception. A relief that was shared by Henry because he, too, had been unsure about attending.

For as well as Ben Tennant and Fred Parsons, both killed with Alexey, and John Croome, the ceremony was in honour of Robert Hamblin. So Jane, Robert's wife, was prominent among the guests. Indeed, in her own way she dominated proceedings - the eye was drawn to her – much as Ingrid had dominated the service at New College. So at first both Henry and Ingrid feared she might be the mainspring, as so often in the past, of resentment among those villagers who were still their enemies.

But no, the locals seemed genuinely pleased to see them. Ingrid, in particular, felt their tribal embrace. She may have been German, it seemed, she may have been a theoretical Hun, but in this context, plainly, she was "one of us."

The villagers saw her as family – and that was the end of it.

She came out of the service feeling comforted. How very different from New College.

Chapter One Hundred

Yet others were less fortunate. Henry, especially, continued on his downward path. For now there was a new factor beyond even Antwerp, Alexey's death, the New College service, and the rest: he was angry with Rupert Brooke.

When they'd met at the funeral (Henry had found Brooke over-impressed by the social aspect) Brooke had thrust an envelope in his hands which contained 'new poems.' In them, he said, before slipping off to the Claytons' reception, he'd 'tried something different.' And, remembering he'd given Henry a view on *his* work, he'd be awfully glad if Henry might do the same.

Which Henry found, as ever, flattering.

But when he opened the envelope, it contained just two sonnets, one entitled 'The Dead' and the other, 'Peace.' And it was 'Peace,' especially, which troubled him:

"Now God be thanked Who has matched us with his hour

And caught our youth, and wakened us from sleeping,
With hand made sure, clear eye, and sharpened power,
To turn, as swimmers into cleanness leaping...."

And so it continued, full of highfalutin phrases (Henry noted that Brooke had finally found a berth for that swimming metaphor he'd dreamed up at Betteshanger) that were, in fact, nothing more than Kitty Clayton's philosophy put to verse. He couldn't believe it. After all that horror, cruelty, unimaginable catastrophe....... to embrace it, revel in it, as if it were some kind of *benediction*? He himself was full of neurosis and confusion but Brooke's work, surely, had the authentic stamp of madness. And the other poem, 'The Dead' was little better.

God help them all, what was happening to the world? What was happening to *Brooke*? Had he not made his name as the great iconoclast, the holy terror of the bourgeoisie? With poems like 'Channel Passage,' which was largely about being sea-sick? And now he was presenting *this* as 'something new'. In fact, it was very old: the most energetic and violent leap backward.

God knows, to an extent, Henry understood what he called the 'Agincourt syndrome'- this desperate need to confuse oneself with Sir Philip Sidney and Henry V. He'd had it in extreme form, himself. But surely realities like Antwerp must cure one of this. It had certainly cured him, for good.

Indeed, the more he thought about it the more it seemed plain that the same horrendous experiences - war generally, the particular terrors of Antwerp - could induce dramatically different reactions in different people. On the one hand responses like Kitty's and Rupert Brooke's. On the other......well, it sounded ridiculous but the only real dissent he could think of, offhand, was his own poem, 'Memory.'

The very poem which had been so lambasted by the publishing committee at Cecil Hampton's! But which still felt, God knows, like the best thing he'd done - even prophetic. Yes, you could place those 'Now God be matched' lines beside his 'Memory' and you would have a true union of opposites:

"But when wars die......" he'd written,
"........What started real, if cruel and drenched in spite,

Decays from that hard truth, and tales erupt;
A thousand lies infest each tale of fight
And glory, legend, honour, all corrupt."

In the blue corner Rupert's 'Peace,' in the red corner 'Memory'....

Although the one thing he *had* got wrong was the notion that time was needed for such corruption to take place. In the case of Kitty and Brooke, and the processes they represented, the switch had been almost instantaneous.

Worst of all, he thought, there was no way his poem's point of view would ever, in the current atmosphere, get a hearing. And this even though there must be thousands - tens of thousands! - of people who felt exactly the same. As did Ingrid, evidently, and now Tom, and even Robert's Jane. Not to mention Alexey himself, before he was killed by this very craziness.

There was simply no way, it seemed, that sanity could prevail.

Chapter One Hundred and One

And so it was that Henry's depressions entered depths unprecedented, with all the drearily familiar symptoms: the rows with Mary, the irritability with the kids, the constant trips out on his own, sometimes all day.

Nor did it help that Anthony Parsons chose this moment to take up residence in his rooms at Westbury, if only, as he put it, strictly temporarily, 'to help hold things together for a bit.'

Yet Mary sensed some further factor in Henry too, some mystery ingredient which was arguably bugging him most of all.

But he wasn't saying anything. What could it be? And she pondered and pondered, but the answer evaded her.

Meanwhile, nevertheless, both Henry and Mary, inasmuch as she shared her husband's pessimism about the poetry-reading public, were arguably underestimating them.

One afternoon Mary came back from shopping and found George, down from Cambridge. He was on one of his increasingly frequent visits to see Ingrid.

For the first couple of hours, as Ingrid was out in the woods with Mary's children, he talked with Mary, and had interesting things to say about his home town. There were many among both dons and students, apparently, who shared the war scepticism of those at Westbury. Some had even seen the same two sonnets Brooke had shown Henry and felt just as Henry did.

There was one young chap for instance, Charles Sorley, son of an academic, very bright, very level-headed ....well, he'd been as violently against the war, from the start, as most people had been for it (Sorley was, incidentally, no mean poet himself.) He'd told George roundly that a poem like Peace had nothing whatever to do with the Brooke he knew, the man who wrote 'Grantchester', and that curious piece of piscine metaphysics, 'The Fish.' "It was almost," he'd said, " as if Peace had been written by someone else."

Indeed Sorley had essayed his own poetical corrective:

To Germany

> You are blind like us. Your hurt no man designed
> And no-one claimed the conquest of your land.
> But gropers both through fields of thought confined
> We stumble and we do not understand.
> You only saw your future bigly planned
> And we, the tapering paths of our own mind,
> And in each other's dearest ways we stand
> And hiss and hate. And the blind fight the blind.
>
> When it is peace, then we may view again
> With new-won eyes each other's truer form
> And wonder. Grown more loving-kind and warm

> We'll grasp firm hands and laugh at the old pain,
> When it is peace. But until peace, the storm
> The darkness and the thunder and the rain.

It seemed that the great divide over the war's horrors, first evident in the funeral row, was breaking out nationwide. Even if the heroic, combative version - as that most suited to those in power - remained dominant for now.

So where did that get the likes of Ingrid and Henry? Nowhere much, not now at any rate, but at least it was a comfort to know there were others, even quite a few, who felt just as they did.

Then something happened which offered rather more than comfort.

A letter arrived for Mary from Cecil Hampton, Henry's would-be publisher.

First, Hampton explained why he was writing to Mary, rather than Henry himself. Quite simply he feared, given his history with her husband, there was little chance that Henry would give him a hearing.

But next - to come to the point - a new view was being taken, at his firm, on Henry's poetry. Opinion among the editorial board had turned. And lo! the alarmist aspect of his work was now seen, in many ways, as only too justified. Remember the poem they had especially disliked - from the 'apocalyptic' point of view - the one titled 'Memory'?

Well, embarrassing though it was to admit it of his colleagues - perhaps it was best viewed with a touch of humour - this poem, above all, was the one they now admired. So different in flavour, they'd declared, from the bellicose spirit of the age, especially as expressed in poems like Binyon's' 'The Fourth of August' or Thomas Hardy's 'Men Who March Away.'

In fact, they had experienced a revulsion of feeling comparable to that which George had described among the sceptics in Cambridge. The result was they would dearly like to print 'Memory' just as soon as they could – indeed, if possible, in the next issue of a new journal Hampton had lately launched, 'Tempo.' And then, perhaps, adding it to any other poems Henry had written recently in similar spirit – maybe putting out the book they'd always hoped for, but with a different emphasis. Although they would of course use Henry's earlier material as well.

Perhaps this spark might ignite a conflagration?

Finally, he must stress again how eager he and his board were to advance along these lines, and to apologise, once again, for the confusion of the last few weeks. Hampton could only offer, in weak defence, the notion that attitudes, like events, had been febrile and ever-changing in this war.

They certainly had, thought Mary. And she was equally clear, the moment she'd read the letter, what she would do.

First: she would accept his offer, in principle, right away. Here surely was a gift from the Gods. She would grab it with both hands.

Second: she would, as yet, say nothing to her husband - there had been too many near-misses and disappointments already. Any repetition of such debacles right now could be disastrous.

Meanwhile.........she wrote back, saying yes, the very same day.

Chapter One Hundred and Two

Certainly, she reflected, divine intervention had come not a moment too soon. For Henry's deterioration was gathering pace. His angers were startling, the rows intense, but what really shook her was the evening he smashed his violin.

She heard a shriek, and a strangled scream, and when she rushed into his room - she thought he'd had an accident – she found him looking aghast. The violin was in pieces on the floor.

Only Mary knew how much he loved it. He would kiss it when he'd finished practising.

It was weirdly reminiscent of that incident Ingrid had told her about, weeks before, when Alexey smashed the clock.

Yet Alexey hated the clock, and Henry adored the violin. 'For each man kills the thing he loves': it was, in effect, a form of suicide, and this was what scared her most.

And now, in this obsessive mindset in which the Thorntons increasingly found themselves, she found herself watching ever more frantically for the post. She was looking for confirmation that Henry's work would definitely get used; the sole thing she could think of, now, that might help.

Time and again she nearly broke her own rule and told Henry what was on offer. But each time she avoided it. Although she did allow herself veiled hints – well, more or less veiled – suggesting that in life, even at the worst, there were always possibilities of recovery. She even quoted Clough's 'Say not the struggle naught availeth,' complete with resounding final line, ' Lo, Westward look, the land is bright' – a poem that had once been one of Henry's favourites.

Then immediately regretted it, as Henry's rejection of such 'facile optimism' was savage indeed.

Nevertheless, the day finally dawned when Hampton's letter arrived. It was long, but not so very thick: Mary ripped it open, and out fell the first number of 'Tempo,' around fourteen inches by ten, with a glossy, four-colour cover. And there, on the front page, was Memory, printed in full. With a large headline above it, saying:

This poem redeems the conscience of the world

Mary gasped with delight. This was more than she'd hoped for, far more – and there was a covering letter, too, fluttering down onto the floor. Hampton was fulsome in his praise for what he'd printed, said everyone at his firm was right behind him, and added that he looked forward, now, to the next step, which was reactivating Henry's material in book form. Especially if Henry could find – or write! - other poems in like genre.

Now, at last, Mary would tell Henry. She rushed over to their bedroom where she had last seen him - but there, as so often, was no Henry, just a scribbled note. He'd fled on one of his walks. But she imagined he'd be back for supper. However black his mood, he had a genius for arriving when food was served.

But he never returned for supper, nor later that night. Not that this especially worried Mary - she remembered the time, months back, when he had chosen to walk back through the night from Oxford and had written the 'Stars' poem en route. And there had been several all-night walks, and unplanned stop-outs, since then.

Even so, compulsion took over, and much to her self-contempt, as soon as it got dark, she once again found herself obsessively seeking possible instruments of self-harm. Not the poniard, this time - she'd dealt with that - but that other weapon, the one she'd long ago discounted, Henry's pistol: she slunk upstairs, she ferreted out the box - no, it was still there. Covered by a cloth.

So she put the children to bed and then followed them, still burdened by a strange weight of apprehension. How utterly ridiculous! She should take a tip from her children - *they* seemed happy enough, and more than ready to accept her explanation: "Daddy's gone shooting with Joe Parsons and will be back God knows when, you know what Daddy's like."

And, surprisingly, the moment her head hit the pillow she was asleep. And only woke up next morning, due to hammering at the door. And there was Joe Parsons, with Phil Brooke and Jim Bewdley from the village. But like Henry the day he came back from Antwerp, their faces said it all.

Chapter One Hundred and Three

Joe asked if he could speak to her alone.

He was very very sorry, he said, but he had to tell her that Henry was dead.

He explained. They'd been out early looking for poachers. They'd found no poachers, but they had found Henry. He was at the bottom of that high rock in the middle of the forest - did Mary know it? – about three miles off.

He'd been slumped on the ground, and they knew instantly he was gone.

Mary sat down on the nearest chair. She stared fixedly with glazed, unseeing eyes. Joe Parsons eyed her with anguish, and asked what he could do. But Mary seemed not to hear, and went on staring into space, clasping hard on the arms of the chair.

"Where is he?" she said finally, practicalities to the fore.

"Still up there at the moment," said Joe. "Tom Cooper's with him - but we can bring him down whenever you like," He winced – it sounded wrong.

"Yes of course," said Mary, still remote, and then, "of course" again, this time with meaning.

Then she turned to Joe, looked him straight in the eye and with an intensity that frightened him, she asked:

"How did he die?"

"Well, like I say," – Joe quailed under her gaze - "I don't rightly know, but it looks like he must have toppled off that rock. It's a good twenty feet.... but how it happened, and why he got up there, God knows. It's a long way down if you do fall. Must have lost his footing somehow. Last night was very dark..."

"*How did he die*?" repeated Mary.

"Well, like I say, I don't rightly know, I mean he fell, that's for sure, it's a long way......"

"**HOW DID HE DIE**!" screamed Mary, and now Joe Parsons jumped.

"Tell me how he died," cried Mary, "tell me exactly, you're keeping something from me, tell me the truth!"

Was Joe keeping anything from her? He'd said all he knew for sure. But Mary plainly had something else in mind. What could that be?

At which moment Anthony Parsons appeared, pulling on his dressing gown, from his rooms on the hill. He'd heard the commotion and run swiftly down.

Instantly he took charge. He couldn't have been more helpful. The first thing, he said, was to get Henry's body down to the camp – which Joe and his friends might do – then he himself would phone Doctor Holm.

So off went Joe and his men while Mary resumed her studied calm. She maintained it, remarkably, when Ingrid, woken up by the commotion, came to join her - and lacking Mary's self-control, went into her own, deep shock.

She maintained it, even, when the children appeared and she told them - reluctantly, but with her usual stolid courage - in answer to their questions:

'Yes, it's true, you'll never see Daddy again.'

And Mary's ruthless calm, and busy activity, continued throughout the day, as she made breakfast for the kids, sent telegrams to interested parties like Henry's parents, and considered exactly who needed to be informed. The doctor? (done) The registrar of birth and deaths? (Tomorrow.) The coroner, even? Well, hopefully, that would not be necessary.

Because as soon as Henry's body was brought back to the camp and laid out in the rooms next to Anthony's, Doctor Holm declared the cause of death was heart failure for sure. His personal guess was that a heart attack had struck Henry while he was standing at the top of that twenty-foot rock. So the fall was a symptom, not a cause.

Which Mary dearly wished to believe. How much she prayed the cause of death would not prove sinister! Nevertheless, the nagging fear that she could be wrong - or right - was a big reason why she then asked if she, too, might examine the body. Which Anthony and Doctor Holm agreed to, graciously and at once.

What could be more natural, if courageous, in a bereaved wife? But the surprise, for them, was when they realised she meant literally *examine,* in near-professional detail. For the moment Mary entered the room she explained she wanted to undress the body, and could they help? Presumably, it seemed, to see if she herself could find the cause of death.

And that was surely what she seemed to be attempting, turning the body gently to and fro, trying hard to see – that much would be plain enough! - if there were wounds. Because what she was looking for, though of course she didn't say so, was knife - or 'poniard' - or even bullet wounds. Something self-inflicted, with all its implications.

Which plainly, as the men began to suspect this, pleased them not at all. "I don't know quite what you're looking for." said Dr. Holm, "but I'm certain heart failure was the cause."

And Mary found no evidence to contradict him. So eventually, after long scrutiny, she left it at that.

But what struck Dr. Holm was the *relief* he then sensed in her - a reaction he'd not seen before in the bereaved.

And Mary's self-control maintained itself, even through the impossible process of putting the children to bed. It was only when she finally found herself alone with Ingrid that she cracked.

And when she cried it had a self-effacing, private quality, quite different from Ingrid's noisy histrionics.

But then. as Ingrid realised, tears, for Mary. were most unusual - above all for herself. If she cried at all - and it was very rare – it was almost always for someone else.

And so, despite Mary's uneasiness, the matter was settled. The cause of death was 'heart failure.' No need for an inquest.

They would hold the funeral in Westbury church. The very same where John Croome's and Robert's had been held, just a fortnight before. And it would, Mary determined, be the opposite of Alexey's. Quiet, unpretentious, and above all else, sincere.

And yet... as soon as they started the preparations, Mary began to have doubts. For a start Alexey's uncle and aunt, away in Wales, couldn't come. Then there was Eric Rother, and Henry's publishers, and the whole Clayton, London mob. Mary simply didn't want them around. Even Henry's parents made difficulties: his mother, as ever, was ill, while his father's letter, explaining this, resurrected all his resentment about the guest list at New College.

Most disconcerting of all were the villagers. For mysteriously, ever since Henry's death, they too had changed. Gone was the relative friendliness of the Tennant / Hamblin funeral. Instead, they'd developed some mysterious reserve, some novel undertone that Mary couldn't place.

Robert's Jane, especially, who Mary ran into more than once (she was staying with friends in the village) had a manner that defied description. Not aggressive exactly – just weird.

In short, for any number of reasons, the mooted service felt more and more unreal.

Above all it lacked any relevance to Henry's life. And it would be conducted in a cultural language which for Henry was alien. What a travesty of his memory to be sure!

Mary talked to Ingrid, who understood. Indeed Paula, George, and even Tom felt much the same.

So slowly, tentatively, a new project was born. Why not develop their *own* memorial service, for Henry and Alexey, and Charles too - not forgetting Ernst - performed in their own way, in their own time and place? That way they could avoid both the extravagances of New College and this mysterious Westbury sullenness. They could hold something with genuine meaning, a real tribute to the dead.

They could even develop their own ritual, if that was the right word. They had the whole field of English poetry to choose from, after all, not to mention the folk-songs Henry adored. As for place, they could perform it – where else?! - in the magical beech grove above Westbury that had been so important to all of them, especially Ingrid, Mary, Henry and Alexey.

And so it was decided. Though there remained one further question. Who should they ask? But the answer was simple: their own tight group of friends. That was the whole point. People who really cared about the dead - real friends, not even relatives. And yet...... if they were truly acting in a different, generous spirit, how could they possibly omit John Croome's mother - so vulnerable and so genuinely devoted to her son, whose death had been the starting point of it all? Her devastation at the village funeral had been plain.

Or, come to that, Robert's Jane, if only as an act of reconciliation? Robert was no less dead than anyone else. And Mary had been struck by her evident misery, at the church service, too.

In the end, Mary undertook to ask these two herself. But as it turned out both refused, though Jane, in particular, seemed genuinely pleased that she'd been asked.

And so it was that three days later Mary, Ingrid, Paula, Tom and George wound their way up to the beech grove on Westbury hill, which for all of them had such history and such meaning.

It was a misty, late autumn afternoon, the sun lost in a blur - more soft September than November the tenth, the date on the calendar.

The beech tree leaves, late turning, were faded and yellow, the ground wet and rank, as Mary and Ingrid read out three poems.

First John Donne's' sonnet, 'Death be not proud'. Then Henry's own 'Memory'. Finally, one of Henry's favourite Shakespeare songs, from Cymbeline:

".. ....Fear no more the frown o' the great

"Thou art past the tyrant's stroke

"Care no more to clothe and eat

"To thee the reed is as the oak.

"The sceptre, learning, physic must

"All follow thee, and come to dust...."

They'd planned a brief eulogy, but no longer felt it necessary. Instead, they stood in silence. And the longer they stood there the more each felt that Alexey and Henry were with them, too.

Chapter One Hundred and Four

Yet there was a postscript to all this, in some ways most remarkable of all.

Two days later Mary was in the kitchen, mending one of Josephine's boots, when there came a knock at the door. It was Jane Hamblin.

She looked exhausted, with a set, mask-like expression on her face, yet strangely agitated, too.

"Could I possibly talk with you?" she said.

"Of course," said Mary, and ushered her in.

Mary offered her tea but Jane refused, with the air of one who must come to her point. Yet she sat there for a good half minute without saying anything, began twice and stopped, till finally, in fits and starts, but with slowly gathering momentum, she said:

"Excuse me if I don't make sense – I've not slept for days. Especially since Henry......died." A stabbing glance.

"...I......well, it started when Robert died, and now Henry.... and the...... his funeral....by the way, I really appreciated your asking me to the ceremony but to be honest I wasn't sure I could get through it........."

"Nor were we," smiled Mary.

"I can well imagine," said Jane, with another frightened glance. "You and I have had rather similar experiences, haven't we?

 "We certainly have."

Emboldened, Jane tried again.

"You see........... I hate to see you so unhappy at Henry's death. It's *devastating*. God knows I know myself just how it feels. I feel so.......*guilty* – you see…. because...... you see .... I know what happened between Robert and Henry and Anthony Parsons." This last in a rush. "And John Croome too, come to that."

What on earth, thought Mary –

"So what did happen?"

"They – he - ……. well, basically, Anthony got Robert to join Henry's squad to bring Henry down."

"*What*?"

 "To bring him down – yes – to ruin him – discredit him – before he ruined Anthony himself."

And so the story came out, slowly and fitfully. And a complicated story it was.

For a start, it emerged that Henry had been quite right in thinking Anthony Parsons had been behind Robert's joining his troop. But now Jane gave the reasons. It was, apparently - she apologised for being so blunt - because Anthony had heard the rumours about Henry and Alexey's homosexual 'predilections' and sought evidence that would, as she said, 'discredit' them. Above all Henry.

"And he could get the information he needed via Robert, if Robert was in Henry's platoon."

Because a new factor had emerged since Henry and Alexey had joined up: they'd formed liaisons, allegedly, with soldiers under their command.

They *what,* gasped Mary? And anyway, why would Robert and Anthony have planned this plot? What was their motive? True, Robert had every reason to dislike Henry. His affair with Jane alone, all those years ago, would have been enough. But Anthony?

Yet Jane had the answer.

"The real reason, quite simply, was that Anthony and Robert had been accused of the same thing, especially Anthony."

People thought, apparently, he'd misbehaved with boys at Westbury and lately things had come to a head. Several boys had made new, specific allegations to John Croome, who they saw as a kind of leader, and they were convincing enough that John went to Anthony and asked him – and got roundly abused for his pains.

"But John refused to be put down. So eventually he gave Anthony an ultimatum. Either he came clean and answered the accusations or John would go the police. Or rather, he'd go to Henry, and get him to go to the police - it seemed a bit much for John, brave though he was, to expose himself to quite that degree. He was still little more than a boy, so he wanted Henry's support.

"Because there was another aspect, too - for years the boys had thought there was something going on between Anthony and Robert. Now *I* don't know whether there was any truth in that, but I was always struck by how close they seemed. And did you ever notice that strange smile of Anthony's - how corrupt it looked, how unlike his expression at any other time?"

And Mary thought, yes, she had noticed that, and so had Henry - though they'd never really taken it seriously

But this was all too new, and too bizarre, for Mary. She sat down and stared fixedly in front of her. Now it was Mary avoiding Jane's eyes.

"I'm so sorry," said Jane hopelessly. "Because the thing is, I knew all this was going on. And I did nothing. And now first Alexey, then Robert, and now Henry are all dead, and I feel responsible, and guilty, and so sad...."

And Mary remembered that when Henry and Jane had had their liaison all those years ago, while Henry's feelings had been intense but mainly sensual, Jane's surely had been love. She too had been bereaved, profoundly so, by Henry's death.

"And worst of all," said Mary, "is that nearly all of it, surely, is just gossip, absurdity - yet look at its effect."

"Especially," agreed Jane, "the stuff they were digging up for the trial. Now that *was* ridiculous, to be sure."

"Trial?" said Mary, wide eyed, "What trial was that?"

"Oh God, didn't you know? Didn't Henry tell you?"

And now, more surprise; for Jane explained that the Army had finally got to hear about all this (Mary would guess how) and formalised it into allegations. A Major Leveson, apparently, was involved. There'd been talk of a court martial....

"Though now, of course, it will be dropped, given everything that has happened, and Alexey's and Henry's deaths."

"Oh God."

This finally was too much, and once again Mary sat down – not least because she realised, now, why Henry had seemed so preoccupied in his final days. He'd thought he might be publicly shamed. Quite enough to shatter anybody, let alone someone in the state he'd been in.

They talked some more then cried a little and embraced. How little Mary had expected such a moment with Jane Hamblin! And shortly afterward Jane hurried back to the village.

And Mary went and sat in the garden.

Yes, this, surely, was the unknown element she had sensed, the final pressure that might have tipped Henry over the edge. And yes, terrible though the thought was, his death might have been suicide after all.

Except, of course, that there had been no evidence of any such thing on Henry's body. She had seen so for herself. No bullet wounds, no cuts, no damage, visibly, at all – perhaps his death had been as innocent as Anthony and Dr. Holm had been so eager to point out. Over-eager, indeed, as if they had been desperate to get Henry buried and out of the way! Though Anthony, in particular, might have had very good reason.

And that was how Mary left it for the next few days – traumatic, grotesque, and sad, but everything guessed at, nothing proved.

Until, that is, sorting out some shelves of Henry's, she came across a small black bottle of potassium cyanide which she had found – and been alarmed by - no less than three years earlier. Then more or less forgotten about.

At the time it had scared her very much - why would Henry have this? And she hadn't dare ask him but had checked it, periodically (when she remembered) in much the same way she checked his poniard and his gun. And it had always remained unopened, the label intact, until finally she forgot about it.

And now she stumbled on it. There it was, with its label from Henry's father's chemists. God knows how Henry persuaded his father to give it to him.

But now - unlike those other times - it had plainly been opened. Quite recently by the look of it. And it was empty.

He could have taken it away.

He might have drunk it at the top of the cliff and then fallen. It could have been suicide after all.

Chapter One Hundred and Five

She told Ingrid about it. She and Ingrid were now each other's confidants. And Ingrid, predictably, was the soul of sympathy. Always generous-minded, she'd become, in the last few weeks, an excellent listener.

Nevertheless, between the two of them, they continued to discount their lovers' bisexuality, sharing their horror at being maligned. They regarded such allegations, however lurid, as mere 'slurs.' Why, just look at the gossips' key source - Robert Hamblin! Who was going to take him, of all people, seriously?

But gradually, the more they talked, Mary realised that there was something else going on in their conversations, something far more powerful than mere mutual self-justification. Some undertone behind everything Ingrid said, some indefinable resonance; reminiscent of how Mary had intuited the very different preoccupations, before his death, of Henry.

Not that Ingrid said anything explicit. It remained a mere feeling. But with this difference: the quality she sensed in Ingrid, unlike in Henry, was not angst, but joy. There was a light in Ingrid's eyes, a spring in her step, Mary hadn't seen for weeks.

Yet in the days to come Ingrid volunteered no explanation. So Mary kept her counsel, confident that Ingrid would tell her when the moment felt right.

Eventually she did just that.

"I have some remarkable news," she said.

Mary had no idea what this could possibly be.

"I'm pregnant," said Ingrid. "It's true! And this time I'm absolutely certain of the father's identity. It's Alexey."

So now more astonishment for Mary - though this time the cause was benign. That 'light' Mary had seen in Ingrid's eyes had plainly been her pregnancy's first symptoms - the moment when the body tells the mind the glad tidings of which it is not yet consciously aware. And when that had been followed by the familiar morning sickness, Ingrid had seen the doctor. And this time had taken the precaution of a second opinion as well.

So now Ingrid was quite sure. And as for her certainty about the father – well, she simply hadn't been with anyone else. Her brief phase of erotic experiment had long passed.

And what she was sure of too (Mary was less convinced, but happy to go along with it) was that this was the product of her exceptional lovemaking with Alexey before he left – those times, she said, when both had achieved a greater depth, and beauty, of connection than either had ever known.

"I felt it then," she said. "Without knowing why. But now I do."

She looked radiant.

"He's not dead," she said. "He's alive in me. I have a piece of him I can cherish forever.

"The story has come full circle. Now everything makes sense."

Chapter One Hundred and Six

Nevertheless, for all Ingrid's euphoria, so much had happened so quickly that in the next few days she would often go off and reflect, hoping that things might settle, somehow, in her mind.

A week after her talk with Mary she made just such an excursion. As so often she went to the beech glade up the hill, which now felt like a shrine.

It was halfway through November. Autumn had set in, and the landscape, quietly elegiac, suited her mood.

Finally, God had blessed her. After all the trauma of the last six months! For that was how she saw this pregnancy, so different from the first: a triumph, a means of sustaining her and Alexey's love. A resurrection.

She found her favourite seat near the summit and pondered.

In front the path stretched down the hill. The first leaves had fallen. They were so small, so closely clustered that their browns and yellows and greens looked like a mosaic. There was a sense of harvest and consummation – yet a hint, too, of spring-like hope. What was the line Alexey so often quoted? 'There lives the dearest freshness deep down things.' For not only was there the joy of her pregnancy, but now, remarkably, people's reactions to it, as word got round.

She'd been surprised how well she'd been supported. By Mary, naturally, by Tom, more surprisingly, but above all by George. His visits had redoubled since he'd heard the news. Indeed, he seemed far more than just supportive; he too seemed to feel some kind of gladness. Dear George! Was there anyone she knew – even Mary - who was quite so solidly, consistently loving, so sanely reliable? It was remarkable, really, in all the circumstances. He might just as well have been upset.

Yet there was one especial piece of news, as Ingrid sat there, this crisp November morning. And that was the most surprising of all.

Five days earlier she'd received another letter from Mr. Crosby. He was ardent they should meet. Ingrid had had 'a rotten time', he said, and he was anxious to do whatever he could to help.

So pressing was he, so tender his tone, that she promptly agreed. And three days later Mr. Crosby appeared. He was without his wife, for which Ingrid was thankful, and they sat down in Ingrid's kitchen.

And what he told her transformed everything.

First, he said how sorry he was that Ingrid had been through such experiences - above all the death of Alexey. But he'd felt for her, too, from the bottom of his heart, when he'd heard about her earlier 'pregnancy,' in the letter from her father. He couldn't imagine how hard it must have been. He'd wanted then to help, but sensed Ingrid's need to stay distant. And when he gathered, later, that her pregnancy had been 'phantom' he'd felt more sympathetic still. But he had no idea what to do.

His heart had gone out to her at the funeral - it was plain how profoundly Ingrid was stricken. But now he'd heard – no matter how, forgive him! - about this new pregnancy, and that this time Ingrid was certain it was Alexey's. He could see what this would mean to her, and she was right to feel this, and he too rejoiced.

Indeed he wept as he said this.

Though she soon understood why. For Mr. Crosby told her two things more. The first was that he must insist on helping her – no ifs and buts about it. He would support her in any way necessary, with whatever she thought best, but this *must* be so. Money, housing, nursing, she would be the judge. Surely she deserved some happiness at last.

And the other thing he explained was why.

For he answered the key question left unanswered back in Germany: the identity of her natural father, her mother's lover, all those years before.

It was David Crosby. It was he.

Of all the shocks the last few months had given Ingrid, this was the greatest of all.

Suddenly, how much more made sense! Ingrid's constant feeling, over the years, of some special connection with this so-called family friend; his tendency to spoil her, to take her side against his wife; his capacity, time and again, to be disproportionately moved by her, notably that time at the station when she left for Germany. No wonder Lucy Crosby had looked so upset!

Then add in the warmth Ingrid, too, had always felt for him. How ironic that she had often thought, when things were difficult with her father, that she would have preferred David Crosby as a father figure, had she the choice.

At least one thing was emerging from all this: there was little wrong with her instincts.

And Mr. Crosby explained still more. He confirmed that the version Herr Uberspeer gave her of her mother's conception was true - her mother HAD been involved with the adventurer, 'Johann', just as Uberspeer had described it. And Johann had treated her dreadfully, and Uberspeer had rescued her, just as he said.

But while this was certainly the truth, it was not the whole truth, nothing like. For what Uberspeer hadn't said - because he hadn't known! - was that he, David Crosby, had had an affair with Ingrid's mother before she ever met Johann: she was already pregnant by him before Johann got involved.

So why hadn't *David Crosby* 'rescued' her? Well, not for lack of wanting: he'd cared desperately for Ingrid's mother. She was his first love.

But the problems were huge. Back then he was studying in Germany, which was how he knew Herr Uberspeer, and was poor. It would have meant either he or Ingrid's mother moving to the other's country. It would have involved Henry giving up his studies so he could earn.

But above all else it would have meant reneging on the fiancée to whom he was committed back in England. Yes! It was Lucy, his present wife – they were already engaged. They had been for two years. His guilt was huge, he couldn't abandon her.

Even so, he might still have married Ingrid's mother, had not Uberspeer intervened, with his own absolute commitment. And, crucially, money.

And then, well, it began to seem that this could be the best - let's say the most *pragmatic* solution. Uberspeer, too, unquestionably loved Ingrid's mother and would provide her and Ingrid with just the kind of security and steady affection he had indeed manifested over the years.

So that was what happened, with neither Johann, nor Uberspeer, in the end, knowing who Ingrid's real father was. Frau Uberspeer, for her part, swore solemnly to keep the secret, and so it remained. But not without endless regrets on David Crosby's part and an absolute determination to see Frau Uberspeer, and Ingrid, whenever possible. Ingrid would remember how often the two families had visited each other over the years.

Bizarre that neither Herr Uberspeer nor Lucy Crosby knew any of this while he and Ingrid's mother knew it all! Quite a situation to have carried on for nineteen years.

Now David Crosby allowed himself a gleam of levity.

"So that *is* the whole truth, pure and simple' he pronounced, "although as the inimitable Oscar pointed out, the truth is rarely simple and never pure."

Dear old David, thought Ingrid, bookish to the end.

They kissed, and shortly after David Crosby took his leave.

And steadily the strange optimism which Ingrid felt continued to grow. It grew despite the continuing catastrophe of the war; despite the practical difficulties and downright silliness of her moral position; despite, even, the extraordinary tiredness she felt constantly.

And it grew still more after her next meeting with George.

Because George, who knew, of course, about the pregnancy, had somehow heard about David Crosby's visit - with some inkling of what it meant - and was the next to offer Ingrid absolute, unconditional love.

He proposed marriage. By no means what Ingrid had expected! But like David Crosby, his declaration, once made, opened the floodgates. He told Ingrid everything he'd bottled up for months. And the fact he did it clumsily, even gauchely, only added to its charm.

He was determined, he said, to make her his wife. He loved her utterly and had loved her from the start (this part Ingrid rather doubted) and it would be an honour for him to act as father to her child. It would be a tribute to Alexey's memory.

He talked about their future. He could wait, he said, just as long as Ingrid saw fit. She naturally needed to adjust. Meanwhile he would help. He was happy to stay on the sidelines for now, if only Ingrid grasped one fundamental truth: he was utterly determined to marry her. He had never been so sure of anything in his life. Meanwhile she must also understand that caring for her, protecting her, cherishing her – till they were finally wedded - would in no way be a duty, rather a joy.

And on that resounding note - Ingrid feeling dazed but undeniably pleased - they parted.

What George did notice, however, despite any clear commitment on Ingrid's part, was how her face changed as they talked. When he'd arrived she'd looked weary – pale, distracted, with shadows under her eyes. Yet when he left the shadows had vanished, all lines and wrinkles were gone, and her complexion bloomed.

Chapter One Hundred and Seven

So George loved her, but would she ever love him? In its current form the scenario was too new; yet the more she thought about it the more she found the idea - and George himself – replete with promise. They had a future.

But what of her friends? Paula for instance? Well, she'd just heard she was in France. She'd eschewed nursing, apparently, and demanded something more 'compelling.' And she'd found it – she was, Ingrid heard, involved with British Intelligence. Or to put it another way, she'd become what Ingrid had always suspected... a spy! Identity crisis, clearly, could express itself in different ways.

Then there was Tom. That poor, pale, shattered personality, that ghost of his former self, had yet to find renewal. Ingrid hoped fervently that he would. After all, even Elspeth – hook-nosed Elspeth as they'd so cruelly called her – had found her own strange redemption. For she had fallen in with, of all people, Paula's ex-lover Celine, that French communist who had, in an earlier phase, set Alexey and Henry at odds. For Celine had come to England in pursuit of Paula, and found, to her disgust, that Paula had left for France. At which point, remarkably, she'd got involved with Elspeth instead.

Praise God for his sense of humour! He'd seen fit to leaven their Greek tragedy with farce.

And then, most poignantly, what about Mary? Well - that could be the strangest denouement of them all.

For increasingly, in the last couple of weeks, she'd been involved with Tom. Looking after him, protecting him, virtually nursing him - in ways that would have been unimaginable previously. For his frailty had lately taken a very particular form. Much like Ernst (no wonder they'd always disliked each other) it seemed Tom's bluster masked what was effectively a little boy. And Mary was nurturing that boy –a relationship the precise opposite of the one he'd had with Ingrid.

Yet plainly he relished it. Perhaps they would both benefit, and a better Tom evolve. As Oscar Wilde once said - that Oscar so beloved of them all - the only thing you can say for sure about human nature is that it changes.

Chapter One Hundred and Eight

And finally there was Alexey, that character who, though dead, still dominated the lives of all.

A week after George's declaration, Ingrid got a visit from the Smolenskys, the first time she'd seen them since the funeral.

Like the Crosbys, she'd exchanged glances with them there, but they'd not spoken. Like the Crosbys too, the Smolenskys had been struck by how forlorn Ingrid had seemed. They'd thereupon determined to visit her, to nurture her in their mutual bereavement. Added to which there was now, of course, a link of blood: for Ingrid's determination to harbour no secrets meant they had heard about the pregnancy, and that Alexey was the father of Ingrid's child.

Unsurprisingly, they and Ingrid got on swimmingly. They were extraordinarily gentle with each other. The three people who loved Alexey most seemed blessed by their connection.

Equally predictably the Smolenskys told endless stories about him, impelled, plainly, by the intensity of their feelings.

There was one particular story, which would never have come out, surely, at any other time.

The key to understanding Alexey, they stressed, was his relationship with his mother. It had been remarkably, almost unnaturally warm. The one thing you noticed, whenever you were with them, was their profound, mutual trust.

Which meant, of course, that when Alexey's mother killed herself, the trauma was all the more extreme. Indeed, it had even led Alexey to deny his mother's origins - did Ingrid know that she was Polish, unlike his father, who was authentically Russian? It was as if obscuring her history could change the truth. Of course, it never worked. Had Ingrid ever noticed how Polish so many of Alexey's mannerisms were, imbibed right back in childhood?

Indeed, she had - it was one of the first things that had struck her.

And there was one other aspect, interposed Alexey's aunt Johanna, of which Ingrid might not be aware. But which, dire though it was, she should know. It was the final key to understanding him.

At which Alexey's uncle, sensing something, tried to restrain her. But Mrs. Smolensky plunged on.

Ingrid knew of course, said Johanna, about the suicide. But did she know how it had happened? No, said Ingrid, not really.

Well, said Johanna, whatever Alexey may have told you, the brutal truth was that his mother hanged herself.

But the still more dreadful fact – so dreadful that for years Alexey had been unable to tell them - was that he himself had been the one who found her.

Tout comprendre, c'est tout pardonner. Now this, too, made a terrible sense. And Ingrid fell once more to pondering.

For three days she felt utterly cast down. Then gradually her sadness evolved into the most profound, heartfelt compassion.

And then she heard from George. He was coming to see her the very next day. And right away – there was no rhyme or reason about it – she began to feel happier.

Printed in Great Britain
by Amazon

6ae9bffa-baff-4fbc-82bc-47c157c09c6bR01